ALSO BY JANE HAMILTON

The Book of Ruth

A Map of the World

The Short History
of a Prince

Jane Hamilton

THE
SHORT HISTORY
OF A PRINCE

A Novel

RANDOM HOUSE NEW YORK

All rights reserved under International and Pan-American Copyright
Conventions. Published in the United States by Random House, Inc.,
New York, and simultaneously in Canada by Random House
of Canada Limited, Toronto.

A signed first edition of this book has been privately printed
by The Franklin Library.

Heartfelt thanks to the Ragdale Foundation, where much of this book
was written, and to C.C. and Professor Jenkins of Northfield, Minnesota.

Library of Congress Cataloging-in-Publication Data

Hamilton, Jane
The short history of a prince : a novel / Jane Hamilton. — 1st ed.
p.   cm.
ISBN 0-679-45755-0 (acid-free paper)
I. Title.
PS3558.A4428S56   1998
813'.54—dc21   97-31627

Random House website address: www.randomhouse.com

Manufactured in the United States of America on acid-free paper

2 4 6 8 9 7 5 3

Book design by Caroline Cunningham

For JMW—for Boonkie

One

AUGUST

1972

Why Walter woke up earlier than usual on August 10, Saturday, he couldn't at first explain. The collies next door were barking at the air, as always, no space for brains in the tiny knob between their pedigreed ears. It had rained in the night and the summer sun was already drawing steam from the moist ground. Walter would later say that he felt *her,* that it wasn't the light cutting through the misty heat or the rumpus of the Gamble dogs that made him sit up. He had gone to the window and looked out. It was like the dawn of the world down below, so green and vapory and lush with fronds, and when the lilac tree shook in her yard he admitted that his foolish heart came up his throat. He was still half asleep, and for an instant—just that long—he expected to see a reptile reeling in breakfast on its sticky tongue or a dragonfly, all veiny wings, the size of a model airplane. Thank God! It was instead Mrs. Gamble snapping at the dying wood of the tree with her red-handled loppers.

Woman, what have I to do with you? Walter thought, words he'd heard somewhere, in a play or from a book. It was five-thirty in the morning, the day of his Aunt Jeannie's and, also somewhat incidentally, his Uncle Ted's anniversary party. He needed his sleep, in preparation for the event. That he was awake and watching Mrs. Gamble must mean something. He was often assigning meaning to moments, saying, Here, and here, and here is a beginning, the opening sequence of my real life. He was fifteen and he was ready for drama even if he had to construct it himself. Ideally he'd take the part of the unlikely hero, or the witty and cunning rescuer, or the artist who is at first misunderstood. And in the conflict, he guessed, he might enjoy being hurt just enough to make an appealing victim, but not so much that he'd actually suffer. How convenient it would be, too, if change was heralded, if an epoch was launched with a clarion call or unusual weather patterns, if Mrs. Gamble could get her dogs to tweet, the birds to bark when there was going to be upheaval.

He remembered how Mrs. Gamble used to sit on her toilet in the downstairs bathroom in the old days when he was over playing with Trishie Gamble, how she smoked her cigarettes and read from her book of astrological charts. The book lay open on her lap, on her apron, her pants in folds around her ankles. Her short dingy hair, as usual, was coiled into pin curls and secured with bobby pins. She had apparently long since given up the habit of shutting the bathroom door in her own house, so what if Trishie and her son, Greg, the neighbors, the dogs, drifted by while she cast their horoscopes. Walter was Virgo, the virgin: "Exact," she told him, "methodical. Industrious. Chaste." She said the word with relish. "Ch-haste." He didn't know what it meant, precisely, and he couldn't tell if it was something he could look forward to being. " 'The Virgoan heart,' " she recited, " 'is not quickly melted, but when once it finds itself in love's furnace it glows with a pure white heat and takes ages to cool.' "

He conceded, to himself, that he was still afraid of her, a little, it was true, afraid to look her right in the eye. Down in the yard she was wrestling with the lilac branch, having trouble making her cut. It was one of the first signals, he would tell his friend Susan months later. Mrs. Gamble, the augur, with her loppers, trying to clip away the canker. When she squinted up at his bedroom that Saturday morning he ducked. He went down on all fours and crawled to his bed. She had felt his gaze—he shivered at the thought of it. He should shut his eyes and dream about a carefree Walter McCloud, a slouch, the life of the party, a boy with a new star, a new planet, a new astrological house. The Gamble collies had already barked at the neighbor, Mr.

Kloper, on his way to work, and so there was no real reason he couldn't turn over and go back to sleep.

Two hours later when Walter went down to the kitchen he found his mother standing by the sink with her nose under his brother's chin, inspecting his Adam's apple. Joyce was wearing her purple-and-blue apron that went up over her shoulders and crossed in the back with an additional sash around the waist, tied in a bow. Walter had been to the ballet the night before with his aunt, and it struck him that his mother was wearing something like a costume. He wondered if a choreographer as sensitive and penetrating as Mr. George Balanchine could translate Joyce's life into dance. What would the genius ballet master do, he wondered, to get at the essence of Joyce? He sat down to his cornflakes trying to imagine what trick Mr. B. used to bring the spirit of his dancers to the fore. In a feeble beginning, he knew, he pictured Joyce rising up and skimming across the floor on the tips of her toes doing bourrées, to pour him orange juice and set out the napkins.

"Does it hurt when I touch there?" Joyce was saying, pushing the pad of her thumb into what she thought was her older son's lymph node.

"Sort of." Daniel had thrown his head back, to the limit, and the strain made his voice sound higher than usual.

"She means, is it pressure, which is not necessarily a bad thing, or is it pain?" Walter said, turning the cereal box over to read the ingredients. He'd pulled a muscle in ballet class in July and his teacher had spoken to him in a similar vein, trying to pinpoint the hurt.

"That's right," Joyce said, "pressure or pain?"

"I don't know, Mom. I just feel it. It's big."

Walter glanced up from the box. "You two may be under the impression that you are alone, in our own house, but in fact you're providing Mrs. Gamble with an excellent view of the examination from her kitchen window. She probably has already figured out what's on Dan's neck. I bet she's on her way over here now with a cure-all, with some organic liver."

Daniel did not mutter a brotherly "Shut up," or try to move away from the sink. His head was still hanging back and he gurgled when he spoke. "*Organic* liver?"

"I'm going to talk to the doctor, Daniel," Joyce said.

"Aw, Mom, it's all right. I don't want to mess up the day."

"Overnight you have a—protrusion—as big as a—"

Walter stood up, to see. He had not ever been athletically inclined but he understood his mother's confusion. There was no ball in any American game that he knew of for purposes of comparisons. "How'd you get that?" he asked, gaping.

"I have a sore throat," Daniel said, as if that explained the vaguely three-sided growth that was slightly smaller than a tennis ball. "I woke up with it."

Over the phone the doctor prescribed aspirin and bed rest and further consultation in a day or two if the pustule hadn't drained on its own. Joyce hung up the telephone and opened the refrigerator to look at the two hundred deviled eggs she'd made the day before. The McCloud family was supposed to drive up to Wisconsin, to Lake Margaret, for Aunt Jeannie's twenty-fifth wedding anniversary. Joyce did not want to leave her son at home with such an odd malady. "Are you well enough, Daniel, to ride in the car," she said, "or are you sick enough for me, at least, to stay with you?"

Walter set his spoon down on the table and turned around to look at her. They had to go. Aunt Jeannie had asked for his help, and Joyce had made the lime Jell-O in the doughnut molds, the orange Jell-O in the fish molds, the deviled eggs, a ham and a kettle of baked beans. He realized that he'd been looking forward to the day. He didn't want to miss the occasion, and he also didn't like the idea of being at the lake, at the extravaganza, without his mother. It was she, it was her presence, that kept a family party from going off center.

There were no ballet classes in August, and Walter and his two dancing-school friends, Susan and Mitch, had been hired by Aunt Jeannie to serve the hors d'oeuvres and refill the champagne glasses. They had been instructed to wear black dress pants and white shirts and black bow ties. Aunt Jeannie had purchased silver plastic bowler hats for the servers and commanded her daughter Francie to sew silver-sequined vests. Walter had told his friends that Aunt Jeannie was a nut case, there wasn't any straighter arrow than her husband, and so there was bound to be some excitement. They'd load the car with grocery bag after grocery bag, sacks filled with buns, cantaloupes, cherries, peaches, whole watermelons, gallons of milk. On the way Walter planned to be in the fold-out seat in the back of the station wagon, squashed against Mitch, across from Susan, all of their legs tangled together, the wind blowing through the car so that none of the other McClouds, neither his parents, nor Daniel, if he made it, could hear the conversation.

Walter had been taken from his Illinois home to Wisconsin, to Lake Margaret, through the summers ever since he was born. His great-grandfather had built the Victorian house, the barn, the pump house, the privy and the summer kitchen. The estate had passed to Joyce's father and after his death to Joyce and her two sisters and two brothers. Weekend after weekend Joyce's husband, Robert, stopped at the iron gate and Joyce and her two boys got out and walked up the wooded drive. That was the important part, to walk the last stretch, to see it all come slowly through the trees: first, in the far distance, the glint of the lake, and then the red and blue of the plaid hammock strung between the oaks, and the stone shepherd boy in the middle of the fountain, the grassy opening, the croquet hoops and colored balls, and finally the house itself, the lovely old white clapboard house, with scallops and latticework, the long windows, the lacy curtains, the swing on the front porch moving in the breeze.

Walter loved that walk, the feeling that you couldn't get to Lake Margaret by car, not really. The place still had the lingering odor of carriage leather, starched sheets and kerosene lamps, and sometimes he imagined that the relatives, all of them who had come before, were still sleeping in their iron beds upstairs under the eaves. They were sleeping, the whiteness of the hot afternoon under their closed lids, the sounds in their ears of the water and the insects, the halyard idly banging against the mast in the soft hot wind. He knew the ancestors because there were photographs on a Peg-Board in the living room, pictures of the jowly great-grandmother and the great-grandfather awkwardly holding a baby. There were pictures of the great-aunts, the solemn young women with their hair piled on top of their heads, and the great-uncles with handlebar mustaches and what looked like barbershop-quartet clothes. It was so strange, Walter thought, that a house could outlive a person; strange, marvelous even, that he could walk up the drive and out of time.

Walter hated the idea of staying home from the lake, missing the anniversary party, and only because Daniel had a goiter and a sore throat. It was Daniel who, point by point, convinced Joyce that they should go and leave him behind. He would be fine in a day or two, he assured her, and, in case she'd forgotten, he was no longer five but seventeen years old, capable of pouring his own ginger ale and putting himself to bed. Actually, he said, he'd welcome the chance to rest up, to get ready for two important swim team races in the coming week.

The McClouds' house and the Gambles' house were the only two homes on Maplewood Avenue that were mirror images of each other, so that kitchen faced kitchen, dining room faced dining room. To set the day to rights Joyce, from the kitchen window, flagged down Mrs. Gamble at her sink. In a matter of seconds both women were out in their yards, standing at the Gambles' chain-link fence. Daniel's little dog, Duke, a terrier and beagle mix, did not seem to realize that it was futile to try to mount the Gamble collies through the diamond links, and Joyce absently reached for his choke collar, pulling him to her so that he was standing on his hind legs, his eyes bulging.

"How's the carport construction coming, Florence?" Joyce asked.

Mrs. Gamble reached over the fence toward Duke. "Give the boy to me." She hoisted him up, and when she had him, clasped to her bosom, she lifted up the flap of his black ear and whispered down into the inner chamber. He stopped scrabbling and went still.

Joyce remembered then that at breakfast Walter had said something about Mrs. Gamble. What was it? A line about Mrs. Gamble giving an examination, Mrs. Gamble knowing more than they did. She couldn't get it back exactly. But it was true, she thought, that Florence was like the headmistress of the block, the dread matron patrolling the corridors. She should have had a career, Joyce supposed, a position that made use of her unusual talents. A postal official barking at the next customer to step up to the window, or a meter maid marking time with her long chalk on the stick. When the children pestered the milkman for ice on humid mornings, out Mrs. Gamble charged from her back door, snapping her bullwhip on the pavement. The urchin pack scattered, gone, not a sound but the burr of the Borden's motor and the echo of the whip. Why she owned such a thing was a mystery, although some said it had come down to her from her cowhand uncle. Why she felt the need to police the children and the milkman was another puzzle. Joyce had found Walter trembling in the bushes once, the ice melting in his clenched fist, water running down his arm. There was probably not enough in Florence's three-story house, Joyce thought, and the quarter-acre lot, to keep a woman with her intellect occupied, and so she had moved beyond her property line, out into the alley, to keep watch and edify. There was no doubt that she was the pioneer with improvements on Maplewood Avenue: there had been the state-of-the-art chain-link fence, and then the rubber straps with hooks that went over the top of the trash cans to prevent retarded Billy Wexler from swiping the lids. Most recently, there was to be the addition of the carport.

Each house had its own matching garage facing the alley, but the Gambles were soon also going to have a driveway up their front lawn, ending in a carport. No one had driveways in Oak Ridge, Illinois, much less a carport. No one had ever dreamed of a carport. "How's the construction coming?" Joyce asked again.

After the update on the project, the slackers who passed for workmen, the crack in the concrete, the broken spotlight, Joyce asked Mrs. Gamble if she could keep an eye on Daniel while the family went off to Wisconsin to celebrate Jeannie and Ted's wedding anniversary.

Mrs. Gamble raised her blond eyebrow. "How long?"

"It will take most of the day, but we'll try to be home before dark," Joyce said. "Daniel knows to call you if he feels—"

"No. How many years? How long has it been for Ted?"

"Twenty-five, Florence. They, Ted *and* Jeannie, have been married for twenty-five years." Before Mrs. Gamble could make a remark about her relations, Joyce reached for Duke, prattling in a motherly way—"Here you come, upsa-daisy."

Mrs. Gamble grinned into the glare of the sun and murmured, "I hope the Jell-Os don't melt on the way."

She always watched over the McClouds' house when they were gone. It was not a hardship for her, no more devotion required to watch an empty house than a full one. Walter imagined her taking the key from her apron pocket, opening the back door, and roaming through their house when they were away, during a thunderstorm, under the pretext of checking the windows. He pictured her moving silently through all of their rooms, transfixed, so that her personal habits fell away and she didn't need to pluck at her shirt or clear her throat. She would not open the drawers or rummage around the attic. Through the simple darkness of the house she'd see into Robert and Joyce and Daniel and himself; she'd see their dreams laid out before her, see their unrealistic aspirations, their daffy ideals and the thin weave of their allegiances.

In adulthood Walter made an effort to refrain from thinking of the scenes of his boyhood as Greek theater, and yet, in spite of his resolve, he could not keep from associating Mrs. Gamble with Daniel's sickness. She was the old lady seer, the one with the pin curls, the X's of the bobby pins spelling out an oracle. It was Mrs. Gamble, after all, who watched over Daniel on Aunt Jeannie's anniversary. In their absence she may have walked through the McClouds' house whispering, *I hope the lawn chemicals haven't leached into the water, I hope the lead pipes haven't poisoned. . . . I hope the pollution from Gary. . . . I hope it isn't, I hope it hasn't.* She might have left in her wake something as insubstantial, as potent, as a dark hope.

As it turned out there was so much baggage on the trip to Lake Margaret that Walter's friends, Susan and Mitch, sat crushed in one foldout seat in the back of the car, and Walter was left with the middle bench seat. Robert McCloud had arranged the two aquamarine coolers, the suitcases and the grocery bags. It wasn't for nothing, he said, that Joyce had been a Girl Scout: she was fully prepared for an ice age, a drought, a monsoon and the invasion of the termites. Walter was pinned against the door by the coolers, it was awkward to turn around, and he had to shout to be heard. The teenagers gave up talking after a few minutes on the expressway. Susan and Mitch fell asleep against each other. Nothing had gone according to plan, and Walter stared gloomily out the window. Just as well that Daniel was sick, he thought. If he'd come they'd have had to tie him to the roof rack.

Joyce glanced back now and then to make sure there was nothing unseemly going on between the two lovebirds in the kiddie seat. She gave her husband a preview of the day to come, quietly, and with restraint, evoking her hysterical sister. Even marking the gestures, not imitating them full out, was funny, and Robert snorted into his shirt and twice said, "Oh, Joycie."

She had enough sense not to ask Walter if he was all right. She could see that he was troubled about something, and he in his turn knew that she had taken note of his unhappiness. Her general sympathy brought him a guilty little pleasure. His thin skin and tender heart were at once a source of pride and anxiety to her. He had asked to study ballet, she had known better than to try to talk him out of it, and she had clung to the belief that his enthusiasm for the dance would shield him from the predictable taunts. It had been such a stroke of luck that his two dancing-school friends happened to live in Oak Ridge. They had been put together in the First Junior Class at the Kenton School of Ballet in Chicago when they were ten years old and together they'd advanced all the way up to the Second Intermediate Class. But through good and bad fortune Walter would always have his own temperament, and Joyce feared that he would feel the injuries of adolescence more keenly than his peers. Still, she hadn't given up on a straightforward future for him, and she wondered if it was Susan, if the leggy girl squeezing against Mitch, was the source of his present misery.

Her conclusion was not exactly off the mark. Walter was thinking about the night the week before, when he and Susan and Mitch had been in the McClouds' living room, dancing and listening to records. Walter had picked out Tchaikovsky's *Serenade,* a piece that had been their favorite since the previous summer. George Balanchine, the greatest choreographer in the history of the dance, according to Walter, had made a plotless ballet to the music, and Walter, in a tribute to both virtuosos, had the volume up so high that the Gamble dogs, in their yard, cocked their heads this way and that, hearing noises in a frequency Tchaikovsky never intended. The dancers rushed headlong in and out of the doors, running the length of the room with their arms outstretched, doing the bits of the Balanchine choreography they had absorbed over the years. Between the three of them they had seen eight performances of *Serenade.* Walter and his aunt Sue Rawson had seen it four times the month before, night after night at Ravinia Park.

Mitch was always the man, intermittently lifting Susan over his head and carrying her around like a barbell. It seemed to Walter that Mitch's strength was inherent, that it was a quality he had not had to work for, no need to lift weights or wrestle or play a lot of catch. It was just there, that strength, a part of him. There were a few hard, fast, unstated rules to their dancing game, principles not to be broken or bent. They were meant for Walter. It was curious, he thought, that he understood the protocol instinctively, that no one had ever had to slap his wrist or say, Repeat after me. Funny, that it was the kind of thing he knew with animal sense. He was not allowed to lift Susan, but he could offer his arm if she wanted support for an arabesque. He was not to turn her; the pirouette business was also Mitch's privilege. Susan, however, could turn Walter, with good humor on both sides. He most certainly was not to attempt, even as a joke, to lift Mitch. But he could touch Mitch if, say, they were dancing in a circle, holding hands. Then they were comrades, the three of them. When they spun there was nearly an absence of possession.

Walter, in the first movement of *Serenade,* threw himself into the wind of the large fan on the dining-room table and struck a pose. He buffeted back and forth, in and out of the steady push of air. If only he had on one of the blue chiffon costumes that Balanchine's dancers wore, a gown that would flutter and billow after him. He was going full tilt—no one could say that he did not have enough feeling for the entire ensemble of twenty-eight girls. "Not having the blue dresses," he panted as he jetéed past Susan, "for this ballet, is probably on a par with riding a motorcycle and"—he called over his shoulder—"finding that it doesn't rev."

"You're right," she said, flying at him, taking his waist in both her hands and spinning him. "Something's missing. Your shorts don't really cut it."

Walter promptly ran upstairs and put on his heavily brocaded velvet suit coat, a genuine piece from Liberace's Mr. Showmanship Collection, an item he had found on a day God blessed him for fifteen dollars at a yard sale. It was his next best thing, in lieu of a layered blue chiffon gown with spaghetti straps. He couldn't help smiling Liberace's stiff jewely grin when he wore the suit coat. As he came back into the room it dawned on him that Liberace, Tchaikovsky and Balanchine were really after the same aesthetic. He threw his head back trying to dance as if Balanchine had first choreographed the ballet expressly for Liberace, and as if Tchaikovsky had written the music only with the Mr. Showmanship suit coat in mind. He was thinking, as he moved, that there was surely a place between the hootchy-kootchy, the watusi, well beyond the hokey pokey, but running neck and neck with the gavotte, the galliard, the courante, and with all due respect to the cha-cha, the fandango, the monkey and the mambo—a place where those forms would meld into something very like what he thought he was doing with his hips at that moment.

"Ow! Jesus! Mitch, you dropped me!" It was Susan, on the floor, hugging her arms to her chest, glowering.

Walter opened his eyes. Mitch was stooped, petting Susan's hand. But he was staring at Walter, shaking, laughing noiselessly. "What?" Mitch finally said. "What the hell were you doing, McCloud?"

Mitch rarely called his friend by his last name, but when he did, the endearment sent a tingle through Walter. "Are you okay, Susan?" Walter said.

"Fine. Just fine." Very little then, besides her feelings, had been hurt. She stood up, did a demi-plié, a battement tendu, to see if all the parts still worked.

"Honest to God, Walter," Mitch said, "what was that thing you just—"

"Would you take that stupid coat off," Susan snapped. "It makes me hot just looking at you."

Mitch sat on the sofa, clamping his teeth together to keep from tittering. Walter knew he had been a success but he puckered up, wouldn't revel in it. He got busy removing the suit coat and hanging it in the closet. Susan stood in the middle of the floor untangling the earring that was caught in her hair. In an effort to bring them back to-gether Walter said, "I'll never forget the performance Sue Rawson and I saw at Ravinia, the time we had the far-left seats and we could see backstage, and one of the dancers was sick every time she—"

Susan, her earring freed, lifted her hands over her head and rose on her half-pointes, just as the fourth movement, the Elegy section, began. She was wearing white canvas pants with holes in the knees, skinny yellowed sneakers, a lavender tank top. The only light in the room came from the Gambles' half-finished carport, the beam from the dangling fixture filtering through the leaded hall windows like the refracted light of a star. *Serenade* was sacred to Walter and Mitch and Susan in part because they knew it was sacred to the company mem-bers at the New York City Ballet, and in part because they had seen it at a time in their lives when they were especially vulnerable to the beauty of the music and the splendor of the ideas. They believed that the ballet was about the spirit world, about evil, and love, death, the triumph of goodness. Susan, only moments before in the living room, had been shocked by Walter wearing the hideous Liberace jacket, and then appalled by Mitch, throwing her around like a sack of flour, and dropping her! Hurting her! She would show them. She would return the dignity they owed to *Serenade,* to Mr. Balanchine, to Tchaikovsky and to herself.

Walter moved to the sofa and sat down next to Mitch, to watch her. She danced with her eyes shut, as if she had no need to see her au-dience or the obstacles—the piano, the rolltop desk, the coffee table, the card table with the jigsaw puzzle of the medieval fortress. There was a quality of liquid gold about her movements, Walter thought, perhaps from the strange light on her long hair, her long arms, her long exquisitely turned-out leg unfolding into an arabesque. There was such eloquence in the simple movement. He swallowed and bit his lip hard with his eyeteeth. It wouldn't do to cry and embarrass himself. He felt, watching her, that he inhabited her body, that given her set of tools, what was such an arbitrary gift after all, he would have danced just as she did. She moved as if there were no distinction be-tween her own limbs and the music, as if her flesh and the sound com-ing from the phonograph had become, in the McCloud living room, part of the same wave.

Walter soon forgot his bloody lip, forgot the tears spilling down his cheeks. Going to the ballet had always inspired conflicting emotions in him. He wanted, often in quick succession, to be the girl, wanted to be the girl with the boy, wanted to love the boy, wanted to be the boy, wanted again to be the girl. It was a confusion of endless change and pairing. But that night, for the length of the Elegy, he felt as if he were inside Susan's skin. He was one character, only one, moving her arms as she did, with each inevitable step she took.

When the music came to the end she slid into the hall with her arms flung back. Walter realized that Daniel must have slipped in at some point, that he was sitting on the edge of the wing chair. He'd been watching Susan too. The record scraped around and around. The boys sat in the gloom listening as the needle methodically crossed the scratches. They could not have said what it was she had done to start the charm. She had used basic steps that anyone could learn. She had kicked off her shoes—they might have done the same. She had put steps together and run around, tossing her head to keep her hair from falling across her face. And yet they waited in the quiet, hardly breathing. They felt they couldn't lift a finger until she did, until she told them to.

She was still out of breath when she drifted back through the wide hall arch. Like an ordinary ballerina she sank to the floor in one motion, and she spread her legs in a V, stretching over her knees, her long limp torso draped along her calves, her hair covering her feet like kelp.

Walter had wanted to reach and do nothing more than clasp Mitch's hand, maybe even hold it for a time. Daniel coughed and said, "Wow." Mitch squatted and went to Susan with his legs bent, his knuckles to the floor, like a chimp, Walter thought. The boyfriend lifted her heavy hair off her shoe, and smoothed it down her back. He lay next to her, buzzing into her ear, "Suze. Suze."

She extended her hand to him with all the poignancy of the dying swan recovering for one last little flap-flap. Walter leaned forward to see them better. It was not wrong, to look upon this scène d'amour, considering his emotion, his—involvement, considering that he could just as easily have been Susan, just as naturally had the right to reach for Mitch's fingers, to kiss them, and hold them to his own flushed cheek.

The lovers in the fold-out seat woke up when the car came to a complete stop at the end of the drive. The McClouds had arrived at Lake Margaret at eleven, well before the party was to start. The cousins' dogs barked and ran back and forth in front of the station wagon. Robert would not have felt truly penitent if he'd run over his sister-in-law's moronic dogs, and he did not slow down much. Susan looked around herself, rubbed her blue eyes, stretched, groaned and slumped back into Mitch.

Walter had not walked the usual final leg of the trip because he was bound on either side with baggage. He opened the door slowly so that none of the goods would fall out, fondly swatted at the dogs, told them, as each of the McClouds always did, and to no avail, to shut up. He smelled the freshly cut grass and the canvas sail from the great-grandfather's sea boat that was drying on the lawn. In the outside air he was sure he could detect the fragrance of the mold and must of the indoors, the cold soot of the fireplaces and the faintest hint of mothballs. He breathed deeply. The old house was in need of foundation repairs and a coat of paint, but for Jeannie's party there was enough to show off in the grounds and the enormous screen porch that looked over the lake. She had wanted her sons at least to spruce up the front entrance before the gala, but they had been busy working at the family grocery store. Walter was glad the paint was peeling. The shabbiness, he thought, made the place seem dramatic and dignified; it commanded attention, in the way a gaunt elderly woman would, the spinster who had lived through the wars.

Walter loved to lie on the swing on the porch, secure from mosquitoes and gnats, and read the nineteenth-century novels his oldest aunt, Sue Rawson, prescribed. He loved the kitchen where the aunts and nieces held on with an iron grip to the Lake Margaret etiquette, as well as to their positions, based on relations, many of which went back to their birth orders and the petty squabbles of childhood. There was only one bowl that melon balls could be served in, no sympathy for the sister-in-law who didn't know better and brought out the orange platter. Aunt Jeannie was obsessive about the refrigerator, and she defrosted it compulsively, guarding the appliance as if it were a beloved feverish animal, the wet cloths like bandages dripping down the shelves.

Lake Margaret held for Walter some of his finer memories of Sue Rawson. Of course his mother had given him life, and yet Sue Rawson, he sometimes grandly thought, had given him his own self, something that may have been even more difficult than birthing a baby. From the very beginning, it seemed, without either the benefit or the obstruction of love, his tall aunt had looked down her beaky nose at him and seen him clearly. She had planned what amounted to a seduction by taking him to the ballet when he was nine; she had known every little move he would make in his seat, how tears would spring into his eyes at the first sight of the ballerinas in their gauzy blue skirts. For him, she knew, the dancers' floating hair and arms and legs would seem like the notes made visible, like music itself running around on pattering feet. *I want to do what they are doing.* She knew the very words he'd say to himself. *I want, somehow, to be them.* She was equipped with the schedule for the Kenton School of Ballet when Joyce called a few days later, inquiring about dance lessons for Walter.

At the lake Sue Rawson often invited him up to her room during happy hour to listen to the opera on her phonograph. The rest of the family was down on the porch with the crackers and beverages and talk of boating, but he was in her room, the late-afternoon light flickering gold on the braided rug, the white curtain fluttering in the breeze. Joan Sutherland, Rosa Ponselle, Renata Tebaldi sang of heartbreak in Italian while Sue Rawson sat in her chair following the score. There was something thrilling in the severe commands she used to make him pay attention to particular passages. When he was older, he understood that she'd been trying to show him the way into a life of meaning with the music. As a child, he knew that regular people, his younger aunts, and his uncles, yapped at the children to pick up their towels, their inner tubes and buckets, but it was plain that Sue Rawson didn't spend her energy for nothing. She was different from other women and not very much like any man Walter knew. Certainly she was leagues apart from his mother, who was small-boned and had soft dark hair that curled at her shoulders. Sue Rawson had thick ankles and large wrists, a gray pageboy haircut, and the pupils in her blue eyes seemed not to expand beyond a prick of black.

Although she was his aunt, his mother's oldest sister, he never thought of her as Aunt Sue. He never called her anything to her face. At home they always referred to her as Sue Rawson. For a long time he supposed that Rawson was a suffix that any parent could add to a person's name to give it a regional distinction. As a boy he naturally did not think about her past history. In his twenties he learned that she'd inherited a considerable sum of money from a maiden Greek professor she'd had at Vassar. They had had a deep friendship, according to his mother, whatever that meant exactly, and they'd traveled to Italy and Greece together after Sue Rawson's graduation.

In Wisconsin she was usually reading on the porch, writing in the margins of her book, and she sailed in the weekend races, fiercely, with a need to finish at the head. For Walter there were long wild summer days at Lake Margaret, swimming with the cousins, swimming until his lungs were heavy with water, his ears plugged, his eyes itchy and red, his nose stuffed. The noon whistle blew from a mysterious source in town, to tell them to go up to the house for lunch. During the quiet time, if the bugs weren't bothersome, he lay in the hammock on the lawn while the cicadas, in the green of the catalpa and oak trees, pierced the quiet. In the still heat of the afternoon, damp, waterlogged deep inside himself, he tiptoed to the porch to Sue Rawson, to request another book.

At dinner the parents drank and argued about politics, slamming their hands on the table, shouting back and forth about the threat of communism, the danger of the beatnik, the hippie, Richard Nixon, Lyndon Johnson, Gene McCarthy, the unfettered female, the New Math. Walter knew very little about his own turbulent times, and he thought the adults behaved like imbeciles. If they'd had a particularly rousing meal, they marked the day and the year on one of the wine bottles with an indelible pen and placed it on the ledge on the porch. The shelf ran around the wall just above the screens and was cluttered with bottles, some that went back as far as 1900. The children, jammed together at the table, all skinny arms and elbows, were noisy and crude, farting, putting peas up their noses and, once, slinging mashed potatoes, like snowballs, at one another. It took three throws for an adult to notice the commotion across the room. Uncle Wally, who died shortly after, scooped up a mashed-potato ball from the serving dish and lobbed it over to his son. It missed his target and hit Sue Rawson squarely on the back as she made her way into the kitchen. Even the youngest child knew not to laugh. Aunt Jeannie leaped up, averting a stunned silence, and in a frenzy began both scolding the perpetrators and with her napkin blotting the buttery smear on Sue Rawson's red shirt. Walter wondered years later if that single ball of potato did it, if, as Jeannie shrilled into her ear, Sue Rawson said to herself, This, none of this, is funny.

"Will you look at that?" Robert McCloud said to Walter, when Aunt Jeannie finally made her entrance at her own party at two-thirty. The unsuspecting guests were standing on the porch holding their shiny silver party plates. The sun, blurred by a haze, seemed not to have moved in the yellowy clouds since noon. It was too hot to be a glorious day and the sky was the wrong color. But the women from Aunt Jeannie's tennis club, wearing girdles and stockings and slips under their flowered dresses, insisted that it was a perfect afternoon for an anniversary party. Never mind that it was impossible to make fans from the little limp napkins that said "Jean and Theodore" in silver cursive, that they weren't much good for mopping a brow either. No matter that there were horseflies down at the lake, not so much as a puff of air from any direction—and who had noticed that the hostess was two hours late? It was a glorious day. A splendid day!

Robert McCloud was the only one who saw Aunt Jeannie appear at the French doors. She was standing with silver tears in her dark lashes, wearing the wedding dress she had worn exactly twenty-five years before. "The celestial body," he murmured to Walter. "The comet streaking across the sky."

The guests turned to look, to see what had glimmered in the corner of their eyes.

"Dad!" Walter gripped his father's arm.

The gown had been stored at the furrier since the honeymoon. None of the beads were missing from the fitted bodice, the leg-o-mutton sleeves were crisp, and the mud had been cleaned off the train that buttoned up the back into a bustle. After six children and twenty-five years of marriage to the manager of the Jewel Food Store in Oak Ridge, it was clear that Aunt Jeannie still had her figure.

She opened her arms. "Welcome!" she cried. "Welcome!" Someone, a plant in the audience, Walter guessed, clapped, prompting everyone else to set their plates aside, to put down the runny Jell-O and the deviled eggs that had been leached of their color in the heat. They all applauded. Aunt Jeannie clasped her hands at her throat and nodded her head, left, right and center. "It is every last one of you," she declared, "who has made me the luckiest, the happiest, and the most satisfied woman in the village of Oak Ridge."

She stepped down, bobbing and smiling, and stood for a moment before the Peg-Board where the family pictures hung. Uncle Ted had been told to get some help and carefully bring it out from the living room that morning. Walter turned to Susan, to explain. "She wants the visitors to appreciate the wonder of a family that has shared such an expensive place for so long and are still speaking to each other. She's posing in front of the photographs, taking her place in the history that might just as well end with her, now, on this very porch."

Walter was unable to pour the champagne, take in the spectacle of his aunt and keep his own sweat from dripping into the clean glasses on the table. His clothes were drenched, including the lining of the silver sequined vest his cousin Francie had made. Where was she? He assumed that Jeannie had not made her children serve, that it was important they be on display as model progeny. For an instant he felt so happy that he was his mother's son, and not his aunt's child. Francie had probably been locked in the sewing room with nothing but loose hay for materials, fretting about how she was going to come up with the vests by morning. He leaned over again, to Susan. "Aunt Jeannie's taking a curtain call, not only for her entrance but for the performance that's lasted twenty-five years."

Susan smacked him on the hand. "She's gorgeous," she said, "and she's not even perspiring."

"Look at Uncle Ted," he went on, unhindered. "Look!" Ted was in the corner drinking whiskey and dribbling pear Jell-O down the front of his tuxedo.

"You really are evil, Walter," she said, snickering into her chest.

"What are you talking about? I didn't invent these human beings. I'm showing them to you, in the same way people call your attention to the tiger and the seal at the zoo. They could do the same to us, except they're too interested in themselves to— Look, look at my mother."

Susan rose up on her toes to see through the crowd. "What about her?" She squinted at Walter. "What? She looks like she always does."

"I know. That's the point."

Joyce McCloud was leaning against a post, staring out at the lake. Sue Rawson had been talking to her, but when Mitch passed with his platter of dates wrapped in bacon, Sue Rawson abruptly excused herself and followed him across the porch.

My mother, Walter thought, is entirely unto herself, serene, untroubled by the lunacy of her family. She was wearing a batik skirt, plain flat white sandals on her bare feet and a cotton blouse. Sue Rawson had been the unattractive smart girl in the family and Joyce had been the quiet, sensible one, the daughter who was at first overlooked, the child with the serviceable intellect. Aunt Jeannie had always had a gaudy suburban glamour. Even as a little boy Walter had felt there was too much of her. Too much blue on her eyelids, too much gold jewelry clattering on her wrists, too much sweetness in the rose perfume she always wore, her large hands stroking, stroking his arm, down, down the sleeve; too much sympathy, too much understanding, suffocating him with her concern. His mother's dark hair was beginning to gray at the temples and her lipstick had worn off, but he couldn't help thinking she was beautiful, and certainly the belle of the ball in the over-thirty category.

"Remember, Wally," Robert McCloud said, "it's your mother's family, not mine." He paused while Walter refilled his glass. "The kooky gene usually skips a generation."

"Uh-huh," Walter said, looking at his father, at the gap between his two front teeth, his short damp hair in spikes, the heavy lids over his brown eyes opening and closing slowly.

"You boys are all right, but you'll want to have your kids checked at birth. Watch for heavy breathing, undue excitement when they come into the world. An overdose of enthusiasm is a dangerous thing, as you can well see."

"I probably won't have any children," Walter said, wiping the rim of his father's glass with a linen towel. "It looks to me like a pretty risky business."

"I'm not raising you to care for me in my old age," Robert said, in no relation to any conversation they had ever had, "so you can put me out on the ice floe when my time comes without feeling guilty."

His father had drunk four or five glasses of champagne from Walter's table alone and perhaps more from the others. At family parties he always drank in a burst at the beginning, and then slipped away to the parlor to sleep in an armchair. Sue Rawson had driven Mitch to the inner wall and was lecturing him on George Balanchine. She was telling him about the time she'd seen Diana Adams, Maria Tallchief and Tanny LeClerq dance *Apollo*. Walter could tell by the way Mitch was nodding and smiling that he wasn't listening to a word Sue Rawson said, that the star male of the Kenton School of Ballet had no interest in a history of dance that did not yet include him.

"Father Flannery!" Aunt Jeannie screeched through the cluster of guests. "There you are." The priest had come out on the porch quietly, without letting the screen door slam behind him. She rushed to him, clutched his arm and bore right into his pink face. Walter noted that two out of the three Rawson sisters on the porch were overpowering a helpless male simultaneously. His mother was the only one minding her own business. Aunt Jeannie had been born into the Presbyterian Church, but she'd converted to Catholicism before she married. It had been Father Flannery himself who had performed the wedding ceremony at Ascension Church in Oak Ridge twenty-five years earlier. He had come up from Indiana, for the repeat performance.

"It's wonderful, so wonderful you're here!" Jeannie's hairpiece was quivering, the stiff curls slipping away from the pins. "Isn't it a glorious day? Did you see the children? They're delighted you could come!"

Walter doubted that his cousins would give so much as a fig for Father Flannery. His black robes looked to have given him prickly heat on his scrawny neck and possibly down below, underneath, on his spongy skin that never saw the light of day. Aunt Jeannie continued to fuss at him and he probably had no choice but to forbear. "It rained on our wedding day all those years ago!" She was so wound up she was shouting. "Do you remember? It poured just as we came from the church, and you carried my train, you, by yourself, to the car. I'll never forget that, never."

Walter could see that even though he had God on his side, the pastor needed rescue. It was precisely for rescue that Aunt Jeannie had hired him. She had given the team careful instructions about circulation. He picked up his tray, made his way to the center of the room, and thrust the drinks between the bride and her priest. "Champagne, Father?" he asked.

"Not until after the ceremony, my friend." He spoke reprovingly, as if it were common knowledge that saying a mass under the influence was not only dangerous but illegal.

"Ted! Ted!" Aunt Jeannie cried. "Where are you? Father Flannery is here! He's here!"

Her husband was already standing at the dresser that had been dragged out to the porch for the altar, standing just as he should have been, waiting for his wife to come forward. The presents, wrapped in silver paper, had been stacked at his side. Aunt Jeannie swept through the porch, the living room, the kitchen. She shrieked down the hill, trying to find her two boys and the four girls.

It took half an hour to round up the six Donleavys and make them presentable. Francie, the oldest daughter, had invited an Oak Ridge boy named Roger Miller to go up to the barn with her to see the bats hanging from the rafters. She was sixteen and had not yet kissed anyone. She was a hefty girl, and her mother worried that too often she hid her sweet face behind her long straggly hair. They sat on the one bale of straw in the barn and Roger Miller explained how a bat uses radar to find its food. It was so interesting, Francie said. He had weak eyes, long pale lashes and fragile wire-rimmed glasses. She had the urge to do something protective, to hold his head to her breast, and she looked at him thinking how to do that, how to take his face in both hands and draw it to her. When Aunt Jeannie, in the search for her children, finally saw the couple heading out to the woods, she ordered five-year-old Peter to snag them. Her anger was immediately tempered by the fact that Francie was with the Miller boy, a young man who had a future in the medical profession and came from one of the

23

wealthiest families in Oak Ridge. "Hello, my dears!" she called gaily to Francie and Roger as they came down the path. "Come, you two," she said, as if they'd always been together. "We're going to have the mass now."

She breezed onto the porch, and then lowered her head, demure all of a sudden, as she made her way to the altar. There was a hush as she slowly went to Ted and took her place before Father Flannery. "A faithful friend," the priest intoned, "is a strong defense; and he that hath found such a one hath found a treasure."

"Does everyone do this?" Susan whispered to Walter. "Replay their wedding?"

He moved close to her so he could speak right into her ear. "No, not everyone does this after twenty-five years of marriage. It's optional. I think it's like those Civil War reenactments. You get to dress up, fire your musket, have a bonfire, run around. It's for fun, I think."

"But it's sort of beautiful. It's not only reliving their day of glory, but it's—"

"A way for Aunt Jeannie to prove that she's thinner than everyone else her age and has a great hairdresser?"

"No! They're renewing their commitment, making a pledge for the next twenty-five years."

"And they get all these great gifts on top of it. Their children bought them a stereo. My mother spent a fortune on some silver teapot—"

"It's a good thing you don't have a sister, Walter. She'd be stunted with you as the big broth—"

"Shhhhh. Please." It was one of the tennis ladies behind them.

"Let us celebrate this union by hearing again the vows made on August 10, 1947," Father Flannery was saying.

It was difficult to hear Jeannie repeating after the priest, although the porch was much smaller than Ascension Church. She was choked up, dizzy with emotion, just as she had been the first time around. Walter reached for a drink, hoping Aunt Jeannie's friends wouldn't object to a minor's having a taste. He drank through the vows, and the prayer of thanks for the day, for the family, for the continued good health of all of those present and for peace and prosperity. He was on his third glass when Father Flannery announced that he would administer communion to the married couple and to anyone else who wished to come forward. Ted's sisters had brought the loaves all the way from an Italian neighborhood in Chicago, and broken them into pieces in the kitchen. When Susan started up to the altar, Walter reached for her hand, pulled her back to him. "You can't," he said. "It's a mortal sin if you're not Catholic."

She stopped and considered for a moment. "This will ensure my trip to hell?"

"Yes, that's right. A mortal sin."

"Good. That's good, Walter." She raised her own glass of champagne to toast him. "I've been pure, you know, up until this point. But if I do this one thing, then I'll be secure. I'll know that we'll get to the same place, that we'll always be together. I love Mitch, but I don't think he'll really last into eternity, do you know what I mean?" She kissed him on the cheek and got in line, swaying a little, closing her eyes, already bracing herself, Walter thought, for the flames catching her hair, burning her face.

After the mass, after he'd been released from his duties, Walter sat on the pier with Sue Rawson. Susan and Mitch had swum out to the raft and were wrestling, pushing each other off, struggling to get back aboard. There was that moment, as they hoisted themselves up, when they were suspended, their elbows bent, their torsos and legs pulled down by the water. After five years of ballet school Walter knew their bodies. Susan had virtually no breasts, two patty pies with penny-size nipples; each rib was clearly delineated all the way up to her clavicle, and in fifth position her legs tucked into each other as if they'd been welded together. Walter was sure that he could draw from memory the pattern of the veins on Mitch's feet, the curves the artery took as it went up his calf, the distance, bone to bone, on his hairless chest. It was hard to say which feature was the most arresting, if it was Mitch's height that commanded attention or the pinkness of his lips, the blush along his jaw, or the blue eyes, with the excessive lashes, and the gently drooping lids. The first time she'd met Mitch, Sue Rawson had said, "Now that's the sort of boy who will catch fish without a worm on his hook."

"Does it sometimes surprise you that Mitch has stuck with the ballet this long?" Sue Rawson was speaking to Walter but she was looking out to the lake.

It had never occurred to Walter that Mitch might quit. "What?" he said. "No, no, not at all. He's a natural. He loves the music, the way Susan and I do, and he always gets encouragement. And his mother makes him go to class, besides. She broke her foot the day she was supposed to dance for Sir Frederick Ashton, in London, so the story goes. It was the end of her future."

"Ashton is a simpleton," Sue Rawson said, as if all along they'd been talking about the British choreographer and not about Mitch. She pointed to the swimmers. "Do those two youngsters think they're in love?"

"Uhh," Walter said, involuntarily, as if he'd been punched.

"It's all right." She seemed about to pat him on the leg, but she must have thought better of it. Instead she reached for her binoculars and looked through, to see, up close, Mitch wrestle Susan to the prickly turf of the raft. "Don't worry," Sue Rawson said in her dry, knowing way. Susan let out a bloodcurdling scream as she fell backward into the lake. "They'll get sick to death of each other soon enough."

When they went up to the house the band was playing on the porch. Walter stood outside on the walk in his wet trunks, drinking champagne out of a paper cup, watching the guests dance to "We've Only Just Begun." He saw his mother at the far end of the porch, winding her way through the couples, walking toward him. For many years to come he could not account for what happened next, shortly after she appeared, drifting in and out of his vision. It was as if the lights went out on the sunny afternoon, as if for a few seconds everyone was tripping around blind in the night, panicking, stumbling over their own shoes. There was a noise, like a sudden clap of thunder overhead, and for an instant the sensation of darkness, the floor giving way. Walter felt the bang once in his heart, and then it echoed out of him, into the silence. The guests stood still, their hands clapped to their chests or their ringing ears. A large woman in a floral muumuu whispered, "Lord a mercy."

The air cleared, became bright again. All at once everyone could see the disaster. The Peg-Board, with the family pictures, had fallen to the floor. What a noise it had made! Joyce, who may have been the only one not stopped by the commotion, continued her walk between the men and the women, the dancers who had burst from one another's arms. She went out the door. She did not acknowledge Walter standing on the grass. She walked across the lawn and onto the footpath that led to the woods.

Aunt Jeannie was too horror-struck to weep or take action. She could only whimper, "How did this happen? How did it happen?" Uncle Ted, useful at last, ordered his brother and his nephews to lift up the board and set it against the porch wall. The glass of every single frame was smashed and the shards lay as they had been broken. The pictures that remained on the board were crooked, or their matting had fallen and dangled below the frames. "Go get the broom, please, Brian," Uncle Ted said. "Charley, mops in the woodshed— watch your step, Mrs. Gardener, watch out there for the glass." Nothing more dramatic than a broken jar of pickles, an everyday occurrence down at the Jewel; he'd seen it all, women's water bursting, cantaloupes in smithereens in the produce aisle, freezer doors left open overnight and in the morning rivers of ice cream and orange juice flooding down to checkout. His aptitude, in truth, was not for managing money or overseeing a complex and perishable inventory, but rather for directing the stock boys to clean up and keeping the ladies from peril.

It was shortly after the mess was cleared away that Walter heard Aunt Jeannie's piteous cry from the living room. "Where is Father Flannery? Didn't anyone show him to his room? Didn't anyone tell him he could stay the night?" Her older sons were dead drunk in the boathouse, and the younger daughters were in the trees down at the lake, jumping into shallow water from dangerous heights. Francie had finally gotten Roger Miller to look her in the eye and the two were necking, tentatively, behind the woodpile. "Where is Father Flannery?" Aunt Jeannie wailed. Her hairpiece had wilted and come off and she was carrying it in both hands as if it were her bridal bouquet. The priest didn't answer. Nobody had seen him leave hours before. He had eaten a sour grape off of the arbor up in the old tennis court, where his car was parked, looked at his watch and told himself he could be back in Indianapolis by dark.

The McClouds were quiet on the way home. Walter and his friends were sunburned and woozy. Robert had slept through the catastrophe on the porch, slept through the noise of the two frightened babies and woken only when most of the guests had gone. He felt refreshed and ready to drive. It had been a hard day for Aunt Jeannie, and he personally was glad to have gotten through it. He was looking forward to Sunday, to some tennis early in the morning, and Daniel's swim meet in the afternoon. His wife was resting in the front seat next to him, and he did not disturb her. Joyce wasn't asleep but she kept her eyes closed, and her face turned to the window, to the hum of the August night. She thought she might just call Mrs. Gamble's son, Greg, when she got home. She might ask him if he would teach her this transcendental meditation business. She hadn't told Robert yet, but she'd had an upsetting conversation with Sue Rawson in the middle of the party. She was going to need something in the coming months, an aid, her own little syllable, to calm her.

They drove up Maplewood Avenue. Most of the houses had a few lights on downstairs and, in the upstairs, the dim yellow glow that came from the children's night-lights. Their own house was black, the windows reflecting the streetlights, as if the place had no heat, no life, no center of its own. The Gambles' house was ablaze and the Missus herself was standing under the light on her front porch, her cigarette burning between her two fingers, her arms crossed, waiting. Waiting for them as if they were truant children. She looked as if she was too mad to shout, too mad to curse; she looked as if she was going to take her time and when she was good and ready she'd whisper, she'd practically spit each word, Where—Have—You—Been?

Two

SEPTEMBER

1995

At the end of the summer Walter spent several days at Lake Margaret trying to envision his future. It was an embarrassment, to be in his late thirties and straining, still, to see what came next. He hoped that no one was spying on him as he sat on the pier watching for a light to shine from somewhere out in the dark years before him. He had struggled to find his way as a teenager and as a college student. It was humbling to be in the future, in the time that should have been filled with satisfying labors and triumphs. How was it that he was sitting in the same chair, trying again to divine the path ahead? Most of the people he knew seemed to have had little difficulty long ago choosing a profession and stepping into the role, using the jargon naturally, looking the part. His cousin's husband, Roger Miller, had decided in the third grade to be an optometrist; Susan had always been on the ballerina track; Daniel had wanted to become a marine biologist.

Through his twenties and thirties, Walter had worked at a dollhouse shop on the Upper East Side in New York City, selling furniture and house kits, and teaching his customers how to install the dinkiest marble tile, hardwood for floors, period molding and slate shingles. He understood the allure of the miniature because he had grown up helping Joyce put together and decorate her three-story town house with a dormer. They'd wired the downstairs with electricity, so that at Christmas the impossibly small candles clipped on the three-inch tree in the parlor filled the room with what his father called a homier-than-thou yellow glow. Walter knew that for his adult customers the simple delight of reducing real life in all of its detail to fit on the coffee table was worth eyestrain and aching fingers. There was also the more complicated charm of creating a kingdom so small that a person could perfect it. What woman wouldn't find it gratifying to make something incorruptible by human beings? No slob was ever going to track mud through the $4,000 Georgian brick town house with twenty-six hundred hand-laid mini bricks, or the English baby house with dentil molding, or the southern colonial, fourteen rooms, full attic, with clapboard siding and a cedar shake roof.

Walter had been sympathetic to some of his clients at the shop, ladies who, like himself, loved the spirit of a house as much as the particulars of design and structure. To his way of thinking there was nothing hokey or Oriental in the idea that a house had a life and sensibility of its own. He would never have said that a building had an aura, but the long and the short of it was that some places felt right and others did not. He indulged himself in the pleasure of communion with his customers as together they bent over veranda spindles and newel posts and finely turned balusters. For a while he thought he might fill his studio apartment at Ninety-sixth and Amsterdam with a replica of his old neighborhood in Oak Ridge. His boss would have given him the materials at cost, the construction would occupy him for years, and when he finished, decades later, the *Smithsonian* magazine could do a feature on him—he, an old man with a hobby. He supposed at the root of the project was the normal longing to fashion his own history and commemorate what was past. A friend had dragged him to the Y, to a seminar on taking charge and living in the moment, but the theories and techniques were suspect, Walter thought. The moment, after all, was a flash in the pan. Life, he knew, had meaning and was fully possessed only as it was remembered and reshaped.

It had taken Walter several years to admit to himself that he couldn't go on indefinitely selling Lilliputian Coke bottles and microscopic toilet-roll dowels. What, then? How was he to spend his days and how was he to earn his bread and butter? Maybe through his childhood he hadn't focused, hadn't crossed his legs at night on his bed, eyes closed, concentrating on Walter in a pinstriped suit, Walter shaking hands with the boss, Walter on the front page of *The New York Times* sealing a $70 million deal with a great American company.

He had not visualized prosperity and fulfillment, and so he was thirty-eight years old, sitting at the end of the pier at Lake Margaret wondering where to live in the years before retirement. The wind blew across the lake, driving off the sailboats and turning the water a darker green. Already some of the leaves had yellowed, drifted to the ground and stuck in the bushes. The neighbors were burning brush and to Walter the air smelled of autumn. He watched the chipmunks darting to the holes in the cracked seawall with wads in their mouths, and he thought that if he were a small animal in Wisconsin he would know by the smell to expect great change. Smoke filled the air, spiraling into the pale blue sky. He used to think there was nothing as sad as Lake Margaret in the fall, and it seemed so again. Summer was over, school would begin, winter was upon them. All green things, the moss, the vines, the children at their desks, would soon experience a prolonged state of near death.

In the daylight Walter sat far into the old white Adirondack chair, drinking coffee, and in the night he sat there also, under the heavens, wrapped in a quilt. He had never been out of doors by himself for that long, and it seemed to him enough of an occupation, watching the water change color, watching the fishermen holding their rods hour after hour in their metal boats. A morning went by, and he had only looked, and remembered, and looked, in the honest labor of smelling the change of season and waiting for absolutely nothing. He looked across the lake to the cow pasture and he looked at the water, where he sometimes saw his ghostly boyish form swim up to the surface. His was an ordinary tragedy, he knew. He had been happy as a child and had not realized it. But happiness was spent so quickly, he thought, and identifying it, feeling it, trying to hang on to it, made him nervous. Maybe it was better to be ignorant of bliss, unselfconscious, and later have the sense to recognize its traces.

In May, Walter had applied for a job teaching English at Otten High, in Otten, Wisconsin. He had been back to school part-time in the last four years for his certification. It had been a marvel in the spring during his inquiries to hear the secretary at the school say "Otten," and then "Wisconsin," as if her vowels, the broad Wisconsin *o,* were on display for a freak show. Walter could have supplied good reason for wanting the job, but he had applied primarily on a whim. It was the secretary, Mrs. Oldenberg, and her bewitching voice, and it was also the fact that Otten was an hour from Lake Margaret. The town of three thousand people had been named for a temperance leader, Samuel Otten, an easterner who had hoped to build a temperance utopia out in the wild Wisconsin territory. Well over one hundred years later there were taverns dotting the village map. Walter didn't know if such an inception, followed by the abandonment of the ideal, was a good sign. He and Samuel Otten were perhaps cut from the same cloth, two men from the East with ridiculous expectations. Maybe it was absurd to imagine he could teach farm boys Shelley's "Hymn to Intellectual Beauty," but from a distance it didn't seem impossible. They might not heckle him; it might be worth a try.

He had learned, a week before, that from the fifteen applications he'd submitted had come only two offers. It was a choice between a school in Queens and Otten High. He had grown accustomed to life in New York, and he wasn't sure he could make the adjustment to a town with a one-screen movie theater, no bookstore, no café, no opera company, not one ballet troupe and no chain clothing stores. It was unlikely, too, that there would be very many of his own kind in Otten. Either pick involved the risk of death, he considered, one literal, the other spiritual. The Queens high school had metal detectors at the door, equipment that weeded out assault weapons and handguns. Box cutters, apparently, were not detectable by the scanner. A math teacher had bled to death after his throat was slit in May.

Walter sat with his feet in the water pitting one place against the other, thinking of irrelevant specifics, weighing the appeal of the mangy city rodents, slinking along the subway tracks, against the type of rat sure to be found in Otten, the sleek, well-fed beast that made its living in the grain elevators on the edge of town. He listed the famous people who had grown up on Wisconsin soil: Spencer Tracy, Georgia O'Keeffe, Thornton Wilder, Harry Houdini and, of course, Liberace. Wladziu Liberace, born in the working-class town of West Allis;

Wladziu, Polish for Walter, had been called Wallie when he was a boy. Surely the Liberace connection was as good as a marker, showing him the right direction.

Mr. McCloud, from Otten, Wisconsin, Walter said to himself. He rolled up his pants and slowly let his legs slip into the lake. If it warmed up he might swim out to the raft. There were very few boats around on the weekdays, and if he got a cramp and started to drown no one would see him flailing. In the years that he had been gone from the Midwest, his father and Uncle Ted had planted cedar and maple trees along the fence line to keep the neighbors from the family's intimate moments. Francie and Roger Miller had gotten married at the water's edge with a string quartet in the grass on one side of them and a brass ensemble on the other. There had been two memorial services, three weddings and numerous office parties. Walter had missed a good many of the celebrations. He couldn't help reminding himself that Daniel would not have strayed so far from home, would not have fled the way Walter had after high school. Daniel had not ever really left the 600 block of Maplewood Avenue in Oak Ridge. He was forever eighteen, forever the child who would not willingly leave his parents for adult life. It was so easy to imagine that Daniel would have become successful in a conventional way, someone who moved confidently through the halls of a venerable financial institution in the heart of the city. Daniel might well have bought a house down the street from the McClouds, calling on Joyce and Robert in the evenings, to ask their advice, to dispense his own wisdom.

It was a trap, rusty, clanking, stinking, Walter knew, to glorify the lost brother, the kind of son who would have driven up to Lake Margaret every weekend to spare his father the trip, who would have mowed the lawn, checked the locks, weather-stripped the windows, cleaned the gutters. Walter tried to imagine himself on the tractor mower, wearing a chambray work shirt, a baseball cap, canvas pants with compartmentalized pockets down the thigh that snapped shut. It didn't require more than five or six minutes to get the picture in focus, to see all of the accoutrements clearly: Walter, revving the engine, wearing a dark blue cap, Ray-Bans, and his new mail-order fanny pack, complete with water bottle, securely fastened at his waist. After struggling for nearly seventy-two hours to imagine a future, and coming at last to the vision—Walter McCloud dressed for lawn care—he said to himself, Maybe. Maybe I could live in Otten.

He had read in the paper that there was a trend, a tide that could be charted, people of his generation who had moved away from their birthplaces and were coming back home in middle age. Walter could be part of a legitimate trend, a pattern that as far as he could see was not harmful to his or anyone else's health. "A trend," he said out loud, as if the word might charm him into casting the deciding vote: Otten or Queens. Aside from the comfort of being at last a part of a movement, he thought that it was probably time to return to a place where he had imagined himself, even if the image was farfetched. He leaned back against the Adirondack chair and pictured himself mowing the slope down to the lake, the sunset in the distance, through the trees, the bats hanging by their little feet in the barn, staying put, and all the summer insects, every one of them, fluttering around the yellow porch light.

On Walter's fourth day at Lake Margaret his old friend Susan drove up from her parents' house in Oak Ridge with her two children. She lived near Miami now, in Coral Gables. There had been very few students at the Kenton School of Ballet who were star quality, and from her beginning there she was best girl. She'd left Illinois for Manhattan when she was seventeen, and at eighteen she became a member of the New York City Ballet. She was one of the last dancers to be handpicked by Mr. Balanchine for the roster, before his illness. At his Russian Orthodox funeral all of the ballerinas stood in the darkness of the vaulted cathedral holding lit candles. Susan, tears streaming down her face, was in the center of the photo that ended up in *Time* magazine. A year later she shocked her friends and relations by quitting the company. She hadn't the heart for it, she said. Didn't like the new management. She failed to mention that she'd met a man named Gary Morgan at a party, that she'd fallen in love with a normal, non-artistic person, the owner of a bookstore in Coral Gables. She moved to Florida, decorated Gary Morgan's house, signed on with Edward Villella to dance with the Miami Ballet and got married. "There's more

Balanchine in Miami," she always insisted, "than there is in New York." When Walter visited her he was always freshly horrified by the tiny lizards that skittered like mice across the sidewalks.

In the afternoon Susan and Walter stood up to their ankles in Lake Margaret while the two boys swam. She had not aged much in the twenty years since her high school graduation. Her hair rippled from her forehead and went all the way down her back just as it had when she was seventeen. "I don't know anyone else whose hair cascades," Walter said. "It wimples. And rumples. I don't think there's any amount of money the average woman could pay to get the effect, right from the roots, of undulation."

"You're getting corny, Walter," she said, pulling the mass over her shoulder and inspecting it for split ends. "Is that what happens when a person is nearly forty?"

Her nose was a little bit stubby, her one flaw, but otherwise Walter thought that, counting the hair, she was close to the ideal. She had large blue eyes, thick blond lashes, the right amount of mouth, curving lips that had a certain elasticity, and she wasn't too thin. He had seen plenty of dancers who had starved themselves and looked like plucked chickens.

"Speaking of old age," she said, "I've been meaning to tell you. I met someone recently who reminded me so much of Daniel."

"That happens to me, sometimes," he said, splashing water up along his arms.

"No, but this man was so much like him. And it occurred to me, afterwards, that you and I, as close as we are, have never really talked about that year Daniel was sick. We avoid it. There, I've said it. Well, anyway, it was startling to be with this person who had some of Daniel's mannerisms and what seemed like the same sort of organizing principle in his brain, if that makes sense. In many ways they are nothing alike, but there was something uncannily similar about, I don't know, maybe their chakras."

"You're getting wonky in your old age, darling. Are your earrings—they're crystals, right? Are they functional? Do they tell you where to go, what to buy, who to trust?"

"It's just fashion, Walter, and we haven't even hit forty, so let's stop this talk, please. I admit to thirty-three in the company, even though everyone probably knows it's a lie. But I've wondered through the years who Daniel would have become—and this man seemed like a good approximation. His face could have been a computer simulation of Daniel's, those renderings of how a person, at seventeen, will look when he's forty-five. Or maybe I'm making it up, and it's only that we're still somehow looking for him, missing him. Is that ridiculous after all these years?"

Walter squinted across the lake, at the pasture that had grazed cows since his grandfather's era. "In books, death is what often propels the plot," he said, "either ignites the action or finishes it. Death or marriage, one or the other. For me, death has always been right under my skin, not doing much to move me in any real direction, no plot device. It's just there, lurking, a spot, the Daniel stain, in every cell. I can't say that such a presence is useful, or has taught me some great lesson the way it would in a novel. The law of thermodynamics, you know, the idea that nothing is lost, that a loss in one area equals a gain in another, was actually not invented by scientists but by the people who write redemptive fiction. Stories that are praised for being a testament to the human spirit. Actually, in real life, we lose things all the time and they're gone. Lost, period."

That was as much as Walter had said about Daniel in years. Susan reached under the water, picked up several snail shells and turned each one, snail by snail, over in her hand. After she had examined all of them she said, "I used to think that Daniel, when he died, had really gone to India or Burma, and that I could go there and find him walking down the street—"

Just then her nine-year-old boy, Tim, stepped on a sharp stone and yelped. She sprang up on the pier and ran down the rickety wooden slats to hoist her son to safety and examine his big toe. Walter climbed the rock steps to shore and went for the Band-Aid box in the boathouse. He was grateful to the child for putting an end to the conversation. He didn't want to speak about Daniel, or Susan's role that year, the year they glossed over when they reviewed their history. The cut toe was bloody. The Band-Aid swam in the wound, wouldn't stick, and in the end they bound it in a rag Walter found in the tackle box.

They hobbled up the gravel path to the house to get warm and find something to eat. The boys huddled in their bathrobes on the lawn, in the sunshine, eating Oreos. "What's this town like, Walter, where you've decided to teach?" Susan said, licking the filling out of a cookie and crushing the rest into the grass. He noted, as he always did in her company, that she used his name when she spoke to him, as if she liked to say it, liked the feel of her tongue to the back of her teeth, making the *l,* anticipating the explosion of the *t.* In college, when he had had no idea what to study in order to have a profession, he looked up "Walter" in the *Oxford English Dictionary.* There was no hope, no consolation in the definition, a rendering that was so at odds with the tidy and productive Virgo Mrs. Gamble had once promised him. "Walter" meant: to roll, to be tossed on the wave; to wallow, or revel in; to move or go unsteadily, totter or stumble; to surge or roll high. He was therefore living up to his name when he was drunk or stoned, a condition he found himself in regularly during his college years, rolling high and tottering at the same time, behaving, without question, like an ass.

"Walter," Susan said again, "what's this town like, this Otten?"

"I don't know much about it, but it strikes me as a barren, inhospitable place, about as cozy as Siberia, although not as far from train service. I suppose in the drabness there are probably fabulous wildflowers and stunning native grasses. It's a sleepy, ugly little town in the middle of nowhere, and as far as Otten High goes, although the management doesn't come out and say, it's basically a technical school. Twenty percent are college-bound."

"Oh no! You'll be casting your pearls before swine!"

"My pearls? Yes, well, there's certainly no harder task than that, is there, but maybe there's no better one either. Imagine those poor pigs having nothing but slop all their lives. The school retains a Latin teacher—how's that for an idiosyncrasy? She's about a hundred and sixty-five years old and of course cuckoo, as all Latin teachers are. Either they haven't the heart to let her go, or some codger on the school board can recite Catullus and values the subject. And, I hate to have to break this to you, sweetie, but you cast your pearls before swine at every performance. There are people out in the audience who are falling asleep, having spent their money on a ticket so they can dress up and be seen doing something high-minded. And there are probably plenty of situations where we're the swine and we don't even know it."

"Oh, all right. You win. But still, why choose Otten? Isn't there a middle ground, a place like Oak Ridge, a suburban school with adequate funding and serious students?"

"Why choose it?" he repeated. "I could go into a hypnotic state with the aid of your earrings and tell you that *it* chose me. The truth is, I don't really have a choice, not now, not this late in the season. I'm behind everyone else, having been in the miniature business half my life and looking for work in midsummer. Fire or ice, those were the options."

"Queens or Otten," Susan murmured.

"It's been easier to justify Otten than you might think. I'd love to get to know my niece, Linda, for starters. For once I'll be close enough to act like an uncle. And I'd like to spend time with Sue Rawson. It's unlikely that she is ever going to die, but in the event that she does pass on, I will be glad to have been in her company. Plus, I'm an hour from Lake Margaret and can help Mom and Dad look after this place. I went up and visited Otten the other night and I got a little bit of an *Our Town* kind of glow. There was a man on the school baseball diamond running his toddler daughter around the bases. That seemed promising. There was a great big retarded girl riding bikes with her younger sister, and that also seemed sort of hopeful in its own way. A real estate agent named Penny took me around and showed me the rental properties, all four of them. I could have a house for six hundred dollars a month, a whole house, with shrubs and tulips in the yard, an island in the kitchen, a living room with windows that look out to woods, to nature. There are deer antlers hanging on the garage and people will think I'm a sportsman. They'll call me Mr. McCloud. I'll buy a compact car and a speed bike and a Weber grill. I don't know, for some reason it doesn't sound that terrible."

The younger boy, Toby, shouted to the older one, "That shovel is mine, I hate you! I had it first."

"And there won't be racial conflict in Otten. I'll have garden-variety discontent to cope with, such as we see here, but not gang warfare." Walter left the children to their mother. He went to the woodshed to find the old puppet theater and the accompanying trunk. He didn't remember ever fighting with Daniel, although they must have occasionally had words and come to blows. They had grown up like ghosts to each other, a shadow in the hallway, a clink at the breakfast table, a breeze coming across the porch. Sue Rawson had constructed the red-and-green plywood box and sewn a crimson velvet curtain for the front and the back of the puppet theater. She had at one time done elaborate productions, in the days when she had only a handful of nieces and nephews, before she realized that they were fundamentally uncivilized. Walter dressed the French hand-carved wolf in Red Riding Hood's cloak and an old pair of Barbie's stiletto heels. Over the years a few stray items had made their way into the trunk, corrupting the contents.

On the lawn Walter lay behind the theater, making the wolf hero-ically sing, in his heels and cloak, and with a strained falsetto, "O mio babbino caro." The performance did not mesmerize Susan's boys, and before the aria ended Tim whacked Toby on the nose, yet another bloody scene. Susan, with no pity in her gesture or her voice, handed Toby a mass of tissues from her purse and ordered both of them into the station wagon.

"Sometimes," she hissed at Walter, "I despise them." She began picking up her things, talking more to herself than to him. "I love them best when they're asleep or when I'm gone—there, that's the horrible truth. When I dance I use that love to set me spinning. But the reality of them, God! I'm not sure I'm cut out for this, Walter."

He watched her gather their towels, plastic shovels, buckets, trucks and wet suits, compressing what was strewn over the lawn into one beach bag. Mothers, he thought, had the ability to rake up pos-sessions and compact them, make the whole impossible load portable. Their proficiency was probably encoded in their genes, the packing skill having been selected for first in nomadic days, carried forward into the covered-wagon era and on into the age of mass-produced toys. Despite her agitation and her comment about mothering he could tell she was a good parent. Her boys were high-spirited, but they weren't cocky, they weren't cruel. She'd wanted a normal life with children and that had been one of the reasons she'd left the City Ballet, given it up. He stood aside, watching, telling her about how the ten Klopers on Maplewood Avenue used to go on vacation, and be-cause seat belts had not yet been invented, Mother Kloper used to cram five into the middle seat, four in the back, the baby up front.

They each had a paper lunch bag with the one plaything they were allowed to take along.

"One toy"—Susan snorted. "Ah, those halcyon days."

"They were halcyon all right," Walter said. She was getting into the car, leaning over the front seat to give Toby the evil eye. "Do you remember Aunt Jeannie's anniversary party?" he asked. "Do you remember how my mother made the wall of pictures topple over, and the frames shattered?"

"No!" Susan held her seat belt halfway across her chest. "Not your mother! She didn't make that happen."

"I wouldn't be so sure. I sometimes think she might have given it a nudge. She was the only one who wasn't shocked by the noise or the mess. Sometimes I think of it, and I wonder." Walter bent down and kissed his friend through the open window. She hardly noticed, immobilized by the idea of Joyce McCloud willfully committing a destructive act.

"I don't believe it," she said, shaking her head. "Why? Why would she have done such a thing?" She let the belt go and pulled it again, this time all the way across herself. "We never gave your mother a literary personality, did we? It's so interesting, to think about who she was in those days. We are her age now, Walter, do you realize that?"

He put his hands to his forehead to make a visor. He studied the sky, trying to look as if he was making an effort to remember. Joyce was outside literature, he thought, not someone they could easily peg. Through high school he and Susan, and Mitch too, had had the habit of assigning one another parts from their current favorite novel. The practice gave ordinary life the weight it would never have, and also lent substance to their own personalities. It was only lately that Walter had seen the obvious: Mitch as Charlotte Stant, and himself as Maggie Verver. But in the old days Susan was always the moral or immoral beautiful and intelligent heroine: Elizabeth Bennet, Margaret Schlegel, Anna Karenina, Dorothea Brooke. Mitch in that era was naturally the romantic lead and Walter the character part. Susan was the only dancer Walter had ever known or heard of who read serious novels.

"It was ingenious of you, to marry a bookseller," he said.

"All the uncorrected proofs I can read," she said, smirking at him. "A brilliant career move. Oh, Walter, you've got me thinking about that anniversary party. Daniel was supposed to come, wasn't he? He had been going to bring the girl on the tennis team—Eleanor O'Reilly was her name. But he got sick that morning. The very day. And the old bag, the neighbor lady of yours, Mrs. Gamble, was so angry at your parents when you got home. She took your mother by the shoulders, said she had no business leaving a kid with a tumor on his neck at home by himself."

"There hadn't been a diagnosis yet," he said, "but she seemed to know already that it would kill him."

"God, she scared me. I thought she was going to attack your mother. Or maybe it was those dogs of hers. They were all going crazy behind her fence." She chewed on her lip and Walter noticed that she had fine lines—wrinkles—on her brow. "Anyway, now you're leaving your old life and moving back here. I hope your students can read other things besides the gearshift panel of their John Deere tractors." She stroked her forehead as if she knew he had seen the creases, as if she was trying to smooth them away. "I'm a lot dumber than I ever thought I'd be. I planned to be a famous ballerina, an artist, and deep down I'm just a suburban mom with a paneled station wagon, domestic problems, two bratty kids who sleep on cotton sheets patterned with trucks. But you, you are going to teach your swine to walk and talk!" She reached both hands out of the window, pulled Walter's head in, and solemnly kissed him on the mouth.

"Ask your mother if she made the pictures smash and why," she called as she started down the drive. "I'll bet you a million dollars she didn't."

"She'll never tell," Walter shouted after her. "That's what I bet. She will never tell."

Before school began in Otten, Walter drove to Schaumburg, Illinois, to visit his baby sister, Lucy. She had been born in 1974, when a good portion of the family's life, in Walter's view, was over. She had missed growing up with his brotherly instruction and he couldn't keep himself from thinking that such an absence might explain why she was living in a place like Schaumburg. He was arrogant, he knew, but he couldn't help it, couldn't help wanting to improve her, to make her see what was hollow about her choices. He was, after all, thirty-eight years old, and she only twenty-one.

There was nothing good about Schaumburg, in his opinion, not the mall around which the town had recently been built, not the corporate headquarters, not the concrete sprawl of it, not even the sweet backward intentions of the planners who wanted to build a Main Street with a mock downtown. He did not like the wide new streets in Lucy's subdivision, with culs-de-sac that were supposed to prevent undesirable people from speeding and pillaging. All of the homes in the neighborhood—a term he used loosely for Lucy's environs—had two-story foyer windows and skylights in the master bedrooms, but they were alike in a way the Oak Ridge houses had never been. Maplewood Avenue, he knew, had once been a tract and many of the Queen Anne–style houses had identical floor plans, but all the same those structures had grace and beauty, and also character. In fact, there were certain houses that seemed to attract handicapped or troubled people and others that assured a type of normalcy. It was as if the buildings themselves determined the owners. In Schaumburg there was probably an ordinance that broadly defined and prohibited weirdos. Nothing, Walter believed, neither a range of owners nor the ravages of time, would add texture or variety or interest to the houses. And where was the alley? In Oak Ridge, Mr. and Mrs. Kloper and the ten girls had lived to the south of the McClouds, and their cousins, the other Klopers, were in the yellow house straight across the alley, all twelve of them, all boys. For years there had been jokes about the water, the air, the soil on one side of the alley versus the other, and the effects those elements had on determining gender. The alley itself was the great divide, the place where the children spent the daylight hours, but after, in the dusk of summer, they split away, each to his own turf, and went to war.

Walter couldn't imagine that there was one personality in Schaumburg as peculiar as Mrs. Gamble, not one woman who would storm out of her house with a bullwhip when the little children begged from the milkman. He was stubborn and not altogether reasonable about his dislike of his sister's town. It was middle-aged of him, he realized, to feel irritated by a place, to be bothered by the fact that there were driveways instead of alleys, that there were no stay-at-home mothers, no tired housewives in curlers, no women who started drinking whiskey sours at three in the afternoon on their porches. Where was that leisured class, the Mrs. Gambles, who took it upon themselves to police the families, the dogs, the village employees? Mrs. Gamble could detect the tantrum of a spoiled child in a faraway house. The squall of a husband and wife. The low rumble of the garbage men, always late, coming from the west side of Oak Ridge. There was no point and certainly nothing attractive in middle-aged despair, and yet, Walter thought, someone had to have angst. It should not have been surprising that the old neighborhood would slowly vanish as the children grew up and their parents moved away and the world changed, but he was on hand to say, I am surprised! I am dismayed. I don't like it!

There was a quietness about Lucy's street, as if each house were stranded on its own lawn. It was hard to believe that men and women were really behind their closed paneled doors, couples thinking, cooking, making love, banging on a piece of wood with a hammer down in the basement, something, anything, for home improvement. The shades were drawn all down the street as if a president had been assassinated, as if one a day got a bullet through his head.

Walter arrived in Schaumburg on Saturday morning, just as his three-year-old niece was getting ready to go to her ballet class at the park district. Lucy had invited Walter especially for the class, because of his interest in the dance. He was standing on the blue mat that said *Welcome!* in red cursive, talking to Lucy before she appeared. "Linda's too young," he was saying as the door swung open. "Do the park district officials look at the feet? Would they know what they were seeing if they did? Who does she take after, you or Marc?" He waved his hands in front of his face. "It doesn't matter—the fact is she's too young."

"Walt," Lucy said, smiling at him. "I'm fine too." She was the only person who had ever called him Walt. He had also once looked up

"Walt" in the *Oxford English Dictionary*. It meant to revolve in the mind, to consider. It meant to fall into anger or madness. His name, in any form, did not portend an easy life.

Lucy took him by the arm and led him into the entry that was as large as the New York studio apartment he had left behind. His sister's house always had the gift-shop aroma of dried flowers and scented candles. Walter took a whiff and coughed. He wondered how a suburban girl had taken to the country craft movement, if it was pure chance, a mutation that had made his mother's home-decorating gene run amok in Lucy. There were plaid bows around the stems of the brass candlesticks on the mantel, checked gingham curtains with tiebacks, and at every turn a fabric goose, a wooden goose, a porcelain goose, a stenciled gaggle of geese. There were pigs too, pink pigs, white pigs, stuffed pigs, china pigs. The house had come with the opulent foyer chandelier, a dazzler, all right, with several hundred prisms hanging from ever smaller steel circles that went up to the ceiling. The fixture clashed with the barnyard motif, but unfortunately it seemed to be attached to the main beam without hardware, a natural and permanent outgrowth from the ceiling. Walter's niece was sitting on the carpet through the way into the living room, picking out bits of pink lint in the white tulle skirt in her lap. "Hello, Miss Queen Dido," he called to her.

Linda looked up, slowly, blinking, as if she'd been asleep. She hadn't rushed to the door, calling his name, spinning around, wriggling with excitement. "Hi, Uncle Walter," she said dutifully.

He thought her terrifyingly well mannered, as quiet and closed as the houses in the neighborhood. To Lucy he said, "Her feet are not ready for ballet. Her bones are too malleable. I looked at them last weekend, at the lake. They're baby feet, soft, like pudding. In Russia they don't start children until they're nine or ten, and only after each one has had a complete physical, only if the child is suited for the rigorous training. I'm serious, Lucy. She's too young."

"You? Serious?" She reached around him with slack arms, and laid her head on his shoulder.

"Take her to *The Nutcracker* when she's eight," he commanded, absently patting her back. He called out to Linda, "Cover your ears." She obediently clapped her pudgy hands to either side of her head. "She'll want to be Clara more than anything in the world," he said into Lucy's silky sweet-smelling hair. "Blue satin dress, golden curls, white pantaloons, pink shoes. After the performance, tell her you can't afford the lessons. Apologize. Keep telling her about your impoverished state, even when she weeps, begs, beseeches. Pretty soon she really will want lessons more than a puppy, more than Barbie's dream house, more than getting her navel pierced. She'll take up religion. She'll pray. When her demands reach a feverish pitch you say, 'Maybe. Maybe, Linda.' Right before she goes over the edge you acquiesce, although grudgingly. It will be perfect timing, you see, because at that point she will be ready to submit to the torture, and find the path to the divine." He took a deep breath. "This park district thing is all wrong."

Lucy had moved away from Walter halfway through his prescription for her daughter's dancing career. She'd enrolled Linda in the ballet class thinking it would please him. She laughed a little as he spoke, as she wrangled the child into her yellow-and-white tutu. "There's no telling what goofy old Uncle Walter will say or do," she whispered. Linda was already wearing white tights and yellow ballet slippers. The yellow headband, with pink and green flowers sticking straight up on a thick wire, wound in a white ribbon, gave her the antennaed look of an ant.

"She loves her class, don't you, Lind," Lucy said, jostling the whole girl to free the skirt of lint. It was not a question and Lucy didn't wait for Linda to answer. She took Walter by the arm again and pressed gently. "Marc thinks she's so cute in her dancing outfit. Relax, Walt, and look at how cuddly she is."

"How what?" he called to her.

Linda followed her mother out the door, her unfortunate knock-kneed walk making the stiff tulle of the skirt bounce up and down. She buckled herself into her own car seat in the back of the New Dodge Caravan Limited Edition, which was a glittery sand color called Desert Romance. Walter wished Linda would cry and buck, get down on the floor and be a head banger. She fastened her seat belt and adjusted her antennas. When Lucy turned on the ignition, Kenny Loggins came on with the air-conditioning.

"You were born too late to enjoy this kind of thing," Walter said. "This guy's voice is clotted with—with goodness and self-satisfaction.

Why aren't you listening to something you can argue with, Mahler, or Björk, or Liz Phair?"

Lucy tilted her head toward Walter and smiled without opening her mouth. He was different, that's how she thought of him, when she described him to her friends. A different drummer who wouldn't hurt a flea.

"Walt," she said pleasantly, "would you please just give up on me?"

She had a knack, Lucy did, of occasionally saying something that betrayed a certain acumen. Walter had actually come to Schaumburg determined not only to nag at her but also to talk. From what he'd gathered, neither one of his parents had wanted to make a set of stories about the past. They had discouraged her questions, nipped her native curiosity in the bud. Joyce and Robert had apparently believed that Lucy could make a clean start if she wasn't burdened by the family's previous history, if she was not encouraged to read difficult books or take up an art form beyond making cakes from boxed mixes. Walter had occasionally wondered if Joyce hadn't had the heart to raise another child, if she had gone through the motions hoping for a healing effect, hoping for something that never came to her. He wondered if his mother had not had the strength to rescue Lucy from her mild temperament and her ordinary aspirations. Joyce had allowed her only daughter to go to junior college and marry at nineteen.

Who could tell what had shaped Lucy or who had given her her best self? By the time she was kindergarten age the neighborhood was already lost. The swarm of children had grown too old to play war in the summer nights and so she had missed shinnying in the Kloper trench after the phantom bounty. There were moments when Walter had truly believed that if the big boys caught him they would slit his throat with their pocket knives and bleed him like a lamb at slaughter. Fear, he'd believed early on, had a metallic taste, and also smelled of dirt. Across the alley, on the safe side, Mrs. Gamble leaned against her fence, her burning cigarette providing the beacon and the scent of the home country.

Walter had asked himself a number of times why Lucy should care about the history of Maplewood Avenue. Why should she be interested in the texture of his boyhood? There was no clear reason, and still he wished that retarded Billy Wexler had not been killed by a car, gone before Lucy had had a chance to see him stealing the trash-can lids. Year after year Billy seemed never to grow older, always a four-year-old in the same adult body. His tantrums, his shrieking, had had the same grounding effect as church bells, a noise that is both heard and unnoticed, day after day. By the time Lucy was in third grade the genius twins were doing liver transplants at competing university hospitals. She'd missed the boisterous secrets the porch mothers told about their husbands, and she'd missed the pack roaming the block barefoot from Memorial Day to Labor Day, as if they were all living on a farm. But it wasn't exactly an elegy that Walter wanted to deliver.

He wanted to talk to Lucy not because he wished to cast a golden light on his past but because finally, in his premature middle age, he was afraid. Afraid, he guessed, of life itself. He was afraid of the boys who sat in their bedrooms in the glow of their computer screens, communing in sentence fragments with people they would never meet. When he thought of all those little zombies his stomach hurt. So many people seduced by a technology that bred impatience and greed. What was good, what had stood the test of time and had value, was being thrown out and replaced with a perpetual present that was slick and speedy and shallow. His stomach juices churned, the muscle clenched. He was well aware of the fact that others before him had been frightened by the next generation's ignorance and bad manners in just the same way. It was certainly not abnormal to believe that the new crop was deficient, but perspective did not make the distress less keen. In his blackest moods Walter feared that the books, music, art—everything he loved—were going to be overlooked by this coming spiritless and nescient generation.

Walter would make a point of listening to Lucy as much as speaking himself. He would listen. He wanted to find out from her that he was mistaken about the next century, no cause for sleepless nights. He would admit that he had become like the old lady shaking her black umbrella at the unruly boys loitering at the bus stop; he had become dowdy and out of touch, as Wordsworth had, mumbling on his walks over the wold, depressed about the general evil of the civilization.

He hoped to find, too, that he and Lucy, even without the old neighborhood, had something in common. He was willing to probe, to take a risk, to see if there was anything, besides duty and the assumption of love, that linked them. If there was not, then he would rest. He would let duty and familial love be enough. But how exhilarating it would be if they had reason for a bond, if there was something that in all of their years Walter had overlooked.

Even when he tried to dismiss his gloominess as something characteristically middle-aged, he could not move beyond his impression that Lucy and her husband, Marc, were lacking in substance, and that living itself would not provide them with insight. They were poorly equipped. They seemed to have missed their chance to build an inner life. They didn't read, they didn't discuss ideas, religion or politics, as far as he could tell. Lucy, he feared, had an interior dialogue that was as still, as silent, as a deaf girl's.

On the way to the park district building Lucy pointed out Marc's favorite features in the new van, which he had managed to acquire below cost from the dealership. There was a white quilted piggy with a red satin bow around its neck hanging from the rearview mirror. At a stoplight she took a deep breath and she said, "I'm so happy you're living close to us. We'll be able to have all the holidays together, not just Christmas. Mom said that even Mrs. Gamble is thrilled to have you back in the Midwest."

"Thrilled?" Walter said. "I didn't know that Mrs. Gamble was capable of registering delight. Indignation, yes. Rage, of course. Is there an emotion that invariably goes along with the act of snooping? What does one feel when one skulks? Titillation, perhaps." He took a tissue from a red-and-white container that had been embroidered in counted cross-stitch, and wiped his nose. "Do you notice that we always speak of her? When we meet, one of us always brings up Mrs. Gamble. Is she like that problematic third party, the Holy Ghost? I never understood what the Holy Ghost was, but maybe Mrs. Gamble is as good a definition as any. Otten is three hours from Oak Ridge and that's surely close enough to be in her force field again. That's the alarming part about moving to Wisconsin."

"She's an old dear," Lucy said.

Walter turned slowly to look at his sister. He was unable to move his mouth, to ask her to repeat herself. He felt as if he'd snorted the words, as if they'd gone up his nostrils and were doing their bad magic.

"But think," she persisted, unaware of his shock, "think. You'll be able to have Thanksgiving with us, with the whole family, at Lake Margaret. And Easter, too. I don't think I ever remember you at any of the Lake Margaret holidays."

He had been absent for most of her childhood, it was true. He had gone far away to college because at eighteen he knew he was in danger of never leaving home, of making his baby sister the center of his existence. It had been a wrenching departure, and even now he couldn't recall the leave-taking without feeling sorry. He regretted the distance and the fact that they had very few overlapping stories. It was funny, though, the way she seemed to think that he'd never had a Thanksgiving at Lake Margaret, that his life before her birth was un-lived. After college at Columbia he'd stayed in New York. He hadn't the vacation or the money to come home, he told his mother. He hadn't the inclination, he told his friends. With a few years between them there was something about his parents and little Lucy that made him uneasy. It was as if his family had died and an all-new McCloud unit had moved into 646 Maplewood Avenue. He didn't know them anymore. He'd had trouble thinking and talking in what felt like the sedated calm of that household.

Without them he managed to have some glorious times in his twenties, in the city. He had partaken of the pleasures consigned to youth, to excessive sex and drink and drugs. He didn't get drunk much anymore and he rarely smoked dope or did cocaine, and as for sex he occasionally went looking for that someone, that high-wide-and-handsome moment. But Lucy, he was sure, had not ever given herself up to either sin or joy, had never conceived of real experience. It was a waste for a person as beautiful and capable as she was, never to have run like a gazelle across the sand on a beach and talked at high speeds about the intricacies of nothing at all, and woken later in the arms of some improbable boy.

Walter and his group had grown up, gotten tenure, or at least regular jobs, developed paunches. A few had bought homes and tou-pees and plastic Christmas trees. Some were dead. Some had come

through, made it so far, nursing sick friends and lovers. The playwrights of his generation insisted that they were hanging on with emboldened hearts. Walter doubted that his heart was emboldened by
either the deaths of his friends or their political struggles to fight the
disease. Still, his young wild life, his secret, lived on in him. For all the
ridiculous and petty intrigues of that spent time, he thought of the secret as a force of its own, a current, strong and clear, that ran through
him, informing his older, wiser, stodgy self.

Lucy had no such thing, and now and then Walter wanted to wake
her, a simple slap, one, two, three, back and forth, hello, wake up, here
you are, twenty-one years of age, on this remarkable and sensitive
planet, a place where single cells suffer shock if the pressure changes.
Suffer shock, he wanted to demand. An old dear, indeed! He remembered that neither his parents nor Daniel had ever suggested that Walter be other than he was, and yet he wanted to grip Lucy's shoulder
and insist that she be different. He noticed, as he reached for another
Kleenex, that the car tissue box said, in red cross-stitch, "Happy is the
house that shelters a friend."

Emerson, on Lucy's tissue box.

"Who wrote this saying?" Walter asked, testing her.

"Marc's mom gave that to me," she said. "I don't think anyone
wrote it. Those phrases, ones that are true, get passed on and on." She
nodded, as if to agree with herself. Looking over her shoulder, she
parallel-parked the van in one dream-come-true Driver's Education
continuous maneuver.

On the blue linoleum strip in the basement of the Schaumburg park
district building, Linda and twenty little girls in spandex and tulle fin-
ery made a line. They scratched their legs and talked to one another,
some of them making the age-old feminine gesture, slapping their
hands to their mouths as they giggled over their three-year-old fancies.
Melissa, their teacher, born and bred in Schaumburg, was sixteen. A
schaumie, Walter thought. He wasn't sure if her hair was supposed to
look teased and in place, a great puff of it in a second tier of bangs, or
if she'd had a nightmare just before she'd rolled out of bed. There was

no telling. She was wearing a black leotard that didn't quite cover the last tuck of her bottom, but the shortage kept her busy, yanking at the material every few minutes. Once her charges were in line she stood in front of them demonstrating the steps. She did not turn around to see if they were bending their legs correctly, or safely, if they were keeping their backs straight, their feet pointed. There was no barre for them to hold. She motioned to her boyfriend in the corner, her extended index finger jabbing the air, the sign that he should hit the button on the tape deck. There were several girls who didn't have any interest in following Melissa, and they wrung their friends' hands and spun until they fell down.

Walter sat on the folding chair on the side, next to Lucy. He tried not to look as if he were watching his homeland go up in flames. In spite of his need to educate, he would keep his outrage at bay and refrain from pontification. He would not keel over into his own lap. He'd sit erect and behave himself. This type of suppression was like holding his breath for a long period, and he intended to see the effort as an exercise, something that would at least firm his stomach muscles and possibly develop his character. When the girls on the dance floor started to turn around and around to the song "I Can Show You the World," tottering on half-pointe, their arms overhead in the shape of diamonds, rather than the elongated classical ovals, Walter clenched his teeth and gripped the chair. It was going to take all of his strength to prevent himself from scooping up Linda, chasing away, kidnapping her from her life of plenty and horror.

"Lucy," he nonetheless found himself saying out of his closed mouth. "Lucy." Classical ballet was the last fruit of Renaissance art. It began in the fourteenth century and came through Russian imperialism into the twentieth century. Imagine if the masters, if Petipa or Fokine had been able to anticipate Linda and all her cohorts and Melissa crucifying the form. "If I had seen this in the future, when I was thirteen," he muttered, "I would have slit my wrists."

She had no idea that he was really overwrought. "Sourpuss," she murmured lovingly.

Walter again turned to gaze at her. She had their mother's slender nose and hazel eyes. Her light brown hair was pulled back in a ponytail, her application of pink lipstick still holding. She was lovely, small-boned, a lightweight girl Marc picked up and spun around. She was happy with her job in customer service at the bank, happy watching her daughter doing what was expected of her, along with her Schaumburg neighbors. Linda, too, might grow up to have run-of-the-mill desires, reasonable expectations. He had watched her only a week before at Lake Margaret, asleep in a bed that used to be his. He had admired the sweaty sheen of her sleeping face. He'd kneeled at her side to look at the line of her eye, the white mother-of-pearl, showing under her slightly open lid. For an instant he believed he might, through that small thin line of white, see into her dreams. It was possible that like her mother she would aspire to a job, central air, a deck out back. There were moments when Walter felt wonder at the feat of his own sister's normalcy. It was so far beyond his notion of average. She and her husband were average to a marvelous exponential power. Lucy and Marc were like a skating pair, all made up, with matching satin outfits, sequined bodices, hair sprayed, in place, always in place, zigging and zagging over the ice, doing their synchronized moves, glowing, smiling, arms up, waving.

Lucy leaned over and patted him on the shoulder. "Maybe it's just not all that it's cracked up to be, Walt, to feel tortured so much of the time."

He had taken her to see *Swan Lake,* starring Natalia Makarova and Mikhail Baryshnikov at the Civic Opera House in Chicago, when she was eight years old. He would have liked to shout at her, to remind her of it, over the noise of "I Can Show You the World." "I don't feel tortured all the time," he said. "I'm one of the happier people I know, except for, maybe, Kathie Lee. I'm not as happy as Kathie Lee, but almost, Lucy, almost."

She laughed and slapped her hip. "Wait! Just wait until I tell Marc that one."

Walter began to say that it wouldn't hurt her to experience a bad day, that a brief depression would do her good. He bit his tongue. At thirty-five she would probably succumb, and he feared that she would have nothing, no good words, no music except Kenny Loggins's lullaby CD, for guidance. He looked out to the dance floor, to Linda, already cursed by her dull name. She was standing, frowning, while all the other girls tried to follow Melissa's combination. She looked small and bewildered. He wanted to go to her and whisper into her ear, offer her a pink-and-white swirling sucker, a new bike, a dollhouse, anything, so that she'd know it was all right, that life wasn't always like this moment, standing in the middle of the dance floor, standing, while everyone else breezed past. But it happens sometimes, he'd say, and believe it or not a person learns to make use of the loneliness.

Walter turned to his sister and whispered, "Linda is very, very cute. She'll be a great little dancer."

When they got back to the house Lucy's husband, Marc, was on the deck, firing up the gas grill. "Hello there," he shouted into the kitchen to Walter. "How's it going?"

Walter came through the sliding doors, grinning at Marc, grinning as hard as he could. "Good, good," he said. "Yourself?"

"Great, just great." He pointed past Walter, back into the house. "How's Miss Dance on Her Tippy Toes?"

"She did everything right," Lucy said from the dark kitchen. "Walt even said so."

At first, during Lucy's courtship, Walter hadn't wanted to like Marc. But as her high school career wore on he found that it took too much energy to repress what he supposed could be called fondness. He admired Marc, especially at a distance, when he was out in the yard mowing the grass or washing his newest car in the driveway. Marc worked eighty hours a week at the Chrysler dealership. He was skilled, giving his customers high fives, remembering their first names, and their children's names, but Walter sensed that his brother-in-law was embarrassed by his calling, that even at nineteen, when he'd started in the business, he'd felt apologetic. He worked out and he had his blond hair styled and he let Lucy dress him in pink short-sleeved polo shirts. His were the honest good looks you'd think you could trust, a man who would not lose his boyish appeal into his forties, who would grow up to be the salesman of the year, time and time again, until at last he owned the dealership.

It was the pleasantness in Marc, always moderated to the same pitch, that rendered Walter speechless. He wondered if Marc was capable of fighting for a school-bond issue, or seriously thinking about a presidential candidate, or feeling a wave of sadness at the sight of poor lost Linda on the dance floor. Walter once dreamed that Marc was dressed in gold lamé, flying on his own power in a powdery sky. When Walter concentrated on liking Marc, on getting to know him, he was bored to tears, and if he focused on the elements of his dream, what might have been an indicator, a peek into Marc's soul, what was lurking and probably forever stunted, Walter fell silent.

"She buys this meat from the Jewel," Marc was saying, "that doesn't have any fat in it. Zip-o fat."

"Wow," Walter said, marveling not at the meat but at a twenty-four-year-old who had already reduced his wife to a pronoun.

Lucy opened the sliding door and stuck her head into the September heat. "Walt, Linda wants to show you what she made at her art class."

Walter excused himself and followed Linda into the living room. Lucy had just bought a white velvet sofa and loveseat, new end tables, and two ceramic lamps with frilly shades. The living room was not large, but there was a vaulted ceiling with rough-hewn beams that was supposed to make the place feel spacious. Next to the rocking chair, the one relic from Maplewood Avenue, there was an antique wooden wagon with blocks arranged inside to spell Linda, Lucy and Marc. Linda stood at the shelf where Lucy stored the ChildCraft set of reference books, and the *Parents* magazines in binders. Perhaps she had so many classes she couldn't decide what handicraft to show him, or maybe, Walter thought, she too was struck by the decor of the room.

"Sit down, why don't you, Linda," Walter said, taking the child by the hand and helping her onto the sofa. "While you're thinking about where you put that art project, I want to show you something. That's right, you get settled, and here, give me that headband, if you don't mind."

Linda watched without a word while Walter first stretched the band and then fit it on his head. "Your great-aunt, Sue Rawson—you remember, the tall old lady who looks like an endangered bird—she used to take me to the ballet when I was little and it pretty much changed my life. She was always changing my life, if you want to know the truth." He adjusted the band again, so it wouldn't pinch behind his ears. "Now," he said, "picture that I'm a swan, a cygnet. Little swans in ballet are called cygnets, which is something you will have to know about if you're going to be a ballerina. A cygnet is the greatest thing you can be when you're a dancer."

He was wearing khaki shorts, his blue paisley boxers sticking out above his belt in the back, black leather tennis shoes, green socks and a matching green T-shirt. "I'm at a disadvantage, Linda, because I'm minus the three other swans in this dance of the four cygnets from *Swan Lake,* and also I don't have a tutu like yours. Don't close your eyes, don't do that, but use your imagination anyway." He hummed a few bars of the music, broke to explain how the four dancers were linked up, arms hooked together in a basket weave, and then he did the entrechats, jumping in place, and retiré, bent leg, foot pointed at the knee, and head to the right, down, and to the left. "In *Swan Lake,*" he said, already panting as he did the jumps, "these swans are girl-friends. They're happy in this dance—but whatever they feel during the ballet, they are together—together in their happiness, and their misfortune, and their beauty. A lot of people like me, not just dancers, but fellows like me—happen to know and love this ballet and espe-cially this variation. I got into big trouble once doing a scene from the third act—but that's another story.

"Anyway," he puffed, "there's a prince, Prince Siegfried, and it's his birthday, and his mom is going to make him choose a wife. She's going to throw a party for him and invite all of the prettiest girls and he's going to have to marry one of them. So he's in a really bad mood. He goes out to the lake—which is what I always do when I'm depressed—you can do it too, when you're older and sad—and in this peaceful glade he sees the most spectacular creature. Her face is half covered in swan feathers, and her white dress is made of this soft—downy swanny stuff."

He was going to have to start an exercise regime once he got set-tled in Otten. He was breathing heavily, but Linda was smart, of course she was, and she was getting the idea. "And, naturally," he went on, "the prince falls in love with this bird-girl. She sees him and she's scared out of her ever-loving mind—she thinks he's going to shoot her and have her for Thanksgiving—"

"Walt," Lucy said, appearing in the arch between the living room and the entry, "what are you doing?"

He continued to move, hopping on one foot, his leg stretched behind him, head down, one arm to the side, the other in front of him. "I took your mother—to see—*Swan Lake*—when she was eight, Linda," he sputtered. "She doesn't remember. Sometimes—that's all I want to ask of her—that she remember." He continued hopping, head to the left, down and to the right. "Am I being overly dramatic?" He gasped. "It was with Makarova—one of the greatest ballerinas—Russia—and the world—for that matter—has ever produced. Do you notice the plié—that bend Melissa was teaching you—it's about the most basic movement there is. In this four-minute dance—there are about fifty thousand pliés. Eddie Villella—my friend Susan's ballet master— believes that the battement tendu—the pointing of the foot—the stretching outward of the leg—is the way to Nirvana—but I differ with him—I prefer the plié as my personal route to the—"

"I do remember," Lucy said. "You wouldn't buy me Jujyfruits at intermission. You gave me a long speech about how movies could be about food *and* the movie, all at the same time, but that the ballet was separate from the body, that going to the ballet was—spiritual, I think you said, and did not mix with Jujyfruits. Sue Rawson probably never let you have candy when she took you to the ballet and so for you it was like a rule or something, a commandment."

His left leg, at that moment, extended in a knobby arabesque, came slowly to meet his supporting leg. He stood breathing out of his mouth, his headband antenna quivering. She had twisted her hair into a French knot, so that she looked grown-up, womanly. "A commandment?" he said. There was sweat running down his forehead, dripping off his brows. He balled his fists and rubbed his eyes.

"You don't have to start crying," she said, holding out a frosted glass of lemonade to him. "I got over it. All those people onstage running around made me hungry, that's all. Take this and drink. And yes, I do remember *Swan Lake*. The—couple, or whatever they are, die in the end, but you're supposed to be happy for them. I've got some lemonade for you too, honey," she said to Linda. "Just think, Walt, if your students could see you now, they'd transfer right out of freshman English into Shop. If they could see you, what would they think?"

Walter looked up to the ceiling, wished for a double Manhattan and then took a long cool drink of his sister's brew, made from a powder of sugar and lemon flavor. He had temporarily forgotten that he was going to be a high school English teacher. "Oh well," he said lightly, "Freshman English is a requirement. You can't transfer out of it." His sister meant no harm, he knew. She had propriety to think of, her daughter's moral upbringing as well as her husband to protect. He was getting uppity on her own turf, and she couldn't condone it. Her reaction was understandable. But if he was ever the instrument of revenge, if he was ever going to have magical and evil power over her, he knew how he would use it. He would wave his wand, and presto, little Linda would grow up to be exactly like their aunt Sue Rawson.

Three

OCTOBER

1972

By October Daniel had already had two operations, both to remove small growths. Mrs. Gamble suspected the worst the day the family went to Lake Margaret, when she'd crept up to Daniel's room, and stood outside, six inches from the door, her arms crossed on her chest, listening. She thought she heard a noise, a sizzling sound, like an apple baking in an oven, the thin red skin stretching and splitting. Her hand flicked to the white wood of the door. It fell open. She held her breath and craned her short neck to see around the corner. The boy was asleep, his head turned on the pillow, so that she had a panoramic view of the protrusion. It had the look of something hard, unforgiving, nothing that would grow soft or oozy, the poison finally draining off. She believed that it was still in progress, continuing to enlarge while the parents drove off to celebrate the marriage of the grocer and his Mrs. Hoity-toity.

A week after the party Daniel was admitted to the hospital for the removal of the lump. Mrs. Gamble did not need to be told that it was malignant. She had seen it. Over the back fence Joyce thanked her for her concern, and the basket of vitamins, and said only that Daniel was much better. In September, another tumor had grown under his armpit, appearing overnight, like an egg left in a nest. At the beginning, Dr. Blume did not know, or would not say, the name of the illness. Although the tumors were cancerous, Joyce and Robert found several reasons to be hopeful. Daniel would have radiation and chemotherapy in a fine teaching hospital in Chicago. He was young and in good shape. It might be nothing that had caused the swellings; they might be isolated freaks of nature. Joyce dreamed that the growths had come from outside her son, carelessly slapped on Daniel by an invisible hand.

By the first of October Daniel had already missed three weeks of his senior year of high school. Walter knew very little about his brother's sickness, but it crossed his mind once that in all of Daniel's spare time he might be thinking about the clang of death's door, the path to heaven, the silence along that unimaginable road. It was what a feverish person might dwell on during the long, empty day. Walter thought about his brother abstractly and without much concern. Both before he had gotten his tonsils out, and in recovery, he'd been afraid his heart would stop, and so it wouldn't have surprised him if Daniel too had worried about croaking on the table. The odds were against it, of course. Worldwide someone died every few seconds, but in America, in Oak Ridge, the odds were generally against death.

Walter's friend Mitch Anderson occasionally spoke about a mind-control program his mother swore by, for health and success, but Walter had never tried either her technique or regular positive thinking to cure his common viruses. What was the point in exerting effort when the twenty-four-hour flu would pass in its own good time? He figured that if he ever had a real disease he would rise to the occasion and think, think like crazy about sunshine and wanton gaiety. He'd watch the Marx Brothers movies, learn to play the piano like Chico, laugh doubled over, holding both his sides. Whatever Daniel had was surely going to pass without the need of Mrs. Anderson's present enthusiasm. Once Daniel was better there might be a memento that would stay with him, Walter supposed, the pink welt of a scar, the cavity inside where the tumors had been, a severed nerve—something that would throb or itch when he was older, to warn him of rain or frost.

In the late afternoons Daniel sat in the rocking chair in the living room, convalescing, an afghan over his shoulders, another for his lap.

He sat in that old-man pose in his chair, before dinner, looking up the street. He watched Walter coming home, the kid brother walking along Maplewood Avenue with his feet turned out like a duck's. Daniel's throat was sore, and sometimes it was hard to get simple words out, even so little as a Hello, hello, Walter.

At the Hendersons' lawn Walter could see Daniel in the window. It was then, almost home, that Walter suddenly and briefly felt sorry for his brother. He put his head down and came quickly. It seemed to him that Daniel had never before been alone, and there he was, glaringly separate from the rest of them because of a few morbid growths. It wasn't the vague disease that disturbed Walter; it was Daniel's forlornness that sent a shock through him. He couldn't stand seeing the desolation in his brother, the sort of quiet wretchedness that had previously been Walter's province. Concentrate, Daniel, Walter willed. Think of your long future: swimming for the gold, a contract with a sportswear company, a college sweetheart. He tried to imagine the girl, her even teeth, her shy nature, her madras culottes, her fair-sized knockers beneath her buttoned-up cardigan. When he got to the Gambles' property Daniel came into focus, a gaunt teenager with jaundice, a person who would frighten a child, a boy who looked like a poetic horror, a Boojum. It was an embarrassment to have to face someone whose luck for the time being had unaccountably failed him. Walter went up the stairs without hearing his brother's raspy hello. The word was stuck halfway up Daniel's throat, and by the time the last syllable came out of his mouth Walter was on the second floor, shutting his bedroom door.

That fall it seemed to Walter that the house had the fake hush of a funeral home, the music turned low in the living room, Joyce and Robert tiptoeing along the hall, so formal with each other, Robert opening the front door for the neighbors and their casseroles, his gentleman's gestures, his friendly welcome, muted. The change had come after the second surgery. The people in the McCloud family were like acquaintances, Walter thought, boarders who shared a bathroom and happened to eat together. Within the house they had apparently been released from their old selves and merely because one person was temporarily sick. There was no trace of the reliable characters they had once been, and no clue about the new and presumably improved selves to come. The large foil-wrapped pots of purple and yellow mums on the end tables in the living room, gifts from Aunt Jeannie, were the only things that seemed to have any chat in them. She blew in once a day, and everyone, even the dog, took cover. When Robert stayed late at his factory, Joyce sat in the window-seat of her bedroom staring at the sky, without moving, like a Yogi. Walter wondered, years later, if by October Daniel understood the nature of his illness. He came to believe that while he was off at his sophomore year of high school memorizing the periodic table, reading *The Grapes of Wrath* and the highlights of *The Peloponnesian War,* Daniel was doing the optional work that all good students of death, all goners, undertake. He was preparing. It was as if he had already grown up and left them.

Four afternoons a week and on Saturday mornings, Walter rode the el train from Oak Ridge to the Loop in Chicago for his ballet class. Susan and Mitch sat in one seat, their arms around each other, and Walter sat behind them, or in front of them, or across from them. The handsome couple might have passed for brother and sister if they hadn't usually been in each other's lap. Their eyes were the same quality of blue, they were slender and they both had a graceful, erect carriage. Mitch, for everyday purposes, had the confident I'm-beautiful gait of a runway model. Susan's hair was a silver blond and Mitch's the yellow of straw. He parted his mane on the side and the long fine strands fell across his eyes every time he moved. He habitually flicked his head. Walter thought, Your Highness, each time Mitch made the gesture.

On the train, suspended between the luxuriant green world of Oak Ridge and the unending pavement of the city, Walter was always aware of Mitch's taunt. Susan might lean against her boyfriend, or kiss his cheek, or stroke his hand, and then, invariably, Mitch flicked that gorgeous head of his. He kept it where the movement landed him, to show off his profile to Walter, and slowly he combed through his hair with his first two fingers. He'd finally turn, and look straight across to Walter. It was in part the size of the blue iris, the roundness of the eye, and the heavy lids that made Mitch's face notable. A showstopper.

He fixed his gaze on Walter as the train lurched forward and moved slowly on.

There wouldn't have been much of a message in a quick glance. For Walter, time gave the look meaning, the stretch along the tracks between Cicero and Pulaski. Mitch hardly blinked and he didn't move his hands or his feet. The sly smile was set. It was as if the boy was becalmed. But in the stillness he was saying to Walter, *I have this great girl on my arm, something you'll never have. See the way she fawns—I can sit here motionless and she fawns! She can't get enough of me; she'll do anything to make me show signs of life. Anything!*

The train passed the housing projects on the West Side of Chicago, passed the boarded-up schools, the burned-out lawns, the rusty jungle gyms, the few garden plots in the narrow fenced-in backyards. The ghetto flashed in a blur while Mitch stared at Walter, while Susan tickled her quarry's earlobes and cheek, her manicured nails moving circles over the ruddy skin of his permanent Irish blush. The red lacquer made Walter shiver. Even if her hands were folded on her lap the sight of the nails gave him goose pimples.

Once, at the Halsted station, Susan sat in Mitch's lap whispering at his neck while a pickpocket was arrested three cars up. Walter pulled on the sleeve of his own corduroy jacket to keep himself in his seat, to prevent a humiliating moment. He might shout, against his will. What happened to love if it wasn't collected, he wanted to know, if it wasn't received? He might ask this question out loud. He might stand and go from commuter to commuter down the aisle, asking each one what he thought about the old unsolved problem that science and mathematics had never tackled and literature and the opera only fleetingly illuminated: Where, he'd ask, does love go? He felt as if his skin were porous, that love was gaseous, leaking out of him, a cloud of stink everywhere he went. It was an element with alchemic properties, sometimes, according to its mood, sweet, heavy, lustrous. The minute it hit the air Walter imagined it became deceptively light, something unseen, like a tubercle bacillus, passing from person to person, taking each one from health to either heaven or hell. Mitch's head was thrown back, his mouth slightly open, Susan trying to sleep on his shoulder. She had her hand on his collarbone, on that graceful curving truss, as if she owned the thing. Walter kept his seat and looked at page 42 of *The Golden Bowl,* the page he'd been reading since he'd boarded the train.

He half believed, in that year, with only occasional relief from his own fresh pessimism, that love was capable of killing a person, and that even a worm, digesting the particularly bitter juices, could distinguish a corpse dead from love. But there were moments, riding the el, walking the school halls, eating lunch, when he felt as if he were singing, singing without realizing. It didn't seem impossible that he might suddenly become an enormous woman belting out a heartbreaking Puccini aria—*Folle amore!* He was screaming at the top of his lungs, wasn't he? *Folle ebbrezza!* How could it be that Mitch was not receiving any of those musical strains? And where did the noise of the shriek, the smell of leaking gas, the melody, the words Lauretta sings, "Have pity, have pity"—where did all of that matter go when it was not absorbed by the loved one?

They walked up Michigan Avenue, the three of them linking arms, Susan between, a phalanx against the wind that swept off the lake. Walter held his collar closed and adjusted his earmuffs. Mitch never wore a hat. He jerked his head, his single defense against the freezing temperatures. If they had time they went to the Artists' Café and drank weak coffee, emptying all of the cream from the pitcher into their cups. They often discussed the problem of the ego and the artist, the artist with the ego, the importance of the ego to the artist, the difficulty of maintaining an ego of healthy proportion, and the possibility of peaceably quelling an erupting ego. They couldn't drive or vote or buy beer but they were virtually adults, they felt, drinking coffee, and discussing the nature of the ego, the id, the artist. Walter usually managed to recite a scrap of verse. He had absorbed some lines of Christopher Morley from Sue Rawson and was able to say, " 'When ego, fantailed like a peacock, can find the needle in the haycock'— something, something, something, 'is that millennium?' "

"Walter," Susan said, after he had been spouting Morley, "if you break your leg in seven places, God forbid, and can't dance, you'd be a great English teacher. You know so much more than Mr. Reynolds."

He felt a burst of love for her years later, when he remembered the conversation. She had allowed him an easy out, a shattered leg in order to get on to a viable profession. At the time he tried to muster a visible shudder. Mr. Reynolds? Mr. Reynolds! The flamer in his prissy bow tie, his yellow shirt, emerald-green blazer, pleated pants, silky off-white ribbed socks, polished loafers outfitted with brand-new pennies? Walter got his shoulders to twitch. He would never have gone so far as to say that he liked Mr. Reynolds or admired him, but he did have a secret sympathy for his teacher. It was true that he had more poetry committed to memory than Mr. Reynolds, and that he knew little-used words such as callipygian, long before it was the MTV word of the day, but deep down Walter was rooting for the man.

Mitch twittered into his coffee. "Great goal, Suze, to be like Mr. Reynolds."

"I *said,* Walter knows a lot more than Mr. Reynolds."

Walter, warming to the idea of himself standing at a podium speaking passionately, began to quote from *Howards End.* " 'Life is indeed dangerous,' " he recited, " 'but not in the way morality would have us believe. It is indeed unmanageable, but the essence of it is not a battle. It is unmanageable because it is a romance, and its essence is romantic beauty.' "

"See?" Susan said, wagging her head at Mitch.

"I know I've been saved by books," Walter went on, ignoring them. "I mean literally saved, and I suppose it wouldn't be such a bad thing to try to help people understand that books have that sort of power. That, ah, redemptive power, if you will." He was pleased with himself, by the fact that he was already quite capable of speaking like an English teacher.

"Yeah," Mitch said, still sniggering, "but Mr. Reynolds?"

They went into the Louis Sullivan Building, into the dim entry that years before had been stately. The marble was scuffed, the brass had dulled, and the gold leaf was gone. Harry, the elevator man, sat slumped on his stool, holding his lever. He was sleeping, his head resting right next to the emergency button, while he waited for passengers. When Mitch stepped in, Harry opened his eyes and began to mutter, seamlessly coming out of his dream into the world of motion and small talk. He took them up to the twelfth floor, his head bowed, talking as he did, day after day, into his stomach, no matter the season, about the bitter weather, the merciless wind. With one lever he drove the metal cage up, slowed and slowed, adjusted, up, up, an inch, another inch, so that finally it met the floor.

The hall on twelve was lit by one lightbulb, and so the corners were suitable for last-minute fondling. Susan and Mitch kissed under the dusty panel depicting the birth of Venus. Walter opened the door to the waiting room, to the smell of sweat and rosin, cigarette smoke, the tinny noise of the piano from inside the studio, the thump of forty girls jumping, landing on the same last beat.

If life for Walter was composed in part of confusion, shame and deception, the ballet was order, dignity and forthright beauty. He could come from the train, from the outside world of his brother's sickness, his own strife and Mitch's cruel taunt, into the studio to the realm of the dance. He could stand behind Mitch at the barre, in fifth position, pulling up his puffy knees with all of his strength, so that they would stand as flat as possible against each other, and stretching his scrawny leg, pointing his long slab of a foot in a battement tendu, he could say, with each movement, *I love you, Mitch.* Their teacher, Mr. Kenton, snapped his fingers and walked the studio, adjusting a student's arm, a neck, a hand, an entire leg. The pupil always nodded, to display understanding and gratitude. And one, and two, and three, and four. On one, Walter pointed his foot in front of him, *I love you, Mitch,* and two, close to the fifth position, *I love you, Mitch,* and three, à la seconde, *I love you, Mitch,* and four, close to the fifth, *I love, I love you, Mitch.*

When they turned around to the other side, to do the exercise on the right leg, Walter was in front of Mitch. He didn't look at the girls along the barre. He closed his eyes and saw Mitch, Mitch in every detail: Mitch's thighs that tapered elegantly to the knee, the slight bulge of his calf, his short feet that were so arched they looked as if they could snap shut. He remembered how Mitch had stared at the ceiling once, with his hand on his throat, how he listened when Walter played Schumann on the piano. He was sure that Mitch was listening intently. And he thought of the notes that Mitch had passed him in geometry class, his irreverent answers to Miss Guest's inane story problems. Walter figured that beauty and wit, good writing skills, and maybe even great feeling were instruments of power, but he sometimes wondered if it was the specific construction of Mitch's spine, if it was that alone that gave the boy the glide and air of a high-ranking church official, a bishop, a cardinal, even. Lucky Mitch! To be Mitch, to have Mitch!

The boys, through their ballet-school life, wore white T-shirts, white socks, black tights and black ballet slippers. The girls changed outfits as they progressed from level to level, wearing different-colored tunics to signify the class and, always, light pink tights and pink ballet shoes. Walter, unable to regally toss his head, rolled up a bandanna into a tube and tied it in a circle to keep the curls out of his eyes.

It had been clear from the start of their careers in dancing school that Susan and Mitch were the two in their age group with natural talent. The older girls kept an eye on Susan, fearful that she would one day overtake them. Ordinarily the misfits of the class formed their own fraternity, but Susan early on claimed Walter as one of the elect. In her childish way she knew only that he was someone to care for. As she grew older she developed a line: He was an unknown quantity. He might not be the most terrific dancer but he was definitely somehow or other going to show his colors.

The three of them had begun dancing in the same year, when they were in fifth grade. Mitch had been tall for his age, and had a robustness that Walter lacked. He had muscle in his rangy legs, but he was also surprisingly light, and could jump. There were several mothers, a club of them, who sat in the front room during the lessons on the sofas with taped-up vinyl cushions, knitting or making tapestries in an effort to soothe their frayed nerves. They did not leave the waiting room while their children executed their demi-pliés behind the closed studio doors. They so hoped their girls were not sticking out their keisters as they bent their knees, that they were sucking in their little tummies! The door was closed expressly to shut out the mothers— The Furies, Walter called them. Although they were not allowed to observe more than twice a year they managed to garner a considerable amount of information. They might be blind to the weaknesses in their own daughters, but they were able to gauge the promise of the other girls. When the class was over and the door opened, they snapped to attention, trying to see on the dancers' faces who had suffered, who had been complimented. Mitch, they said, was an adorable boy. He was safe to admire, nothing he could do, really, to outshine their daughters. They had heard Mr. Balanchine's famous quote, "Ballet is woman," and taken it to heart.

Mitch would be strong enough to support the girls when it came time for the pas de deux class. In addition to his brawn he already knew how to play the gallant. They could imagine his dancing Prince Siegfried, or Prince Florimund, or the Duke of Silesia. When they spoke about his vigor they meant in part his masculinity, and without passing words they nodded in understanding, in agreement: *he* was not going to grow up to be a homosexual.

On the way home on the train one night Walter wondered out loud if The Furies planned their wardrobes over the telephone. It seemed to him that they all wore the same beige cashmere cardigans with pearl buttons, the same plaid wool skirts, and underneath, no doubt, the constricting panel of the eighteen-hour girdle grimly doing its work. He made the mistake of asking his friends what they thought the mothers said about the three of them. Susan muttered, "I hate them, every single one of those women." Mitch, sitting next to his girl, blurted, "What they say about *us,* you mean?" Walter realized then that in Mitch's drama the mothers didn't even consider Walter. They didn't see any boy except Mitch. They looked at the place Walter stood at the barre, and saw straight through to the mirror. Susan, in Walter's defense, shook her head at Mitch and said democratically, "They talk about everyone. They tear all of us to shreds."

It was a gamble for any mother pushing her child to the dance. There was no telling who was going to come through adolescence. The girls, especially, might have potential, and at thirteen stop growing, or start growing, develop large breasts, become wide in the hips. It was unfortunate, and sometimes a travesty, what puberty did to the girls. There was the added danger of rebellion: even the delicately built dancers got tired of the discipline, ate whatever they pleased or went astray with boyfriends, alcohol, parties. A boy with a solid foundation, with the goods in place at the start, was not as susceptible to physical ruin. By the teen years, if he'd held on that long, he might well have become accustomed to being called queer and built his defenses. Mitch's teachers had high hopes that his last growth spurt and the thickening of his chest would not spoil his nearly flawless form.

To have a boy, a serious boy, was unusual in any regional ballet school, and both Mr. and Mrs. Kenton believed that Mitch had the talent for a top-flight company. Not only did he have the right build but he had innate musical sense. They were ecstatic to have such a student, and the mother as well, a woman who had wanted to dance, who had ambition for her son. She did not often sit in the waiting room, but every quarter she paid an extra sum for a private lesson, and she phoned periodically for a progress report. Mrs. Anderson had been Maureen O'Kelly before her marriage, an Oak Ridge girl who had almost made it to the Covent Garden stage, when she broke her foot in several places. Mr. Anderson, the Swede, had died suddenly in Terre Haute, Indiana, when Mitch was two, and his widow had come home to live with her mother and her older sister, both of whom had had a hand in raising Mitch. Because he was the object of so much attention and hope, and because his body adapted without difficulty to the classical ballet technique, he could afford to be lazy and good-natured. Walter wondered if Mitch believed that everyone else's wishes would carry him to stardom. Mrs. Kenton had the habit of shaking her head, dismissing his sloppy steps, pardoning his forgetfulness. She snorted daintily, and murmured, "*That* Mitch." It was clear to Walter that Mrs. Kenton would never say dreamily or otherwise, *That* Walter. He knew that neither his character nor a few choice expressions had currency, that a crooked smile, a sweet hangdog look, would not excuse a defect or a lapse.

Susan Claridge was small for her age at ten, but she had legs that every mother at the studio wished for in a daughter. It was inevitable that the women invoke the horse when they had the chance to watch her chassé across the studio floor. They dubbed her Suzie; they were intimate enough with her, they thought, to use a diminutive. Suzie, they sighed, had limbs like a filly. Suzie, they regretfully acknowledged, had no trace of little-girl flab. The prosaic name, Susan Claridge, could be changed. Look at the New York City Ballet, at Roberta Sue Ficker, who had become Suzanne Farrell, or Nelly Guillerm, rechristened Violette Verdy. A name was disposable. Suzie was lean and muscular and lithe. She had proportion, from head to toe, nothing oversized, and she was undersized in all the right departments. She had shiny blond hair, which she did up in two braids right before class, standing in the middle of the waiting room, in front of a rapt audience. With the pins in her mouth she stared at the wall, at the autographed pictures of Margot Fonteyn. She carefully coiled the braids on each side of her head, and one by one she removed the pins from between her teeth, securing the buns. She wouldn't let her own mother touch her head, much less any of the ladies who would have so loved to give her a pat.

Walter had always squatted on the floor watching that ritual without trying to conceal his fascination. She did not seem to notice any of her devotees, women or children. At ten she inspired awe when she did something as simple as braid her hair, or stretch, her head to her knees. She had presence, something the mothers feared their girls would never be able to acquire or imitate. Like Mitch, Susan also had a body that tended naturally toward the lines of the classical ideal. Her knees were hyperextended, her long arms were lyrical in any position, and when she was older her feet, disfigured by corns and bunions, were pliant and smooth in her pink-satin pointe shoes. She seemed, furthermore, to be innocent, kind and not at all snooty or temperamental. Many of the mothers were grateful to her for her goodness, and it was difficult for the more imperious and resentful women to bad-mouth her. They knew it was not dignified or appropriate for grown women to pay homage to a child, and yet they couldn't help themselves. For three years in a row, when she was eleven, twelve and thirteen, Susan played Clara in Chicago's production of *The Nutcracker*. She was so unmistakably on her way. For two of those years Mitch was her prince, her consort. The four times that Walter auditioned he made it past the first cut, but he only once progressed to the third round, in spite of the word that there was a shortage of boys.

In his late teenage years Walter realized that had he been a Russian or a New Yorker, had he applied to the Bolshoi Theater in Moscow or to the School of American Ballet, he would not have passed the preliminary interview. At both of those schools a prospective must have a physical and an audition. Each dancer is evaluated for strength, for aptitude and for inherent structural weaknesses. Walter had feet that were not technically flat, but they had very little shape, and his thin legs brought to mind a horse with spavin. At a school dedicated to producing professionals of the highest caliber, Walter would not have gone on past the doctor's examination. Mr. and Mrs. Kenton, former soloists of the Ballet Russe, had high standards, certainly. They demanded effort at all times, and excellence if possible— but they did not turn away pupils at the door. All were welcome to try their luck.

When Walter first took lessons, he was convinced that Margery and Franklin Kenton, natives of Edinburgh, Scotland, were related, both of them, by blood, via the Romanovs, to the House of Windsor. They had impeccable BBC accents, they'd been to Russia, Franklin wore an ascot, and Margery had perfect posture, which she tried to duplicate in her students by holding a cane to their backs when they did their demi and grand pliés. She wore her dark hair in a bun like Walter's favorite near-royal figure Mrs. Simpson, and she wore a black silk skirt that came to her knees. When she demonstrated an exercise she demurely raised her skirt an inch or two, to show more of her leg, to show the line. It was vaguely mysterious that she had no babies, and yet she seemed not to have missed loving a child of her own. None of the pupils could imagine love from someone so remote and exacting. It was her praise, the smallest word, that would mean more than a kiss or an embrace. She kept the beat crisp, clean, snapping her fingers severely and counting sternly out loud. There was never any doubt where the beat began and where it ended. Walter couldn't imagine her lingering over anything, savoring a peppermint stick or reading a sentence more than once. Perish the thought of her bathing. He was certain that she never shed her black leotard down to her skin, that lying rigid in her single bed, next to Franklin's single bed, she still wore her dancing skirt.

Walter dreamed about breakthroughs, in his own technique and in the appetite of the ballet world. What he would have given to be the dancer, the understudy, who happens to be in the audience when the Prince fractures his kneecap! *Walter McCloud,* the paper would report, *was overlooked at his ballet school but he studied the part on his own and after a slight delay for warm-ups and stage directions made his stunning debut.* He lived in that fantasy for hours at a time, making adjustments to his costume, his curtain call, the flowers given, the accolades in his dressing room following the performance. In fact, Walter knew he was better off than many of the girls at the Kentons'. He was fortunate to be a boy, to have the status of a rare one. Both of his teachers encouraged him and he was usually called to the front row during the center work, a sign of favor.

Mr. Kenton was less remote than his wife, but when he engaged with the students he was often harsh and sarcastic. He persecuted the girls who were clumsy, who had large rear ends, who made mistakes, who seemed to be dim-witted. The class seized up when he yelled at a stupid clod. *Thank God, thank God it is not me,* each one thought. Ballet school was a brutal society, no doubt about it, but Walter believed that the cruelty was necessary. It took a caste system based on body type, and a dictator, to make artists out of a few talented long-legged suburban girls. Although the Kentons disliked different people, multiplying then, those who were shut out, they were united in the dancers they chose to love. If you were favored, how the sun shone down upon you!

Before class the fat and the short and the ungainly gathered around the baby grand in the corner to listen to the piano player make disparaging remarks about famous ballerinas and about her employers. It was terrifying too, when the Kentons shouted at Mrs. Manka. Sometimes her tempo was sluggish or she played a mazurka when a waltz would have been more fitting. The Kentons' tone was like a good whipping. When they shamed her she turned red all down her neck and her arms, and she sputtered apologies, frantically leafing through her binders to find an alternate selection.

It was Mrs. Manka who took in the branded girls, who comforted them and gave them fresh hairnets for their slapdash buns. The haughty girls, those with promise, didn't speak to her, didn't need her ministrations. By Walter's rough calculations Mrs. Manka was no more than two hundred pounds overweight. What torture it must have been for her, to be the pig in an order of plucked chickens. He loved watching her little head bob and sway as she played her schmaltzy melodies, she, who could make Bach sound like lounge music. It was her beloved Chopin, he guessed, who carried her along through the tedious hours of class, Chopin who made the misery worthwhile. She had mastered the art of smoking with no hands, and she puffed away at her cigarette as she played, the black holder sticking straight out of her mouth. She leaned back, always in the nick of time, so that the ashes fell into the dish on the nearby table.

Walter wasn't scorned by Mr. Kenton; he told all the gossip he could think of to Mrs. Manka before class and he was not stigmatized for the association; and to top it off he was friends with Susan and Mitch, even when he did not get a part in *The Nutcracker* year after year. He was in every one of the camps at the Kenton School of Ballet, an accomplishment, a feat, to be able to move like a journalist across the borders. In his sanguine moments he told himself that if he'd been in a primitive society, more primitive, that is, than the Kentons'—if he'd lived in a tribe, in the jungle—he would have been a magic man, someone who was worshipped.

As they grew older his two friends recognized that Walter had, not talent exactly, but certainly something, a flair, you could call it. First of all, he had an encyclopedic knowledge of ballet and music history. He had such strong opinions about productions that had taken place in the thirties and forties that they half believed he'd seen them with his own eyes. It was Sue Rawson who had witnessed early Balanchine and passed on the lore to Walter. She also lent him books—with grave admonitions to return them with no stains or dog-ears or smudges. She had books about Diaghilev, Nijinsky, Fokine, Petipa, about the male in ballet, the female in ballet, about Lincoln Kirstein, Pavlova, Markova, Fonteyn and Tallchief. By the time Walter was thirteen he had read all the ballet books in Sue Rawson's library, and he had an enviable collection of LP's, many of which his aunt had given him. He carried the music of the great ballets around in his head by day, and at night he fell asleep to the strains of *Swan Lake* coming from his cheap portable stereo. When he woke to Sunshine Gamble's barking in the early morning, he felt as if his heart had been beating in waltz time through his dreams. He could sing on command all the variations of *Sleeping Beauty, Raymonda, Les Sylphides, Giselle* and *Coppélia*.

When he went to Susan's or Mitch's house they often played the music game. One of the friends put on a record and Walter was to guess the composer, the title and the soloist, and if he knew the soloist he could often say the record label, because prima donnas had their contracts with specific companies. At the height of his powers and if he was on a streak, he could name the orchestra and the conductor. Sometimes they played the game as a contest, Mitch as the MC, Susan versus Walter. None of them paid much attention to the Vietnam War or to President Nixon's reelection campaign. They didn't know anyone who had been touched by the war and the boys assumed that it would be over by the time they reached draft age. Walter sometimes poked his head into Daniel's room to look at the poster on the wall of Mark Spitz in his skimpy little suit, all seven medals hanging around his wet neck. And he had read at the dentist's office that J. Edgar Hoover might have been a homosexual. If he had been questioned about major figures in current events he would have been hard pressed to think of anyone besides Nixon, Kissinger, Hoover, Mark Spitz, and a senatorial candidate Sue Rawson said was dangerous, a man named Helms from North Carolina.

In addition to his wealth of ballet and music lore, Walter could imitate, down to the smallest gesture, any of The Furies, Mr. and Mrs. Kenton and Mrs. Manka. He was the jester, he knew, responsible for delivering the truth and maintaining good humor. He took the job seriously. Into Susan's living room he walked, snapping his fingers as Mrs. Kenton did, counting punctiliously and viciously correcting the posture of Mrs. Claridge's highboy. The next minute he was Mrs. Manka, sitting at the piano, one of Mr. Claridge's cigarettes hanging from his lip, banging out Rachmaninoff with exaggerated tempestuousness. Enter Mr. Kenton, ripping off his ascot, screaming at the pianist, "Slut! You gelatinous slut! You, you stout-bodied killifish! You slab of cold flummery!" Mrs. Manka again: cowering, mashing the cigarette into her mouth, trying to flip through *Teaching Little Fingers to Play* to find another piece. Susan stood at the bookcase laughing, but Mitch—Mitch rolled on the floor and wept until he'd exhausted himself. Walter never broke character, never cracked a smile. How he loved Mitch's laughter! Susan thought Walter brilliant, and she also believed that he was free of vanity and pride, free of ego. Such a thing, in and of itself, she said solemnly to Mitch, was unique, something that should be treasured.

That fall Daniel was sick Walter got in the habit of walking the couple to Susan's house after ballet class, after the trip to Oak Ridge on the el. He left them nuzzling at her door and slowly he made his way south to Maplewood Avenue. He couldn't get in the door at home, couldn't reach the top step of the front porch without Joyce appearing, pushing Daniel's dog across the floor, telling Walter to take him for a walk. The animal's legs were locked, its claws scratching across the gray paint as Joyce nudged him from behind. Walter had hit Duke a few times in his puppyhood, when he deserved it, and the dog still had the nerve to cower. If communication had been possible, Walter would have asked the mutt to be reasonable, to consider that he and it saw eye to eye. He, on the whole, didn't like the idea of the leash any more than the dog did. The leather strap offended Walter's sense of trust, and furthermore he was not interested in playing the role of the master. It was the arrangement, was it not, he said to Duke, that man and dog were companions, and therefore the beast had no business acting like a tyrant? If Walter put the mongrel on the leash the runt strained at it, making ghastly noises, so that Walter wanted to gag in commiseration.

Long before it was the law or the badge of refinement Mrs. Gamble, always tidy, walked up and down the alley and with her silver trowel she prodded the dogs' stools onto the scoop and deposited them into a sandwich bag. Walter didn't want to have to do that; he wasn't equipped to do such a thing. Night after night Duke at first trotted beside him, free, as if they were on good terms. When the animal, the mutt, got to the hydrant at the end of the block, he lifted his leg, watching Walter out of the corner of his nearly lidless left brown eye. Walter had no interest in looking on as the dog pissed, and he'd glance at the sky and back to the dog, a shrub and back to the dog. For just a minute he'd spy on a dinner scene, or a family around the television, and in that time Duke would streak off into the night. Walter would turn back to check him and find nothing but the dying grass on the parkway, the drip down the hydrant, the empty street. Duke, vaporized in the space of a heartbeat. It wasn't the vanishing act itself that irritated Walter but the fact that the dog understood him and could anticipate his movements. It was unnerving the way the animal knew exactly when it was safe to bolt. Although it was not difficult to track him, the task set Walter cursing, pulling leaves from the neighbors' shrubs as he ran. It was predictable that the dog would try to hump the Gamble collies through the fence, or try to mount poor old Billy Wexler's leg out in the alley, his clutching paws crossed in the back of Billy's knee. The dog had supposedly been neutered and he was still a sex fiend.

"I hate you, I hate you," Walter chanted as he roamed the block, alert to the smell in the wind, trying to find the dog. If Duke hadn't been Daniel's, he thought he might have tried to kill him, might have picked him up and slammed him against a cement wall. "I hate you, you shitstorm. You goddamn shitstorm. What I would give for Mrs. Gamble's bullwhip so I could reduce you to a bloody smear."

Walter did not usually swear and he had never before threatened to beat any living thing to death. Duke, he guessed, appealed to the deeply buried brute in him, the Harley-driving, tattoo-armed, leather-jacketed real man, someone who would take great satisfaction in beating the tar out of the demonic little dick-bastard of a dog. Once he got started talking hatefully to his brother's pet he couldn't stop. It was amazing, he knew, that the eight-inch-tall dog with a white-tipped tail, the animal the Kloper girls called Poochie, could make Walter feel so extravagantly foul.

Some nights he used the leash and ignored the pitiful and repulsive slathering. He walked to the center of town, to the whole-food store, Nature's Health. He would not yet have had his supper, and in all the world what he wanted was to sit at the snack bar and order a tiger milk shake, a drink that had a lot of coconut in it and a secret ingredient that would absolutely give him physical strength and mental vigor. Walter felt guilty going over to Nature's Health when Uncle Ted's Jewel Food Store was two blocks away. There was an intimacy at Nature's Health, not only because of the size of the place but also because of the curious, nearly unpleasant odor. He felt as if he were in someone's poorly ventilated house, that he was smelling a stuffy bedroom. The stink Walter both didn't quite like and wanted more of came from the muddy beans in the cedar bins, the herbs and roots in paper bags, and the dusty whole grains, the noodles, the nutritional yeast, the granolas and the exotic nuts in the white buckets on the floor. Back at the deli there was always the woody sweetness of fresh carrot juice. The smell of the place was mysterious and close, and it drew Walter in, to the counter where he ordered a tiger milk shake for clarity and vim.

Mrs. Gamble shopped at Nature's Health for all her groceries, except cigarettes, and in the evenings she was often making her way down the narrow aisles stocking her cart with vanilla-bean ice cream, acidophilus milk, potato-flour bread, and peach kefir in swollen cardboard containers. She always wore her apron, the strip of heavy fabric around her waist that had pockets for her tools, her wallet, the trowel and the Baggies. She bought organic beef for the dogs, an Adele Davis brew for extended life, as well as everyday nutritional supplements: wheat germ, niacin and folic acid, the Vitamin B complex, Vitamin E capsules and time-release C in 1000 milligrams. She'd come to Walter, lean against the counter and look over her glasses into his face. He had always felt as if he was supposed to hold still, as if her scrutiny was a privilege.

One night that October she approached the snack bar, and instead of chastising Walter as she usually did for tying Duke to the meter, she narrowed her eyes and said, "I think Daniel has pellagra." She cleared her throat, plucking at her shirt between her breasts and waited, this time for him to question her. He knew he should inquire about the specifics of the disease, about which she naturally had superior knowledge. When he didn't speak she continued to squint at him over her bifocals. He was determined not to say a word, to stare her down, to make her feel that he could see clear past her eyeballs, down her throat, into her own black heart. He hated her, too. "As— I'm—sure—you—know," she said, slowly and contemptuously, "pellagra is a disease caused by the deficiency of niacin and protein in the diet, and characterized by skin eruptions, digestive and nervous system disturbances, and even"—she leisurely hacked twice—"eventual mental deterioration."

"Gosh," Walter said, "you mean the shortage of one little vitamin and Daniel might lose his marbles?"

She was going to come very near him, call him "young man" in the menacing way she reserved for boys who spit in the alley, who teased the dogs. Her movements were like smoke, the waft of her right in his face. "You," she purled, "none of you, are looking for the right signs."

She didn't mean astrology, he knew that. When she read her book and made her pronouncements she was straightforward about the business. Walter supposed she was trying to tell him that there was no reason for Joyce to spend her time and money consulting doctors when she lived next door to Mrs. Gamble, a person who could over her own counter dispense niacin and organic lamb-burger patties.

"It's essential," she spit. "Niacin is an essential vitamin."

"Essential," Walter repeated. "I see."

She began twisting the cap off a small dark brown bottle. She removed the wad of cotton from the top and shook out half of the contents, about twenty white pills. "Take them," she ordered. Before she could explain the regimen, how many a day, with or without food, he obediently stuffed all of the tablets into his mouth, chewed, chewed, and washed them down with his tiger milk shake. Well fortified, he swirled off the stool and skimmed out the door. He did not glance back to see Mrs. Gamble stricken, her little eyes bulging, her hand at her throat. He unwound Duke from the meter and dragged him wheezing and gagging all the way home.

—————

Walter did not bother trying out again for *The Nutcracker* that season. He had been to the auditions at the Arie Crown Theater the previous four years, dancing the combination the ballet master demonstrated without making any errors. He was good at picking up combinations, and he could reverse complex steps without having to think them out first, the way his friends did, without using his hands to mark the movements. Susan and Mitch went off to the theater after class one Saturday to see if they could again land a part in the annual Christmas extravaganza. By three o'clock in the afternoon Susan was both a snowflake and a waltzing flower. Mitch, much too tall for the prince and too young for the character roles in the second act, graduated to the part of the Mouse King. After the call from Mitch, Walter shut himself in his room and listened to Montserrat Caballé sing Elisabetta in *Don Carlo*. He sang the Italian and at the same time read the English from the libretto that came in the boxed set.

> *You who knew the vanities of the world and enjoy in the tomb profound repose, if they still weep in heaven, weep over my sorrow and carry my tears to the throne of the lord.*

But it wasn't enough to suffer the simple humiliation that came with being the worst on the team, so bad there wasn't any reason to try to hit the ball. No, not enough to be flat out rejected, repeatedly, without so much as a thank you, try us again. The last week in October, Walter suffered a deeper humiliation. Just as class was ending, as they were taking their final bows, Mr. Kenton announced that he'd like to see Walter in his office. Walter, bending to the floor in the révérence, said to his shoes, "Me?" A summons was usually a portent of good fortune. It meant a promotion to the next class level. He stood up, his heart banging in his chest. It was suddenly not beyond Walter's wildest dream that he should be moved to the Advanced Class, without Susan or Mitch, leaving them in the Second Intermediate Class, to work up to his level. He'd been too close to his talent after so many years to be a real judge. Mr. Kenton was going to tell him that only now had they, he and Mrs. Kenton, realized that Walter had a special ability, so rarefied they had heretofore been unable to detect it. But they had seen! They saw! They had been initiated!

"You'd like me—?" he said, his fingers like prongs poking into his chest.

Mr. Kenton's cigarette was hanging out of his mouth, his arm extended to usher Walter through the door of the studio and into the musty inner sanctum, the place where Mr. Kenton smoked and talked on the phone and Mrs. Kenton worked at the books and sewed the Advanced girls' recital costumes.

Something fantastic is about to happen, Walter thought, stepping into the office. His teachers had finally felt his passion. Never mind that he had no technique, that he hadn't the basic tools most dancers need to convey in the classical mode the complexity of human feeling—that was of no consequence and was actually limiting to Walter's type of artistry.

"Have a seat," Mr. Kenton said. The pate that he was going to wear for Herr Drosselmeyer in the Arie Crown Production of *The Nutcracker* was for some reason on a wig stand on his desk. It was as if there were two people present, a baldy and a slick-haired Mr. K., to tell him the good news. Walter sat on the edge of the chair and folded his hands. When he realized it was his own shuddering legs that were making the chair wobble he clutched his knees. The chair continued to clatter, so he put both hands on either side of him, bracing the seat, holding it firmly in place.

"I got a call from the Rockford Ballet this morning," Mr. Kenton said. "From a Miss Amy. She's looking to put together a cast for her *Nutcracker*. She needs a teenage Prince and she's not having any luck. You came to mind right off."

"The Rockford Ballet," Walter echoed. He shut his eyes, squeezed them tight. "The Rockford Ballet." Perhaps he was snug and warm in his bed, fast asleep. It was a joke, a funny, funny prank—the whole class was going to jump up from behind the desk and yell SURPRISE! Wasn't that hilarious, Wally? Wasn't that the most reckless joke—THE ROCKFORD BALLET! Bet you didn't even know there was a town in northern Illinois called Rockford. Here is the church, here is the steeple, here is the studio called Miss Amy's Dance Emporium, up above the Main Street Bar and Grill. Here is Miss Amy in her red-and-white polka-dot bandanna, Miss Amy who has dedicated her life to teaching jazz, tap, gymnastics, ballet, modern and the fine art of the hula hoop. She's got every mother within the city limits sewing satinet costumes for the production that's going to be in the Rehabilitation Center's Gymnasium. They'll just push the bars aside, the contraptions they use to teach the paraplegics to walk.

"It would be a nice opportunity for you," Mr. Kenton was saying.

Walter nodded. A nice opportunity. Certainly. Nice as Topeka. Nicer than the dusty town of Ogallala. Nice, the way it's nice to be put in a sack and dropped from the top of the Prudential Building.

"I'll give Miss Amy a call, then," Mr. Kenton said.

Walter managed to stand up, to exit, through the waiting room, out the studio door. He thought he heard Mr. Kenton say, "Congratulations." He made his way through the hall to the boy's bathroom. While the strains of a girl singing down and down the scale came through the walls of Mrs. DeBenedetto's Voice Studio, Walter stood over the toilet trying to vomit, or at least retch.

When he took Duke for his walk that night, he snapped on the leash and set off across the lawns. It was dark and cold, and he considered that in all probability no one would know until morning that the dog had been hanged from the middle branch of the Gambles' mulberry tree out front. He wasn't sure, however, if he could stand the choking sound, and as they had recently finished a unit on Poe in his American Literature class, it occurred to him that he might, if he murdered Duke, have to live with the sound of the dog's speedy little heart coming from under the floorboards. He undid Duke's collar, and just as the mutt began to shit, his back hunched and trembling, Walter took off, pounding down the alley. The asphalt hit hard with each step. It was the glee that Duke must feel when he escaped, the pure rush of defiance, nothing short of jubilation.

Walter made it to his own backyard. He fell to the grass, and he lay, panting, looking up into the cloudy sky. There was a pink haze to the night, all of Chicago to blame, he thought, for spoiling a thing as vast as the heavens. He could have the role of the Prince, but the rub was Rockford. It was a test of some sort. He was in a fairy tale and there was a right course of action and a wrong course of action. He could have the kingdom but the princess bride was a midget. The ugly mutt would turn out to be the clever one, the Puss in Boots type who could guide the oafish hero to the conclusion. The story was probably really about the smart-ass pup, a dog who had already proved by his escapades that every night he achieved happiness, something that the master would never have in Rockford or in any other godforsaken outpost.

Four

NOVEMBER
1995

Joyce believed that it was she who had kept Duke alive for seventeen long years, that it was her devotion and her will not to lose him that had given him spirit and strength. Mrs. Gamble, privately, took the credit. She was sure the dog's longevity was the result of the nutritional yeast she had encased in meatballs and slipped through the fence directly into Duke's mouth. On the family-history wall up at Lake Margaret there was a picture of him, standing on his short black legs, looking slantwise, figuring when to run, his tongue hanging down to his knees. In his prime, he had brought in squirrels that rivaled him for size, and for all of his years no punishment could keep him from rolling in dead fish on the pebbly shore.

On into his thirties Walter continued to be surprised by his own heart. The morning Joyce called to say that Duke was dead the unpredictable pounding began in Walter's chest before she'd finished the sentence. The dog had died standing at the fence, looking, Joyce said, as if he were waiting for Kingdom Come. Walter had had to get off the phone quickly, put his head to his knees and steady himself. It was one of the mysteries of life, he supposed, that a person could suddenly feel love for a thing he had once despised. He would miss that clear gaze, a look that seemed knowledgeable in a creature that by rights should only have had instinct to rely on. He would miss the one last link to Daniel. Walter had always thought, in spite of himself, that the animal understood something they did not, that there had been, not exactly a channel open from Duke to Daniel, but at the least a mutual sympathy. His fancy was ridiculous, he knew; the point had been to love the dog because Daniel had felt strongly about him. Still, the possibility was gone, the wild chance that Duke would come to Walter's feet and drop a rolled-up, spitty note from Daniel, a message with one last plain truth.

On Thanksgiving Day of the year he moved to Otten, Walter sat in front of the fire in the parlor at the lake. Thirty-two of his relatives were scattered over the house and grounds. The older women and the mothers were cooking, the college girls secured themselves in a cold lakeside bedroom to gossip about the family, and one of the cousins Walter's age claimed the heated nursery, waiting to hear Francie tell a secret she could no longer keep. Outside, the men and teenage boys chopped wood and the children ran in a pack from leaf pile to leaf pile, and in one sweep were down the hill, striking matches and throwing them flaming into the icy waters.

Walter's students were required to keep a journal, to write about the texts they were reading, and also about themselves, if they were so inclined. He had 130 spiral notebooks to read and comment on by Monday, as well as a stack of as many essays. He was a first-year teacher and had inflicted this misery, this bludgeoning, upon himself. In the next quarter he would try to stagger the assignments, spread the due dates among the classes. He had chosen to work, in the hours before dinner, in the drafty front room, a place where very likely no one would interrupt him. From the living room the ancestors and Duke looked down upon him from the sacred wall. The long Peg-Board had been bolted to the door frames, never again to be removed, after the disaster at Aunt Jeannie's party, after Jeannie had paid nine hundred dollars to have all the photographs rematted and reframed. In the parlor Walter wrapped himself in a quilt and sat as close to the hearth as he could without catching fire.

His freshmen were writing about *Romeo and Juliet* in their journals. There was an occasional entry with life and spark and wit, and it was the lure of just one more good piece that kept Walter reading. He hadn't imagined he'd have pets, but his favorite, a student named Betsy Rutule, wrote that Juliet was much more beautiful in the mind's eye than any person could actually look, because of Romeo's awesome descriptions. A girl back then, she said, probably wouldn't smell so good or maybe even have very nice teeth, what with the Dark Ages' hygiene. She wondered how she could get a boy to think of her in the way Romeo so generously thought of Juliet. "Are any of us even made that way anymore?" she asked. She concluded by saying that when she got her braces off maybe she'd get lucky.

Walter prodded the logs, thinking of what to say to Betsy that would not smack of false cheer. She played the trumpet in the marching band, a round-faced girl with silver hoop earrings, third row, fourth from the left, in the crush of brass instruments. There was at best a remote chance that someone was going to think that her "eyes in heaven would through the airy region stream so bright that birds would sing, and think it were not night." Walter wasn't ruling it out, that she could move a suitor to similar sentiments. There was a studious, unnoticeable boy in his second-hour class who might have both the gift of poetry and the love of girls, but would he know enough out of the starting gate to concentrate those talents on Betsy? Walter told her that she had discovered something important about the power of language and the imagination. He wrote in the margins of her journal that the high school boys he knew generally did not speak in Shakespearean couplets to their girlfriends, but that true love usually did make people of all ages, in all times, say impetuous and poetic things, usually working in figures of speech that included starlight, moonlight, the depth of the deeper oceans, the many grains of sand the world over and the far reaches of the universe. He forgot for the moment that he had never had braces and he wrote, "I remember how difficult it was to eat popcorn and apples when I went through my orthodontia experience. I hope yours will be over soon."

In red pen he wrote *See Me* on top of nearly half the essays. He had promised himself in his student-teaching days that he would never do what his homo English teacher, Mr. Reynolds, had done to him. *See Me* meant a fifteen-minute session alone with Reynolds, listening to him ramble on about the use of which and that, lie and lay, good and well, bring and take. Mr. Reynolds's dandruff fell to his shoulders like slivers of asbestos even with the gentlest movement, when he cleared his throat or leaned forward to pencil in a semicolon. And yet there Walter sat at Lake Margaret, unable to keep himself from printing the command *See Me,* the words that would make some of his pupils feel disdain, and others dread. He reasoned that some of them needed him one-on-one to piece their shapeless thoughts together, and with a little concentration to progress to the point where he could explain the transgressions of the comma splice, the passive voice, the dangling modifier. That many of the students obeyed him, and came during their study halls, surprised Walter. It was remarkable that he, Mr. McCloud, wrote *See Me* on the assignments, and a day or two later they stood by the door at eighth hour, or before first hour, and wondered if he had a minute. The girls tended to be all nervous attention; the boys looked at the floor and nodded without making eye contact. He enjoyed getting to know them without the chaos of a whole class, and there was sometimes gratification, struggling with them to bring the subject and the object into focus, to find clarity. In the quiet of the empty room, Walter meant to treat every student, no matter how blank, as if he or she were withholding a concise paragraph, as if each one had the secret desire to write complete and grammatically complex sentences. He had tried both to have stature and to be something like himself. He meant, too, to keep his inborn English-teacher didacticism to a low roar. His class, he recklessly hoped, would be like a buffet filled with gorgeous food, so tempting that the students would lose their appetites for Cheez-its and glazed doughnuts.

The fall had been a blur of faces, so many blonds, so much white skin, pimpled skin, so much denim, so many bad haircuts. Walter felt as if he could hardly keep up, hardly maintain his self, much less his stature; he felt as if he were running uphill, pulling at the shirts of his students to make them stay in one place while he remembered their names and got through the tasks in the squares of his daily lesson-plan book. At night he fell asleep on his couch with their papers on his chest and the anthologies on the floor, and in the morning he woke too early with flutterings in his stomach. He knew that he was steaming through his classes on very little besides the force of his own personality, that he was trying to win his students with bravado. He tossed in bed, well before the sun rose, worrying that he would not have the strength or the courage to last the day.

It wasn't that the students as a group were cynical or disrespectful or violent or stupid. There was battle to do because many of them saw no reason for an English class. They had no interest in books, no interest, it seemed, in thought. There were studious girls and indifferent girls and bad girls; there were lean boys with offensive T-shirts and baggy pants, as well as nerd boys and athlete boys. Some were huge, boys with round, pink faces, butter-baby farm boys, their bellies already spilling over their jeans. He wondered how they could do anything through their growth spurts but dream of fried chicken and mashed potatoes. They all looked as if they were sleeping while he tried to put it to them, obliquely, of course, that the shame Reverend Dimsdale experienced was probably not so far removed from the shame they felt within the confines of their own dark bedrooms. Or was shame a thing of the past now that a person could advertise his naughty deeds on television talk shows? Walter's students weren't sure, or didn't want to say. He had to read a good deal of *The Scarlet Letter* out loud to get them to take it, as if the words were bitter medicine he was making them swallow, drop by distasteful drop. He strode back and forth along the blackboard wall in his room making pronouncements, declaring that from out of the last century Nathaniel Hawthorne was writing to them in Otten, Wisconsin. "Is there discrimination in any form in our town?" he asked them innocently. He did the shuffle-off-to-Buffalo to wake them up, he tried to get them to think about what held a society together, why adultery was considered a heinous crime, why Hester Prynne was heroic. He sat for long periods of silence waiting for them to develop an opinion, venture a comment. The energy it took to make them laugh, to get them to speak!

He designed his freshman course around the theme of justice, with books and plays he had expected would provoke the average fourteen-year-old. For every bleak work he planned to follow up immediately with a piece that was comic or hopeful, so that they'd get the idea that there was in life the potential for fabulousness. In the Shakespeare unit he was going to teach *Romeo and Juliet* first and then *A Winter's Tale,* in spite of the fact that the department chair disapproved of the second play. It was all going more slowly than he'd imagined, this tricking his students into appreciation and wonder. In his seventh-hour class he had had to jettison the program and improvise day by day. There was one diabolical boy, Jim Norman, who, with the nod of his head, was capable of starting an insurrection. Norman's sneer, his pen tapping, the fag jokes—each part of the contempt set Walter's bristly neck hairs on end.

Walter had suffered humiliation in every stage of his life, and he had anticipated having his share of it in Otten. A person had to get out of bed in the morning; that, after his years of teacher training, was the best advice he could give himself. In those first overwhelming weeks he walked around his own backyard in the evening, raking aimlessly, thinking about his seventh-hour class, the group that was in danger of unraveling because of one mean-spirited punk, a few regular troublemakers and a future madam named Sharon. In Jim Norman there was a menace that Walter could not easily dismiss. The boy was brittle and knowing and had no mercy. With his evil glare he as good as said to Walter, I see you are a measly little faggot—you're someone I can mess with. Walter reminded himself that if he really wanted to he could get back on the train to New York, reclaim his job at the dollhouse shop, volunteer at the soup kitchen and reopen his charge at Tower Records. The thought of his other life fortified him and made it possible for him to face another seventh period in Otten.

On the third day of freshman English Walter had told Jim Norman that as penalty for writing obscenities on the desk he could not return until he had written *Fuck You* five hundred times in neat printing. "You might come to understand," he explained, "just how bored I feel when I see those words on the woodwork." On the fifth day when Jim made first a lewd gesture and then a threatening remark, and the group laughed and whooped, Walter calmly divided the class in half. The right side, he said, were prisoners applying for parole, and the other side was the parole board. The students looked so taken aback that Walter wanted to point at them and say HA. He had them; he'd temporarily outfoxed them. Sharon couldn't believe she was a prisoner, and at the same time she was trying to think what sort of crime she would like to have committed. Walter appointed Jim Norman head of the parole board and some of them cheered. It was Jim's duty, with his staff, Walter directed, to draw up a list of rules by which they'd judge the prisoners, not in relation to the crime but in regard to a person's usefulness to society. The jailbirds were to write a letter explaining why they deserved to be let out, and what they'd do with their lives if they were given a chance on the outside. Many of them rose to the bait and came to life at his bidding. He had scored, even if it was a far cry from Shelley's "Hymn to Intellectual Beauty."

Walter remained unflappable in those first months. He had bursts of creativity, he devised inspired group activities, and yet Jim Norman usually sat with his pen between his fingers, keeping a beat with it on his desktop. Walter managed to move the class through *The Crucible* and *To Kill a Mockingbird,* as if Jim's mutterings and his pen made no noise, as if nothing would suit Walter better than to become in all of their minds the archetypal fruitcake English teacher, alone in Otten, wearing the trademark paisley bow tie, with shiny pennies in his new loafers. He recited poetry, he sang from *South Pacific,* the musical he would direct in the spring; he had them up and putting on scenes from the play they read. His efforts caused him a pulled neck muscle and a spastic colon at the start of November. In his bed, watching the clouds, having taken the last of his Valium, he wondered if anyone would notice if he left town, if he never returned.

On most weekends Walter drove over to Lake Margaret to check the grounds. He was at last doing a son's duty. It had been a dry autumn and the grass did not need cutting once. It was a relief not to have to fool with the tractor mower, although he still warmed to the idea of getting decked out for lawn care. There had not been many occasions so far to use his new fanny pack or his pants with the loop for the hammer. He roamed the property with the intention of inspecting the boathouse, the woodshed, the barn, the garden and the pump. He hardly had to look, he knew so well the curve of the hillside, the tilt of each stone step, the chipped bricks in the sidewalks. He got out of the car in the circular drive, closed his eyes and felt a peace settle over him.

He often brought a sandwich and a box of cereal, his books and papers. He stayed the night. He felt that, as much as anything was his,

that house belonged to him. He understood the nature of his ownership, that it was his in a way that did not include but went well beyond
a deed and the transfer of money. His uncles had died, and his mother
and two aunts were the shareholders in the Lake Margaret Corporation. When he stayed on Saturday nights he slept in the four-poster
bed in Sue Rawson's room. He imagined her bulk on the mattress, her
sound sleep, her guttural snores. He wondered if she allowed herself
the slightest rapture when she woke in her girlhood bed to the sound
of lake water out the window. After two stiff whiskies one night, the
thought came to him that he was exactly like the large still house itself,
the house that was filled with antiques, family paintings, letters and
photographs. He tried to imagine taking a lover through the house,
pointing at each object and saying, This, and this, and this, is a part of
me, something you must look at if you are to understand who I am, if
you are to know who it is you love. And he would have to do the same
for the beloved, an exhausting labor for each, visiting the sacred
places, looking and trying to know.

Walter had expected to be lonely in Wisconsin, but he found that
the loneliness was a different strain from the other types he had experienced. He didn't much miss anyone, or wish to be elsewhere, or
yearn to be better dressed and wittier than his neighbors. He didn't
wonder, as he had in the past, what he could do to make some kind of
long- or short-term contribution. It was more than enough, trying to
win the stubborn hearts of his fourteen- and fifteen-year-olds. In
Otten, he was using himself in a way he never had before, and as a result of his exertion he sometimes felt a novel satisfaction. Giving Jim
Norman an F on his midterm had not brought Walter happiness or
the temporary delight of revenge. He was surprised to find that he
wanted to go after the boy with the slit eyes and cruel mouth, to have
him wake up, to voice a perception, to meet his match in literature. It
was a fantasy, that Jim Norman see himself in a piece of writing. He
might grow up to be someone with the glittery hardness of Gilbert
Osmond, without, of course, the refinement, or he might go the other
direction and become even more slovenly, his evilness pared down to
stupidity, like Gatsby's George B. Wilson. Although Jim didn't always
show up, Walter had no intention of letting him off the hook. When

he didn't come to school Walter called him and left the assignment on his mother's answering machine.

He sometimes thought that after a long day it would be nice to have someone waiting for him at home. He was grateful he'd been born in his own era, that his orientation hadn't required him to take shelter, to become an anthropologist studying remote cultures in the bush, or a priest, living in a friary with the excessive camaraderie and what-have-you of the other fathers. He realized one night at the lake that what he missed at the moment was his brother's dog. He would have liked to see Duke chewing, with his nauseating snorting noises, on some repulsive bone. When he went back to Otten, for his week of teaching, he'd recall his time at Lake Margaret, and he felt the house to have an almost human comfort, as if the wood, mortar and brick had the pliancy of a good companion.

At Thanksgiving, the smoke from the burning leaves blew in every time the kitchen door opened, to mix with Aunt Jeannie's rose perfume, the roasting turkey, the baking bread and the fourteen acorn squashes steaming on the counter. The musty smell of the house was temporarily overpowered by the fragrance of Pilgrim fare and drugstore cosmetics. Walter had to shut the parlor door so he could concentrate on his students' journals for an hour or two before he joined the party. He sat hunched over an illegible piece of work, and he didn't hear Sue Rawson in the room until she rustled a magazine.

He dropped one notebook and let loose a soprano shriek that sounded something like Hi!

She was perched on the arm of the sofa, flipping through an old issue of *Military History*. "How do you find it?" she asked. Her diction had grown more patrician through the years. Everything about her had become sharper, more severe. Age had not stooped her. If anything she seemed taller, her bony nose longer. The gray of her eyes had not grown misty with cataracts but had become dark, shiny. Walter knew her well enough to understand what her question meant. Had she been a conventional aunt she would have said, "How's your job?"

He was panicking even before he'd recovered from the jolt of her arrival. He was short of breath after that foolish yipping Hi; he was panting! How was he going to explain his life to Sue Rawson so that she'd be pleased, so that she'd show her approval with a caustic sentence or two? What should he say? She had always valued an artistic sensibility above all else, and he had known, since the early days at the ballet and the symphony, that she believed him to be the only gifted one in the pack of nieces and nephews. He didn't want to disappoint her, but he hadn't had time to anticipate her question and fashion a comprehensive or poetical answer. He could tell her it was difficult, as he had expected, but that was not the exceptional reply she had come to hear. There were times when living in Otten had both the tragic and comic elements he had experienced as the Prince in the Rockford Ballet's production of *The Nutcracker*. As his panic intensified, Walter suddenly remembered that once or twice he had been rewarded when he talked openly with Sue Rawson, when he behaved as if they were intimate. In theory, he did feel intimate with her, in spite of the fact that she was steely, formidable. He had always had a sentimental affection for her when he was far away. He had a hope that before she died she would tell him a choice morsel that would open the door to her secret self. She still intimidated him, although there was also something in her that made him want to try to wrestle her to the ground. She could almost have passed for an uncle or an older brother in her blue jeans from Sears and Roebuck, a model she had purchased back in the fifties, that snapped at her big waist.

"Well," he began slowly, setting his stack of papers on the floor, placing his foot over his comments on the first page so she wouldn't see. "How do I find it? I'm not sure I'm doing a respectable job, but I'm engaged in it. I can't honestly say, you know, as my dental hygienist does, that I *love* my job. And I don't think I'm going to be a *To Sir with Love* sort of teacher. But I wanted, I guess, to be consumed by something. That was my idea in getting certified, anyway." He leaned back in his chair to watch her, so he could try to gauge her response. "I spent my twenties indulging myself, believing that it was right and good to be happy, sexy"—he said the word lightly, quickly—"to give in to everything beautiful and sunny, to have rich friends, to make sure I got an invitation to the Hamptons on the weekends. I was Lily Bart, minus the face, the figure and the hats. There were seasons when everyone I knew wore the same thing: blue turtlenecks, button-up blue jeans, stone-washed to an exact shade of blue, and navy blazers. There was a specific way and direction you were supposed to twirl your foot when you sat with your legs crossed just so." Her mouth had not yet once twitched in disapproval. "My life was about survival," he bravely continued, "grim survival, on one hand, at the dollhouse shop, and on the other hand it was about pursuing pleasure. There was love all around me, at the opera, even up in standing room, or probably especially up there, at the ballet, at every concert I went to. It was love, you could call it, in the park, on Fire Island. Everyone seemed most of the time to be dancing, singing, playing, acting love. Love! Then of course some of us began to get sick. We grew up or we died. None of us stayed the same."

He had found himself well beyond their usual boundaries. She was immobile, and he began to talk faster, if only to quickly get to the finish. "I realized I could live a moral life, that I should, as an adult, live a life dictated by duty. If I chose I could find beauty by living in the real world; I could probably find beauty by working day after day at meaningful drudge. I often had that anxious, desolate feeling that I was wasting my time, that I was wasting an afternoon, a weekend, a whole life, by not choosing to do the right thing—the work that would simultaneously wear me out and sustain me. I was striving for the, ah, mature life. Here, I said to myself, I've been waylaid by the most sinful temptations, and if I don't change now I might wander around forever wadded up with stupidity of my own making. I'd gotten distracted by laziness, by narcissism, and I'd also become clever in a despicable way, clever like a mild version of Milton's Satan, Satan-lite, if you will. I could think rationally, but without any sort of spirituality. I was disconnected from anything moral, or from a sense of awe. Finding the straight way so naturally led me to Otten, Wisconsin, to teach sexually active, uninterested fourteen-year-olds poetry." He raised his voice one notch below his yelping Hi. " 'Margaret, are you grieving, Over golden grove unleaving?' "

Sue Rawson sat staring at him, her little finger hooked over her upper lip and her thumb under her chin. After a brief silence she said, "I see."

Walter nodded. He poked the grate with the iron, already regretting his every word. She had not changed her position on the sofa. He had probably been a disappointment to her since the Rockford Ballet, when she had such high hopes that he would dance. She had short gray hair, cropped bangs, still, in her seventies, a boyish look. He suspected that with one of her muscly arms she could lift him in the air, turn him horizontal, hold him over her head. He would think about her heft, her thick waist composed of almost eight decades of bread and butter, and her undeniably butch coiffure, rather than reproach himself for babbling about the moral life. He would try to forget that he had in effect come out to her, that he had violated her code by speaking of that part of themselves.

She continued to stare, and Walter, bending to re-tie his double-knotted new brown utility boot, blurted, "I'm glad to be here. Especially glad to be close to Lake Margaret. I don't really have a home anymore, and this place means as much to me as—"

Aunt Jeannie's cackle sounded from all the way down the long hall. "Really," Sue Rawson said.

She was going to do her best to remain inscrutable until she took herself away to the next world. She'd go quietly and efficiently, like a cat. Walter kicked the log in the fireplace and it fell apart, the embers scattering onto the hearth. It was too late in the conversation, no chance for redemption, and he guessed he might as well go for broke: he would remind her of their bond. "Do you remember," he said, "how you used to play Tebaldi's *Madame Butterfly* for me in your room, here, upstairs? God, I loved Renata Tebaldi! You used to stand at the window, as if you were waiting for Pinkerton. 'Che dirà! Che dirà?' " He sang outside his solid baritone range, squeaking and wringing his hands in front of his chest. " 'Chiamerà Butterfly dalla lontana.' I'd feel like bawling and you'd let me have a sip of your gin."

"I did no such thing. I despise *Butterfly*." She was snarling. "The most mawkish drivel he ever wrote. I don't know why he composed such a sickly—depraved"—she drew out the *a,* hammered both *d*'s— "depraved opera. What was he thinking!"

It was one of Sue Rawson's hallmarks, Walter remembered, that when a piece of art offended her she spoke as if the writer, the painter, the composer, had made the work principally to irritate her. There was that old thrill in the air. "Who cared what she was singing?" Walter said meekly. "You were listening to Tebaldi, to her voice."

Sue Rawson rolled up the military magazine and raised it, as if she were about to paddle Walter in lieu of Puccini.

Walter would not have been rude to his aunt under any circumstances, but he would have liked to shake her, to make her remember those afternoons of slow time and heavy sunlight just as he did, to admit that she had enjoyed his company. "No, really," he said, trying both not to quail and to laugh as the magazine came slamming down on the back of his chair. She would scoff if he said, *I loved those days,* or, *I treasured those afternoons.* She'd make him feel like an old biddy who pressed corsages in the dictionary. "That was where I discovered the great singers," he said. "You introduced me to some of the most important people in my life."

She whacked the arm of the sofa. "Mawkish drivel," she said under her breath as she stalked from the room.

Just as Walter was beginning to decipher Peter Labatte's handwriting, his mother turned the doorknob and stuck her head around the corner. Peter was a short, freckled boy who found the feuding families in *Romeo and Juliet* an excellent springboard for discussing the baseball strike. His writing was so small and so smeared that at first Walter thought that the word "baseball" was the name of Romeo's friend, Benvolio. He had finally gotten on the right track with the mention of George Steinbrenner. "Can I interrupt?" Joyce asked.

Each time Walter saw his mother he had to adjust to the fact that she was in her middle sixties. She had had shingles in the summer, and she did not yet look well. She had lost weight; she walked as if something in her center had seized up, and her hair, her shoulder-length, wavy hair, had gone completely white. She looked older than Sue Rawson, who was ten years her senior.

"Dad's out there chopping wood with a tool called a Monster Mall," she said. "I don't guess you think I should try to stop him."

"He's probably hoping it will tire him out and he'll have a legitimate excuse to sleep through dinner."

"He's been a good sport through the years, putting up with all of us. I don't know that I would have been as chipper about going to spend every summer weekend with his sisters."

"I remember when I realized, when I had the horrifying realization, that you and Dad hadn't always lived together, that when you were little you weren't even living in the same state. That scared me, made me for the first time, you know, think about the hostile and indifferent universe."

Joyce lowered herself to the sofa carefully, as if it hurt to bend, and when she was finally sitting she smiled at Walter's remark. "Speaking of hostile and indifferent, are there prospects for real friends in Otten? Can you tell? Are those other teachers warming up?"

Walter had met a man in a box seat at Orchestra Hall in Chicago the week before. He had gone anticipating only the pleasure of hearing Maurizio Pollini give a recital of Beethoven sonatas. But in the box there had been a man named Julian Wright, sitting apart from the four others. Julian had struck up a conversation. They were talking before Walter had taken his coat off, before he was properly in his seat. They might have left at the intermission if the performer had been anyone less compelling than Pollini. Looking into each other's eyes, they had balanced the joys of a hand job against the forthcoming storm of the three sonatas of Opus 2 and the Opus 7 in E flat. There was time for both sex and Pollini, they silently concluded, just as the lights went down.

To his mother Walter said, "I've been too busy to really look around. I feel as if I've had a successful week if I've gotten through half of my lesson plans, and if I make it to the grocery store."

"Mrs. Gamble wanted to be remembered to you. She keeps asking me when you're coming home. I haven't told her you've come twice so far. How she's missed seeing you, I don't know. She rests now in the day. She naps. I've reminded her that you have a very challenging year going on, that you've had no preparation time and that you have papers to grade."

"Remind her also that she never liked me." He laid Peter Labatte's masterpiece aside. "I tracked mud in her living room once and she made me vacuum. Every crumb. Every dust mote. Tell her she is never far from my mind, and that I'll sleep on her couch when I come to Oak Ridge next, provided she can remove all the dog hairs. Those hairs, as I recall, had the penetrating quality of volcanic ash. We can do tarot cards right before bedtime so that she'll have her usual satisfaction of freaking me out. Explain to her, will you please, that I'd have to have an exorcism done to expel her from my soul."

"Oh, Walter," his mother said, laughing and rubbing her eyes. "She is unusual, I'll grant you that, but she's harmless, after all."

"Harmless? She never cast spells on you from the toilet. I have sometimes thought that if demons ever did come from the underworld into our realm they'd do it during a purification ritual, right into Mrs. Gamble's house, up, up into the john, through the water and out past her rear end, free! She forced me to take an overdose of niacin once. I broke out in hives everywhere, went itching and scratching for days."

"Ah well, she still is a health nut—"

"Who smokes," Walter put in. "A true health *nut,* yes indeed."

Joyce smiled at him. "There was never a truer saying than 'Good fences make good neighbors.' It's pretty quiet now on dear old Maplewood Avenue. We're all getting old. The Gambles are the only children who never left home. Trishie's having a show at the library, in January, I don't think I told you."

"It makes sense that Trishie has become a photographer, that she's inherited her mother's skill for observation."

"She invited me up to her attic—her atelier, she calls it—for a preview. There are an awful lot of dog photographs, I guess that's not surprising. They're black-and-white and look artful."

"Arty, I think is the word, Mom. Aren't there any stark shots of that narrow downstairs bathroom, the ashtray on top of the toilet tank, the stack of books—"

"She took the nice one of Duke, the one I sent you, with his paws folded over each other, sleeping on the back porch. I like that one a lot."

"It did capture his sweet side," Walter said.

"And Greg Gamble, imagine, he's forty-five, he has his mail-order business at the house still, and Florence says he cleared fifteen thousand dollars last year on the incense alone."

"Enough money to rent a little place of his own, you'd think."

"There was a time, believe it or not, when I seriously thought I might ask him to teach me to meditate. He goes to some group and has learned to levitate." She tightened her lips and shook her head in small quick motions, as if she was shuddering. "Far be it from me," she said, "to pass judgment."

Walter coughed. "Oh, come on, Mom. You're allowed to pass judgment. You've always passed judgment—granted, it was in your own quiet way. It was magnificent, for example, the way you made the pictures fall down that summer, at Aunt Jeannie's anniversary party. You can't tell me that that wasn't judgment in its purest form."

She scratched her nose severely. "Well," she said slowly. He realized that they had the same inflection, the same rhythm when they said the word "well," that they used it to stall for time. His mother was outwardly dutiful and good, but she too had a secret life. It was as if she occasionally brought out a plain wooden box, held it before him, and opened and snapped it shut, just enough time for a glimpse of the black stone, one sniff of the exotic scent. He waited. Her knobby hands, he noticed with a pang, were red and chapped from scrubbing carrots and apples in the unheated cookhouse. She raised herself up. "I don't know," she said. "There are plenty of mysteries, aren't there? Some are best left unsolved, the reasons for them best covered. I think the craze to unburden ourselves of our feelings, all of them, is a mistake, that our deepest urges aren't always those we can be proud of, aren't the ones to share. Here's another example: I've always wondered who ruined Mrs. Gamble's lovely new carport roof. There's a puzzler for you. We woke up one winter morning when you were, what, fifteen or sixteen? And that roof was covered with the primary colors, as if someone had hovered above and dropped balloons loaded with paint. Yes, I believe there were bits of balloon in the spatters of paint."

Walter stared at her, his mouth open, his hand to his breast. After all this time, she was still curious about the prank he'd played on Mrs. Gamble, that year he was fifteen. He and Mitch, on Valentine's Day, had in fact creamed the carport roof with paint-filled balloons.

"Hmmm?" she was saying.

Maybe he would tell her, sometime, about that night that changed his life, maybe, when there was the leisure for a long story. "Mother." He drew the word out, resting in the *r*. "You know I love Mrs. Gamble."

She bent to his ear and said so softly, "But not, my dear, as much as I love my sisters."

Lucy was the third to make an entrance, not two minutes after Joyce managed, even with her infirmity, to prance out of the room. She brought with her a tray piled high with silverware, the polish and old rags. "Here, Walt," she said, handing him a spoon and a rag that had already been dipped in the chocolaty polish. "We're having an argument in the kitchen, about who should get married next so we can have a family wedding. Sally is five years older than me and she claims she's still too young. All of Aunt Jeannie's kids are married, and so are Uncle Wally's. Phil is supposed to be getting a divorce, but hasn't everyone been saying that for years now? There are a few distant cousins somewhere who haven't done it, but would they invite everyone? Aren't these spoons disgusting? They're black! Marc went off to chop wood with Dad, even though the dust aggravates his sinuses. Linda doesn't need me now that she's so big. But I said to myself, I'm not doing this job on my own. Make sure you get the part with the initials, the engraving, clean too."

Walter assumed that Lucy knew enough not to suggest, even behind his back, that he get married. It was very likely that Aunt Jeannie asked at every gathering if he was dating. Aunt Jeannie, at seventy-two, like Sue Rawson, had not become diminished in any way. Her voice was shriller, her holiday sweaters jazzier, her fragrance had a greater range, and her exaggerated red lip line went far beyond the curves of her own fine mouth. She had hair that looked like spun copper, so airily spun it shone through to her clean white scalp. Walter didn't want to think about how his mother responded to Aunt Jeannie's questions. Joyce would probably say that Walter didn't confide in her about those things, but that there'd been a girl back in high school, Susan, the dancer. Good old Susan was so multipurpose, the kind of friend who could be used for any occasion.

Walter had never discussed his preferences with his mother because he felt it was so obviously understood between them. It was a conversation that was beneath their dignity, he sometimes thought, and at other times he could see no reason to hurt her out loud. He didn't want to talk about it with her and he didn't want to plan talking it over with her in the future. They appreciated each other, no need to dwell on what was neither here nor there. When he someday met the man of his dreams he would be only too glad to bring him home to Mother. They would sit around the table and talk about miniatures, the old neighborhood, what a good dog Duke had been. His father would pass through the room, deliver an endearing non sequitur, find his magazine and shuffle off to the sofa.

Walter could very well imagine the conversation that was taking place in the Lake Margaret kitchen. Those who had good instincts would be silent while the others rattled on, wondering and wondering why he hadn't plucked some nice girl off the street. The thought of those conversations pained him, for his mother's sake and for Lucy's sake, too. That the rest of them had not figured him out, after all those years, that they continued to hope, made his heart tighten and his hands sweat.

It was in part his brother's fault that Walter suffered at family functions. Walter blamed him. He couldn't boast that he had known Daniel, as either a friend or an adversary. Still, the boy, in his various stages, in health and in sickness, haunted him. Sometimes in the dark bedroom Walter heard the sound of Daniel's light tenor seventeen-year-old voice. It pleased him that in over twenty years he had not lost the tone and timbre of his brother's speech. Two friends of Walter's had died in their thirties, and yet Daniel's death often seemed more recent. Walter couldn't say one way or another that he had either liked or disliked Daniel, but surely he had been a commendable person, not to have mocked Walter, never to have beaten him up. There were times when Daniel had had every right to pound him, to punch him in the nose. Walter wasn't sure why or how they had inhabited different worlds. Joyce had probably helped to engineer it, or maybe they had had nothing in common so that they had naturally, as young children, taken separate paths. They must have made a truce early on, knowing the limitations and potentials of each other, coexisting without needlessly going over the same battles day after day. Walter liked to think that they had been smart, that they'd consciously made an economy in their relationship. It was pointless to project what Daniel would have been and done, but even so Walter often punished himself with images of his brother, the do-gooder. It was illogical and unfair—he knew it—to be irritated by the dead boy, and yet he sometimes felt a fleeting, dim anger. Daniel had left Walter alone with the burden of passing on the family name, the one act he would never be able to accomplish. It was convenient to blame Daniel for the wounds that Walter necessarily had to inflict on Joyce, at just those times, when his mother had to deal with Aunt Jeannie's probes about Walter's luck with girls. Lucy probably had to deflect the questions, too.

"Daniel would have married," he muttered to the tarnished butter knife he'd picked from the tray.

Lucy was vigorously rubbing her spoon with action that involved both her hand and the wide sweep of her forearm. "Daniel who?" she said. "Would you look at this rag? Oh!— Daniel! Mom says he was smart and very sweet and that the girls all liked him, but you never know." She held up an old undershirt that had moments before been white and had quickly become wet and black.

Walter stared at her goggle-eyed. " 'Daniel who?' " he repeated. Where was the reverence, the curiosity? How could she say, "Daniel who?"

He remembered all at once the feeling he had had as a child, asking an adult a simple question, an important question, with great interest. "Why, Daddy, is the sky blue?" His father had given him a terrible answer about electrons and ions and light refracting. He'd gone on incomprehensibly for ten minutes, when what Walter wanted was a short story. He'd wanted to know in a way that he could understand, that made sense: the sky is blue to match Calvin Klein's spring line; blue because overhead you need a color that doesn't threaten, that soothes; blue because sky-green, sky-orange, sky-red, doesn't sound right when you read it on the spine of a Crayola. Walter realized that he had overwhelmed Sue Rawson by telling her honestly about his life, about his yearning for meaningful work, just as his father had told him more about the atmosphere than he'd wanted to hear. It might pay, then, to take a different tack with Lucy. She was dipping her rag into the neck of the bottle, soaking the cloth with polish.

"This is The Story, more or less, of Daniel," Walter began. He tucked his leg under himself and abandoned his knife on the armrest of the chair. "The Story of Daniel—or Daniella, if you must—goes something like this." Lucy was polishing the daylights out of her spoon, and he couldn't help advising her before he launched into the body of the tale. "You might want to think about saving some energy for the rest of the utensils, but then again you know best. Anyway, The Story of Daniel." He cleared his throat, breathed in and out. "So there were once two sisters. They were good in different ways and pretty in different ways. One of them got sick and became more beautiful, because of the sickness. She lost weight, and her cheekbones became more pronounced, her eyes grew very large—she was exquisitely fragile—and also, she grew introspective, long-suffering, and probably religious. She became almost perfect in everyone's opinion, as she languished, and when she died she was suddenly, in the collective memory, the smartest, kindest, wisest and most ravishing person who had ever lived. As the years passed, she became even more perfect, if that's possible, although no one ever talked about her. Still, she was there, everywhere, always present. Her sister, who was ordinary, but good in her own way, could never forget the radiant and morally superior dead girl. She never married, even though everyone discussed her wedding in the kitchen. She always imagined her sister's wedding, and it came to take the place of her own, this wedding in her dreams. No detail went unnoticed in the fantasy. All of the bridesmaids, for example, had large firm breasts that were useful, like Velcro, when it came to holding up their fuchsia strapless dresses. She even understood that when she talked about the ghost sister she was really using her to understand herself. She realized that dead people serve as a kind of measure, that you look back to them to find yourself. She accepted that. You must know that the living sister was happy enough. She had a real job, she had lovers occasionally, sometimes people she knew and cared for, but more often she had the squalid encounters in the john you hear about, the one triumph, a truck driver, so handsome, very little English, ten minutes of bliss in the can in a bar in the East Village—and she lived until Thanksgiving Day, when she choked on a bone right at the dinner table. It spoiled the party and no one ever forgave her, even in death. But she forgave them from heaven because she knew they were regular old human beings who worried about propriety and gravy boats and the silver being polished. And so they all lived happily ever after, especially little Linda, who grew up to be a famous ballerina despite her busybody uncle's warning about starting her training too early."

Lucy dropped her spoon on the tray. Walter had never seen her look astonished before. It became her. Her tongue was blue from a candy she'd been sucking on and her bottom teeth were straight and very white. He remembered that as a teenager she'd worn a metal cage around her head at night and that when he came home he always found rubber bands on the kitchen floor that had sprung off her braces. He had a fine view of her two fillings. "Waaaaaaalt." She finally laughed down the *a* of his name.

"It's a true story," he said, gathering up his notebooks, tossing his head, making for the door, satisfied that at last he was having his turn to make a dramatic exit.

At dinner Walter drank a lot of wine because he'd brought several choice bottles, and also out of mortification at his own wagging tongue. He wasn't sure why he'd told both his aunt and his sister the key facts of his life. He had been discreet for thirty-eight years and in one afternoon blown his cover. After several glasses he got into a lively discussion with Uncle Ted about sexual mores in the United States. The art of conversation had never been Uncle Ted's strong suit. But Ted had also drunk nearly a full bottle of Merlot and so he began not only to talk but to have opinions. It turned out that he hadn't ever gotten past blaming Betty Friedan and the entire state of California for the decline of the family and the sexual revolution.

"But, Uncle Ted, you have Jeannie," Walter said. "Not everyone has that bulwark. You're never going to have decline of any sort going on within ten miles of your backyard."

Francie had just taken a drink of water and she had to spit it back in her cup. "Over Mother's dead body," she said, sniggering. "You've got that right, Walter."

Uncle Ted was all in favor of this Newton Gingrich, he called him, as if calling the new Speaker of the House Newt was disrespectful. Walter took him seriously and tried to raise his consciousness. "Yes, but you see," he said, gesticulating wildly, knocking the tongs from the salad bowl, "the sexual revolution was on its way long before Haight-Ashbury. For example, what changed the public's attitude toward whores after World War Two wasn't a change in morality at all but the availability of penicillin. Syphilis was now under control. The prevailing attitude had absolutely nothing to do with lax morals."

"Blame it all on the feminists, Dad," Francie muttered. "Blame it on the women who are tired of the bullshit, excuse my French."

"Walter," Joyce said, moving the dried flowers in the pumpkin vase so she could see him across the table. "I forgot to tell you my friend Paula—you remember, the reference librarian from way back—saw your old friend Mitch in town the other day."

He understood his mother was trying to change the subject. He had been thinking, in relation to morality, about the time he'd caught crabs from the Sicilian longshoreman, and how that affliction had made him chaste as a nun for a while. He also was noticing that Francie had lost a fair amount of weight, and was uncharacteristically petulant. "What did you say, Mom?"

"Mitch Anderson. My friend Paula, the one who loved going to *The Nutcracker* every year—Paula saw him in town."

Walter hadn't heard from Mitch, hadn't ever tried to contact Mitch, hadn't seen him since high school graduation. He didn't admit to thinking about Mitch. Susan had gone to her tenth reunion and the fifteenth, and found no trace of him. She had hoped to visit Mitch's mother, but the woman had either gotten an unlisted number or moved, or had died.

"He's a developer in Southern California, Del Mar, doing quite well for himself, it seems. Two little girls, I think she said."

"Huh." It was the best Walter could manage. He put a chilled pre-cut square of butter in the depression of his steaming mashed potatoes and watched it melt. I'm shellacked, he said to himself. He tried to focus on the yellow pad becoming liquid and slowly filling the reservoir. Uncle Ted had turned to the other side and was talking past Francie, telling Lucy's Marc about the phony organic produce that came from the West Coast and was triple the price of so-called commercially grown vegetables. Mitch, in Del Mar, two girls, a developer. Walter thought of Mitch standing before a zoning board, flicking his bleached hair. His skin was probably leathery from the California sun, with rugged-man creases around his eyes. Maybe he wore cowboy boots, a bolo tie, a big silver belt buckle, a hunky drag and slouch to his walk to suit the terrain where just beyond the pass there were mesas. He would have the power to charm the elderly women into deeding over their farms, the power to make the men on the water board reroute the rivers so that his personal property of twenty thousand square miles became arable.

"What happened to that girl, you know, the one who went off to the New York City Ballet, the one you used to bring up here?" Walter's cousin Vicki asked.

"Miami Ballet," Walter said with his mouth full of potato. "More Balanchine down in Florida than there is in New York." Susan had called him the night before to tell him that she'd fallen in love with a man other than her husband, the man who looked so much like an older version of Daniel. She wanted Walter to travel with her to Chicago in January so that she could possibly commit adultery. "She's doing great," he said, the potatoes slogging down his throat. "Star of the company."

The twenty-five adults were sitting around the Ping-Pong table that had been assembled in the living room for the occasion. Aunt Jeannie had brought her festive pumpkin-and-turkey-print cloth to cover the rough green surface. The children were in the kitchen at what had always been called the cat table, almost out of earshot. The meal, as usual, had begun with a brief group conversation, about potential purchases or recent acquisitions in the dog, car and computer departments. Marc was the expert in the vehicle line, and he was sure to sit next to the husbands who would want to pick his brain. Cousin Maxi sat in the corner talking to the college girls, the two education majors, about the success of her second-grade students in a program called Reading Recovery. Roger Miller, Francie's husband, had recently begun to raise orchids, but he couldn't seem to find anyone who wanted to hear about the delicate process of hand pollination. Sue Rawson was next to Robert McCloud at the far end of the table, bent to the work of eating, carving the thigh of the turkey with a serving fork and her pocket knife. Robert trusted Sue Rawson's financial instincts, and they often sought each other out to discuss their mutual funds. Aunt Jeannie, from the head of the table, broke through several of the conversations and called down to Walter, "Your mother tells me you're going to direct *South Pacific* at the high school. That sounds so special!"

He drained his glass. Without a trace of mockery he exclaimed, "I bet it will be! It will be very special, Aunt Jeannie."

"What's the best part about directing a play, I wonder?"

"The best part, the best part." Walter covered his eyes with his napkin as if the subject warranted complete concentration. His aunt, he knew, would never stop speaking to her adult children and relations as if they were preschoolers. "Well," he said, leaning forward so she could hear him. "I've already cornered a couple of boys in my freshman class and told them if they're in the chorus I might sneak a plus into their grade. At the least I'd give them a brownie. I dared them to learn the Charleston after school one day—fourteen-year-old boys with sloppy steps and goofy grins, but they did it, and I got the sense, unspoken of course, that they were grateful to have moved in a way that didn't involve running down a field after a ball. I've got my eyes peeled for talent. There's a girl named Sharon in my seventh-hour class who's built like a barge and has no fear. I may have to blackmail her to try out, but I'm thinking she'd make a lulu of a Bloody Mary. The school recycles the musicals every five years, because they already have the costumes and thirty copies of the play, so I'd like to try to figure out a way to make it seem new and unusual."

Jeannie's red lipstick was called Congo Madness, and with that color and a black lip-pencil she had learned over the years to create a big enough mouth for what she herself called her extra-large personality. Her smile was certainly still the focal point of her dazzle. "That is just so wonderful," she was saying to Walter. "I remember the way you loved your dancing. We all kind of hoped you'd grow out of it, and you did!"

Mitch, a developer in Del Mar, two little girls, a wife. It was a pre-dictable enough life, no reason to dwell on the shock. Walter was de-termined that no one rob him of the charity he meant to feel toward everyone in the room. "I loved the ballet all right," he said, "but I stunk. I mean I was really lousy. My ankles, my knees, my feet." He grimaced at the thought of his legs in black tights. "I could turn on a dime, though. It was the one thing I could do. The girls used to gasp in class when I got turning. And I had a noble head. I've realized lately: a noble head. I didn't know it then, but I had just as much no-bility as the next guy. If I could have been amputated at the neck I would have been a great dancer."

Aunt Jeannie slapped her hand to her mouth. "Oh, sweetheart"—she tittered—"surely not. You don't mean it."

Before he could assure her that he was exaggerating, Sue Rawson loomed over the table demanding quiet, banging at her water glass with the serving knife. She boomed, "I have an announcement to make." Lucy and Maxi were clearing the table, but everyone else abruptly stopped their chatter and turned to the person many of the younger ones only grudgingly accepted as the matriarch. "I'll make this brief," she said. "And thereafter I don't want to hear another word about it until we have our next family meeting. In the meantime you can decide what you want to do." Joyce covered her nose with the triangle her hands made, the weight of her head resting solely on the tips of her two index fingers at the bridge of her nose. Even Lucy stood still then. She leaned against the mantel, her arm around the largest bowl in the kitchen, full of coleslaw. No one in the family liked coleslaw, and every year Joyce shredded three cabbages and emptied two full jars of mayonnaise.

"As you know," Sue Rawson said, "I own well over a third of the stocks in the Lake Margaret Corporation. I believe it's time either to pass the property down to the next generation, or sell out altogether. I can't force this upon my sisters, but I can sell my shares. I'd like my money. We elders need to be relieved of the financial burden, the taxes, the maintenance and so forth, and let you youngsters, if you're up to it, take on the responsibility of ownership. I haven't used the place for years except for family affairs such as this one. I've had enough. The house is falling into disrepair and I don't like it. We're

valued here at about nine hundred thousand dollars, you can figure
what my shares are worth. I've got fifteen more than my sisters. You
can call my lawyer, Mr. Giddings, when you've a proposal put together. This transaction will require thought, creativity, cash, and I
dare say put you all to the test. Nothing wrong with that. Let's say we
come together June first. That gives you plenty of time to consider the
options. All right, then? Where's the dessert? I like to see it on the
sideboard, gives a person reason to carry on. I hope there's enough
Cool Whip. Last year you girls didn't bring enough."

She sat down, picked up her drumstick and went back to the
work of gnawing at the bone. There was only a moment of silence before Aunt Jeannie's youngest daughter, Mary Beth, began to wail,
"Lake Margaret? Lake Margaret?" Aunt Jeannie herself cried, "What
are you saying, Sue?"

"You heard me," Sue Rawson barked. "I spoke plain English. Do
we need an interpreter next to me, to make my sentences into gestures? Anyone know the deaf alphabet? I want to sell. I want the
money. *Je veux l'argent,* for you French speakers. We can sell the
whole place if none of you want to buy me out. I've got more shares
than the other two. My brothers left me more of their portions for
their own good reasons. I own a larger chunk of this place than anyone else."

No one dared to murmur or cough or stir. They sat, each one, staring at the pumpkin men and gobbling turkeys on the tablecloth. Most
of the cousins felt as if they'd been evicted from their own homes, as
if they were squatting on the sidewalk with a few belongings thrown
willy-nilly in boxes. Walter could think only that from the single
speech of his aunt Sue's would begin the dissolution of over a century
of one family's life. He didn't think, I must fight her, or She is wrong.
Aunt Jeannie had carved smiles on some of the miniature pumpkins in
the centerpiece and she'd found long-burning birthday-size candles to
put inside them. They seemed to be winking at Walter. He said to
himself, Here, then, is the awful beginning.

It was Joyce who first moved, who put her hands noiselessly to the
table and stood up. She tapped her shiny silver spoon on her wine-
glass, an unnecessary call to attention. She was growing old, Walter
thought again, but she was full of grace, a quality that had completely

bypassed her sisters. She stood before them, glancing over the table, meeting each person's eye. Sue Rawson would know better than to deny her, the dignified baby sister who had had her share of loss. "You want your money," she said quietly. "We all understand that." In truth, most of them were appalled by the notion. "There is something, however, that you must realize, Sue. I'm asking you to think about our heritage, about the fact that none of us paid any money, not a cent for Lake Margaret. Our parents did not have to pay for the privilege of this property. It has been given to us, handed down, from generation to generation. There has been a trust fund to assist us with the up-keep. The idea of exchanging money for its use is foreign to us. You are asking your nieces and nephews, and your sisters, to pay for some-thing that was free to you. Free." She let the word settle for a minute.

"You talked to me about selling the place years ago, at another gathering, at Jeannie and Ted's anniversary. The subject does put a damper on the party spirit, I might add. All these years I've been wait-ing for you to bring it up again, and for some reason you haven't. I'd come to think that after the—discussion—we'd had that day, you per-haps, after all, saw my point of view."

Walter remembered the anniversary party, that hot afternoon, his mother walking across the porch, through the dancing couples. Hav-ing a Catholic mass at Lake Margaret, Jeannie dolled up and behaving like a starlet, must have inflamed Sue Rawson and may have been the last straw. He remembered his mother and his aunt talking in a corner. He understood at last that it was Sue Rawson who had provoked Joyce, or maybe a corner of his mother's skirt caught on the edge of the Peg-Board, it fell over, and she thought to herself, Why not? I could claim responsibility for this, like a terrorist who phones in, who is suddenly dangerous without having had to lift a finger.

"So all along," Joyce went on, "you've been thinking of the house in terms of your rightful inheritance, your nest egg. That—makes sense. Except, you see, most of us probably have not thought in those terms. I may well have been the only person who realized what you've meant to do." She brushed a white curl from her forehead. "We have not been brought up to speed. Forgive us, then, if we are taken aback."

Aunt Jeannie murmured, "A-men."

Joyce tapped her spoon slowly on the table. "I think you will have to anticipate three things in the coming months. Right or wrong, the family, many of them, will hold this against you. There is a lot of emotion about the house, and now we have a next generation that is attached to it. Second, there will be factions, no doubt, because this is going to be a complicated transaction, as well as an expensive one. I'm not aware that any of us have twenty-five or fifty or what?—two, three, four hundred thousand dollars to spare? The young people are most of them burdened by their own house payments and growing children. Last of all, you must know that we will never be whole again. That has been our great blessing, our strength, as a family. Goodness, the three of us, you, Jeannie and I, have managed to stay in our hometown, to be close to each other. How unusual! Nothing, of course, ever stays the same, but through great change we have remained together. How lucky we have been." She wiped her mouth with her napkin. "We have real whipped cream this year, by the way, and four choices of pie. They've just come out of the oven and so they are not yet on display. And why the real cream, you may ask? No reason except the exhilaration of dangerous living."

She sat down and looked straight across the table at Walter for a disarming number of seconds. Sue Rawson had moved on to her generous portion of dressing and was eating as if she were in the privacy of her own kitchen. No one glanced in her direction or spoke. In their lives together, they had not ever been speechless simultaneously, with the exception of the time right after the family pictures slammed to the floor. That silence had been prompted by something outside themselves. With the dishes cleared away they did not know what to do; they were embarrassed to be in their own company.

Walter gazed up at the wall of photographs. He settled on a picture of himself with Sue Rawson thirty years before. He was seven, missing his front teeth. She was covered in a dark Oriental wrap with dragons on the lapels, standing behind him, not touching, her arms at her side, looking far beyond the frame. It seemed to Walter in the disquiet of the living room that he didn't belong in the photograph, that he had been like a milkweed seed that floated in front of the camera just as it clicked.

He wished that Joyce would speak again, that she'd jump up and say, Oh, by the way, I did it. I knocked the picture board over that time, at the party. I wanted everyone to blast out of their skins to see clearly into the future, to know the spoiler in our midst.

Walter didn't know what such an admission would prompt, but it might at the least serve to revive conversation. Lucy spoke first, asking her father to pass the turkey platter. Her request did not interrupt the deeper silence. Walter hoped that over dessert his mother would tell the family a soothing prophecy: Sue Rawson might after all die before the property changed hands. Joyce could tell the group that their aunt was a difficult woman who nonetheless deserved affection; it was possible she wasn't repelled by tenderness, let any who dared try to prove the point.

His mother was staring at the fireplace and patting a dog without realizing her hands were moving. The sorrow in her features had settled there long before, and was such a part of her eyes, the shape of her mouth, the sag of her cheeks, that it was hard to remember that the expression wasn't just the look of her face. Not even Lucy's birth all those years ago had brought Joyce McCloud back to her former self. Walter drank one last swallow of wine. He thought there must be a place, like a dead-letter office, where everyone's longing went, yearning that was sent out, day after day. He thought it must collect somewhere, in a dank basement room, the mass of it rising and rising like water, and with no end in sight.

Five

DECEMBER
1972

When Walter first loved Mitch, he loved without the claptrap of words. Music filled his head, fragments of concertos and sonatas and even show tunes, but the melodies generally came without lyrics. A few months into his devotion he tried to write poetry, but the long, florid lines seemed to fix and abbreviate what to him was fluid and fathomless. He felt, looking at his verse, that he had trapped some great rare bird, that he'd stuffed it in a pint container, his hand smacked over the top. Never having been farther away from home than Wisconsin, he had written that his own heart was like the echoing nave of Saint Peter's Basilica, that the love itself was as ornate as the Forbidden City, as hortatory as a Beethoven symphony. Wishing for his original wordless rapture, disgusted with his efforts, he ripped the pages out of the notebook and shredded the paper. Years later, when he was a chaperone for the Otten High Prom, he thought that the gym, gussied up in streamers and little white lights in potted trees, was actually a fair representation of his teenage idea of love. The baskets at either end of the court were wound with crepe paper and tinsel, and the balloons and tissue flowers strung from the ceiling were as lush as tropical vegetation.

At fourteen, Walter wanted more than anything to believe in grandeur. He had no use for his mother's on-again, off-again stab at becoming a Unitarian, saw no reason to put his faith in a faceless guiding principle. The Greeks and Norsemen had surely been better off with their temperamental gods, gigantic men who wore magic belts, who had teeth of pure gold and threw red-hot hammers, who ate greedily in a realm where the food was more varied than loaves and fishes. Walter decided that if he was going to worship anything, it would not be the milksoppy emotion that was God's love but rather the extravagant and occasionally tormented feelings that roiled within the breasts of the happy-ending heroines in his favorite Victorian novels. He was certain he loved in each moment, that not a beat passed by when he did not know that he loved. His was a pure love in the beginning, a love without the paraphernalia of hope and expectation. He might just as well have said *Mitch* to mean the word *love*. It was girlish behavior, perhaps, to give up the rest of the language, to seize on his name. He didn't care. He whispered "Mitch" into his pillow; he opened his closet and said it louder; he sang it softly in the shower; he filled a few notebook pages with it in different scripts. When he moved about the house he felt as if there were two Walters, the one in front who talked and ate and played the piano in the dream life of every day, and the other, who hovered, guarding, always guarding what was real, what was true.

He no longer knew to eat or sleep or brush his teeth. He had lost any instinct that might guide him. He would have skipped off a cliff if his beloved had beckoned him across the abyss. That first spring of his adoration Walter walked from his house to Mitch's, down alley after alley, lilacs, wet after the rain, dripping over the back fences. He made his way without narration, without phrases or sentences running through his head. There were snowball bushes in the yards, syringa, honeysuckle. And a few tulip petals drifted along the pavement, stripped by one gust from their long straight stalks. Soon the fluff from the cottonwood trees would blow down into the grass, into the shrubs, the sandboxes, the gutters, the screens, onto the car windshields and under the wipers. Walter smelled neither the blossoms nor the garbage in the ribbed galvanized cans. He could not have said what sort of day it was, what he'd had in his lunch, what he'd seen on television. He felt the privilege of walking the alleyways as if they were private, as if he were riding the dumbwaiter up to the king's bedroom.

He walked and walked, thinking only of Mitch and Walter in various indoor and outdoor settings: Mitch and Walter dancing bare-chested, in an empty room, high ceilings, a silver fixture, tall double-hung windows, the morning light falling across the floor. No sound but their breathing. Or Mitch and Walter in the forest, the dank loamy smell of woods, Walter running without shoes, but over the softest moss, streaking through the underbrush, Mitch fleeting over the ground, behind, trying to catch him.

It had begun on what seemed to be an unexceptional day in the September of Walter's freshman year in high school. Walter was sitting on the floor in the waiting room at the Kentons', as he always did before class, his legs spread, looking up periodically, watching for Susan to come and stand before the mothers and wind her hair into her twin buns. He was naturally stiff, not much suppleness anywhere along his rigid spine. He was straining, bending to his toes. It was painful to watch him grope for his shoes, and the mothers avoided turning his way.

He was struggling to lay his cheek to his knee when the boys' dressing-room door clicked open. He saw Mitch's feet, the short thick feet packed into the worn leather slippers. He glanced up the legs, the calves, the thighs, his eyes resting farther, on the bulge, beautifully packaged because of the dance belt Mitch had recently decided to wear. The smell of him, the sharp boy odor went up Walter's nostrils, oh how good it was, the sweetness of Right Guard, the sour dance clothes, the talcum powder inside his shoes, his hair, his hands, the fresh face. *Mitch.* All at once the fine poems and songs Walter had learned through the years left him. *Mitch.* He inhaled, held his breath, closed his eyes. Nothing to say, nothing to breathe or understand or look at, nothing except Mitch. One name. That single word.

He put his head back and he let the pinky glare of the fluorescent lights shine down upon him, and it was as if the long white tubes were burning, as if they had the heat of the sun. The warmth, and the word, were in him, and he felt even then that the syllable would hold him through the length of any siege. He did not know how much time passed before Mr. Kenton walked from the office, clapping his hands, his cigarette hanging from his lips. Mitch was holding on to a chair, slowly sinking into a full plié, slowly working through his leg muscles to pull back up to a taut first position. Susan had fixed her hair and was at the sink with the heel of her shoe under the water, to make it mold to her foot. She had stood in front of Walter, braiding her hair, and he had not seen her. The waiting students all followed Mr. Kenton, crowding like sheep through the door into the studio. Walter got himself up, smoothed his hands down his legs. *Mitchell Dylan Anderson.* The full name. He didn't see the mothers, the sofas, the photographs on the wall, Mrs. Manka coming to get more coffee. He had always loved Mitch. It wasn't something that had just happened. He had loved without knowing, without identifying the feeling. That meant he was something like the retard on his block, Billy Wexler, who had no nerve endings in two fingers and was always getting them cut and blackened by twig fires without registering pain. Walter stumbled into the studio. It was so simple! What he wanted to do, what he really wanted to do, right away, right before class, was fill huge balloons with paint, good paint, expensive paint, and drop them out the window. The balloons would burst on the cement twelve stories below; they'd burst, spattering amber, spattering liquid gold and silver all down Michigan Avenue. The swift drop, the break, the color— all of it would reveal how he felt.

It was enough for quite some time to be in Mitch's presence, to say, with every plié, every battement, *I love you, I love you, Mitch.* If the boy's jacket or a book was left behind at Walter's house, he smelled the thing, he tasted it, he ran it across his cheek, he held it against his clavicle in sleep. When they were alone, without the distraction of Susan, there was a quality about their friendship that now and then made him tremble, that brought him happiness. Walter sat on his bed and Mitch sprawled on the floor, running his fingers through his own hair. They talked idly of the Kentons, of the girls in class, their teachers at school. And they talked in earnest, too, about the dangers of adult life, about corruption, cynicism, fakery. How they hoped they would be strong enough to stick to their principles and not sell out, not end up doing chorus numbers in some saccharine Broadway musical.

They argued over the merits and flaws of Ivan Nagy, Erik Bruhn, Nureyev, Edward Villella, Anthony Dowell, Peter Martins. To make his point, Walter sometimes imitated the dancers so that of course

Mitch laughed. Walter had him then, and he knew so well to build the comedy slowly, to let Mitch chuckle for a while before he pulled out the stops, before he gave in to slapstick. Poor Mitch rocked back and forth on the floor, howling, holding his stomach. In a quieter mood, they listened to music sitting side by side, against the bed, so close, Tchaikovsky flooding the room. They opened Sue Rawson's coffee-table books on ballet and pored over the photographs, feeling the other's rhythm, knowing when to turn, on to the next page.

There was no formal declaration when Susan and Mitch took up together in January, in the middle of their freshman year. The friends had been a threesome from the beginning of their dancing careers. There was no prologue, no portent of fracture. They were riding the train one day and Walter was looking out the window. He turned, about to say, I wonder if Mrs. or Mr. K. will teach class today. He got as far as, "I—" They were holding hands. Mitch and Susan. He had to stare at the fingers, his, hers, mixed up in the clasp. "I—" he said again. He had to think why they might be touching each other in such a manner. He followed Mitch's hand, to his arm, to his neck, up to the taunting smile.

"You—" Mitch said. "You what?"

"I didn't know." Walter managed to say that much. He looked back out the window. If they were holding hands they must at some point have made declarations of love to each other. Without him they had sat together, said clever and suggestive things, gazed moonily and groped around in the dark for who knew what all. He felt as if he might not make it to the journey's end. When he glanced again at the two-some, Susan had her rippling head of hair on Mitch's shoulder. There was nothing he could do but sit and wait for the ride to be over, nothing to do but hold the horror inside, smile and nod, smile and nod.

Privately he called them Mr. and Mrs. Mitch Anderson. Bitterly he referred to them as S&M. It became their habit to kiss at length in front of Walter. Theirs were long, elaborate kisses, with murmurs and saliva glistening on their mouths when they paused for purposes of respiration. Walter remembered that he used to wish for drama, for tragedy, a little torture, and here it was, the wish fulfilled. He didn't know if their necking was supposed to be a tribute to him, if they meant to include him in their intimacy, or if they were showing him how comfortable they were in his presence. He didn't know then that telling a third party is essential for most lovers, that after a while the couple needs to see itself, to admire itself, through another set of eyes. They intimated that they'd been up in Mitch's attic, and Susan said something, through her giggles, about the creaking of the grand-mother's pine bed. How then could Walter keep from putting them through their paces in a number of different positions? He envisioned their slender firm bodies naked under a musty quilt; he could hear Susan's petite yelps; he could see Mitch going faster and harder, so pleased with himself, with his performance. It occurred to Walter that after the momentous release they'd think of him. They'd think of his picturing them and they'd go at it again, with more gusto. They wanted, after all, to imagine just how it was that Walter saw them; it was for Walter that they moaned and called for God, for Walter that Susan lifted her hips to meet Mitch's thrust.

He supposed he might be paranoid or deluded or crazy. It would never have occurred to him to tell anyone about his feelings for Mitch, and so the impulse to chronicle and reveal was a mystery to him. He used his strength to hide his love, to protect it. It was possible that there was nothing complicated about the display, that the two of them couldn't help it, or they were only bragging as they kissed, waving their wealth and their wares right in front of his face. Walter watched them because he couldn't do otherwise. Susan, always, after the kiss had been going on for a while, put her palms to Mitch's cheeks. It was a gesture Walter waited for, as if she had to keep Mitch at bay before he overwhelmed her. That first day on the el when they held hands, Walter began to imagine that he could slip inside Susan, zip himself into her skin. It became a preoccupation, fantasizing that he was one with her, both his and her hand petting Mitch's soft cheek, both of them in effect putting their lips to his singular mouth.

When they were grown, Walter often told Susan that he no longer re-membered much about his high school career. She took him at his word. What came to mind, he said, was the travel, back and forth, on the el or riding in the car with his mother, day after day, to Rockford.

And also, day after day, his mother's urging Daniel to eat, to eat breakfast, lunch and dinner. Walter's epicurean friends in New York believed that food had been invented for entertainment, and in their
galley kitchens they spent the weekends simmering liquids, making
sauces and syrupy reductions. Walter always felt that eating was in
part duty, and he often heard his mother's pleading voice, as if it were
a grace, when he sat before his dinner. She once broke down and wept
over Daniel's TV tray.

Walter doubted that he would ever fondly remember the scenes of
that December, the season of the Rockford Ballet. As he grew older
and he came to love his awkward and earnest young self he still could
not laugh over the Christmas party, the time he fell down the back-
stairs, his head banging on every step. Mitch had bent over him on the
kitchen floor, Mitch, as concerned and loving as Florence Nightingale,
holding an ice pack to his wounded forehead.

Daniel, in fact, was better in December, as well as he would ever
be again. Walter was given selective information about the treatments,
but he also overheard enough telephone conversations to piece together some parts that had been omitted. At the time he did not realize that his parents were trying to keep some of the details from him.
They had never been garrulous, that was all. He assumed that the
therapies were going to make Daniel well, and in the meantime there
was nothing much to say. Daniel had had radiation in November to
take care of a mass of some sort in his chest, and there had been a
complication with the second surgery. At the urging of the family
lawyer, Joyce and Robert were thinking about taking legal action
against an incompetent doctor. This bit Walter found out because
Aunt Jeannie asked him about it. The surgeon had stitched up Daniel
in a way that was troublesome but apparently not life-threatening. So,
Good, Walter thought. A lawyer and a team of doctors working for
Daniel. Everything would eventually turn out just fine with the professional people on his brother's side.

He might have asked Joyce about the sickness in the hours they
spent driving to Rockford for the *Nutcracker* rehearsals. But she did
not seem to want to talk, and anyway Walter had homework to do by
flashlight in the winter darkness. Joyce was living her life in the car, he
knew, driving Daniel to the hospital in downtown Chicago several

times a week, and then many afternoons she turned around and shuttled Walter the other direction, an hour and a half to Rockford for his rehearsals and an hour and a half back home.

The Rockford Ballet wasn't entirely a nice opportunity, as Mr. Kenton had promised, but well before the run was over Walter admitted that it was probably worth doing. He told himself that it was good training for some future career, exploring third-world countries or rocketing to airless, cratered planets. Miss Amy, the director, producer and choreographer, had put out a talent search for a teenage boy, for the leading role of the Prince. She had choreographed her own version of the ballet, and while she meant to use many of her own dancers, she had no intention of depending on little children to enthrall the audience. She had zero tolerance, she said, for cuteness. Hers was a serious, full-length ballet featuring emerging and mature talent. The Prince and Clara were demanding roles for advanced students. Clara had several variations on pointe, and it was imperative that the Prince have partnering skills. There were no older boys in Miss Amy's school, and it turned out to be more arduous than she'd anticipated to find a boy who was both suitable and willing to travel to Rockford.

At the audition, it did not take long for Miss Amy to see that Walter would suffice. She had grandiose ideas but flexible standards. Dancing alone on the parquet floor in the studio above Debbie's Beauty Shop on Kishwaukee Street, he had no sense that he, Walter McCloud, really did have physical appeal. His dark curly hair, his dignified, slightly aquiline nose, the red lipstick he'd found in the car and applied to his mouth as an act of defiance—against whom, for what, he wasn't sure—all gave him a theatrical look, somewhere between grieving Edith Piaf and loopy Carol Burnett. He extended his leg à la seconde, tragically, and spun around and around with his head thrown back, like a skater.

Miss Amy was the first person to see possibility in Walter's dancing. It wasn't exactly potential that he had, she said, trying to explain to the stage manager after the audition. "I can't describe it exactly, except to say that I think he's got this raw kind of possibility."

It seemed to her that he might be an actor. He was her last candidate, and she considered that it might not matter much if he couldn't point his foot. The boy from Peoria who'd tried out could jump, but he'd had no expression, no vitality. What counted, in the end, she said, was that Walter had moved his arms and legs as if he believed he was a prince. She'd asked him to walk across the floor in character, and although he'd overdone it slightly, so upright he was in danger of falling backward, she felt she could rein him in, subdue him.

Walter would never go so far as to say that Mr. Kenton had done him a favor by showing him the way to Miss Amy. But two weeks into the rehearsals he began to nurse along a hope. There was a chance—remote, to be sure—but a chance nonetheless, that what happened at Lincoln Center, or at the Arie Crown Theater, could also take place in Rockford. It was not out of the question. The lights might go down on opening night, in the theater, the little box of a room black for an instant just as the canned music came through the speakers, and the world, all of life beyond the stage, might dissolve. There could conceivably be enchantment right there in Rockford. It was Miss Amy with her frizzy blond hair tucked into a lavender silk scarf, walking across the floor with him, correcting his posture and praising his princeliness, who gave Walter the idea that Magic, after all, did not have to be expensive.

He did not speak about his "nice opportunity" with his friends. They were absorbed with their own performances. He certainly did not tell them that he was one of two leading males. The other, the Sugar Plum Fairy's cavalier, a stuck-up thirty-eight-year-old named Philip, from Milwaukee, didn't talk to anyone except Miss Amy and the stage manager. Aside from Philip, who rarely came to rehearsals, Walter liked the troupe. He felt at home in the makeshift theater, home to the Rockford Community Players. When they first started rehearsing they had to dance around the set of the current production, *Bye Bye Birdie.* Walter got a charge out of being a prince from timeless fairyland in a living room with an orange plastic sofa and a pink phone. He amused his fellow dancers by playing a galliard on Conrad Birdie's electric guitar, Renaissance for most of the way, with a Buddy Holly twang.

The girl who danced Clara, Nancy Sherwin, had thick thighs, which her skirt would obscure, and large breasts, which her chemise would not. She was a big-hearted floozy at sixteen, a girl who couldn't

even take her own stardom seriously. Walter guessed she realized she
was in Rockford, no reason to get excited. She laughed whenever anyone meant to be funny, a great musical flutter on one note. She
laughed if the joke fell dead. She was generous that way, her flabby
mouth hanging open, waiting for the punch line, waiting to spring her
cadenza. She laughed when Walter put his hands around her size-
sixteen Spanky Pant waist, when she wobbled around in her nearly
motionless turns. On the lifts she meant to help him, getting a running
start where she could, coming at him like a bag of wet cement.

Despite her size and her heft, she was graceful. In the slower variations, if she took the time, she occasionally moved Walter with her
poignant and miraculously elongated arabesques. What he chiefly admired her for, however, was her unrelenting exuberance, her notion
that everything was equally hilarious and the apparent absence of any
deeper self that was sensitive to injury. He thought she would have
found it funny that he borrowed Daniel's weights and lifted them
every morning before school in order to get in shape for their pas de
deux. He knew she would have laughed not at the need, not at herself,
but at the thought of scrawny little Walter shaking as he hoisted the
barbells overhead and held them there for three short seconds.

Every evening Miss Amy led them through a few warm-up exercises to the music on a scratched record. When she taught them the
steps to the ballet, she sang the melodies, keeping the beat going by
clapping if she had to interrupt the tune to call out a correction, picking up the strain at its proper place when she came back to her role as
accompanist. In later years Walter likened the project to a Special
Olympics event, the dancers' persistence and enthusiasm in part com-
pensating for their disabilities. In the course of the rehearsals, he felt
that he shouldn't be enjoying something that was so far from being
even second-rate. And yet when he forgot to worry about the production as a work of art he threw himself into it wholeheartedly. He loved
his blue velvet tunic that came midthigh, the matching blue blouse
with cream-colored satin cuffs and a silver sequined V at the neck,
and his tights that had sequins sewn in clusters all the way to the
ankle.

The first time he put on the suit he stood on the toilet seat at the theater, kicking at the stall door to keep it open, so that he could see the

mirror over the sink. He couldn't take his eyes off himself. Miss Amy finally had to call from the outside, "Walter, hon, have you died in there?" Kicking the creaking stall door open wider so he could see his whole body in the coming gesture, he put his hand to his breast and finding a lower voice, an imperious tone, he said, "Be out in a moment."

He thought to talk to his mother about the quality of the production. He couldn't have said that he needed someone to give his participation in *The Nutcracker* a blessing. He knew only that he wanted to ask Joyce a question he hadn't yet framed. Every day, when she dropped him off outside the theater he turned to her, wanting to ask, Is this really all right? She was always staring out past the windshield, as if she'd come to a stop for no reason, as if she might start up and without thinking drive until she got to the West Coast. "Well," he'd say, "bye, Mom. See you at nine-thirty." She'd turn to him, remembering that he was with her. He could see that she hardly knew what he was doing: she sometimes could not remember why they were in Rockford. She'd leave him on the curb and drive off, to the library, she said. To do what? he wondered. He pictured her sitting in a carrel, putting her head down, like a high school student, and sleeping until whatever was left of her mother instinct told her to wake.

A week before the first performance, on a Sunday night, Walter walked over to Sue Rawson's to return a stack of *Dance Magazine*s he'd borrowed. He could see her in the living room through the sheer curtains. She was on her chaise longue, her half-glasses on her nose, looking at the ceiling. He could hear Maria Callas singing Violetta through the brick walls of the house. Sue Rawson had always professed to be a Renata Tebaldi fan, and therefore she couldn't love or even listen to Maria Callas. It was impossible. The two divas were archenemies, and a serious opera lover had to choose. Was Sue Rawson a secret worshipper of Callas? He considered leaving the magazines in her mailbox on the porch, or else slipping them between her door. If they got stolen he would be in trouble, but if he interrupted her holy and treacherous moment he might be in bigger trouble. He would have to take the magazines back home and return them another night, face charges of their being overdue. He was standing on the stoop, thinking of those things, shifting back and forth, when she opened the door.

"I thought I saw you out here," she said.

"You're listening to Callas!" he bleated.

"And you are standing on my doorstep. I wish you'd come in."

He wiped his feet thoroughly, squatted to take off his shoes and tiptoed into her foyer. "Do you like her?"

"Like? I don't know if I like any of them. I don't think it's ever been a matter of liking. But now I think I've grown weary of idols."

"Oh," he said. She had never spoken of fatigue, never wavered in an opinion. He hadn't known before that she believed in opinion, that such a thing existed for her. "Oh," he said again.

"You're tired." She came closer, removing her glasses to get a better view. He could see that she was concerned, and he remembered that all of the relatives were worried about Daniel, and that maybe by association she was worried about him.

"I've been having a lot of rehearsals," he said. "For this *Nutcracker* thing I'm in."

"*Nutcracker*—thing? What does that mean? Either it's *The Nutcracker* or it isn't."

He squinted at the green tile. He didn't think he had the skill to describe the Rockford Ballet to Sue Rawson. He glanced at her quickly and looked back to the floor. Her mouth had softened, perhaps as a result of the music, or his own presence. He wasn't sure he was seeing straight. He hadn't ever noticed such a kind expression on her face. She looked almost warmhearted. He had thought her charitable on occasion, and always knowledgeable, always interesting. That benevolence might be a part of her character, an inborn quality, had never occurred to him.

"I—I—I'm not certain what it is, or if I should be in it," he said. "I'm a little confused about it, actually."

He shut his eyes, waiting for her to snap at him. He had committed the sin of doubt, and in addition he had misjudged her. She had never been tender in his company. He felt her bony hand on his shoulder; she was saying, "Come in—here, let's turn this racket off, and you tell me about it. Why shouldn't you be in the company?"

They were in the living room, and she was lifting the needle off the record. He sat on the edge of the blue-and-cream-striped sofa that happened to be the exact colors of his Prince costume. He had never spoken confidentially to her before. He didn't know how she could suddenly have learned to look so concerned without practice. "Well," he said, considering as he drew out the word whether he should go any further. "It's just that—" The new soft and anxious droop of her lip made him want to confess. "It's just that it's a tacky little production."

He'd said it. Those were the words he'd tried to say to Joyce on all the trips to and from Rockford. As he spoke he knew that he could not stand having Sue Rawson watch him partnering his ton of bricks. He did not want her to see him in his tights, pointing his bargey feet. *Oh, God, what could keep everyone he knew away?* That friends and relations would come to see the performance had never been real to him until that moment. "I mean tawdry," he cried. "Really tawdry."

She said calmly, "And you're embarrassed, like to want to die, is that right?"

He sniffled and nodded.

"Is there anything positive about the production, anything at all that's worth your while?"

"There is! That's the perplexing part for a snob like me. I sort of enjoy it. I hate to admit it, but I like the people. And I have a pretty good time at rehearsals. If I were going to see it, I'd know right as the curtain rose that it was terrible. But being in the middle of it I imagine that there's a little bit of, well, magic. Luster. I'm probably deluding myself; I know I am." He looked down at his black socks. "I really hope you don't come," he said to the floor.

"Why do you dance, Walter? Why do you take lessons?"

He was panting from the strain of the conversation. She was asking all the difficult questions. "I know I'm not any good," he whispered. He lifted his head and saw, across the room, the far wall with the Degas prints in gilt frames.

"So why do you keep on," she persisted, "if you think you're not any good?"

"Because," he choked, "I *feel* it."

"Yes, that's it."

"I feel the ideas and the patterns and the abstraction of the beauty, and—"

"Yes, you do. And if you feel the meaning strongly enough you'll no doubt convey something of it. I don't think you can help it. I'd wager that you enjoy the rehearsals of this so-called tawdry production because you're communicating. In other words, you're succeeding. What part do you have?"

His mother had not even told her own sister that he had the starring role. "I'm, ah, the Prince."

"That's what I thought. You'll make a splendid Prince. You have the right sort of nose, and perfect hair." She tilted her head, smiling, as if nothing were more natural. "A prince," she declared, "should always have curly dark hair."

He couldn't think whether to say Thank you or How do you know? His ideal was the blond, blue-eyed type. He nodded at her requirement. "I guess," he said. "That's been the fun of it—trying to act as if everyone should pay homage, make an obeisance as I pass. It hasn't been all that hard, really, to imagine that I'm—"

She laughed, and then he laughed too, at the idea of the latent prince in him so close to the surface, so accessible.

"If you'd like me not to come I certainly won't, but do let me know if you change your mind. I wish that ballet school of yours had recitals for students other than the most advanced. We relatives are always looking for excuses to get out."

He could almost have nestled in her bosom. She was delivering great comfort, comfort of the sort normally dispensed at the eleventh hour by fairy godmothers and deities. Inviting her was the least he could do. "No, no," he said. "You can come if you want." He immediately wished he could take his words back. "It's not much, as I said, not really much of a ballet, even though our hearts are in the right places."

"I look forward to it." She slapped her hands to her knees. She stood up, and in that motion the pliant lips went tight. Her former self, the Sue Rawson in which everything is cut and dried, wiped her glasses with a man's cotton handkerchief. "You caught me listening to Callas, didn't you?" She looked at him critically, waiting for his admission.

"I didn't catch you—I could hear it from the—"

"I only listen to her so that when I go back to Tebaldi I appreciate her gift. I listen to Callas, in other words, for perspective."

He wasn't ready for the real aunt to speak to him. He wanted the other to stay, even if she was an impostor. He would have liked five more minutes of the intimacy that already seemed long ago, that seemed exquisite in his memory.

The night of the first performance, Walter's family drove out to Rockford in the station wagon. Daniel, Walter and Joyce sat in the backseat, and did not speak, and Robert and Sue Rawson sat in the front discussing their declining stocks in the Jewel Food Corporation. Aunt Jeannie and Uncle Ted had so many children of their own participating in Christmas activities that they were not going to be able to attend the ballet. Walter, pretending to sleep, prayed for his father to lose control of the car and drive into the median. It occurred to him that he was often wishing for death or thinking of death. He should try to kick the habit and become more cheerful, become someone like his Aunt Jeannie. He opened his eyes just as they were driving under a viaduct. *Drive into it,* he willed. *Hit it! Smash! Break!*

They arrived at the theater, each of them in one piece. As Walter was getting out of the car Daniel said, "Good luck."

"Yep," Walter said.

"At the New York City Ballet," Sue Rawson instructed, "they say '*Merde*' for luck on opening night."

"This is Rockford," Walter muttered.

He stood on the curb watching them speed away to the Howard Johnson coffee shop. He gave up a short prayer, again for saving grace, for a hoodlum to come and gun him down. And he could finish off Franklin Kenton too, put a bullet through his sinewy gut. It was cold, and he finally turned and went into the building. Without speaking to anyone, he did his pliés at the barre Miss Amy had installed in the greenroom, put on his costume and makeup, and his terry-cloth robe for warmth, and went out into the dark theater to wait. It was a shallow stage, and the set, a Victorian living room, only made the dancing more difficult. The plastic tree in the corner had arrived two days before and the performers hadn't adjusted to its presence. In forty-five minutes the lights would go down and the pageant would begin, taking Clara from the Christmas Eve party, through the land of snow, to the kingdom of candy and love. The little girls in their dresses and ruffled pantaloons and new ballet slippers, their hair in ringlets, were onstage skipping and shouting. One of them knocked a red bauble off the tree and it shattered. Louie, the stage manager, shouted at them and shooed them back to the greenroom.

Nancy Sherwin was charging around the theater, indiscriminately giving everyone kisses and flowers. Walter slunk into his seat in an effort to avoid her and also to get into character. I am a prince, he said to himself, beginning his meditation. "Where'er I walk," he sang under his breath, "cool gales shall fan the glade. Trees, where I sit, shall crowd into a shade. . . . And all things flourish where'er I turn my eyes." He felt better by the time Nancy spied him and came rushing to his seat. "Walter, Walter, Walter," she cried, "there you are! You're practically on the floor. Are you hiding?" She thrust a posy at his nose, threw her chubby white arms around him and breathed heavily into his chest as he sat. She was assaulting all of the cast members and there was nothing to do but bear her embraces with princely stoicism. "Where'er I walk," he repeated, "cool gales shall fan the glade." He was as ready as he was ever going to be. Let his parents, his brother and Sue Rawson come forth and see him in his courtly sequined tights and blue eye shadow.

Right before Walter went on, he thought of his father. Robert McCloud had always professed to live and let live, but he had every now and then made it a point to give fatherly advice. It was important to attack a job, carry through and be precise. Whatever a person chose to do was immaterial; it was Process, not Product, that built character. Robert delivered the talks as if he really wanted to say et cetera, et cetera, as if he was going through the motions of his paternal duty, giving the required speech. Walter understood that the message was at once stuffy and true. The family had watched a television special once called *Dancing, a Man's Game,* a show that compared male ballet dancers to great athletes, and Walter knew that Robert at least had respect for the Process of ballet. It would be all right, dancing in front of his father, Walter thought, as he waited for his entrance.

He performed that first night expressly for Sue Rawson. He checked himself in the mirror when he was offstage, and he thought his curly dark hair actually gave him a touch of the rogue. That was all to the good. He wanted his Prince to be decent, self-effacing and dignified in the face of folly, but not so decent that he was deadly. Surely he looked worthy of a princess, and in fact worthy of a higher-class princess than Nancy Sherwin could ever be; he was a young man any queen would be happy to have as a son-in-law.

It went well, until the second act, when Nancy and Walter were sitting on their bench, the throne, watching Madame Bonbonnière in her voluminous hoopskirt. Walter turned to his partner, to whisper conversationally, as Miss Amy suggested they do. They were supposed to be delighted and absorbed for forty-five minutes, for the remainder of the ballet. He bent to meet her glance, trying to be lofty and loving at the same time. Her eyes were misty. She was gazing at him with a terrible hopeful look in her eyes. "Walter," she murmured.

"What?" he said abruptly, out loud.

"Wouldn't you like—"

He pointed to the stage, to the little children coming out of Madame's enormous skirt.

"Walter," she drawled again.

If he wasn't mistaken she was after him. He edged away from her, making a mental note of the exits, including the fire door. Everyone, from the peasant on up to the nobleman, needed individual space. He scraped at a crusty spot on his tunic, wiped his nose and mumbled something about the cute dancing kiddies.

"Yes," she said, snuggling into his side.

He could drop her in their last pas de deux, he thought, when he hauled her around the stage, she with her dimpled legs crossed. She would sustain a blow to her head, and Miss Amy could on the spot choreograph a next act, Clara goes to Oz. Why would Nancy want him? he wondered. They'd been thrown together like two people left in a shipwreck, but that did not mean they had to fall in love. Maybe she was the kind of girl who liked it any way she could get it, the sort of good girl who gave blow jobs to boys no matter their preference, and still thought of herself as virginal. If she tried it on him, if she came at him he'd draw his sword, he'd sic Mrs. Gamble on her. A prince, of course, would put a brotherly hand on her shoulder, and then run for cover. He was going to bolt the minute the performance was over, get out of the place before she could corner him and crawl up his doublet. There was the possibility that he had developed a swelled head and that she wasn't making advances. He had not had any experience with girls, but he could detect a new quality in her husky whisper, a different pressure in the way she leaned on him, leading with her breasts. She squeezed his hand and breathed on him all the way up to the curtain call. "Where'er I walk, cool gales shall fan the glade." He kept singing the Handel to himself. He remained in character until the bitter end, bowing only with the nod of his titled head.

The family waited for him in the vestibule. He quickly gathered his things in the greenroom. He had never kissed anyone, much less let a person touch him underneath his clothes. Recently he'd found a men's magazine and it had given him all the pleasure he could stand, no need for Nancy to leap from the folded curtains and goose him. Without saying good-bye to the company, he slung his bag over his shoulder and darted out the door. He had removed all his makeup and put on a stocking hat in the hope that no one would notice him, that he could ditch and somehow find his own way home. He'd walk if he had to, or jump into a boxcar, or hitchhike with a kindly truck driver.

Before he'd taken three steps into the lobby his father was beating him on the back. "You all did a lot of dancing up there," he was saying. "A lot of complicated dancing. It must have been hot under those lights, but you looked cool as a cucumber. I don't know how you learned that fancy footwork with nothing but the music to tell you what to do."

"We're so proud of you," Joyce said, flashing that wide, false smile she'd been using for every occasion since Daniel had gotten sick.

Like a convoy, his family encircled Walter and moved him toward the front door. Walter was suddenly grateful for their protection, grateful for his father's direct, ignorant compliments. There was nothing wrong with his father's simplicity, and he forgave his mother her stock phrase, her unconditional pride.

Under the lights of the theater's marquee, Sue Rawson shook Walter's hand heartily. She was wearing a navy cape and a navy box hat that made her look like a Salvation Army sergeant. He was afraid to look at her, to read the message in her eyes: *It was awful.* Instead of receiving her silent communication he began to talk. He talked about Daniel's loan of the graduated barbells, about developing strength in his upper body and lower back, about the little girl who tripped during the Bonbon variation. He did not stop talking. Halfway home he talked, in one continuous run-on sentence, about Miss Amy. What he didn't know he fabricated. He leaned forward, his arms resting on the front seat, and spoke to Sue Rawson. He told her about Miss Amy's short stint with the Joffrey Ballet, her knee injury, her marriage to her high school boyfriend who became a dentist, her gift to him of a ride in a hot-air balloon for his birthday, and the crash that killed him, the accusation by her in-laws that she'd murdered him, the opening of the studio, her desire to have a company. Daniel finally shook his arm and said, "Breathe, Walter. Didn't anyone ever tell you that you're supposed to stop to take a breath now and then? I've been trying to get a word in, to say that you were good."

"Yes, Walter," Sue Rawson declared. "You were."

What had she said? She thought he was good. Had he heard her correctly? It was Sue Rawson who had said so. She'd come out and said that he was good. Sue Rawson never lied, not even for the purposes of standard politeness. She didn't know how to lie; Joyce often made the comment that Sue Rawson's frankness was refreshing only up to a point. She had said he was good. She wouldn't have said he was good if she hadn't really believed it. "She said I was good," he whispered. "I was good, she said I was." He did not speak for the rest of the trip.

He went up to his room that night, took off all his clothes, climbed into bed and hugged himself. He had danced onstage with a woman; no one had laughed at him—Miss Amy, on the contrary, had praised him, praised his gestures, his turns, his necessarily shortened leaps across the small stage. She had been with the Joffrey Ballet, or maybe she'd just gone to a few performances when she'd visited New York once. In any case, she knew what she was talking about. And Sue Rawson had admired his dancing. He wondered if he was better than he'd given himself credit for after all his years of practice, and he considered that governing his life there might be a spiritual or religious logic. It might be that a person was not allowed to have desire, the way he did, to do a thing, and in the end not be given the ability to carry through. Maybe there was some kind of God, the great I AM who did not tolerate the sort of misery Walter had so far suffered on his path to adulthood. He was a dancer, in his heart, in the pith of his soul, never mind his feet, his ankles, his knees. He had become a prince, in spite of the vehicle, in spite of the Rockford Ballet. He had come through with flying colors, Arie Crown Theater be damned.

Perhaps the all-merciful God also did not allow someone to love another person as much as Walter loved Mitch, and not have the feeling returned, strength for strength. He wondered if he had taken leave of his senses, or if self-satisfaction always came at the expense of sanity. He said out loud, "I don't care." He felt across his chest and along the ruff of black hair that ran down his stomach, and he thought that his skin was nice to touch, that his was a fine, responsive body. He wondered why on earth he shouldn't hold out a hope for happiness.

***

Susan and Mitch could not come to see any of the five performances of Walter's *Nutcracker*. They were dancing thirty-two of their own on the cement stage of the Arie Crown Theater at the McCormick Place in Chicago. Their production was sponsored in large part by the Chicago Tribune, and there were in addition many distinguished benefactors of the performing arts who had made the ballet possible. The Christmas production was Chicago's seasonal pride and joy. Because Walter did not talk about his role, because he saw very little of his friends that month, he wondered if they might possibly have an exalted opinion of Miss Amy's *Nutcracker*. He hoped they did. They may have imagined that all of Rockford's resources went into the costumes and sets, that it was a semiprofessional production in a high school auditorium, on a real proscenium stage, rather than the makeshift sheets of plywood with incongruous joints at the Community Theater. He once tripped on an uneven seam and almost broke his neck. He never told Mitch or Susan that he was the Prince, that Nancy was as heavy as she was flexible. He felt a little smug, holding the secret of what seemed to him to have some aspects of triumph. It was too bad, of course, that Mitch, the Mouse King down at Arie Crown, had to wear a cumbersome headdress that came to his nipples, and a stuffed gray velvet bubble around the rest of him that made him look like a tub. It was a shame that no one could see him for himself. As for Susan, she would be a dead ringer for a snowflake in Act I, dancing as if she'd come sifting from the chill blue heavens. She was to wear a white cap that was all wired up with pom-poms. Forty minutes later, in Act II, she'd reappear as a dewy yellow rose, wearing a petal on her head, no trace of her Arctic beginnings.

When Walter was ordering a ticket from Susan over the telephone for the Arie Crown production, Daniel turned in his chair at the kitchen table and waved one hand. "I'd like to go," he called.

"Huh?" Walter said.

"Could you please get a ticket for me?"

"What for? You already saw *The Nutcracker.*"

"No," Daniel said. "I didn't see the one downtown." He was fighting a sore throat, and when he swallowed he winced. "I saw yours, but not Susan's. I didn't see the professional troupe."

Walter held the receiver to his chest. He stared at his brother. "You don't even like ballet," he finally said.

Daniel coughed, swallowed, grimaced. He took a deep breath. "I like it now," he said. "I like it a lot."

"I'm getting complimentary tickets, you know. She might not even have extra—"

"You there?" Susan said on the line, her voice going into Walter's brown sweater.

"Could you, ah, make that two?" Walter said, looking away from his brother. Daniel was sitting with a blanket over his lap, dwarfed by his enormous bowl of Life cereal. "I don't know why," Walter said into the phone. "He says he wants to see it."

The Rockford *Nutcracker* ran for only the first two weeks of December, because Miss Amy had to go to Florida to spend the holidays with her aged parents. Susan had invited Walter to use one of her precious complimentary tickets for the Chicago production, and he couldn't think of a good excuse to decline. When Daniel wanted to go along she'd said, "How wonderful! Of course I can find another," and it was settled. There was no way out. They went on the third Sunday of the month, a matinee, and it was no great occasion for Walter to sit through another version of the same old thing. Act I: overtired children at a party, the arrival of a cranky bachelor uncle who messes with magic, a battle with the mice, good versus evil, a prince is born, the journey through the snow toward Intermission. Act II: The interminable entertainment. Dancing Chocolates, Coffee, Tea, Russians, Marzipan, Bonbons, Waltzing Flowers, the Sugar Plum Fairy and her Prince, the End.

He put on a pair of blue jeans and a sweatshirt with cut-off sleeves. He couldn't have said why he felt so irritated when Daniel came down the stairs wearing light gray wool pants, a starched white shirt, a nubby green tie and the Harris tweed sport coat Robert had brought him from Scotland the year before. The radiation had made some of his hair fall out, and he had combed and fluffed it to cover the patchy areas. He stood in the hall waiting for Joyce. It seemed to Walter that Daniel was always waiting for Joyce, that there was nothing he did anymore without Mother in tow. He looked so scrubbed and pressed, as if he were heading out to teach Sunday school or sell brushes and knives door-to-door. Walter thought of asking him why he was dressed like a John Bircher. Instead, he made an elaborate show of putting on the old wool jacket he hadn't worn in a couple of years, the one cousin Maxi had dragged through a puddle up at the lake a few Thanksgivings before.

Joyce either didn't notice Walter's clothes, or she didn't have the strength to care. It all boiled down to the same thing in Walter's book: she was out to lunch. She did say that there were too many germs on the filthy el train for Daniel and that she'd drive the two of them downtown. As they got into the car Walter mumbled, "Right, Mom. We sit for thirty minutes in a hermetically sealed automobile so we can spend hours in a closed room with ten thousand people, ten thousand conduits of any number of viruses, bacteria, airborne- and moisture-borne single cells traveling from person to person as we enjoy the ballet."

Joyce said, "Make sure your door is locked, will you please?"

When he and Daniel walked down the aisle at the Arie Crown, Walter said to himself, It isn't that exciting. Nothing that terrific about the blue plush seats, the long blue curtain, the orchestra warming up in the pit, the hawkers in the lobby trying to sell the pricey ballet programs with glossy photographs in color. It isn't really so much, the velvet, the live music, the little stagestruck girls spinning in the aisles in their Sunday best. It doesn't after all add up to something far greater than the sum of the Rockford Ballet. The accessories can't replace spirit and originality. Or pep. He'd never been much of an advocate of pep before, but it had its place, as did determination and grit. He'd stand up in favor of pep and grit any day.

Daniel went out before the ballet started and paid five dollars for the program. He sat next to Walter as they waited, reading the magazine intently. Walter had brought along *A Passage to India* and was furiously underlining with his yellow marker. When the lights went down he again went through his catechism: It's not so much, the music, the larger stage, the conductor wearing a tuxedo, the balconies, the fifty-foot Christmas tree.

During the first ten minutes of the performance Daniel leaned forward, straining to see around the heads in front of him. He sat back when he realized that no one he knew was going to appear for a while. The padded seats were restful and he was pleasantly warm in his suit. He fell asleep, and so he missed Mr. Kenton as Drosselmeyer, missed the exaggerated hobble, the triangular fake eyebrows and the painted frown that gave Walter's teacher the look of the Devil. Daniel's head rolled around from side to side and came bouncing down his brother's shoulder and arm.

Walter shook him off. "Wake up," he whispered. "You wanted to come, now snap to it." He could not remember ever being so uncomfortable. His big brother's head was heavy on his arm, and furthermore he was drooling on Walter's sweatshirt. He couldn't keep his eyes open for more than ten seconds at a shot. "Close your mouth," Walter said out loud, moving away so that Daniel's head jerked back. A woman from behind snarled at both of them for the disturbance. Walter wondered for the first time if Daniel's spit had the sickness in it, if the illness, the unidentified disease or plague, or whatever it was, could infect other people, could get him.

He did not fail to notice that when Susan appeared onstage Daniel suddenly came to. It was as if Daniel had a homing device,

Susan radar. She bourréed through the falling snowflakes and his eyes popped open. He sat up, leaned left and right to see, and poked Walter for the binoculars. "I'm not done," Walter said, shutting his eyes into the opera glasses, seeing nothing but the darkness of his own hateful self. It was far more important that *he* watch Susan up close, he whispered, so that he could comment on her technique, give her pointers.

He had seen the Arie Crown Production four times, in previous years, and he could have said halfway into the fifth occasion that he was not particularly impressed. There was nothing unusual about it or interesting, he remarked afterward to Daniel. And weren't they all a little off? Mr. Kenton hit one note as Drosselmeyer, had no range. The children were cloying in their sweetness. The Sugar Plum Fairy was chilly in her delivery, and had lousy balance. As for her consort, he looked as if they'd found him in a doorway on South Wabash, as if they'd hardly washed him off before they'd propped him up and pushed him onstage.

They were making their way out of the theater as Walter gave his critique. He was speaking as much to the crowd at large as he was to Daniel. "You rely on children to enthrall an audience and you really don't have much when all is said and done. Did you hear the horns, by the way? Did you hear the squeak during the Grand Pas de Deux? Those guys are making union wages and two of them fired off in different directions at the same time! I'd feel much more secure if it wasn't live, if the music was canned. That way a person doesn't have to worry about an overpriced professional blowing it."

Daniel was studying the ballet program while they waited in the crowd to get out into the lobby. He said to Walter's back, "I thought it was good."

"You would," Walter snorted.

Once they'd squeezed through, out the theater doors, Walter pressed forward toward the North Exit, where Joyce had said she would wait for them. Daniel clutched at his brother's sleeve, holding him in place, saying, "Aren't we—can't we go backstage to see Susan? And Mitch?"

"What are you talking about?" Walter spoke with indignation and disbelief, as if Daniel had suggested they rob a convenience store. He couldn't help it. He had no desire to see his friends in their makeup, the relatives and admirers circling them, girls in pigtails reaching out to touch the hem of their garments. First, his brother had developed a lump, and another, and then he'd become some kind of goody-goody ballet aficionado. Maybe Mrs. Gamble's theory was correct: Daniel was deficient in niacin and on his way to losing his mind. Walter stopped and faced Daniel while the crowd banged around them. "There is no point in going to see them," he said. "They're probably already gone."

Daniel took hold of Walter's arms, to steady himself as much as to implore. There was a tear trembling on the edge of his lid. Walter noticed for the first time how large his eyes had become. They used to be smaller, before he got sick. "You slept through most of it," Walter accused. "What would you tell them? Great place to sleep off a cold? They don't want to know that you missed their dancing. They worked hard and you sat snoring."

He couldn't believe that his brother was about to have a breakdown, in the Arie Crown lobby, that they were both in danger of being trampled by the stampede of balletgoers. It was sophomoric to weep in public, and over what? It was infantile. "Get a grip," he growled, and he took off into the crowd, jostling children's heads and their mothers' shoulders, weaving as fast as he could against the stream of people. He was talking out loud to himself, saying that he couldn't get over Dan, Danny Boy, bawling at the Arie Crown, his brother who was an athlete, not an artist, a seventeen-year-old who dressed as if he were going to distribute *The Watchtower* with the Jehovah's.

"There it is," he said to the stage door. He said it before Daniel caught up to him, while he was still at the end of the corridor. "Here," Walter called. "You wanted it, now we wait." He had no thought for the others standing by, friends and autograph seekers who were staring at him while he ranted. "They frisk you if you go through," he went on, "some never return. We do nothing while everyone inside takes showers and puts their flowers in vases and tells long, hideously boring stories about every detail of their performance. Poor Mom is probably getting a ticket or, worse, getting towed. She'll be taken to a hellish junkyard next to the projects, and when she tries to get out, some thug will beat her over the head with a crowbar. But that's okay, it's fine, we'll take our time so we can pay our compliments to the stars."

The dancers were already coming through the door. Daniel said reasonably, "Let's just wait a few minutes. Mom will know that we'd want to talk to them."

"Sure, Dan, sure. I always assume Mom reads my mind. I figure she's there to serve us, and besides she's so much cheaper than a limo driver. I'm thinking about giving her a raise this Christmas, but she'd probably just spend it on booze."

Daniel was about to ask Walter why he was so annoyed when Mr. Kenton came through. He touched his hat to the boys and passed on down the hall. It was the sort of flick of the hand a real celebrity would make to acknowledge his fans. Walter couldn't believe it! That gesture was so phony on a person like Mr. Kenton. What a joke his Drosselmeyer had been! He'd overplayed it, he'd murdered the part. "What a fake that was," Walter started to say.

"Hi, you." Susan was talking to Daniel. "Hey, Walter. Look what *you* have on! You used to wear that old jacket when I first knew you."

"Hey?" he said. She had never in her life said Hey, as far as he knew. Or Hi, you, for that matter. And she didn't have the habit of talking to him as if he were a kindergartner: *Look what you have on!* She was wearing the purple coat that came to her ankles, a white rabbit fur hat with black flecks, and she had in her arms a dozen long-stemmed red roses. Mitch was right behind her, and the four of them fell into line walking toward the exit. Walter, Mitch, Susan, Daniel. Susan chattered at Daniel, telling him she'd gotten flowers from someone who hadn't signed a name to the card. "I wish I knew who sent them," she said, "so I could thank the person. They are the prettiest things. Here," she said, filling his face with the bouquet. "Smell." She went on to tell him how slippery the floor was when the confetti rained down on the dancing snowflakes. "I'm telling you, it's dangerous! We've all fallen on it. The stuff gets up your nose, and makes you sneeze, and it finds its way down your throat. It's so distracting I sometimes wonder if I've actually danced, or if I've just dodged the paper the whole time."

"You d-dance," Daniel said. "You—it was so beautiful."

"Jesus," Walter hissed. He did not congratulate Mitch. Without a word the two boys turned away and went out different doors, to their waiting cars.

The weekend before Christmas the McClouds had their annual party for the neighborhood. It was Daniel who asked his mother if they could have the celebration on Sunday night, rather than Saturday, so that Walter's friends might be able to come. Walter had sneered into his toast. *Where the hell are your friends?* He wanted to have a blowout, finally, after all the years growing up in the placid household of 646 Maplewood Avenue. *Get your own company and stop dressing like a lost Bible Belt boy.*

Walter didn't think he had ever before felt hateful toward his brother. He wondered if he was making up for lost time, hating with abandon morning, noon and night. He hated Daniel's meek suggestions, hated the fact that on most days he looked like a softly lit oversized photograph of a big-eyed kitty cat. Walter hated how fast his own heart beat when he felt especially mean-spirited, when he was about to say something unkind. "Go get your own friends," he said under his breath, on the way to the sink.

Mitch and Susan arrived at the party at five-thirty, after their matinee. Susan's makeup had a gluey look and her hair was still in its tight bun. Mitch had two red marks on either side of his face where the Mouse King's headdress had rubbed. Without taking off their coats, they tagged up the stairs behind Walter. He went slowly, carrying a large platter of cheese cubes, crackers and miniature charbroiled wieners on toothpicks that Uncle Ted had brought from the deli at the Jewel.

Sue Rawson had only moments before given Walter a crate of records that no longer interested her or were worn-out. When Susan threw her wrap down on Walter's bedroom floor by the box she said, "Where'd you get these?"

"My usual source," Walter said. "They just arrived."

"Do you know what they are? Have you looked?"

"My father hauled them in here about five minutes ago. I have no idea what she's discarding this time."

"I know we should go mingle, but you realize that this is the perfect time to play the music game? Right now. Do not get near them, Walter. These will be so fresh, for guessing the composer and everything. Stop, don't come any closer. Mitch, guard them so he doesn't peek. I'll go find Daniel and he can put the records on, so it's really fair, so we don't have to suspect each other of cheating." She draped her coat and scarf over the box. She put Walter's cast-iron doorstop on her clothes, as if those things could keep strong and dishonest boys from surveying the goods.

She ran down the stairs, and into the living room, wending her way through the adults. They were standing in groups, talking, holding their drinks and their china dessert plates. She was so happy to be at the party, to be at the McClouds' house trying to find Daniel. She'd had a great performance and afterward a talent scout from New York City had come backstage to see her. She was going to have a chance to prove herself, to dance, perhaps, for Mr. Balanchine. She had thought that someday such a thing might happen, but not so soon, not yet.

None of the guests knew about her good fortune. They were standing in clumps in the living room chatting about their children and their holiday obligations. Aunt Jeannie was playing "O Holy Night" on the piano with the right hand and motioning with the left to Francie, to come sing. Joyce McCloud's dollhouse was on the coffee table decorated for Christmas, with wreaths at the windows outside and tiny electric candles inside. There was a glow in the toy house and a glow in the real house too, even if Sue Rawson was chiding a neighbor child for picking the Brazil nuts out of the party mix.

Mrs. Gamble was still at home, in her apron, keeping an eye on the festivities from the safety of her living room. She had let down her curls and blotted her wart with powder, almost ready to make her appearance at the party. She could see the guests; she could see Billy Wexler, rocking back and forth in front of the platter filled with mints, reaching to take one, pulling back, repeating the trajectory, again and again. Susan, in her search, watched the grown man for a minute, and she wondered if she could make him take a candy. She knew enough about him to understand that he wasn't predictable, that it was easy to make him cry, and that his crying could escalate into a full-scale tantrum. She pushed the kitchen door open. "They're good, Billy," she said over her shoulder. "They're really good."

Daniel was in the kitchen, at the table, sitting by himself, holding his dog. He had felt so tired it was all he could do to drag Duke up into his lap.

"Oh, Daniel," Susan said. "There you are. I've been looking for you. Could you help us? Would you mind?" She knelt at his side, by the chair, and fingered Duke's ear. "What an adorable little dog you are."

Daniel almost reached and stroked her hair, she was that close to the dog. It would have been so easy to put his hand out and touch her head.

"We'll go up the back stairs," she said, as if he didn't know the way around his own house.

In Walter's room the three dancers shut their eyes while Daniel chose a record from Sue Rawson's box, and then moved the needle to the first band. He put a cardboard against the turntable so they couldn't see the record spinning. Mitch was sitting on the bed, Walter stood at the dresser with his back to the stereo, and Susan crouched at the far end of the room by the bookcase. When they played, Mitch rarely made a winning guess. He didn't care about the game. And that night, especially, he didn't need to prove anything in Walter's stupid music contest. A talent scout from the Big Apple, two hours before, had just about invited him to join the New York City Ballet. He ate from the full tray of crackers and cheese and sausages, and on the easy selections he called out preposterous names, Prokofiev, when everyone knew it was Bach; Richard Strauss, when it could only have been Handel.

Susan had always taken the game seriously. She was competitive, lashing out at Walter when he won too many in a row. She'd stamp and beat the bureau; she'd accuse him of studying specifically to win, or cheating, stacking the records in an order he'd memorized. He was careful to let her win now and again, both because he couldn't stand it when she was angry and because winning pleased her so much.

That night he gave her time to get Janet Baker, a cinch, although she didn't know the cantata number, and she didn't get Neville Marriner and she certainly didn't get Decca. On the second selection he let her have Kathleen Ferrier, but she surprised him when she called, "'Return, O God of Hosts'!—*Samson,* Handel, um, um Sir Adrian Boult, conductor!" On the third turn she got the record label before she'd come up with the conductor, the artist or the composer. She had never been privy to Sue Rawson's collection, as far as Walter knew. A person had to be a genius to know the label first, or at least have read the Schwann catalog backward and forward the way he had. She was smart, but no prodigy, and she had limited knowledge when it came to composers. He couldn't account for her new skill, unless she had been cramming in the last several weeks, unless she'd cozied up to his aunt, plotting her revenge. She was clapping her hands, jumping like a cheerleader with a scissors kick, and in an old house with suspect floor joists. The whole place was quaking.

When the fourth record came on, Walter put his foot forward, as if it were a little bit over the line, as if he could race ahead. He shut his eyes, thinking, thinking quickly, but before two notes had sounded she was shouting, "RCA!"

"Beethoven's Fifth Piano Concerto," he cried. Her voice, her first answer, had rattled him, and instead of focusing on the soloist, instead of concentrating on the qualitative difference between Horowitz and Van Cliburn, he thought, Is it RCA? What pianist records with that label? He had a fleeting thought that she was somehow duping him, but wouldn't she be quiet and smug if she was pulling the wool over his eyes, rather than so genuinely exuberant? "Horowitz!" she hollered. "New York Philharmonic!"

She started to dance her American Beauty Rose steps to Beethoven's piano concerto, yelling in three-quarter time, "I got it! I beat you, Wa-a-a-lter!" He turned around, and saw, through the blur of Susan's waltz step, Daniel's thin face, his blue eyes and the blond lashes magnified behind his new glasses. Before his illness he'd been robust, a nearsighted teenage boy with good teeth and a chiseled jaw. He'd been handsome enough for ordinary purposes. Now the skin on his face had a gray cast, and it sagged under his shining eyes, puddled to his chin, as if the bones underneath had melted away. Susan was laughing, kicking up her leg, shouting, "RCA, I knew it!" The dog barked at her heels. "Oh, Duke, Dukie," she crooned, scooping him up, trying to bury her face in his short, steely fur, "I knew it just by the sound. I love you! I knew it!"

Mitch was alert now too. He had stopped chewing. Daniel had somehow been feeding Susan the correct answers, that much suddenly came clear to Walter. No one knew the label *just by the sound.* Daniel was flashing the jackets at her or else there were signals: two fingers, Decca; three fingers, Georg Solti; a pinkie, CBS Masterworks; a thumb, Leontyne Price. Walter understood the setup by the way she was blabbing to Duke. She was talking to Daniel through that butt-wipe of a dog. She was telling Daniel she loved him. She loved him! She was probably going to thank Dukie for the dozen goddamn red roses. And what's more, his brother loved her back, his just-about-dead brother, eyes all shiny with the light of dear Jesus, the crowbait was head over heels in love with the snowflake-dewdrop, Mrs. Jekyll-Mrs. Hyde, the ying-yang girl.

Daniel had never crossed the line before going to the Arie Crown *Nutcracker,* never entered Walter's dancing-school life or tried to engage with what Walter considered his real self, the other self that tried to take hold outside of the house. Walter looked at his brother carefully replacing the record in the jacket. It was as if the Trojan horse had been set in his bedroom, the enemy creeping out of the trapdoor. He had not paid attention to the warning signs, although he had registered fear early on, when Daniel asked if he could go along to see Susan dance. He knocked over his own desk chair. He hated all of them, couldn't stand the sight of their smiles, their stupid, gloating, happy grins and Mitch's cavernous pink mouth stuffed with the masticated powder of a whole package of Saltines.

It wasn't the force of rage that propelled him down the back stairs headfirst, bumping his eyebrows, his mouth, his nose, his ears, along each step. He ran out of the room without tying his shoes, unsure where he was going or what he meant to do, and at the top of the uncarpeted stairs with metal plates on every lip, he tripped on the shoestrings and went spiraling down. It was Mitch who followed him from the bedroom, who saw, and then screamed, in Walter's stead; screamed, Walter later remarked, like a bunny under a lawn mower. He must have swallowed all of that cracker dust in a hurry to let out a shriek like that. Mrs. Gamble had just arrived and was standing on the rug in the kitchen, looking the place over. She did not, as was her custom, remove her coat. The McClouds suspected that underneath her good winter coat from 1936, with the fox pelt draped over her neck, she always wore her apron; the trowel, flashlight, Allen wrench and screwdrivers straining the pockets. When Walter came to a standstill by the dishwasher, she ran clanking to the freezer compartment of the refrigerator and hauled out the ice, muttering as she went about the benefits of an immediate application of Vitamin E to the wounds.

Walter lay groaning, his head in a pool of blood, and his feet up the stairs. He looked into Mitch's eyes, and he thought that if he weren't so dizzy he'd take both hands and smooth away the red Mouse King marks on either side of his friend's heavenly face. Mitch, who was already jilted, and didn't quite know it. Walter could see past the stars whirling around and around over Mrs. Gamble's pin curls. He thought he could see beyond the walls of the house, that his vision was improved because Mrs. Gamble was in the room, her oracular powers sparking from her aura to his vulnerable, open self. He could see the future: Susan, the widow, crying down the hall at school after Daniel's death, all the girls and boys following at a respectful distance, following the lover who had been left behind to live. Daniel was dying. Susan knew it, and that minute he did too. He had received several knocks to his skull, but very likely they would not kill him. He would live on and on after his brother was gone. Mitch seemed so far away, and it was with great effort that Walter whispered, "I'm still here. Hold it, my head. It's yours."

Six

JANUARY
1996

Twenty-three years after the fall down the stairs Walter still had a scar above his eyebrow. He had had to go to the emergency room and have fourteen stitches. When one of the neighbors wondered out loud, in the McClouds' living room, if the kids upstairs had been drinking, Mrs. Gamble came to Walter's defense. She had smelled nothing, she said, and seen no broken vessels in the whites of the eyes. In the hospital Walter was so agitated he tried to get off the gurney. He wanted to go home, to find out for himself what Susan and Daniel were up to in his bedroom, if Mitch had stayed to fight them, if there was a duel planned, the prospect of a frosty morning, the pearl handles of the pistols with their dull gleam on the tray, the bravery, the fear, the blast, the bloody swatch on the snow. He was raving, struggling with the orderly, and might as well have been drunk. The nurse finally gave him a shot to knock him out.

At Christmas break, home in Oak Ridge, away from Otten, Walter stood at the top of the back stairs just once and thought of his fall. He remembered the cutting edge of the steps, how slowly he had tumbled, how difficult it had been to grab hold of anything solid. He had been able to anticipate each hurt before it happened, crack after crack to his head. Mitch was the only person who had seen the spill. Walter was first upright and seconds later he was on the floor in the kitchen. But he too had been able to watch himself after he went over the edge, and all the way to the bottom; he could see, as if from above, the humiliating dive, every blow delineated in the near stillness of his motion. Why nature bestowed clarity and helplessness on a person at the same time remained a mystery to him.

He wondered if somewhere far off, defying the laws of science, Mitch's two screams were still echoing, if those vibrations had traveled into space, if they moved on and on like rays in a light-year. There might be other forms of life who were receiving the noise and trying to interpret the tones. Walter had always thought that Mitch had cried out for his sake, involuntarily, because of the accident. As he stood at the scene it occurred to him that Mitch might not have been reacting to the fall, that he was instead warning Daniel, warning Susan. The high-pitched womanly screeches may have been Mitch's way of threatening both of them, daring them to go any further.

Walter didn't approve of the use of the present participle in the verb "obsess." He didn't like the way it was so casually used, as if every normal person had clinical obsessions. Still, he let himself say, "I've been obsessing about my brother, obsessing about Mitch." He suspected that the year of Daniel's death was vivid to him because he was living again in high school, faced each day with ninety freshmen and sixty sophomores. He sometimes felt that his Otten students weren't in the current story at all, that he was using them for his own purposes, to illuminate his own past. It wasn't that he was sloughing off, or was in a stupor, or fretting about mistakes he'd made more than two decades before. He was nowhere, he sometimes felt, floating through his own years backward and forward inside the 1937 brick building that took up a block on Otten Boulevard in Otten, Wisconsin. He wondered if he'd always been in Room 209 listening to lockers slam, seeing visions of the old life while he waited to begin preaching, while he waited for a semblance of quiet.

In January he started to go to the basketball games at the high school, not only because there was nothing else to do within a seventy-mile radius, but because he found he enjoyed the spectacle. With the exception of a few of Daniel's swim meets, Walter had not gone to sporting events as a teenager. The heroism of the boys out on the court was a revelation to him. He soon understood—watching Otten's Bill Pierce fly up to the basket, hover in midair, slam the ball through the hoop—why athletes were worshipped in town and in the larger world. He wanted young, handsome Bill Pierce to tear down the court, trample the opposition, score and steal and score. Walter whistled with his thumb and index finger clamped between his teeth when his team made their points, and he leaped to his feet when a player dodged his way through the defense, driving the ball, hooking it into the basket.

He usually sat up in the bleachers with Betsy Rutule from fourth-hour class, after she'd done her part in the pep band. She had stood out in the first week of class because of her forthright comments. Unlike many of her peers, she had complex ideas, she had strong feelings, and she didn't seem to be embarrassed by her zeal. Walter wasn't sure if the others called her ass-kisser. He hoped not. He hoped they could see that she was ingenuous, that her curiosity wasn't about grade-grubbing. If only he could enlist his beautician friend in New York to come to her aid, to help her with her thick stiff hair. It had no body and looked as if it was meant to lie flat, nothing for her to do but try to mold it around her head, tamp it down with clips and pins. At first glance, everything about her seemed out of proportion. Her nose was too short, even for her round face, her wide eyes were set too far apart, her eyebrows needed to be hedged back. Walter thought this until she opened her mouth and made a breathtaking observation. Suddenly she became a stunner. Each expressive feature, in the second glance, was a charming length and thickness, no place for a cosmetic surgeon on Betsy's horizon. Walter was crazy about her, and he felt privileged to be in her company at the games, to listen to her pronouncements on the players, the school staff and the parents.

The coach was not beloved by his townspeople—mothers, fathers, uncles, many of whom had had him as a history teacher when they were in high school. The word on the street: Sullivan was blind to the talent and squandered what he had. Unforgivable, to waste height and strength. Both Betsy and Walter, going against the grain, were his defenders. Coach Sullivan loved the boys and the game, Walter insisted, a person could see that. It was a pressure-cooker job, sitting down, standing up, flailing around, trying to get his point across. Sullivan had to know the rules and the fine print, had to holler out the technicalities over the noise of the unruly public. And he had to wear a suit and tie, when practically everyone else on the court was running around in shorts.

The assistant coach, Mr. Henlow, both the chairman and the one teacher in the Psychology Department, had thin blond hair, the comb tracks always running clean through it. He wore pleated pants, beige polyester shirts with nothing underneath and cheap leather shoes that were supposed to look like expensive calfskin. He lived far away, in a town called Platteville. Walter knew his type, the sort who spoke harshly to the players, who patrolled the shower room, who professed to be making men out of boys. Betsy Rutule said, "There's something about Mr. Henlow that scares me, Mr. McCloud. It's not because he's always yelling, and it probably isn't fair, I mean, it's not based on anything I know. I can't explain it exactly, but he kind of looks as if he's got this whole other body, a messy, burping, fat pig of a person inside his neat, tidy one. It's like everything is zipped up to keep the real guy from bursting out. I know I shouldn't say that about a teacher, but whenever I see him I keep thinking I'll blink and—pop—someone else will be standing where he was."

Walter wanted to pound her on the back and tell her she had an automatic A+ for the rest of her high school English career. There was fortunately a spectacular play and they rose to their feet, shouting and waving their hats. Mr. Henlow was mean and cowardly, as dangerous as they came, someone never to look in the eye. There were plenty of present and future homosexuals in Otten, and sometimes Walter stared at them briefly, sometimes there was mutual recognition in the checkout line, on the street, and in the most sexually suggestive place of all, the Laundromat, with the three types of washers: the Troy, the Trojan and The Big Boy.

"Your big boy working?" He could so easily have asked the most obvious target, the man with the scant permed hair, the tight, buttoned-up jeans. He imagined all of the Otten perverts having sex outside the city limits, beyond the *Welcome to Otten* sign in school-teacher cursive. The town men and boys were never going to be a group, a political force, a club, having their own barbecues, their own choir, their gay pride unit in the Memorial Day parade. It was curious to Walter that with television's inclusion of gay culture into prime-time programming, Otten still ignored the existence and the concept of homosexuality. It was more startling than he'd anticipated, to be in a place that turned its back on the facts of life. One of the checkout ladies at the grocery store said she still couldn't believe that Rock Hudson had been *that* way. Out of the blue as she bagged his food, she told Walter that she didn't care what anyone said, Rock loved the ladies. He realized that in his sheltered life in New York City he had forgotten about the wild interior of his country.

To be sure, Otten tolerated a poofter if a boy was homegrown, if he behaved himself, if he didn't show his colors. The residents didn't treasure their oddballs, but within reason they protected them. There was, out on Highway H, a goat farmer, a third-generation farm girl, and her tax-accountant lover. Walter watched them sitting in plain view side by side at the basketball games, two unmistakable lesbians: tall women, heavy in the hips, drooping breasts under their Shetland sweaters, Sorel boots, cropped hair, a fresh look about their weathered faces. Betsy Rutule referred to them, innocently, it seemed, as housemates.

Walter had never lived in a place as an adult that he could think of as his community. When he sat in the bleachers, sharing popcorn with Betsy and Cassie Klingmeyer, he wondered if he could call the town Home. It seemed a stretch. He had not expected the Welcome Wagon to come to his door with samples of products from the local merchants, but the quiet of his fellow teachers after his arrival, their lack of interest and common courtesy, surprised him. Only the Latin teacher, Mrs. Denval, invited Walter to her house during his first month. At Sunday brunch, over cheese Danishes and instant coffee, she described Napoleon's Russian offensive, and she spoke lovingly of Talleyrand and his gimpy walk. Walter didn't know if he had room in his life for another eccentric older woman. He guessed that without much trouble he and Mrs. Denval could fall into a mutual adoration society, but he wasn't sure he was up to it. He felt as if she was wooing him, that she wanted him for her pet, when she recited the opening stanzas of *The Inferno,* when she stood on a footstool in her living room and with a baton conducted the Italian national anthem as it played on an old 78. She was the only intellectual in Otten as far as he could see; she was a widow, she was lonely, restless and hungry for gossip. They were probably meant for each other, Walter thought a little wearily.

As he was leaving she said, "You'll give this place a kick, a run for its money, if you don't let it stand in your way." With her parting words she confirmed his suspicion that he had not done a very good job blending in with his fellow Ottenites. "We don't have anyone of your ilk here, and you do so look the part."

He drove home in his new two-door car that would be paid off in ten years. He didn't want to think what she had meant by her farewell: *You do so look the part.* He had tried to look as much like himself as he could in Otten, and still every morning as he shaved he had to give his standard pep talk. "Be not afraid," he said to the mirror. "You are funny, Mr. McCloud, and insightful. You once danced the part of the Prince. You have your secret: you sold a miniature set of lawn furniture to an intelligent, gorgeous, nearly divine movie star and her sculptor husband of twenty years." He didn't want to become Mrs. Denval's traveling companion—she, the wealthy dowager, he, the queer, carrying her baggage down the narrow cobbled streets of Florence, Rome, Milan, Venice.

He would think about his car rather than about Mrs. Denval in her aqua chiffon robe with the matching slippers. Walter had never owned a car before, and he felt in awe of the thing. It seemed to him to be alive, to have digestion and spirit, to be a creature who had come to share his life. It was shaped like an egg, and had no legroom. It sputtered and groaned, it warmed to his words of encouragement. He stroked its smooth blue curve down the hood when he left it in the garage in the evenings, and on the weekends he washed it on his driveway. Most important, his brother-in-law, Marc, approved of the model and Walter's maintenance schedule. As part of the Sunday ritual he dragged his canister vacuum out on the cement and cleaned the short gray shaggy upholstery, and he was always sure to have a Chap Stick and fresh water in the driver's right-hand receptacle. On his bad days he told himself that it had been worth coming to Otten if only to experience becoming a car owner, if only to go through one of manhood's most important rites of passage. In his darker moods he tried to remember that he had a few potential friends.

The band director, Cy Burns, wore his hair in a braid, the only adult in town who had the vestigial radical-sixties do. He and his wife asked Walter over for dinner on one of the last warm weekends in October. The four children ran around the backyard while Walter chased them. They threw sand in the salad. They pestered Walter until ten o'clock, when they were at last put to bed. When he finally sat down at the piano to accompany Cy on his sax, the wife, Stacey, came downstairs and told them they couldn't play, it was too late, the party was over.

Walter liked Cy and his bossy Stacey, but they were busy with two careers and four children. Otten was a town for families, most of them descendants of the funeral-parlor family, the Stegemans, and the grocery-store family, the Ketterhagens. Children went to school and grew up and got married and some stayed on the farm, and many others found employment at the Quaker Oats plant by the river, or they drove twenty miles away to jobs in the munitions factory. Walter felt like a spinster, a witch, living on the outskirts in his ranch house with the deer rack, the six-pointer, hanging on the front of his garage. He was related to no one. Mrs. Denval wanted him to come to brunch every Sunday, and she wanted him to fight the proposed four-lane highway with her, to go to board meetings, to drive to Madison and speak about the rural charm of Otten. Walter didn't yet know if Otten was a place that had charm, and supposing it did, he might not then be the appropriate champion, if it was true he looked his part.

With very little company to choose from, Walter found himself rabble-rousing after school. He revived the Forensics Club and marshaled his bright freshmen and sophomores into active duty. He volunteered to cook in the cafeteria for the senior pancake breakfast and the madrigal dinner. In January, after four months of teaching, it still took considerable energy to repair and maintain what he supposed was his self-esteem, particularly after his seventh-hour class. It was restorative to have his six top students, those who more or less saw the light, gather at 2:37 in his room to prepare their dramatic readings. During Team Spirit Week he helped Betsy Rutule paint slogans with bad puns on the dentist's office window and the Laundromat. In the spring he would direct *South Pacific,* and the rehearsals would keep him in school long past supper.

There were a select few who inspired Walter, who kept him going, and there were occasions when a group moved him, when the basketball team ran down the court like a flutter of leaves, when the earnest pom-pom girls, all ponytails and leg warmers, rehearsed in the gym, when the music from the chorus drifted into his room during fifth hour. At the madrigal concert in the cafeteria at Christmas he had felt like a ninny, trying to fight back his tears. The singers were lost in their harmonies, absorbed by their own sounds, leaning to their conductor, quieting at the first motion of her hand to her mouth. Their sweet, untrained voices would never be more beautiful, and standing still on the risers they looked at once so vulnerable and all-knowing and unaware. He slipped out at intermission, drained by the simple fact of their youth.

Walter could readily find fault with the town. There was no place to buy a decent cup of coffee, the movie theater carried family films at the seven o'clock showing and real-man movies, blood-and-gore movies, at the nine o'clock. One hundred percent of the population was of Anglo-Saxon descent; there were hardly any sidewalks; the local library didn't have *The Great Gatsby,* or *To the Lighthouse* or *Middlemarch.* He felt, too, that the place exerted its own strange pressure on him, that it was the townspeople who first looked with a critical eye at the oddity that was Mr. McCloud, and then, when they had sized him up, taken what they thought was his full measure, in one small stroke they erased him. He did not belong in a category that was of use to them. In his lamb cake of a car he made his way to work, parked, locked up, got out and felt along the shiny hood as he whispered, "Good-bye." He had the peculiar sensation, stepping onto the sidewalk, that he made no sound, and when he crossed the grass he noted that his feet made no impression in the wet Wisconsin ground.

There were ten inches of snow on January 17, on the morning Walter was to meet Susan in Chicago. It was always quiet along his road, and when he woke up he did not sense the silence farther off, the stillness of the town. He had not gotten into the habit of listening to the country noises from his bed because, for the last two months, both when he went to sleep and as his waking dream faded, he had thought of Julian Wright. He had made a ritual, a prayer, out of Julian Wright.

When he had met him in his box seat at Orchestra Hall in November, in Chicago, and after Pollini was done playing and the applause died down, Julian had turned to Walter and said, "You're coming with me, baby." It was all Walter could do to get his coat over his trembling arms. Julian had hailed a cab, and they'd sat primly behind the barrel-chested driver, who didn't look as if he'd put up with any hanky-panky. They didn't dare reach for each other, couldn't have left it at one touch or a clasp. When they got to the apartment, Julian fumbled at the doorknob, pushed, pulled, heaved his weight against the glass. The key wasn't turning in the lock. Walter, clutching Julian's back, pressing against him, didn't help. "Oh God, oh baby, open, open, open," Julian said, rattling the large brass knob. The two of them, Walter thought, out of their skin with impatience, were comparable to nothing but themselves. They were two starved men who couldn't stand the wait, couldn't bear the last long minutes before they slammed the door shut behind them.

In bed, in Otten, Walter tried to bring Julian's face to mind, as he always did in the early morning. When he should have been thinking about how best to make his sullen students take to the selected great works of literature, he instead conjured Julian, feature by feature, as best as he could recollect them. There had been no hint of a killer or masochist in the light brown eyes, the small oval glasses, the brown hair cut long on one side, short on the other, in the style Mitch used to favor. Julian had kissed Walter into the corner of the foyer that first night, "beautiful mouth mouth," Walter kept trying to say, the literal and most appropriate translation from Italian to English of one of his favorite eighteenth-century Italian songs. But he could only manage "mouth, mouth—mouth—mouth" as they dropped to the floor in each other's arms. They had both felt an urgency as they stripped each other, but they'd been tentative too, Julian lightly touching Walter's face, Walter smoothing Julian's dark hair across his chest before he admired farther down the long torso. This will soon be over, he thought. He would have liked to give himself up to the stranger and his sumptuous lips, and yet he couldn't dismiss the voice saying, This will soon be over.

Later in the evening, Julian put on Patsy Cline and on the bed that time they'd gone leisurely through "That Wonderful Someone," "Hungry for Love," "Too Many Secrets," "Don't Ever Leave Me Again," and at last, during "Ain't No Wheels on This Ship," Julian again brought Walter off.

It was remarkable, what they had in common, and that was not counting their love for Pollini and Beethoven. Walter examined Julian's CD and record collection and believed that groove for groove in the classical section they had trenches in the same places. They owned many of the same books, they both exercised on a skiing machine, they were teachers. Julian was soon to sublet his apartment and move to New Orleans for a year, to teach poetry at Tulane. He liked to bet at the horse races, something that Walter could probably work up some enthusiasm for, and he was a poet, a sanctified poet, with not only a book of poems called *Until the Last Stop* but the Walt Whitman Prize to his name.

At four in the morning Julian sat at his piano playing a mournful piece by Aaron Copland. Walter, reclining on the sofa, thought how pleasant it was to have a cat moving like a wave against his bare legs. He was wearing Julian's plaid bathrobe, admiring his lover's bare back, the slender waist, the nicely rounded small ass in the white cotton boxer shorts. He stretched, feeling what he guessed was contentment. In fact he'd had an unusually prolonged sense of happiness, and for a little he let himself imagine waking up every morning on Belmont Avenue, in the old apartment with high ceilings and cornices very like those in the living room at Lake Margaret. It was Julian's grandmother's apartment, and although she'd been dead for seven years it was every bit the home of someone who had been born in 1898. There were antimacassars on the upright stiff cushioned chairs, a still life over the mantel, an armoire in the bedroom. The damp smell of the basement came up through the heat registers, gracing the house with that familiar mildewed fragrance.

Walter sat scratching the cat behind the ears. It purred and seemed to like him. He thought of a morning with Julian, eating toast, reading the paper, the cat up on the table daring to sniff at their plates. There might be another morning like the first, and then another, and another, another, another—suddenly he could see a lifetime of mornings, flipping past him as if they were pages in a book. It came to him in a bolt that if he lived on Belmont Avenue, he might never get out of Grandma's black cherry bed with the purple duvet. The tinkly china clock across the room would chime seven, eight, nine, ten, eleven, and he would not move from under the covers.

Walter would love Julian's large lips, that extravagant mouth, so shapely it looked like wax. He would love the intelligent eyes, the fine soft brows, the poet's words waiting on his tongue and in his hands. He would want to hold on, in that bed, to Julian Wright, and Julian Wright would spring up and make coffee, thinking of daylight and cat food and publishers and public readings and talented students. Julian Wright had a calling card as if he were a nineteenth-century man, a stack of ivory cards on heavy stock in a leather holder with his name, Julian Michael Wright, engraved in wedding-announcement script.

Walter would love and love and love; he would think he could love forever, and he'd say so. He would love until one of them changed, until the terrible moment. It might for once happen to him. What was so dear in the beginning—the hole in Julian's red-and-blue-striped sock, the cat hairs on his wool pants, his untucked shirt below his waist, the hairy mole on the elbow, the habit of leaving cups on the piano, his lateness, his imperious nature, his laugh in the wrong places, the compulsion for betting on the wrong horse—what had been endearing to Walter in the first place would in one swoop lose its appeal. It was unbelievable the way, just like that, love stopped. He had seen it happen before, seen the shine go out of a lover's eyes within the space of a few minutes. More often the love leached away slowly, painfully, over a period of weeks or months. No, he advised himself. Don't start. Get out while you can. It was best to be leery of love, best to distrust the erratic heart. "Get out while you can," he said under his breath.

He had shaken himself, pushed the cat off his lap and gone to the piano to begin another tender embrace. But even as they hobbled together back to the bedroom he felt the burden of their complicated future together. He found himself thinking through each sentence before he opened his mouth, so that by breakfast he could not speak. Julian, looking anxious at first over coffee, and then hurt, and finally angry, had let Walter go without asking for his phone number or his address.

Every morning since that November concert Walter had thought about Julian, and he wondered, too, about himself, about why he had become paralyzed at the thought of a regular life with a man who was clearly decent, knowledgeable, affectionate and also enviably well hung. He knew that if he went to a therapist he'd have to delve. He guessed he'd find out that in his occasional sexual encounters with strangers in bathrooms or parks he was after a fragment of an early profound experience. He could cook up a summary, a punch line. He'd have to pay a large sum of money and do a lot of talking to come up with one ridiculously simple statement. When he slept with someone, he'd say, with whom he might develop real feelings, the blaze of the future intruded on the glow of long-ago splendors.

Walter first thought of Julian as usual on Saturday morning, on the seventeenth of January, but after he brought his face into focus he remembered that he was supposed to go to Chicago, to help Susan. Back in November, in that first flush of information at Orchestra Hall, Julian had said he'd be commuting between New Orleans and Chicago, that he'd have to come back to Illinois on weekends to finish his job at an advertising agency. And so it was not impossible that Walter might see the poet walking into, say, Marshall Field's or the Stuart Brent Bookstore. If they met on the street Walter might then give his life over to God, or decide to endorse fate as a life principle. It would mean something if he bumped into Julian. Of course it would! If there was any such thing as a signal, that would be it. If Julian would have him this time around, Walter might well have to follow because there was no banking on a third chance.

A bird whacked into the picture window and he sat up to listen. In the distance he heard a scraping noise. He peered through the slat of his broken blind. It had snowed heavily in the night, the starlings were disoriented and a plow was moving through town. The roads were going to be slick or impenetrable. He might go off into a ditch on the way to the train station, might have to eat the cushions in his car to stay alive in the blizzard. It was unlikely his automobile insurance would pay for a seat that had been ingested or his health insurance cover the removal of his intestines stuffed with fiberfill. He'd been looking forward to seeing Susan, even if she was on the verge of wrecking her life. She was in love, she'd said, with a man whom she had seen for only three hours six months before. It was love, she insisted. Surely, Walter had thought, someone was soon to develop a mathematical formula with x's and a y or two, measuring the relationship of absence to ardor. He had been invited to the first assignation, and he was supposed to either foil the husband or else bear witness to her ruin. He wasn't quite sure of his role. If he could get to the city without damaging his car or killing himself he'd be glad to see her, happy to help.

He packed a small bag. He was going to allow himself two hours to get into the black one-piece snowsuit Lucy and Marc had given him for Christmas, put on his old snow boots, clear the Otten drive, get back out of the snowsuit, take a shower after all the exertion and drive to the train station. The grueling labor, the trouble, was the bit about country living the magazines didn't show. He was suddenly in a state, running around his unfurnished house, looking in empty drawers for things he knew he didn't have, for a beret, a red silk thong, onyx cuff links, a pale peach linen shirt. He wondered what he should wear for Julian. Imagine meeting Julian outside Union Station, wearing all of those fantasy garments he didn't own. Between Otten and Chicago, Walter would try to think of something to say that was equal to a prize-winning writer. He wondered what Julian would think of him in his shiny black snowsuit, including his black wool mask with the orange trim around the eyes and the mouth and the nose opening. He looked like a yeti in his outfit, something to stalk, something you'd fear finding in a cave, a monster you'd brag about murdering.

He was leaving Otten for the weekend, leaving his snowsuit behind. Susan would choose a restaurant for lunch, and she'd explain how he was to assist her adultery, and later in the afternoon he might buy clothes that he would want to be seen in for his God-ordained coincidental meeting with the darling labiate one, the man who had an endearing hole in the heel of his sock and silky black cat hairs all over his tight wool pants.

———

At noon Walter met Susan in the unprepossessing lobby of the Richmond Hotel, north of the Loop, on East Ontario. It was a small middle-range hotel, a quiet inn with no flash, a place an angry husband wouldn't think of if he had to track down an errant wife. She was sitting in a wing chair looking to the untrained eye as if she was only waiting for Walter. He could tell that her calm was studied, but someone as new as her beau, Lester, would never have suspected a deeper agitation. She was wearing brown-and-white-checked leggings that drew the eye up and down the unbelievable length of her legs, a thick white oversize cotton sweater, and laced fashion boots that evoked a hiker, although one who walked only on marked paths. She could easily have just come in from the slopes, her hair pulled high in a ponytail, a white headband covering her ears, her white fuzzy mittens still on her hands, folded in her lap. A person who was not distracted would have removed her outerwear in the warm lobby. In her usual way she took hold of his face, this time with the mohair mittens, and kissed him on the mouth. "I'm so nervous," she whispered.

At lunch, in the hotel café, she said she was too overwrought to eat. She ordered water and a minute later asked for herbal tea, changed her mind and wanted coffee. When Walter's deluxe bacon burger came, she absentmindedly ate his French fries, the detail that made the deluxe what it was, the thing he had been looking forward to out of the whole meal. The fries were zigzagged and shiny with grease. He loved the fact that she didn't even realize she was eating them. "Tell me the plan," he said, "for your liaison, so that I can be ready, at any point, to catch you, if by chance you fall."

"The plan, the plan," she said, her outstretched fingers quivering at either side of her head. "I'm so out of practice at this kind of thing. I'm going to meet him at six o'clock at the Palmer House, and then, and then, we're going someplace for dinner. This is the extent of the plan. Why so early? I guess that's when his meeting is over. Do I know what will happen? No, I do not. Will we talk about the *Bible*—he's sort of Christian, you know—'The Song of Solomon,' perhaps, until dawn? Will we skip dinner altogether? Does he have in mind what I have in mind? What if we run into my mother? Will he let me crawl into his shirt and slide down his pants? Or will we sup, shake hands and part? Will I join you in front of the video of your choice in our tasteful room with the one regulation-size double bed at the Richmond Hotel?" She reached across the table and shook his shoulders. "I DON'T KNOW."

"Tell me again what Gary thinks we're doing here in Chicago, so I've got the story straight," Walter said. Although he would always be on Susan's side, and certainly on the side of love, he liked her husband. He had read more novels than anyone Walter had ever known, being as he was, in the book business, and in spite of the fact that he was always at his store, he seemed to love his family and his wife.

"Oh, dear God"—she groaned. "I lied to him, Walter. I lied to lovely old Gary. How does that line go? 'What a tangled web we weave when first we practice to deceive.' I know some poetry, after all, you see? I've talked myself into thinking he deserves to be cuckolded because he works eighty hours a week. I told him I just had to see you, that there were important matters we had to hash over, issues, you know, issues, that had been bothering me for decades, about Daniel, about that awful year we don't speak of. He thinks I'm here to clear my head! He never asked why I couldn't go up to your place in Otten, why we had to meet in Chicago, spend money on a hotel. I was prepared to tell him a preposterous lie, that you and I needed neutral territory. Can you believe that one?"

"It does sound pretty suspicious," Walter said.

"If I had Lester and Gary, both of them, it would be like having a party dress, very special, an Armani, as well as a nice baggy denim dress for every day. Both are useful, a person wants each at different times, to be perfectly relaxed and ordinary, and then to light up, gad around."

"This experience has turned you into something like a poet—"

"Something like! I'm a jerk, is what I am. I've talked myself into thinking I have to fool around with Lester because I made bad choices years ago. I got myself stuck in Miami and now I've got to blow my stack. Or maybe I want Lester only because I want Lester. Maybe it's not any more complicated than that. Does desire always make a person go wrong, do you think?"

"It's not one hundred percent reliable, but—"

"You have to live wildly, every now and then, so you can sleep at night, and have interesting material for your dreams. Don't you? I figure it's for the dream life that we have to really live. That's what I told Daniel near the end, that's what I already knew. I guess that's why I had no shame, falling in love with him. We both knew good dreams applied to the long sleep, his forthcoming one."

It was noteworthy, he thought, that she brought up Daniel whenever she talked about Lester, that the two of them seemed to be linked in her mind.

"Walter, how do we live when we're so young and stupid? Do you realize that I still don't know what Daniel died from? No one ever told me. I didn't think anyone knew. It seemed beside the point, at the time, to ask. He never said. Who cared what it was; it was killing him. Cancer, my mother said, but cancer of what? Which kind? With each passing year I can't believe that I still don't know, that I've always been too embarrassed to admit that I don't know."

"It was Hodgkin's," Walter said. He spoke with deliberate slowness, in an effort to calm her. "I asked my mother about ten years ago. It irritated her to have to tell me, but I think she was angry with herself, for being so secretive about Daniel's prognosis. I knew, generally, that it was cancer, too, but I never gave it a name. There was a faulty diagnosis at first, I guess, a mishap with one of the early surgeries, a month or two in the winter when he was stable and then the slow journey to the end. My parents eventually sued the doctor, and although they never said explicitly, part of that money paid for me to go to college."

"Oh, Walter," Susan said.

"I don't think Lucy really believes that she had an older brother, that I didn't just make him up as a way to tell her amusing stories with morals. I don't think that there were very many people at the time who knew what was going on. Sue Rawson probably got the details by talking to my father in a businesslike way. She was never nicer to me than she was that year, all concern and flattery. Mrs. Gamble received the word telepathically, I'm sure. I remember being told that Daniel was having radiation, but I didn't really understand what it was for, or what the odds were."

"We didn't know anything outside of ourselves," she burst out. "We hardly knew there was a war going on. I'll have to read old *Time* magazines so I can answer my children's questions about the sixties. How would I know about any of that strife? I was a bun-head dancing while the world fell apart."

"My students don't pay attention to anything but themselves either, but it does seem remarkable that we weren't interested, considering all the excitement. I spent three hours in the car every day with my mother that winter Daniel was sick, driving to Rockford, and we never talked. Not about Nixon, not about the war, not a mother-son chat about how cancer cells mutate. I assumed Daniel would get better. He was my brother, brothers didn't die. He was going to the doctor, they were taking care of it. Joyce had this uncharacteristic ferociousness, her clenched hands on the wheel. She scared me to death. She'd park banging into the car behind her and the car in front of her. The modern age gives us a certain number of false promises, I think, and so when the horrible truth rears its head we go to pieces."

"What do you mean, exactly?"

He looked past Susan, out the window, down the street. "It seems to me that grieving the way we have is a luxury, of our time and place, that it's a privilege and a burden of our era, that we hold our dead ones so dear. With all the energy we've spent mourning we could have built a pyramid to assure Dan an afterlife. People die in other countries like flies. There are women in the third world who still have babies every year, just as they used to in the old days, because they know most of them won't survive into adulthood. We're wimps, is what I'm saying. Certainly my mother took a son's death harder than Jeannie would have, or Mrs. Gamble. I'm not saying she indulged herself, but she was not equal to the task. She was not prepared for failure."

Susan shook her head. "I don't blame her for anything, you know that, but the secrecy caused everyone so much pain."

"It was a different time," he said. "They didn't know better. They didn't realize that I could have used psychoanalysis, or at the least a little family therapy. It wasn't a reflex, the way it would be today."

They held their coffee cups in both hands at their chins and assumed the other was remembering all those years back. Susan thought again about what she should say first when she saw Lester. She knew it was hopeless to try to be witty, but if she didn't think of something she would be sure to act like an imbecile. She clicked her cup against her teeth. She should try to think of a line, something glib, but what?

Walter checked the window to see if Julian happened to be passing by. Julian was tall and he had magnificent lips. He'd stand out in a crowd. You wouldn't miss him if he was anywhere on the street. He'd as good as call out in his yellow-and-green plaid cap with the earflaps, his long tweed coat, a gold cashmink scarf.

"Do you think I'm tempting fate, Walter? I have two healthy kids, a moderately glamorous career, a good husband, who, besides you, was the person who educated me. Gary still makes me read hard books, won't take no for an answer. He quizzes me every time there's a new DeLillo, a new Toni Morrison, a new Milan Kundera. I haven't ever had a major injury, knock on wood—"

"Suzanne Farrell coaching you for 'Diamonds.' Don't forget that," Walter put in. The former New York City Ballet prima ballerina had been their idol since they were ten years old.

"The highlight of my career. Sometimes it still amazes me that I have been allowed to dance her role. Her role. And here I am, wanting to turn the whole thing upside down by running off with Lester. Maybe I'm doing this only because, goddamn it, sometimes I just want to read Barbara Taylor Bradford." She lowered her voice. "Do you know that in Saudi Arabia I'd get stoned to death in the village square for committing"—she whispered—"adultery. I'd be put to death."

"But there have to be four witnesses, I think it is. That's how the law goes over there. The stoning thing sounds barbaric, but actually it doesn't happen as much as you'd think because of the witness clause. And anyway there's just me here, and I'll never tell."

"It's serious, Walter, that's what I'm saying. It's a big deal. I'm really an old-fashioned girl when it comes down to it. I've always worked hard, done the right thing, more or less followed Mother's orders. If Lou Ann knew about this, she'd come after me with her claws out. She'd disinherit me. She'd gladly help Gary kill me. A lot of people have affairs without a second thought, but I can't pretend it's just a roll in the hay." She closed her eyes for a minute, thinking of that roll in the hay. "Oh well," she said, sighing, and then she clenched her fists, gritted her teeth. "Do you know what I hate? I despise it when dead people admonish you from the grave or lead their perfect lives in death. I can't help thinking that Daniel would have appreciated his lot, that he wouldn't have screwed it all up. It's so easy to think that way, and yet the dead have a point: we have so much and we're not grateful, we want more and more, one last little thing, and then that, we say, will be enough. Isn't it enough to have the life I have?"

"That depends," Walter said. "If you're not taking this thing lightly, then I guess you have to ask yourself a few questions. Such as, what is it, exactly, that you long for?"

She was holding a French fry like a cigarette and she had been about to take a bite. "What is it I long for?" she repeated. She stared at him with her mouth open. "What is it I long for?" She said it haltingly that time and as if she were speaking only to herself.

Walter had asked the right question, he knew, could feel it in the tautness of the line between them.

"Lester," she said at last. "Lester might say that I'm really longing for God. Could that be it? Wouldn't it be fantastic if lust was that lofty? So maybe my attraction to Lester has nothing to do with the disappointment in my career, or my boring husband, or my upbringing. Maybe all this yearning is a longing for God himself." She smiled, marveling at the idea. "Wouldn't that just be the limit?"

"I bet there are a lot of different routes to God," Walter said. "And it's probably a lot more fun and more worthwhile if you take the crooked path and the longest. I think it's probably not harmony we're after, not until the bitter end, anyway."

"What do I long for?" she said again. "I want relief from drudge. Get up, get breakfast, make lunches, send the boys off, go to the studio for class, rehearse, call the sitter after school to make sure Toby hasn't drugged her, rush home, grab a snack, nag Gary to leave the store, go back to the theater, perform until eleven o'clock, eat dinner, go to bed. This is my life, Walter, my life as a supposed Artist. I want relief, I want—"

"Adoration, and a bit of sweetness? Passion, adoration and a portion of sweetness?"

"Yes, yes," she hissed, leaning over the table. "That's what I want. All of it. I want the sleepless nights, the ten-pound weight loss, the drunk feeling of love." She set her cup down, held her own face in her hands, and said pleadingly, as if she were asking Walter for it, "Sweetness. I want sweetness with a fiddle player. He is everything that Gary isn't, I know that, Walter. He's gallant and corny and mildly Christian and a little bit vain. The fact that he's a stud is probably much more important to him than he'd ever admit. He's a gentleman caller, is what he is. I think it was the way he spoke to his three spaniels in Houston that got me. He walked in his house and said, 'You-all dogs want to eat?' "

" 'You-all dogs want to eat,' " Walter echoed.

"I know it's not much to go on but it charmed the life out of me. And his Christian-ness made me think he might readily be naughty, that he might be itching to be just a little bit wicked. And yes, all in the name of sweetness."

Walter shrugged. There were different rules governing her world. In his sphere, giving in to temptation made him feel good, and then sometimes bad—or worse, indifferent. Immorality could be lethal, it was true, if you weren't careful. As an adult he had never felt he'd sinned, that he'd burn in hell, never felt he'd done something that rent the social fabric. He could see that she had the idea that sleeping with Lester, the Houston Symphony concertmaster, might cause her house to blow up, her children to drop dead on the playground. And she would think it served her right.

"When I first met Lester I thought he seemed like Daniel. I told you that, didn't I?"

"You did," he said. "Although I hate to think that Daniel would have gotten religion and become a Texan."

"You'd like Lester, you really would. I realized later that I'd made the Daniel connection to myself, as an excuse, as a reason to get to know Les, to write him letters, to like him in a legitimate way."

"He reminds me of a dead friend, therefore I get to have sex with him?"

"Oh God, Walter. That's terrible."

Walter ran his finger along the plate, in the spot the French fries had been, in the grease and the salt. His remark was a little harsh, he knew. "Maybe," he said, "you don't have to think of the comparison in terms of exploiting a person, but a way to tap into memory. Perhaps you could call it remembering."

"No." She shook her head. "That's too generous. I remember plenty." She was quiet for a minute, nibbling her bottom lip with her front teeth. "That Christmas party your parents had, for starters? I always think of it in the winter. I can't hear 'O Holy Night' without seeing your Aunt Jeannie trying to get Francie to sing along with her at the piano. You fell down the stairs that night, and I fell in love with Daniel. I didn't even care that you got hurt. I knew *you'd* survive. Daniel looked so sick in the kitchen. I remember how he stared at me, as if he was taking stock of my strength, as if he was admiring the life in me. He looked at me as if I could save him, and I thought I could, I really did. I thought the power of"—she coughed out the word— "love, could cure him. I think he was an unusual person, Walter. He saw things through this sort of scrim of goodwill, and it wasn't that he was an obnoxious brownnoser, and it wasn't only his innocence. He already had the bemused patience of an older, wiser person. I like to think he wouldn't have lost that quality as an adult."

At Christmas only weeks before, Walter had looked down the back stairs at his parents' house. He had remembered how angry he'd been at Susan, how the minute his head hit the last stair he'd understood that she was going to use Daniel's sickness for her own purposes. He had sometimes believed it was his neurosis that had made him think ill of her, that she herself had only been a sixteen-year-old in love. He had despised her, hated the sight of her, for nearly five months.

She was in distress across from him, wiping at her eyes. "You're not lying to Gary after all," he said. "We are hashing over the past. You wouldn't believe what a nightmare it is to be in high school every day, how the smallest things, a paper punch, a milk carton, Reese's peanut butter cups in the grubby paw of some boy—how one small image brings back an entire horrible day twenty years ago." He noticed a speck of nail polish on her engagement ring, and he took her hand in his and with his fingernail chiseled at the spot. "You might want to take this thing off, you know, before dinner. So anyway, if we were back there in Oak Ridge, doing life over, with our knowledge intact, nothing, not one person, would be recognizable. This is how I see it, through my rose-colored scrim: Mrs. Gamble, true to her real nature, would be a dyke with a crew cut and Dobermans instead of collies. She'd be a dowser, or maybe even a surgeon, or a plumber, something that requires hunting down an error, finding a source, following a pipe or a vein through a system. Sue Rawson would live with a buxom blond biker and be completely under her power. Trishie Gamble wouldn't exist, but if she did, she'd be out in the yard sucking on Quaaludes, handing them beyond the fence to all the little children, to counteract her mother's vitamin campaign. We didn't know that what we did in high school would actually mark us, would stay with us, change us. Choice, action, fate, only affected people's lives if they were characters in Greek theater or a Henry James novel. I used to take everything, every last move, seriously, partly so that I would feel a sense of drama that I didn't think really existed in my life, or would ever exist. I couldn't go through the car wash without pretending it was something significant, a rite, a purging ritual. There was terror, real Aristotelian terror, I made believe, when the water came thundering across the car, and the smell of detergent went straight up your nose and behind your eyeballs, and finally the quiet, the white sign lighting up, the light that absolves and urges you out into the world, the black words: DRIVE AHEAD."

"We were such geeky teenagers," she said fondly.

"Nerds of the highest order, and so unaware. It's shocking to think that while we were doing our demi-pliés at the barre up on the twelfth floor of the Louis Sullivan Building the Cultural Revolution was going on. Parents in China were made to watch their children jump from the top of buildings to their deaths. What defined my childhood wasn't Kennedy's assassination, and Bobby's assassination, and Martin Luther King's assassination, those great divides, the tragedies that determined the befores and afters. My defining moment was seeing *Serenade* at Ravinia, with Sue Rawson. What was one president's death, a martyr or two, compared with seeing angels, getting a glimpse of the spirit world?"

Susan smiled across at him, and withdrew her hand. She thought that Lester probably wasn't as interesting as Walter, that even supposing he was the love of her life, if such a thing was actually possible, he would never know her the way her old friend did. He was looking out into the street, watching each person pass. "You must miss the city," she murmured.

"Sometimes," he said absently, without turning from the window. "Do you remember that night you danced to *Serenade* in our living room, by the way? You were possessed. You bewitched us. You hocus-pocused Daniel from some far corner of the house and he came to watch. Mitch went crawling on the floor after you finished, not just to claim you, but also to try to absorb some of the magic, hoping it would rub off on him. He had previously thought he was the next great star in the making, but watching you he realized he didn't have it for the big leagues. It was that night that determined his future as a developer in Southern California. You didn't even have a skirt on, you were wearing jeans, and yet there was this feeling of billowing fabric. If you dazzled Mitch and me, think what Daniel must have felt. He'd never seen anything like it, never dreamed—"

"But do you know what was awful, Walter, so painful for him? When he couldn't go to school, when he couldn't swim, he found he didn't have friends. They fell away, abandoned him. He couldn't talk to anyone, not only because they didn't know what to say but because he realized they weren't capable of meeting him at his level. He didn't feel arrogant. He was just lonely, sad. We used to talk about that. We had some good conversations in those months—at least, I remember thinking they were profound discussions. Teenagers are deep, anyway, sifting through right and wrong, justice and injustice. Only we had an immediate reason to think about God and death, the nature of love."

"Some of my students don't believe in love," Walter said. "A lot of them live with one parent, which probably explains their skepticism. I suppose I learned about real adult love from my parents. Not about ecstasy, per se, but about the quiet, unheralded splendors of a shared history. There are kids at Otten High who have nothing but cynicism for their own bodies, for their own lives. I have to constantly remind myself that I don't care what they think of my teaching performance art—how much energy it takes, not to care! The other day, just for the hell of it, I recited 'To His Coy Mistress' to my toughest class, the seventh hour. And Sharon, the head slut of the school, says audibly, in a fakey under-her-breath way, 'So why didn't she just fuck him?' On one hand I was pleased that she'd listened and understood, and on the other hand the whole place went to pieces."

"God, Walter!"

"That class is always on the edge, just about to explode. But if I can snag them, if I can harness their energy, sometimes they actually go forward. It takes all my might and my cunning. In the middle of their uproar I ran around the room handing out paper and pencils—I have to provide for them because half of them don't come prepared. I told them to write a love letter, a letter of persuasion, to try to entice someone to go out with them, without using any profanity, without being vulgar, I'd flunk them on the spot for crudeness and swearing. The idea was to use wit to get what they wanted. You can see every teenage emotion cross their faces at a time like that. Some don't know what to say, how much to give away. Some go blank and some can only think of their dicks. The good girls start writing and don't look up until the bell rings."

"Can you imagine Mr. Reynolds reciting a love poem or giving us that assignment? It would have made him blush."

"Yes, but we were well behaved and somewhat eager and furthermore we could read. He didn't have to veer from the textbook to appeal to our imaginations."

"You've given me an idea, do you know that? I'll buy the *Norton Anthology* this afternoon, and at dinner I'll open it, like it's the Bible, and read out loud, 'To His Coy Mistress.' "

Walter sat up straight and with the rectitude of a clergyman recited, " 'Let us roll all our strength and all / Our sweetness up into one ball, / And tear our pleasures with rough strife.' "

"And don't think of your wife and three children, Lester, Lester, Lester." She pulled her hair out of its rubber band, and it fell around her. She had more hair than Walter thought could be contained by one thin band. "I wonder," she said, "if he loves me. Lester's an awful name, what you'd call a pig if you were a girl growing up on a farm."

"Has he seen you dance?"

"Once. The time we met, in Houston."

"And what was it? What were you performing?"

"*Jewels.*"

" 'Diamonds,' you danced 'Diamonds'?"

"My part. Farrell's part, and my part."

"There's no doubt, then. He loves you."

They walked up Michigan Avenue, arm in arm. The gold candles wound with plastic greens were still strapped to the streetlights, along the avenue, left over from Christmas. The sun was shining and the wet sidewalks were crackly underfoot with salt. Susan was wearing a long, heavy camel coat that was too big for her, and on anyone else would have looked dowdy. She was all elegance in the coat and her white beret, just as she had been at ten in a black leotard. She could not possibly have needed the coat in Florida. Walter wondered if she'd lugged it from home, or, miraculously, found it in the closet at the hotel. She had always seemed to have what was appropriate, necessary, he thought, and then, amending that idea he said to himself that she had always had the enviable ability to claim what she needed.

"You know," she said, pulling him closer, "I finally figured out that you let me win some of those music games. It was nice of you, by the way."

"It made you so mad to lose," he said. "I had to give you victory sometimes, purely out of self-defense."

She frowned, looking at him. "I used to have to win back then. I thought I had hidden that unpleasant trait, but you've always known me. I think Daniel's death forced me to sort things out, to realize that winning is beside the point. I did love beating you, though. I cheated to win, Walter. Sometimes, I cheated."

"I know you did, darling."

"I would have hated me, if I were you. Do your parents still have the neighborhood Christmas party? I loved all those strange people, poor Billy rocking back and forth with his hand in his mouth, drooling into the candies. Your aunt Jeannie trying to get her children to perform. You could just tell Sue Rawson always wanted to drive a spear through her heart."

"Exactly," Walter said. "That's the whole problem with Lake Margaret. Sue Rawson wants to punish everyone because God gave her a twit for a sister. She's had to share the place with Aunt Jeannie for so long and she has finally come to the end of her rope. If she knew she wouldn't get caught she'd just go over to Ted and Jeannie's house after dark. With her concealed weapon in her pocket, she'd walk in the basement door, make her way to the bedroom and blow her little sister's brains out. But even that wouldn't be as satisfying as this Lake Margaret deal. She's going to torture Jeannie slowly, make her pay. Either she thinks that everyone in the family is somehow going to understand why she's doing it, and not take it personally, and excuse her, or she figures we'll all be mad at her forever and she won't care, because she'll have so much personal, lifelong satisfaction from skewering Jeannie. Whatever happens, she's going to make about four hundred thousand dollars and possibly get revenge on top of it."

"It's so sad, to lose a place like that."

"It's not gone yet," he said, "but it's a lot of money to raise. I haven't told you the latest twist. It's as if all of this, in a perverse way, has come, not exactly full circle, but close to it. So, my cousins, those who are professionals, are in hock in the suburbs and don't want to go deeper, and the others don't have money, period. We are carpenters, aspiring actresses, teachers. I have about five hundred dollars in a savings account in Oak Ridge. My parents can spare maybe fifty thousand, but they have to think about their retirement. Aunt Jeannie and Ted have blown a lot of money on trinkets for Jeannie, and they've had to educate six children, and let's not forget the obligatory cruise in the Bahamas every year. Couldn't do without a big pleasure boat. At my mother's behest I went to talk to Sue Rawson a few weeks ago. 'If anyone can sway her, you can,' Joyce says, which, believe me, did not make me feel hopeful. In I go to my aunt's coach house, she sits me down in her pink Louis Quatorze chair, the way she used to when I was six years old. She cuts me off the minute I bring up the subject. 'This is not a country shack,' she says to me. 'Do you realize what kind of responsibility is involved, taking care of an estate of this size? Do you understand what sort of expense is required, for maintenance, for taxes, what time commitment you will have to make?' "

"I've never liked her, Walter!"

"No one can stand her, but I've always insisted that she has a secret sentimental heart. I know she does. When I was eight she took me to see the bronze dancer girl, the Degas in the Art Institute, and she could hardly control herself. She has great feeling, truly. I refuse to give up my opinion, even though by the end of the conversation she had reduced me to a pip. There was no point in telling her how important Lake Margaret is to me. I'm penniless! There was nothing I could say.

"I went home in a complete depression, but it wasn't long after that Francie and Roger Miller came forward. Enter Dr. and Mrs. Miller. Center stage. Poor Roger, cultivating his lady's slippers. He's an eye doctor and doesn't have anything else to do with his money. Raise his orchids and, yes, save Lake Margaret! It is Aunt Jeannie's son-in-law who apparently is going to step in and rescue us floundering, useless nieces and nephews. And then, you see, Sue Rawson will have to live with the fact that the majority of the shares are going to belong to Jeannie's faction. Everyone will have to tithe to Aunt Jeannie to use the bathrooms."

"That's almost more terrible than selling the whole place. It won't ever feel like it's yours again if that happens. I can just about hear the saccharine speech Jeannie makes about how much everyone is welcome to use the property as they always have."

"It will bring tears to our eyes. Before we're done blowing our noses and thanking her she'll be screaming at the ingrates to pick up the wet towels on the floor."

"Do you think," Susan said, "do you think a person can manipulate destiny? No, no, no, forget I said that. I know we're not supposed to ask questions like that now that we're past sixteen."

"Sure," he said, answering it anyway. "Especially if you have a lot of money."

They left it at that. They kept walking south, into the wind, holding on to each other and their hats. They stood outside the Louis Sullivan Building for a long time, looking at the stone, the mosaics in the walls and the grillwork on the doors. It had never occurred to them, when they were young, to look at the details. They peered into the Artists' Café, where they used to drink coffee and talk about fate. It seemed not to have changed much, although the orange booths had been reupholstered with pale green vinyl. From the menu taped to the door it looked as if the management still served no-nonsense Hills Brothers coffee, that it hadn't succumbed to flavored brews that required expensive machinery.

Susan and Walter knew that the Kentons had moved the studio years before to the west side of the city, but they wanted to see where it had been, wanted to see through the window of the antique book dealer's shop, back to what was theirs. In the hall on twelve they took off their coats and sat on the long wooden bench, under the same dim light, smelling, they thought, the same dust that was still circulating through the dark corridors. A single voice singing scales came up from the eleventh floor, and there was a violin in the distance, the sound of a Vivaldi concerto.

"It's eerie, how the building hasn't changed," Susan said. "I wonder if I'll ever see Franklin and Margery Kenton again. It's so strange to think that there are certain people you won't ever come across in your life, that for your purposes they are already dead. I don't think they ever forgave me for leaving them for New York. They didn't get to put their finishing touches on me."

"No, it wasn't that," Walter said. "They held you responsible for Mitch quitting. That's my theory, anyway."

"That makes absolutely no sense. I have no idea why he stopped, when he had a full scholarship in New York, a dozen people at the school awaiting his arrival." The voice student on eleven sounded like a ghost at her thin, endless scale. Mitch had quit, Walter knew, because he had spent enough time in the faggot world of the dance and he was ready to put on his britches, go after manly pursuits. He started to say that he thought Mitch had been afraid to be called a homo, but it wasn't a conversation he really wanted to have and thankfully Susan interrupted. "Walter," she said, "I don't think I ever thought about your feelings."

"You mean because I was the worst in the class?"

"No! You weren't the worst."

"That's right, I hadn't had polio like the Russian girl, Svetlana, with the humpback. The second worst, then."

"It must have been horrible, not being in *The Nutcracker,* when we were. I knew, intellectually, of course, that you must have been hurt, but I couldn't have begun to imagine how it felt."

He noted her use of "We," the old twosome, Mitch and Susan. "You missed my shining moment," he said. "I was the Prince in the Rockford Ballet's production. I was the star, not least because I had to partner a girl named Nancy whose real calling was the rodeo. She was a frisky three-hundred-pounder and I had to lift her fourteen times in the course of the first act."

"You never told me about that! Did you? Did you tell me?"

"Of course not. I had a shred of dignity. And I enjoyed hiding that part of my life. My major secret, liking boys, was not only shameful, but I didn't know how I was going to carry it forward into adulthood. I sometimes figured I'd live with my mother, both of us like old ladies eating rump roast on Sunday afternoons, buttoning up and taking a walk in the park. The secret of my *Nutcracker* seemed, in comparison, legitimate, clean, something to prize."

"We should have come to see it—"

"Oh no, you would never have stopped laughing. I wouldn't have lived it down. The only lie Sue Rawson ever told me occurred directly after the performance. She praised my dancing. She said I was good and I chose to believe her. She was being especially nice to me because Daniel was sick. It was her good deed, on a par with helping a senior citizen across the street or having a sick dog put to sleep. After her compliment I got this idea that you thought about the Rockford Ballet, that you glorified it."

"I don't know what was on my mind," she said breezily. "Do you think Mitch wonders about us? Do you think we cross his screen every now and then?" She leaned against Walter, waiting for his answer.

"I like to think," he said, "that he's forgotten about us entirely, just as we never, not even in the deepest sleep, not even in a waking dream, give him a moment's thought."

———

They took a cab back to the Richmond Hotel. At four-thirty Susan got in the tub. She talked to Walter through the closed bathroom door. "Lester's not like you think," she called. "He's not a Texas Holy Roller type, afraid to take the Lord's name in vain, none of that. He's even secretly pro-choice, something he says he can't tell his wife. And he doesn't feel persecuted, the way so many of those Christian types do. Among other things, he has doubt."

"Ah, doubt, that's good," Walter said. He was looking out the window, down into the alley from the seventeenth floor of the hotel. She was splashing in the tub, running more water to froth up the bubbles.

"Could you iron my skirt?" she yelled over the noise of her bath. "Do you know how to do pleats?"

"Yes, ma'am," he said.

"We haven't really talked about Otten, you know. Tell me about it."

"I have to concentrate while I'm ironing because my mistress is particular," he said, setting up the board. "You'll have to come visit so you can experience the breakfast scene at Lee's. I take my papers over there before school sometimes and I sit at my table in the corner, if I can find it through the smoke, and have coffee, do my corrections. You walk in and the men at the counter turn as one and give a nod. Their plectrons are going so you can practically hear the car crashes as they happen. Underneath that noise is the murmur of complaint and gossip and old-guy boasts. Basically it's a story contest down there, a continuous battle of Can You Match That? There's about six regular full-time stool sitters. I figure if we lose Lake Margaret I'll move down to Lee's, take my place at the counter, smoke three packs by nine A.M., talk exclusively about accidents and learn to figure out how many fire trucks are going out on a single call."

He knew she wasn't listening, that she was thinking of Lester, but he went on anyway. "I found a ladder out in the backwoods. If you live in Wisconsin, by the way, you have to say, 'Out in the backwoods.' Mr. Brodie, my neighbor, told me it was a tree stand, meant for climbing up so you can sit on a limb and wait for a deer to happen by. Then you shoot it. I was under the impression that slaughtering an animal requires stainless steel and a drum or so of Saran Wrap, not something as regular and unhygienic as an unpainted wooden ladder. It's not exactly a comfortable feeling, knowing that most of my students, the boys at least, own guns and go hunting with their fathers, that they've killed an animal or two by the time they're fourteen."

He was still ironing and talking when she emerged in her plush terry-cloth robe, her hair wrapped in the white bath towel. "Let me see how you did the creases." She leaned over the board, and the heady mixture of soap, shampoo, gel and cologne penetrated his clogged sinuses. A whiff of her and he could breathe again. "I don't think Lester is going to decide whether to jeopardize his career and his marriage based on the way I've ironed these pleats. You just tell him how hard it is to get good help these days."

"Okay, okay, you're right. They're fine."

She paced up and down, going over, again, her tenuous plan. "I'll either see you later, or I won't. I could call you at some point, so that you know I haven't been stabbed or anything. I should call Gary now, in case, for some reason, he'd call me later. Except he doesn't know where I am. I never call when I'm away, and so that would be strange, wouldn't it? Oh, Jesus, Walter, I've never been this nervous."

"Watch your language, for one thing. You weren't beside yourself when you danced for Mr. B. that summer you went to New York?"

"It's absurd! I know it is. But how often do you meet someone who lights up all of your circuits? I've generated lust for various people along the way, but it's been three times all told that I've experienced this intense, animal reaction to a person. Daniel did it for me. Gary. And now Lester. It's a rare thing. Oh, all right, Mitch did too, but that was only because he was the first. It's still a rare sensation. I'll admit it's making me crazy."

Walter stood by the sink as she applied her makeup, advising her to tone it down, keep it natural. He told her she was stunning, and did not mention that she had a fevered, glassy-eyed look. He kissed her, redid her lipstick, and held her hand on the way down in the elevator and out to the curb. "Good-bye," she said as the cab pulled up. "Have fun," he called, and as she drove off he felt obliged to whisper after her, "Be careful."

In the hotel restaurant he found a window seat, and as he settled himself he ruffled up his curls and smoothed the lumps from his bulky gray sweater. He would have liked to have worn something flashy, but he had left his New York dress-up clothes with his beautician friend in the city. His Wisconsin wardrobe was plain, lackluster, one part interchangeable with the next, most of it meant to jibe with what he supposed was an Otten parent's vision of an English teacher. He ordered a forty-dollar bottle of wine and the salmon. To his waitress, Joanne, he said, "I know this is gauche, but what I really want, to go along with the meal, with the new potatoes, is an order of fries, like the ones they have in the café next door. Is that possible?"

Joanne laughed at his request and said she'd use her clout to get him an extra-greasy heap of what amounted to pure fry. Walter was accustomed to being alone, but he had half a mind to ask her to sit down with him, to forget the other tables, to speak to him about the politics of waitressing at the Richmond Hotel. He would have liked her to talk to him while he waited for dinner, while he waited for Julian to materialize out on the sidewalk. He wondered if anyone in Otten ever drank a bottle of wine that cost more than five dollars and fifty cents. Not on his salary, they didn't, he said to himself. He wondered if they imagined what they were missing. He wondered for the thousandth time if Mitch and Susan had slept together in Mitch's attic in high school, and if Daniel and Susan had done it in the sickroom. He wondered if Julian was going to walk into the restaurant and see him eating French fries and drinking a forty-dollar bottle of Cabernet. He wondered if Susan was seducing Lester, and he hoped, if she was, that the happiness would stick, stay with her like permanent ink on her skin, like a tattoo, never fading. He wished Julian would walk into the restaurant and see him eating French fries with his forty-dollar bottle of wine. Julian might later write a come-hither poem for Walter, about what it was like standing in the doorway and seeing his baby sipping wine from a good year, eating potatoes from a season that had for once had enough rain.

At the beginning of the evening back in November, when he had first met Julian in the box at Orchestra Hall before the concert started, Walter had stood outside of himself, pleased that Mr. McCloud was attracted to someone, that there was again the possibility of love, that he was capable of feeling, capable of sustaining heartbreak. Months had passed and he was eating supper alone in Chicago, watching out the window. He knew he didn't have to wait for change or miracle to bring Julian. He was neither a fisherman casting a wide net into the sea, nor the wife wringing her hands waiting at home. He could find Julian if he wanted to. He could call his office at Tulane, call his apartment on Belmont Avenue. He could write a letter and send it to both places, for insurance.

He picked at his fish. Around him the couples paid no attention while he nursed along his wine. He told himself he should stop the nonsense, stop waiting. He was as daffy as Susan and her wildly improbable Lester. He thought about Julian's visiting him in Otten. Walter could give him an architectural tour of the town, of the storefronts with their façades and the long, plain brick buildings behind. He didn't think they'd dare go to breakfast at Lee's. They could drive to the Piggly Wiggly and buy dairy products and fresh beef. They could invite themselves over to Mrs. Denval's for Sunday brunch, for instant coffee and doughnut holes. Julian would recite his poems for Mrs. D., and make her want him for a pet, too. And then what? How would they fill the hours? Walter didn't think he knew how to do activities with another person anymore. He didn't relish the idea of biking, or shopping, or working an elaborate jigsaw puzzle simply for the purpose of being in someone else's company. They would have to make a construct of time, pursue hobbies if they were to become a couple. Walter would bang on the study door while Julian worked at a poem, informing him that their decoupage class down at the town hall was about to start.

When Susan came back, if she returned, maybe he should tell her about Julian and ask her advice. Julian not only had nice eyes and inspiring lips but he and Walter had felt the same way about Maurizio Pollini. Julian too had sensed Beethoven's rudeness at the end of the adagio, in the Opus 7 in E flat, the noise of the D flat against the C. He was someone who might have had holding power, the sort of man to make a life with. At eight o'clock Walter surrendered his watch. He looked out the window one last time. *Come to me, bend to me, kiss me good day.* There was a little bit of wine left in the bottle and he took it with him, walking up the seventeen flights to his room.

By eight-thirty he was in bed watching a movie—what, he didn't know—a black-and-white film with obscure actors. It was something sad, he could already tell. He might have gone out, to a theater, to a concert, but he felt it was important to be ready in case she showed up. He had papers to grade and *The Great Gatsby* to read, but he couldn't stand the thought of work. The movie was about thwarted love, and so he removed the full box of Kleenex from the bathroom dispenser and put it beside him on the pillow. His arms and legs were sore from shoveling in Otten, in a time and place that seemed far away, long ago. He began to cry before he knew what was happening in the movie, before he knew exactly who would lose what. He put his head back and did not wipe the tears as they fell.

At nine-ten the key turned in the lock. The door closed behind her. She spread both arms out and leaned against the wall. The collar of her coat was up to her temples, and her beret was pulled down over her ears. It had begun to snow again, and the coat was covered with tiny dark spots.

"You're back," Walter said, pressing the off button on the remote. There was a pile of crumpled tissues by his pillow, and he quickly collected them and threw them in the wastebasket. He climbed out of bed and went to her, unwrapped her from her coat, lifted off her hat and led her to the chair.

"Did you drink that whole bottle of wine?" she whimpered.

"Not all," he said.

"You look cute in those jammies."

He glanced down at the blue-and-white-striped pajamas, a Christmas gift from his mother. "Thank you," he said. "Tell me about your evening, please."

She folded over, the way only a dancer can, her long arms draped on the floor, her head at her feet, her breasts resting on her calves. "I love him. I love him. I love him without knowing what love is. I would take any little thing he gave me, and tell myself it was enough. I would do it with full knowledge, knowing it was what fool women do for fool men." She stood up, her hands to her mouth, and murmured, "He has silver hair, and he's swarthy."

"Swarthy?"

"I learned that word in high school, when we read *Lord Jim*. Why did I ever think he looked like Daniel? He doesn't look a damn thing like any of you McClouds. Lester's mother was Peruvian, and his father is British, so you get this man with silver hair, brown skin and green eyes, a Texan! How can I love him, I don't even know him?" She took off her pump and threw it at the bed.

"And then what happened?"

"He wouldn't have me," she shouted. "He's—honorable! He said we both had too much to lose. Do you think there's another man like him anywhere in the world? Or do you think it means he doesn't, you know, fancy me? I don't think that, I don't think that. Isn't it my luck? As a teenager I love a dying boy, I grow up slightly, marry the first heterosexual I meet because I figure being in the ballet world I'll never meet another, and then someone I really love, heart, soul, body, won't have me!"

He gathered her up and held her, and she took to him, collapsing in his arms. "I'm sorry," he whispered. "I'm sorry, Susan."

She reached behind him for a tissue and blew her nose. "How is it," she said into his neck, "that I can know him, and not know him? That we can sit down and talk to one another as if we're picking up where we left off? Do you think we'd hate each other in real life?"

"Probably not for at least two weeks." The radiator knocked and hissed as if it were censuring Walter's answer. "Maybe three," he said, after a minute.

"I'm so cold. I just want to get into bed."

He handed her the white flannel gown from her suitcase. "Other than that, did you have a nice dinner?"

"Yes," she said quietly. "It was lovely." She turned away from him and lifted her sweater over her head. He had seen her in leotards since she was ten and he knew her shape better than his own. She was fiddling with the hooks, having trouble getting out of her bra.

"Do you really need one of those things." He spoke to the carpet about her brassiere.

"Thank you, I do not discuss my cup size or anything else about my breasts with anyone other than my gynecologist. You are as cynical about love as your students are. If you must know, I bought new underwear specifically for this night. Here, look at it." She threw the strip of black lace over her shoulder.

Walter picked it up and examined it. "There's not much here in terms of support," he said.

"I thought it might add to the fun," she said plaintively. She fastened the four white lamb buttons above the yoke of her nightie. "I suppose, really, at the root of this, Walter, I'm worried about what happens next, when I've got that made-up, shellacky look of middle age, when I'm not the star of my boondock company, when I'm not Mr. V's best girl, when I'm at home without a performance." She bent over, let her hair fall to the floor and vigorously brushed it. "Maybe that's it," she said from her upside-down position. "I used to think I'd go gracefully, but I'm not so sure. I think I might be scared, really scared. I think I'm terrified. And you're right, I'd probably be complaining about Lester after two weeks, or else one of us would die of cancer."

"You might find a whole new avenue when you retire," Walter began, helpless, he knew, to comfort her.

"I'm so tired all of a sudden," she said, straightening up. "I haven't slept in days, thinking about this night, and fretting about my foundations. Will you hold me, again, when we're sleeping?"

At 9:45 they got into the double bed, turned out the lights and kissed, puckered lips to puckered lips. He pulled the covers over her. She was on her side, with her back to him. He moved closer, and without the rest of him touching her he put his arm around her waist. He guessed that she must feel rejected, twice in one evening, by Lester, and also by himself. It was illogical of her to feel spurned by him, but that did not make the sensation any less keen. It wasn't that she had ever wanted him, but she might think she was repulsive to him. He probably shouldn't touch her foot with his foot or get any nearer; feet were intimate and he was already close enough. He should try to let her know how generally desirable she was. Daniel came to him then: Walter imagined for a minute that he was his brother, alive, in bed with his wife, the high school sweetheart, that their marriage had evolved to a fond and nonsexual relationship. He kissed her hair, and stroked through it with his fingers. It seemed right to touch her hair. Daniel might have done such a thing before falling asleep. "That's nice, Walter," she said. "That feels good."

He wondered if she would have cheated on Daniel. She would have been his very own sister-in-law, and he would have been forced to forgive her for her high school transgressions. He wondered if Julian would knock at the door of Room 1709 at the Richmond Hotel. He felt a small knot in her hair and he carefully pulled it apart. If Julian appeared at the window, hovering there seventeen flights aboveground, Walter would explain that he was still a homosexual even though he was in bed with a beautiful woman. It occurred to him that it was fitting that he and Susan had come for something they both hoped for, and thought they wanted, and found only each other. They had always been stuck with each other. If they'd known that at the end it would always be just the two of them, how much sooner they would have arrived at their destination, at their quiet sleep, their long blank dream.

Seven

FEBRUARY

1973

Although many of Daniel's friends were preoccupied that autumn and winter he was ill, it wasn't true that every one of them had fallen away. It seemed so to Susan, seemed that they had abandoned him, that they couldn't claim to be sincere and faithful if they didn't call him at night or stop by several times a week. Daniel's friends—the Overachievers, Walter called them—were athletes, musicians and National Merit finalists. They were busy at their senior year, at the business of football, swimming, school government, homework, the orchestra, the student newspaper and college applications. Some of them who had visited infrequently in October and November had been given a talking-to by their parents in January, and had come to understand the gravity of his situation. Chris Nelson played basketball that winter, and he often wrote Daniel from a few blocks away, giving him blow-by-blow accounts of the games. Maura Peterson copied her European History notes and delivered them at the end of each week, and David Horton came over on Saturdays, at first to catch Daniel up in calculus, and later, when they let the math go, he came to play chess.

Susan felt as if Daniel were in a tank, and the old friends were looking in on him, their faces pressed against the glass, their noses squashed, their lips flattened and enlarged. They thought they could approximate real life while they observed him. She hated the way they tried to shoot the breeze, as if in the McCloud living room they were so charitably dramatizing the schoolyard scene, waiting for the first bell to clang. She hated the blowzy entrance, lots of stamping of the feet, and the hearty question, How's it going? Walter too could feel their enthusiasm, all the way up in his room, but he didn't hold their cheer against them. Good humor was in short supply around the house, and in his book there was nothing wrong with importing a little.

At school in January, one of the friends ventured to say, "He's so sick he might die." The word "die" silenced the group walking down the hall. There was no echo in a sound like *die*. It was heavy, a real sinker. They walked on without talking. What does he think? They stood at their lockers, wondering, trying to turn the dials around and around through their sticky combinations. What does he feel? How will he look? When they went to visit Maplewood Avenue some of them did come into the living room all nerves and bravado, gibbering about wrestling, the student-council vote to ban smoking in the court-yard, the coming orchestra trip to Italy. Susan was right about their being frightened, frightened both of Daniel and of the thing that was taking him. As the disease progressed their coming required courage. What Susan believed she saw, and what galled her, was their fake largesse, their phony selflessness, their belief that they would return to their classmates transformed, charged with knowledge after the contact.

On the occasional days Daniel made it to school he walked slowly through the corridors. His clothes, no matter that Joyce continued to buy smaller sizes or shrink his pants in the hot dryer, seemed to drape over his bones and trail after him. In the seven minutes they had to change classes Susan rushed to meet him, to walk him to his next room. Her own teachers excused her habitual tardy slips and did not mark her down a grade when her work was late. Mr. Reynolds bought her lunch in the faculty cafeteria, and made her sit in the meeting room and eat while he watched over her. That special treatment confirmed for Walter that Daniel was already exerting a power that was normally associated with ghouls, sneaks who did their work during nocturnal visits and through Ouija boards. Who could tell, then, what additional benefits might shower down upon Susan when Daniel actually died, when his spirit was set loose into the night air?

She wore long rayon skirts to school, and pearl- or pink-colored blouses in a fabric that had a sheen, and her black patent-leather slingbacks. It looked to Walter as if water would roll right off her slick front. She and Daniel walked the halls, her arm through his, and it would hardly have surprised anyone, or seemed out of line, if she had put up her hand, all the fingers firmly together, and turned it slightly back and forth, a royal wave along the parade route. No more movement in that wave than the quiver of a dog's nose catching a scent in the wind. Walter went in a circle around the building rather than pass the imperial couple going to European History or German. He would have liked to pitch a bowling ball at the two of them, as well as the attendants, the old friends who followed at a respectful distance. In one strike the whole entourage would go down. But he also half wanted to drag along the hall, calling, nearly out of steam, like a lacerated soldier, "Susan! Susan!"

She would be unable to do anything for him, he knew. She was like a character in a horror film, the first victim in town whose soul is plucked from her body and taken to another planet, nothing left behind but a zombie in lustrous silks. From his back-row seat Walter watched her in their American Literature class. She stared at the anthology until tears ran down her cheeks, the poor girl with real adult problems, or else she shut down all together, put her head on the desk, resting for that next long, slow walk with her Casanova.

In the afternoons Walter and Mitch rode the train together into the city without her. She did not go to ballet school that winter. The Kentons never asked after her, and Walter assumed that she had phoned in, giving them her eloquent excuse for giving up her art. She had a patient to nurse, a higher calling than the dance. Maybe she talked to them every week, with updates, with blood pressure and temperature stats, the white-cell count. There was no telling how far ahead she tried to see, or what she spoke about in her Planet X brainless state.

Walter once said to Mitch that Joyce might as well formally adopt Susan, to get a little payback from the additional teenager she was constantly feeding. Mitch had looked so pained Walter craned his neck to see better, wanted to go closer, to catch the expression that was so novel, wounded pride, the little bubble of the self punctured. Walter dropped his book, sputtering something about how Susan wasn't over that much, it only seemed as if it was every single day, including weekends, breakfast, lunch and dinner.

In fact, she was always at his house. Joyce had gained something like a daughter, and in addition the acquaintance of Susan's mother, Lou Ann Claridge. Walter had never warmed to Mrs. Claridge, a woman who played games, golf and cards, a housewife who spent her summer mornings on a lawn chair out in the yard, baking in the sun. Joyce seemed to think that with the bit of strength she had for the outside world it was important to cultivate Susan's mother. It occurred to Walter in a horrifying moment that Joyce had the impression that Susan was the sort of girl who would get the ballet out of her system in good time, and make an excellent wife and mother. She was courting Susan to be Daniel's bride, to be Walter's sister-in-law, a permanent fixture. "Oh God," he said out loud in his bedroom. "Not that. No! Please help Daniel marry a nice sorority girl, a waitress, a librarian, a reformed prostitute, anyone but her. Please, not *her.*"

In later years Walter wondered how both the McClouds and the Claridges could have stood by while Susan came to a complete stop at Daniel's bedside. Joyce, he imagined, lunching with Lou Ann in the dining room, discussing draperies and the country club set, was trying, wordlessly, through the elaborate salads, fruits and marshmallows suspended in the Jell-O, to communicate her plea: let us have Susan, for a time, give her up to us. Walter thought that under normal circumstances Joyce would have been protective, not only of her son, but also of a girl who stood to lose her reputation. She would have been polite and distant to a frivolous person like Lou Ann Claridge. But Joyce was not following her own general rules that winter. When Susan came over she sent her right up to Daniel's bedroom. It was puppy love, she must have said to herself, nothing wrong with it. When the couple was downstairs it never occurred to her that Mrs. Gamble, in her living room, running the Hoover, was watching the make-out sessions through the small square panes of the leaded windows.

One afternoon in February, Mrs. Gamble hardly had to strain to see Susan stretched out on the sofa, her head in Daniel's lap, while the boy traced her features. He was memorizing her nose, Mrs. Gamble theorized, the arch of her blond eyebrows, the bulb of her lower lip, so he would recognize her in their next incarnation. When he bent over and kissed Susan and she clasped her arms around his neck, Mrs. Gamble's heart constricted. No parent was at home at 646 Maplewood Avenue, and the girl was hoisting herself up, climbing into his lap, her legs to either side of him, her little man in the boat no doubt smack against his John Thomas. It was appalling that what seemed delicate and tight in a girl would open, come alive, take on a hunger of its own. She was clutching his head to her breast, and beginning, slowly at first, to rock against him, and then faster, and he, with his head turned, his fluttering eyes closed, gasped and moaned, and at long last gave one anguished cry. Right there for the world to see! Mrs. Gamble heard the noise of it through two sets of storm windows and the twenty feet of grass between them. In spite of her indignation she felt her knees buckle and she had to sit down. All through dinner she could not say a word, couldn't banish the memory of Susan's rippling skirt, and underneath, she imagined, the fresh tear in the girl's sacred membrane. "It is not natural," she said out loud, "that a boy, as sick as he is, can rise to the occasion."

Joyce came in with groceries that afternoon and she thought how relaxed and happy Daniel looked on the sofa. "Another month," she said at night, and in the morning. "Give us another month." Later on it was, "One more week." She told herself that she was strong enough to hold out hope, to beg for an allotment of time, to live with the uncertainty, to go on asking day after day. With their love, with Susan's love, anything was possible. It was the girl who could get him to sit up and drink some broth; she who made him laugh, who made him extend his forecast to the spring. He planned to be well enough to take her to the prom in May, to escort her to the last dance of his senior year.

There were evenings in February when Walter walked into the kitchen to find Susan and Joyce standing side by side at the counter like best friends, chopping up chicken breasts and celery to put in the broth. The ingenue and the mother were bent to the task of keeping the sick boy breathing, conquering his illness with cooked spinach and the salutary power of romance. Walter avoided going home, avoided stepping into a scene that should already have played itself out on daytime television. He went to the health-food store and sat for an hour at the counter like a drunk, in front of his tiger milk shake. Or he went to the library and slept in the oversized chair in the company of Oak Ridge's crazy man and the woman with open sores on her legs. Most often he went to Mitch's house. He could go in secret, shinny up a post onto a roof outside Mitch's room, and open the broken window, climb in, so that Mrs. Anderson would not know just how often he was over, so she wouldn't think he was wearing out his welcome.

From what Walter could gather, Susan had not felt obliged to tell Mitch that she was casting him aside. It had been clear, the night of the Christmas party, that she was moving on, that Mr. and Mrs. Mitch Anderson were henceforth a part of history. With the specter of death hanging over the McCloud household, Susan apparently believed that she did not have to abide by the rules of courtship and civilized behavior. Everyone would naturally understand. It was a bewildering situation, a cruel fix, Walter thought, but for him there was something about all of the relations that made a pleasing symmetry. Susan had jilted Mitch. It was too bad, an absolute shame. Susan had also deprived Walter of a mother and a brother so that the two boys could both, in a sense, call themselves orphans.

Through January Mitch sat on the el without exerting any pressure against the ride, so that on a particularly bumpy trip Walter feared Mitch would slide off the seat. The two sat facing each other, staring at the floor or out the window. Walter wondered how long it would take Mitch to understand that they were together under the same evil star. He hoped that one day on the train Mitch would glance across to him and see his own sorrow reflected in Walter's face. They both looked beat up, they both weren't getting enough sleep. Walter saw his image in the train window and he thought there was misery in the way his own curls seemed to have unraveled, the way they hung in the dry heat of the train as if rain had flattened them. The sight of Walter might fill Mitch with pity, something he might have felt on a few previous occasions, when he'd seen handicapped children on the street or blind people. Although Mitch was wounded, as good as missing a vital organ, surely he would realize that Walter had also lost something, a hand, an ear, several toes, small losses as opposed to a whole beating heart, but parts missing nonetheless. Conniving Susan, the schemer, had robbed both of them, taken what was rightfully theirs.

They didn't talk about her. At the Andersons' house Walter sang along with the record player. There were arias in *Tosca* that described his own unhappiness, and he sat with his legs crossed and his eyes closed, belting them out with Renata Tebaldi. Mitch lay on his bed with his hands pressed against his abdomen. He was having stomachaches and chest pains, what felt like bitter digestive acids leaking into his rib cage. "Ow, ow, ow," he moaned over the noise of the singers. Above all of that clamor Mrs. Anderson went unnoticed, calling to them from the den to turn down the stereo.

Walter understood the signal that in January seemed to beam over the land every five seconds from the McCloud house, from the snug little company that was working with such industry to restore Daniel's health. Mitch came calling for Walter one Saturday morning and he too felt the warning. It was a bad day for Joyce—trouble feeding Daniel, trouble cleaning his wound—and when she saw Mitch standing at the door she said, "What in heaven's name are you doing here?"

"Nothing. Just passing by, but no, I—I don't need to see anyone."

The message from Joyce was clear. *We don't want you.* But there was also the fine print: the world was not going to let Walter or Mitch rant or rail in the face of Susan's goodness. She had come into Daniel's life, had found in her heart love for a person whose patchy skin fell off in flakes onto her hands and her lap. She might save him—so the idle boys be off. Mitch and Walter were well. They had lives ahead of them, and in that future the assurance of strong bodies. During this time they were to be quiet, they were to wait, until there were results, until the something, the thing that was not within their poor power to affect, took place. Then, in the great afterward, there would be more time than a person could spend to sort out the mess.

It seemed to Walter that as the days passed, clauses were added to the original message, sections that contained threats. *If you so much as think to smash the streetlights, to club the ducks in the park, to steal and pillage for attention, you may not live to regret it.* There was not much choice, no alternative but to give up the girl, the mother, the brother, without a squeak. Walter considered that someone, sometime, much later, might see through to their nobility, might understand what they had sacrificed, but in his own room he did not feel much heroism. His parents might just as well have taken him into the forest under the pretext of gathering wood and left him.

Through the winter the two boys went through their usual motions. They met at school, they went to ballet class, they traveled back to Oak Ridge on the el, and then one way or another, by climbing in the window or walking through the front door, Walter usually wound up in Mitch's room. He would have stayed the night on the floor if he could have escaped Mrs. Anderson's watchful eye for the length of twelve hours. Between seven and ten o'clock in the evening they sat on Mitch's brown coil rug side by side, leaning against his bed. They opened the windows, and smoked Mitch's dope, a new hobby for both of them, and they spoke in a desultory way about food they'd like to eat and movies they'd seen. Ever since Christmas, when Walter tumbled down the stairs, they could hardly think what to talk about. It was ironic, Walter thought, that they finally had hours at a time in each other's company and there was nothing much to say. The dance no longer seemed like a large enough subject, and the Susan topic, on the other hand, would lead them through dark twisting lanes, every one a dead end.

If the grass didn't make Walter feel isolated or recklessly hilarious, it sometimes loosened his tongue, and after several hits gave him the freedom to speak about any trivial thing that came to mind. He lectured Mitch one night for forty-five minutes about coffee, about all the facets of production. They were smoking hash, good hash, "organic," the dealer, a fourteen-year-old punk, had said. Walter made a note to tell Mrs. Gamble, if it ever came up in conversation, that they were not polluting themselves, that they were partaking of a chemically free product of the finest quality. After the third toke he very badly wanted a cup of coffee. He got to thinking and talking, simultaneously, about drip versus percolation and the variation in filter paper. His uncle Ted loved coffee, and had thrown what energy Aunt Jeannie spared him into becoming a connoisseur. He was one of the first grocers in the nation to have a grinder available to his customers, so that they could take home the roasted beans freshly ground. Through the years at parties Uncle Ted had casually dispensed facts about the coffee bean in the pause between the main course and dessert. Walter heard himself taking the story back, further and further, to the place where coffee thrives, in the rich volcanic soil of the world's largest archipelago in Indonesia. He knew things on dope that he didn't realize he knew. "Imagine," he said with his eyes closed, "a couple of thousand years ago, the Toradja people of Indonesia, who believed that their ancestors came from the stars." He sang a long, repetitive aria about Capella forming, forty-six light-years away from Earth, and dripping people, like silver rain, down into Southeast Asia. Eventually he made his way back to the important differences between washed coffee and dry-processed, to the problem of tariffs, the longshoremen and the questionable romance of the beverage. He felt as if he might never shut up.

Mitch, taking another hit, looked across at Walter. "That bitch," was all he said.

⸺ ⸺

Daniel marshaled his forces and made it to school on Valentine's Day. He was wearing a red sweater that a few months before had stretched across his chest and been put away for Walter. It hung in pleats down the front and the back. Susan, at his side, click-clacked on the tile in her black heels. She looked worldly and rich in her crimson sleeveless linen dress, her hair done up in a French twist and secured with a rhinestone clip. When Walter saw the pair coming down the hall, looking like two human-sized red-hots, he almost shouted, Fire! He guessed in that moment that he was capable of becoming a thug and that he'd enjoy the subterfuge. It would be nothing to walk to the end of the corridor and pull the alarm. He'd smash the glass by the extinguisher, too, and then he'd join a line somewhere along the way, filing calmly, courteously out of the building, an upstanding citizen. Susan was dressed as if she thought Driver's Ed, American Lit, Geometry, Civics, Chemistry and French were going to have cocktail wagons, in place of the teachers' desks, and bands, playing slow jazzy tunes, the curtains drawn for that hazy late-afternoon happy-hour feel.

Mitch and Walter walked down the hall looking at the waxed floor, at the thousands of little brown and green speckles in the tiles sliding under their feet. They had met in the alley before school and smoked a joint in celebration of that little dick Cupid. They smoked out in the cold near the baseball diamond at lunch, in continued observation of the holiday. Walter fell asleep in his World History class, and the teacher, Mr. Windberg, crept up behind him and squawked in his ear. It was an amusing moment for the other students: Walter jumping in his desk, the wooden top holding him like a straitjacket against the force of his shock.

By four o'clock he and Mitch had gotten themselves to Chicago. They both ordered the hamburger platter at the Artists' Café. They ate every scrap, down to the wilted lettuce and the orange tomato. "Do you think we're straightened out?" Mitch said. They never asked each other personal questions. And Walter certainly had never before been a part of the royal We. He swallowed his coffee, stared at his friend, averted his eyes, tried to take another sip from his empty cup. The question implied a shared history; they might have gotten out of bed together that morning. To think—an entire night with Mitch, sharing the privacy of sleep. They might have lingered under the covers, unable to sort out their own smell in the warm pocket of the bed, Mitch's unruly bangs falling over his closed eyes, creases in his cheeks from the pillowcase. They might have risen to the prospect of a long, difficult day, and having come near the end, there was the reasonable query: *Do you think we're straightened out?*

"I—I'm all right," Walter said. "Are you? You okay?"

"Fine." Mitch slapped a quarter for the tip on the table. It was a father's gesture, and when he stood up he jingled the change in his pockets with his hands like a salesman. He could handle anything, and he walked the yellow line on the linoleum out the door to prove it.

They both did well in class that evening. Walter felt that in general he was making progress. It wasn't only that the Rockford Ballet experience had given him confidence. Susan was gone, ding dong the witch is dead, and with her absence came an unexpected freedom. Walter hadn't realized how much she'd constrained him until she'd flown the coop. There was nothing tentative now in the bold strike of his battement frappé, *I love you, love you, Mitch.*

During the center work, Mr. Kenton told the twenty girls to go off to the barre and work on their trouble spots on their own. It was rare that he singled out the boys and gave them their own masculine high-jumping combinations. For fifteen minutes Walter and Mitch, starting at opposite sides of the room, leaped and turned, doing jetés, glissades, cabrioles, ballonnés. As Walter started across the floor one of his earliest fantasies about Mitch flashed before him: the two boys, without much clothing on, dancing alone in a room, the hairs on Mitch's arms sparking gold in the sunlight, Walter moving in and out of his love's clasp.

The sweat spun off their faces as they turned past each other. They stood panting, watching from either side, counting to themselves, their feet and heads marking the beat, waiting to spring after Mrs. Manka played her introductory measures. They took off, flying to the center, meeting for an instant in a landing that was itself the beginning of the next jump. "And two and three," Mr. Kenton called, "point your feet, Walter, one, head up, Mitch, and three, arms through first, and plié and finish." In one sequence they bumped into each other. It was Mitch who placed both of his hands on Walter to set him firmly upon his course.

After class they stripped off their wet clothes, carelessly mopped themselves, rubbed at their wet heads with a towel, wrestled their pants over their damp legs. "Good night," they called into the office to Mr. Kenton.

He was standing at his desk, studying his ledger. He looked up, started to speak, removed his cigarette from his mouth. "Good night then, boys," he said.

The door slammed behind them, but they didn't mean the noise, didn't mean anything in their loose easy motions. "Good night then, boys," Walter whispered. Mr. K. had taken the butt from his mouth so he could speak distinctly, so he could give them his full attention and his benediction. Walter felt as if he could jump down the shaft and land on his feet twelve stories below. "Let's not wait for the elevator," he said to Mitch, lightly touching the sleeve of his friend's blue nylon jacket. "Let's walk."

"Yeah," Mitch said, "fuck the ride."

As if they had been released at that moment like birds into the great wide open, they made for the stairs, arms outstretched, taking them three, four, five at a time. They whooped as they vaulted down and at each floor rushed headlong around the corner to the next flight. When they got to the lobby they pushed past the girls who were just getting off the elevator. They burst into the terrible cold of the night. The air itself seemed to have made all the lines of the city straighter, cleaner, as if the cold with its own mysterious power had gone and hacked away at the stone and metal, trued up the buildings, the parked cars, the traffic lights. On the way to the el station they ducked halfway down the stairs that led to the Grant Park underground garage and rolled a joint. Maybe the grass was a mistake, Walter thought, sucking in the smoke that scratched down his throat. He was elated and the hit might make him feel giddy, or else drowsy, rather than cranking up his mood to the ecstatic.

He was right. In the heat of the train, ten minutes later, they fell asleep, sitting across from each other, their heads banging on the window with every jolt. Their mouths hung open. Walter felt the thin stream of saliva trickling down his chin and could not stop it, could not shut his unhinged jaw. The train went past Cicero, Central, Austin, Ridgeway, Parkview, and their stop, Elmdale. They did not get off. They slept past Oakland and Division. They slept as the train stood at Radley, at the end of the line. The conductor, walking through, checking the cars, had to shake them. "Hey, pal," he said to Mitch, "time to get a move on."

They stood on the platform waiting for the train to reverse itself, to start back to the city. But they didn't get back on. They were awake, out in the still, clear cold, out in the dark. So what if they had missed their stop? What was two miles on a sub-zero night, the goods in their pockets? When the train passed the outer wooden section of the station, they both took a long toke, and another, and one more. They were on their way to getting good and stoned, Handy Spandy, Jack-a-Dandy. Down the long cement stairs, pocked with pigeon crap, wheeee, they hardly touched the steps, and out into the street. Mitch was shaking, holding his thin collar closed with one hand, the other slapping at his left ear, and right ear, back and forth. They would have liked to piss in the snow, to see if they had some steam left inside.

It was the hardware-store window, filled with gallons of paint and a dusty display of brushes, that brought the memory back to Walter. He stopped and stared at the white-and-green tins stacked in a pyramid. It was Thursday night and all the stores were open in Oak Ridge. An old image came to him, and from it, in the blink of an eye, a plan of great beauty. "Ah!" he cried. It was a scheme that surely had been foreordained. "Oh!" He was practically speechless. Mitch was already ahead, at First Fidelity, but he turned when he heard Walter. He was hopping from foot to foot, clapping at his head. His jacket looked to be stationary while he jumped up and down inside it. "Mitch!" Walter called. He never used his friend's name in front of him. He shouted, "Mitch!" He flapped his arms and ran. "Here," he said, pushing a wad of bills into the boy's glove. "Go across the street to the toy store and get us some balloons, some of those big party things, the helium kind. Get a bagful. The biggest bag." He thrilled to his own words.

"What for, what the—"

"I'll tell you, I'll tell you in a minute. My mouth is so dry I can hardly talk. I've had an inspiration, a gift, maybe from G-God, I'm utterly serious. I've got to get some paint back there, at the hardware store."

Walter went into Gilman's. The cold had penetrated his coat, gone through his sweater and his clammy T-shirt. He was freezing and thirsty, but he was so excited the discomfort did not matter. How he loved the worn oak floor of Gilman's, the rows of wooden drawers with washers and drill bits, the nails and screws, the outlets and lightbulbs, the brooms, the hammers, the hoes, the posthole diggers. Everything in the store was a promise for improvement, all around Walter the raw materials of hope. He stood in front of a bin of copper piping and he let himself remember first loving Mitch, first knowing he loved him. He'd had the urge, not to remove Mitch's clothing or kiss him or sidle up close. He'd wanted, instead, to fill balloons with paint and drop them from a high place. He'd wanted to watch them break. It didn't matter that he was bonged out at the moment; he was in command, he knew that the balloons bursting, spilling their colors down the avenue, had been, and was still, the expression and celebration of the feeling that had run so pure through him. He could be potted, pickled, stewed, and all through the merriment and the cloud over his senses he could maintain his standards, keep his eye fixed on the truth.

He picked out four gallons of paint, the primary colors and also white. "Thank you, thanks a million," he said to the gentleman at the counter. Joyce had given him enough money for a month of lunches, for el fare and also a new pair of ballet shoes, and Walter counted all but thirty cents of it into the hand of the storekeeper. "I love paint, don't you?" he said, smoothing the paper labels on the cans. "My grandfather McCloud was in the business. The Nubian Paint Company, it was called, ever hear of it? Black paint and varnish was the specialty. Nubia was some godforsaken kingdom in the Nile River Valley, I think. All over the map with religion and conquered the pants off of Egypt way back when. Got Jesus sometime after B.C., but then the Moslems captured the entire nation-state, or whatever the heck it was, no more Christmas, you bow five times a day to the east, or else. Some dam project, excuse me, a dam project, and also a damnable one, flooded the whole place a few years back. Anyway, thanks a bundle, and you have a good night!"

He whistled as he walked out the door—God, but he was feeling fine! He could sleep through history class and educate Mr. Gilman all in the same day. The brittle air was sharp in his nostrils and went stinging down into his lungs. Who cared? Who cared! Under the heat lamps in the bus shelter on Lake Street, Walter explained his plan to Mitch. It took sixty seconds. Like the proofs their geometry teacher, Miss Guest, so loved, this idea too, was simple, inevitable and elegant. They took off at a run, home to the McClouds', each boy swinging two gallons by the wire handles.

When they got to Walter's block they slowed. Heads down, the cans to their chests. The fact that they were supposed to be model young men for the duration of Daniel's sickness came back to them only briefly, and then was gone with Walter's whisper, "Who cares?" They noted that the McCloud house was dark except for the light in the back, the light over the kitchen table. Good. They slipped in the front door, closing it softly behind them. It was Daniel, Joyce and Susan there in the kitchen, they could tell by the boy voice, the light voice and the squall of the slut. There was the smell of fish. Duke's tags dinking his pan of water. Robert McCloud would be at work until ten or eleven, busy with a season of rush orders for the invaluable nut and bolt.

Susan's glittering laugh obscured the noise of the marauders creeping up the front stairs. "If I was dying, fish is the last thing I'd eat," Walter murmured as he opened the attic door. "The place stinks like the reedy waters where the fat perch—"

"Sh—shush." Mitch shook Walter's arm. "Shut up."

The attic was just as cold as the enormous outdoors. They stood in the middle of the floor and took a hit. The genius of their project was droll all right, droll as hell freezing over. Walter couldn't help sniggering, the laughter coming out of his nose like blasts of steam. "Sh, sh, sh, sh," Mitch kept on between his own giggles. "Should we take off our shoes?" Why they hadn't thought of that detail was funny in itself, and Mitch had to clap his hand over his mouth in an effort to swallow his horselaugh. They stumbled around trying to keep their traps closed, trying to find a screwdriver so they could open the paint. The attic was lit by the thin bluish lights coming up from the alley. There was no reason a screwdriver should be lying around on the attic floor. Walter walked in circles, appealing to God. "P-p-please, God," he chattered, "a f-f-f-ucking screwdriver." And, as if He were looking upon them, Mitch went straight to the windowsill and found a file.

"Ask, and it shall be given you," Mitch recited, knowledgeable after years of Saturday catechism class. "Knock," he said, prying off the lid of the red can, "and it shall be opened unto you."

They couldn't see very well, and their hands were stiff. Walter had enough clarity to move the rug so they could spill on the floor. They'd cover the mess over with the green wool piece of shit when they were done. He found an old cracked plastic bowl they could pour over. They were thinking! Ace derelicts even if they were wearing shoes. They weren't so swacked they couldn't fucking think! A funnel would have been nice, but you couldn't ask for everything and get it at the snap of the fingers. Mitch held the balloon necks open with his thumb and first two fingers, and Walter poured the paint down, the rubber growing, swelling, the body of each balloon dipping to the floor. The two boys smirked at the lewdness of the ripe balloons, the pregnant balloons, the knocked-up-with-no-husband balloons. The red house paint covered Mitch's hands and ran down the arms of the jacket.

"Mom probably thinks we're the squirrels in the attic," Walter said. They opened their mouths wide and screamed under their breaths. "Squirrels!" Mitch managed to say once, before he doubled over. "Jesus, Walter," he gasped. "You are so fu-fuh—" But he could not finish the sentence. It was hilarious, and he, himself, Wally, Wally McCloud, was priceless, funny ha-ha, hysterical. He was going to die laughing, perish, he thought, go dead in the water, kick the bucket, meet his Maker and bite the dust; he was going to be like a cat with nine lives, nine deaths, so he could use all of the expressions for his untimely end.

They gulped the air. They cupped their hands at their mouths, trying to feed oxygen to themselves, trying to get a shock by ingesting the cold. It didn't help. They couldn't stop. They laughed under their breath, in a stream, as if they were humming. How they filled and tied the twenty-five balloons with assorted colors they could not account for afterward. They vaguely remembered mixing the shades in the bulb of the balloon and Walter tying the knots, cursing and blowing at his fingers. The finished product went into an empty cardboard box that had once held a chest of drawers. Their sleeves and arms and hands were a brownish purple by the time the balloons were all filled. "We're ready, pal, oh pal," Walter said. He had never called anyone pal, and the sound of it in his own mouth made him feel very far away from himself. He thought that he'd perhaps been acquitted of being Walter McCloud, and that he could use train conductors' expressions freely, without being false, without recrimination. *Time, pal, to get a move on.*

He carefully opened the window, Mitch saying, "Sh, sh, sh, sh, sh, sh," at every creak. Leg over the sill, hop, other leg over. The sleeping-porch roof was flat, no danger of slipping down an incline, falling three stories to the ground and killing themselves. The box of balloons was inside, right by the window, within easy reach. They looked over the neighborhood. Outside the hardware store, when the vision had come to Walter, there had been no question about where they'd do the balloon toss. He had not had to explain why the Gambles were their target; no need to justify what had long ago been laid out for the carport roof in Mrs. Gamble's heavenly chart.

For once in twenty years the Gambles' yard light wasn't on, and the carport spots were also off. It had to be the work of the Lord. They shook each other's painty hands.

"Congratulations, Anderson!"

"Congratulations, McCloud!"

"Her roof will be like a Jackson Pollock painting," Walter said. "She'll love it. She'll be crazy about the top of her Shrine that will look like it came from the Art Institute, in the bargain extra-satin finish of latex supergloss."

They lay down on the shingles, writhing, holding their wide-stretched mouths and their empty, aching stomachs. Mitch's laughter was so thin and high it sounded like whining. Walter curled up, his cheek against the shingles, against what felt like the skin of a pineapple. He was panting or he was laughing, he couldn't tell which, each spasm coming up from his worn-out, racked diaphragm. It was funny how it wasn't even funny anymore. They had to get up and start whacking the Gambles' carport roof with the party balloons or they'd freeze to death with their mouths open, still laughing; both of them dead and laughing, something on the order of chickens running around after their heads are gone.

Mitch was still groaning, holding his gut, when Walter went to the window, reached for a balloon inside, in the box, tiptoed to the edge of the roof, and dropped the bomb down on Madame's precious carport. It made a satisfying *flump* along with the splash. He couldn't see the results in the dark, but he knew it had hit the seventeen-by-fifteen-foot target, eighteen or so feet below. All it took was the first shot to sober up Mitch, to get him doing a soft-shoe number across the shingles to the arsenal.

Some balloons they let drop, straight down, no grace in the fall with the dead weight of the paint. Others they hurled, the smash brought on by their own hands. The Gambles in their breakfast nook, eating their shepherd's pie, were watching a news segment on Patty Hearst. Walter tossed one balloon up into the air, using the underhand throw he'd learned out in the alley playing Horse with a basketball. The balloon was heavy and didn't make much of an arc. Walter, watching it rise just a little, and slam down to the roof, lost his balance. He felt himself lurching, in slow motion, of course, tipping, a hand, an arm, his head, going over, no strength to fight gravity, no hope to cling by his fingernails to the downspout. In daylight he would not have been alarmed. He wasn't as close to the edge as he felt himself to be and he was casting left rather than forward. There was Mitch's hand, in Walter's own hand, pulling him back from the gutter, pulling him to safety.

"Fuck," he breathed, holding tight.

"Fuck," Mitch gasped, letting him go.

It seemed to both of them a nearly fatal slip. Later they joked about Walter falling and becoming a part of the Pollock masterpiece, the cream of brains and intestines, the purple of liver, the deep brown stain of blood, in one shining blot. Out on the roof they quickly dispersed the rest of the balloons. "Careful," Walter said, as if they needed reminding. They climbed back into the house, and while Walter slowly, inch by inch, let down the creaking window, Mitch put the lids back on the paint. They hid the cans underneath a piece of furniture Walter referred to as the old chifforobe, in honor of Harper Lee. The green rug would cover the spills nicely, and like good children folding laundry they each took two corners and carried it to the disaster. They stole down the attic stairs, one at a time, their hearts beating in the great hollow of their heads. They stepped. And they waited, listening, breathing. They took another Mother-may-I baby step toward the bottom. In the upstairs hall forced air from the register blasted them square in the face and they opened their mouths to it, as if it were water. They squatted and pressed their numb hands to the flood of warmth. There was absolutely no feeling in their hands, but so what? They were red and cracked and when the blood inside them thawed and the slurry began to run they'd sting and smart. So what!

"That bitch is still laughing her goddamn fucking head off," Mitch said. They could hear Susan, from the kitchen, singing, rather than laughing, singing "Shall we dance?"

It was not easy to make their way down the front steps. They walked as if they had no body between the tips of their toes and their shoulders. Their arms were out for balance, and all of the action was in their pecking heads and their big toes. Susan was trying to teach Daniel a dance—ballroom figures, Walter said to himself, for people who are trying to patch up their marriage. Some spazzy rumba. They could hear her saying, "One, two, three—that's right." Walter froze at the door when she said, "You've got a better sense of rhythm than your brother! You're good, Dan." He was about to open his mouth to protest when Mitch yanked him out of the house. The door slammed, ringing clear through the night. They heard it slam again and again, as if the noise had its own continuous source, as if it were making ripples, out and out, into the yard, the parkway, the street. Both of them ran down the porch, jumped over the railing into the bushes, where they crouched for a minute, side by side, and did not breathe. Sunshine Gamble took her time finishing her business, and when she was done she trotted to the fence and barked. At her alarm the boys tumbled against each other, Walter on the hard ground, Mitch on top of him.

Joyce did not come to the door. They waited. She did not turn on the porch light and open up. She did not call, "Is anyone there?" Mrs. Gamble did not flick the one switch in her kitchen that activated front spots, back spots, garage and carport lights. Only Sunshine Gamble had heard. They lay still, Mitch's head down over Walter's left shoulder. They gave themselves the luxury of breath. Walter's chest rose up against Mitch's chest. He felt shy breathing a little more deeply, rib against rib, those bones, it seemed, even through the jackets, as articulated as fingers. It was Mitch who shifted so that he could kiss Walter; Walter has never forgotten that it was Mitch who kissed his upper lip and his lower lip, Mitch who licked along the fuzz of his coming mustache. When he tilted his head to follow the beauty boy's mouth Mitch pushed him down. He kissed Walter's face, small, feathery kisses at first—worshipful, Walter might have said—and he went on, kissing down his cold white neck. With the cotton glove from his pocket he wiped the one tear falling sidewise to Walter's ear.

Time stop, Walter wished. Hold and hold on. He was trembling so that the stiff brown grasses next to him waved, as if a little wind had come up. Mitch was at his lips again, playing over them, flicking his tongue, deft and quick, lizard motions to Walter's open mouth. Fill me, Walter meant to say with the gaping hole of his mouth, I'm ready,

ready to catch the wet pulse of your tongue, my body beating in time, meeting the rhythms of your body. This is how, this is how, this is how we will be one: mouth to mouth, sweet tongue to tongue, flittering hearts below and, farther down, throbbing cocks alert as hunting dogs, straining at the lead.

Without warning, there was the wide sky overhead, Mitch was gone, through the bushes, running low, like a sniper. The cold swept through Walter, through his unzipped jacket, his sweater, his undershirt, the air clinging, like a haze, to his skin. He wasn't sure he could move, wasn't sure it might be better to freeze at this point, like an Arctic explorer, having come so far. If he returned, back to the journey, he might have to do something barbaric, abandon the other loved ones or eat his own pup. He was careful not to move his tongue over the smallest ice crystals that had formed around his mouth. There would from now on be a whole new realm to want. He would no longer care for the forest dreams or the comfort of the sun. He would wish again and again for that strip of cold earth under the bushes, the cold stars, the small white crystals around his own lips that had been left as proof. *Mitch was here.*

He felt the chill through him, swirling to his center, the mist of it leaking out and in and everywhere like dry ice, like something you should be able to see. He shinnied slowly along under the porch, kneeled when he came to the grass, stood straight, and walked up the stairs, shoving his telltale hands into his pockets. He was brand-new, improved, unrecognizable even to himself. He threw open the door. "Hi," he called from the hall. "Hello, everyone. I'm back. I'm really home now."

Eight

MARCH
1996

Walter drove to the Easter celebration at Lake Margaret wondering what bit of truth he would dress up in a cockamamy story, what scrap he would inadvertently tell Lucy this time around. Some morsel that would give her that lovely shocked look. He remembered how idiotic he'd felt at Thanksgiving babbling at anyone who sat next to him, and he vowed to keep his mouth shut, to say nothing. He'd try to act like a regular guy and talk about sports, offense, defense, no harm, no foul.

Uncle Ted and Aunt Jeannie were going to the Bahamas in April, over the real Easter Sunday; Jeannie had therefore sorted through her children's busy schedules and decreed that the family celebrate the holiday at the lake on March 2. Sue Rawson made no bones about telling the relatives that it was just as well to get it over with, the sooner, the better. On that rainy Saturday the relatives gathered to prepare the crown roast, the twice-baked potatoes, the string beans amandine, the pineapple salad and the traditional Lake Margaret Easter dessert. The cake, baked in a lamb mold, was a family recipe that had been traced to a Frances Rose Rawson of Lebanon, New Hampshire, 1816–1903.

Aunt Jeannie had made Ted order brown eggs through his distributor at the Jewel for the cake, and while she beat the yolks with the

1950 MixMaster in the Lake Margaret kitchen she rhapsodized over the ritual. She had eaten the cake every Easter for seventy-three years; she'd baked it herself for more than four decades; she'd never had a failure, never changed the receipt, she called it, by as much as a drop of vanilla or a grain of sugar. The secret, if anyone wondered, was lard. She had looked all over the house for Francie, in the hope that her oldest daughter would come watch the preparation. To Walter she said, "For goodness' sakes, it will one day be up to her to carry on the tradition, and I'm not sure she knows how!"

Francie hated yellow cake and had gone to the woods, in the rain, with her cousin Celeste. At Thanksgiving, Francie had told Celeste about Skip, her twenty-six-year-old lover. Celeste was not a risk taker and she was drawn to the danger of Francie's story. They walked close under one umbrella and scuffed up the thick carpet of wet leaves. "How long," Francie asked her cousin, "can a woman put up with a doctor husband who spends all his free time in a greenhouse pinching back leaves and mixing potting soil in a bucket?"

Francie wanted Skip, and she was bound to have him, to leave Roger to the sex life of his stamens and pistils. No one but Celeste knew how far from the fold Francie had strayed, and in her absence Walter stood by the counter watching his aunt sift the sugar onto a square of waxed paper. He was a little bit embarrassed by his contribution to the meal, and he thought he might redeem himself if he paid homage to Jeannie. The rehearsals for *South Pacific* had been going late and he hadn't had time to make real hors d'oeuvres, to whip up some spinach puffs and stuffed mushrooms. He had sliced carrots, broccoli and celery, and in the center of his sectioned tray he'd placed the plastic carton of grocery-store dip. "I'm sorry about my—crudités," he said.

She was engrossed in her cake and didn't care what he'd brought. "Some moments are historical," she said, folding the egg whites into the batter. "The forty-fifth time I've done this, right here, on this exact spot. It should make me feel old, but it doesn't!"

Walter hoped, as he nodded and smiled, that she would never become feeble or depressed or senile. He hoped she'd make a good end, that her lights would go out when she was her vibrant self, dressed for a party. As soon as the cake was in the oven and the show over, he excused himself and went into the living room to help his father build a fire. It was not a job that required two grown men, but Robert had asked for a hand. They knelt side by side, crumpling up the paper and blowing on the kindling. It seemed to Walter that his father was suddenly grayer, his brown eyes a little bleary, but when he cracked his smile, his gap-toothed smile, there was that same old light in his face. Walter told Robert that Otten's basketball team, the Braves, had gone to regionals, and so far won every game. They were almost certainly going to make it to state, led by their star, Bill Pierce.

"Anyone make a stink yet about the team name?" his father asked companionably. "Politically correct and all that?"

"Not yet. No, not in Otten. There's a scowling redskin over the basket, too. He's got the scalping look in his eye, definitely not the peace-pipe sort. He's not someone a self-respecting Injin would want to claim as a Native American."

The smoke from the fire drifted into the room before it got sucked up the draft and the two men coughed and waved their arms at the haze. Robert slowly got to his feet and went to open the windows. Walter sat back on his haunches and breathed in the fine ash and must and mildew. He figured he was in good shape and could afford to inhale as many Lake Margaret dust mites as he wanted. Every night after school he'd been going at it on his Nordic Track, to the music of *Swan Lake, Serenade* and *Giselle.* He supposed that skiing in place with a soaring heart, his hips banging at the gray padded support, was a disappointing end for someone who had once aspired to be a dancer. Some might say he was pathetic, a flop, clattering away on his exercise machine. On the bright side, his calves were firming up, he'd gained strength in his arms and he'd lost a few pounds. The workout was strenuous enough to drench his clothes and clear his head. He was far from the ideal, but it was the best he could do. His new fantasy was to become Bill Pierce out on the court, and he always closed his drapes so that no Peeping Toms could witness his stab at a jock's life.

Lucy appeared at Walter's side as the papers in the grate curled and turned black. He and his father had almost asphyxiated everyone downstairs, but the fire was taking to the wood as if the twigs had been laid by the Boy Scouts. Lucy bent down, warming her knees and her hands. Walter noticed a gold locket the size of a nickel between her breasts, nestled in the pink fuzz of her sweater.

"Did Aunt Jeannie give that necklace to you?" he asked. It did not seem impossible that their aunt, at seventy-three, might unburden herself of some of her less valuable reproductions.

"No," Lucy said. "Marc did, for Valentine's Day." She smiled down at the burning wood, thinking about her Valentine's gift to Walter, the box of tulips that she'd had sent to his school with a mysterious note. "From your admirer," she'd written. If he didn't bring it up, if he hadn't figured it out, she might tell him later in the day. She had spent a fortune on the mail-order flowers, and she had no idea if he would think of her along the way or if he'd never guess. With her long thumbnail she opened the heart and stretched the chain to show Walter. On one side was a tiny head shot of Marc, and on the other, the whole length of little Linda in a tutu.

"Ahhhh," Walter said.

"What did *you* do on Valentine's Day, Walt?" She snapped the locket shut and patted it in place against her sweater.

"What did I do?" He felt remiss, as if he'd forgotten that Valentine's Day was a family holiday, one that required a meal with specific foods, an outing, offerings at the temple. She stood up, and she tapped her foot on the brick hearth, her arms crossed over her chest, waiting for him to answer. She looked imperious all of a sudden. "What did I do?" he repeated. She never asked him questions about his romantic life and he had always credited her with knowing better. "As, as always," he said, "I waited around from morning until night for that certain someone to put a token of affection in my decorated shoe box."

She was still tapping her foot. It was the wrong answer, he could see. What, he wondered, was the correct response? What would Marc have said to make the buzzer go off, to win the grand prize? The question deserved a retort, and a proper man's retort should probably include something raunchy, a smutty joke set in a sports arena. Marc was sitting in the next room reading *Popular Mechanics,* and Lucy, humorless and strict, with her hair ratcheted into a French braid, was standing over him, waiting. He wondered later if in fact his answer was for

Marc's benefit, if within his cobbled psyche he was stupid enough to want to impress his brother-in-law.

It seemed as if he should use the words in a sentence. "On Valentine's Day," he began. "On Valentine's Day those of us without loved ones in the immediate area lit a bonfire on the football field. We tried to talk the freshmen girls into sacrificing themselves, but not a one was a virgin, so we gave it up."

"Uuh," she said. "You're not funny anymore. That's disgusting." She slapped the box of matches on the table and went down the hall.

Had she ever thought him funny? She had been lighthearted only moments before, showing him the locket, and without warning, without cause, she'd had a mood swing. He was confused by her censure, not only because of the criticism but because he had gained something, her past high opinion, and lost it, in the same breath. If he'd been his usual sunny self, instead of a tired English teacher at mid-semester, he would never have made that remark to Lucy. Robert had returned and was both blowing into the logs and fanning the flame with the bellows. Walter, to his horror, found himself saying, "I don't understand that—woman." He realized right away that he had paved the way for a man-to-man talk about the inscrutable females in the family, about what it takes to manage them. He would have to hold up his end in the sort of discussion Daniel as a matter of course would have had with Dad at the holiday gatherings.

Robert slapped Walter's back and gripped his shoulder. The universal father hold, Walter thought, and the palsy-walsy smack that was the preamble to talk. His father had made his way through parenthood admirably, without much formal pedagogy. Still, Walter waited, for the advice, the personal testimony, the warnings. He had asked for it. Robert held on for a minute, and when his hand came away it rested so quickly, so gently, on his grown son's cheek.

At Otten High, Valentine's Day had passed more or less without incident, as far as Walter could tell. The Spirit Committee had decorated the lunchroom with pink and red and white balloons, and at a table by the office the band had sold flowers with the promise of in-class delivery. Walter had woken up that morning wondering if his students were celebrating by getting high, or were already in the sweaty grip of a loved one. He hoped those few who had read the last chapter of *Great Expectations* had enjoyed Estella and Pip's exit into the starlight. He thought through the spastic movement of his day, first hour through eighth hour, freshmen and sophomores, prep period, Swiss cheese sandwich for lunch, more sophomores, more freshmen, hall monitor duty, a buzz every forty minutes, change, change, change, and after school *South Pacific.* He would sit erect on the one folding chair in the gym during rehearsal, watching his cast stumble through their lines, moving helter-skelter, flagrantly disregarding the blocking he had shown them so painstakingly time and time again. He would walk them through their moves with the patience of an ant, and he would also praise his leading lady if she showed any detectable improvement in her dance numbers, if she got herself across the stage just once without evoking the camel heading into a sandstorm. He naturally would not be able to keep from singing along to "Some Enchanted Evening," "Bali Ha'i," and his favorite, "I'm Going to Wash That Man Right Out of My Hair."

He sometimes wondered if he wanted Mitch to hear about him through some extraordinary small-world encounter. Trishie Gamble might run into him at a gallery opening of her photographs in Del Mar, and she'd tell Mitch that Walter was teaching English at Otten High, as well as directing the school musicals. The danger lay in the fact that Mitch might possibly have developed a sense of irony in his twenty-odd years away from Oak Ridge. He'd laugh out loud, so glad that his old friend was condemned to remain within the walls of an institution that not only had the age-old smell of B.O. and fried food kept warm under heat lamps, but was also a place that came right out and marked the poor loser's painful anniversaries. Walter, running the scene through his mind with Trishie Gamble as the messenger, always concluded that it was better for Mitch not to know what had become of him. He would have to satisfy himself with the thought that Miss Amy, wherever she was, would approve of his directing ability as well as the dances he had choreographed for Nellie and the girls.

Although he never celebrated Valentine's Day as Lucy might have wished, Walter had always observed February 14. She couldn't fault him for ignoring the date. He had kept it, privately, trying to mark what was long gone, trying to hold up to the light what he knew had existed, however briefly. In spite of the passage of time he had not been able to reduce his teenage prank on Valentine's Day, 1973, and the aftermath, to an anecdote. He never told it. He once had begun to whisper the story to a lover, but the man right off had not been impressed by the concept of a paint-filled balloon.

In Otten, Walter had lain in bed that Valentine's morning, and he thought that if he was religious he'd light a candle every February 14 or burn a stick of incense. It seemed to him that there should be some ritual, a lamb cake, a string of ancient words to mutter, in order to observe the day with respect. He would pay his dollar for the votive candle and light it, not for the dead and not strictly for remembrance. Why, then? he asked himself in the pearly winter dawn of his bedroom. Why light the candle at all if not for remembrance? The past was swallowing up the year and becoming more real than the present, and he might as well acknowledge that it was so with a cupcake, a sparkler, a handful of candy hearts.

He jammed another pillow under his head. There was nothing in his room except the futon and one painting on the wall of a pink butterfly, the work of a dead friend from his New York era. He had spent years at the dollhouse shop and he could reduce it to a fifteen-second dream. The Oak Ridge life intruded like a pushy woman sticking her nose into Walter's business. He could sometimes shut it out by thinking of the round, earnest face of Betsy Rutule. Or he could close his eyes and hear Kimmy Roth, the inert girl with a voice like a charm who played Nellie Forbush in *South Pacific*. She opened her mouth and Walter got chills down his spine, but every time she moved the spell was broken and she was simply herself, a tall ungainly girl with the gait of a pack animal. He would have liked to tack on a prologue to the play, a short scene where Nellie gets her leg blown off by a land mine so that she could zip around the stage in a wheelchair for the rest of the show. The kid he'd cast as Emile could sing and he delivered his lines with confidence, but he was hampered by being about a foot shorter than Kimmy, and with his partially shaved head did not have the look of a debonair Frenchman. Walter didn't know what he was going to do about that hair, beyond making Emile wear a pith helmet for the entire evening. He'd managed to get his seventh-hour problem girl to try out, and he'd brazenly given her the part of Bloody Mary even though she was not much of a musician. It looked as if she was going to have to talk her way through the songs in her grass skirt and the red bikini top that he'd decided should be covered with a sheer blouse, to play it safe.

In bed he clapped his right hand around his left wrist, as if he meant to catch the thirty-eight-year-old Walter McCloud. It was proof, wasn't it, that Mitch and Daniel were distant if he was troubling himself with the particulars of *South Pacific*? Were his students less real to him than the characters of his high school career? From the vantage point of his futon that early in the morning they were all remote, all equally insubstantial. And yet if he didn't build a bulwark against the images, he looked across the room and Otten, the Braves included, faded away. He saw himself more than twenty years before, waiting to hear from Mrs. Gamble. The fact that it had taken her three days to discover her newly decorated carport roof still had shock value.

Walter could not remember the incident without marveling, each time, at the delay. How could she have missed it? Trishie and Greg Gamble's bedrooms looked down on the flat surface that did somewhat resemble a Jackson Pollock painting. Walter inspected the roof first thing when he woke the day after the happening. He hadn't anticipated that their—work—would look quite so vivid. Even the concoctions they'd made at the end, when they were getting carried away, when they had mixed up murky browns and purple, were surprisingly lively in the morning light. The splatters had the cartoon look of open mouths spraying angry words. He and Mitch, the two of them, together, had done an impressive job making the colors in the dead of night. Twenty-five brilliant bursts, some overlapping, some distinguished. The fragments of the broken balloons were stuck in the smears of paint and gave the splashes an interesting textural touch, and in the winter sun the supergloss latex had a plasticky shine. Walter was pretty sure that Pollock would have approved. One of the tosses, he noticed with a gasp, had hit the side of the house. Perhaps that was the pitch that had made Walter almost fall to his death. Mitch had rescued him; he vowed never to forget that Mitch had grabbed his hand and pulled him from the edge. The enormity of such a thing, a friend saving your life. He couldn't dwell on it now, couldn't comprehend his debt of gratitude until they'd gotten through the next phase, until after they'd been discovered and punished.

He had gone down to breakfast and sat straight in his chair in front of the boxes of cereal on the table. He had thought that he'd loved Mitch before, but that old feeling, he realized, had been nothing. As usual he saw through Mitch's eyes, so that everything he touched and looked at and heard and read recalled his friend, his Romeo. His beloved. He never thought himself alone, and even in private he did the simplest tasks and ablutions for Mitch's benefit. That was one of the chief powers of love, he'd learned, that it could so beautifully erase a personality. He had lived with the condition for several years, nothing new about carrying Mitch just under the skin. But that night, hidden in the shrubs, it was as if Mitch had opened a door for Walter to step through. Each kiss had brought Walter closer to the threshold, until he believed that he'd safely crossed over into Mitch's every moment and every thought. He hardly dared to think it was possible, and yet it had been Mitch, after all, who had moved to kiss Walter. Mitch, when he woke in his bed at home, might think of the friend, the Romeo—the beloved—with the lush head of curls and the sincere and poignantly tapered brown eyes. He might put his foot over the bed and think, *Walter,* and feel down through the pile of the carpet to the skin of the rug and breathe, *Walter,* and put his hands to the imaginary form in front of him and say, *Walter.*

Joyce was at the sink scrubbing a pot, talking to herself while Walter sat at the table yearning and feeling himself yearned for. It was more than double the longing, different from everyday multiplication, and he had to hold his stomach with one hand, his chest with the other, to contain the ache of it. Mrs. Gamble was going to discover the roof and find him out and have him arrested, but he wasn't going to care because he had love on his side, love of the sort she had never known with her dingy hair pinned up in curlers and her flat, low-slung serviceable buttocks and her nicotine-stained fingers. She may have been wooed, routinely, by Mr. Gamble, but while he said his pretty words she'd have been thinking with pleasure about cleaning up after the future dogs of her married bliss. There was no passion in the gray flesh of Mrs. Gamble, and never had been, and when she came after Walter he could effortlessly dip back into that scene under the bushes; he could surround himself, protect himself, with the blinding shield of tenderness and desire.

He didn't pour his cereal. He sat with his hands folded in his lap, waiting to use his new might in the crisis. The siren would sound, not from the police station, but from some gadget in Mrs. Gamble's apron pocket. His mother dried the pot and put it away and began to scour a frying pan, shining the copper to its original luster. Mold was overtaking the house, hairy green circles in the bread box, white patches on the oranges, a dark rot along the counter seams. The refrigerator smelled of decay, but Joyce wasn't going to let any of her pots show the least sign of use. Years later Walter told Susan that the seven pieces in the Revere Ware collection, hanging on the rack by the stove, were Joyce's own sweet way of wearing her heart on her sleeve.

He had planned to wait for as long as it took Mrs. Gamble to come, but after some time without any notice he got hungry. Better to eat some Cheerios, he figured, keep up his strength for the incarceration. He chewed, paused to listen, chewed. He expected a cry from the other house and the slap of footsteps down the back stairs and the brattle of the gate. She was going to pound on the McCloud door soon, of course she would. How could the neighborhood sorceress fail to sense the change over her own roof when she usually sniffed out marital problems and canine diseases before the husband had a clue, before the puppy had its first itch?

"Come over here, you little fucker," Walter whispered to Duke when Joyce went into the bathroom. He spoke to the dog in a way that would have made Mitch laugh. "You say a word about the business to that dumb blond Sunshine next door and I'll put you through the meat grinder." Duke averted his eyes and curled up on the rug, his wet nose to his long, mousy hind feet. Walter could hear Mitch's laughter in the room, and he reached across the table to touch the hand he could so easily conjure down to the pale hair between the joints and the knuckles.

When Walter walked to school that morning it was quiet all down the street. Either no one was watching or everyone was. It was hard to say. Through his first two classes he waited to be called down to the office, to his dean, Mr. Wilson. After the accusation he would shake his head and say, "Mr. Wilson, I'm afraid I don't know what you're talking about." It was more difficult to anticipate what he'd do when he saw Mitch, in third hour, in Geometry. How, for example, would they look at each other? Would Mitch smile coyly and pick up his pencil, and turn back once more for an affectionate glance before they had to plunge into their proofs? Should Walter go to his desk while all the students were taking their seats and squat there, and ask softly, intimately, How are you?

In World History, Walter had the horrifying thought that he'd imagined the kiss in the bushes. Was he the fool, dreaming that Mitch could love him? It had happened, he said to himself, it had! He looked at the photograph of doomed Nicholas and Alexandra in his textbook and he resolved that he would approach Mitch in math class. There was no need to waver, to be unsure. There had been frost on Walter's upper lip the night before because of Mitch's advances. Mitch had had the courage to make the move, and it was the least Walter could do to go to the desk and say, *The night was so cold and there was danger. Are you all right this morning?*

When the bell rang at the end of second hour Walter couldn't keep from running through the halls, running to that moment when he'd look, and he'd ask, and in return—in return wouldn't there be a signal, unintelligible to everyone else in the room, a sign for Walter? Was it too much to hope that Mitch would hold his gaze?

Walter was still outside the class waiting when Miss Guest began the lesson. Mitch wasn't very often late, but after yesterday, carrying the gallons of paint all those blocks, his arms would certainly be sore. He was probably standing at his locker, fumbling for the right book, readjusting his load. Miss Guest had to go to the door and ask Walter if he hadn't heard the bell, if he didn't realize that they had three difficult theorems to prove in thirty-five minutes.

We can't start without Mitch, Walter wanted to say.

"Is there something the matter with you?" Miss Guest asked. "Are you unwell?"

"Am I unwell?" Walter said, tripping into the room behind her, making his way to his seat in the M section by following the usual smell of chlorine from Samantha Martin's wet hair.

Five minutes passed and Mitch didn't rush in with a tardy slip. Walter couldn't find the right page, couldn't remember what he'd done with his homework. *Where are you, Mitch?* Had the paint on Mitch's sleeve given him away? He'd been interrogated by his mother, that was it. Walter's pencil kept falling from his grip. Would Mitch squeal? Would he lie to save his friend? Ten minutes, fifteen, twenty, and the seat remained empty. Walter stared at a triangle Miss Guest put on the board. Good for Pythagoras out in the Italian countryside inventing his syncretistic philosophy. Music and math are related to everything under the sun. Susan plus Mitch plus Walter equals a triangle. Susan and Daniel and Mitch and Walter expands to a square. They could double-date. There would be harmony, surely what Pythagoras had in mind all along. *Where are you, Mitch?* What if Mrs. Gamble had zeroed in on Mitch, what if she'd gotten him? Walter imagined her yanking Mitch's hair, trying to get the truth out of him. Mitch would capitulate in a minute. He would think he could withstand the torture, but Walter could tell anyone that the solid young man of Swedish-Irish extraction was sensitive, and had a low threshold for pain. He'd scream once and let everything out of the bag.

That first afternoon following the prank Walter skipped ballet class. It wasn't only that he'd spent his el fare and his lunch money on party balloons and four gallons of paint. He could get by for a while on his birthday cash and he had a savings account at First Fidelity. He could forge Joyce's signature on the withdrawal slip that required parental approval. It wasn't for lack of funds that he stayed home. For one thing, he didn't feel so good, and for another he was worried about his partner in crime. He needed to find a way to make contact, to see how the land, in all possible directions, lay. His father was at work, his brother was getting a transfusion with the girlfriend and the mother, and he must seize the day, make a plan, arrange for communication.

He wasn't inside his own back door when the phone rang. "It's you, it's you, it's you," he whispered, running to the phone.

"Hi," he said, breathlessly.

"What's new?"

Mitch, Mitch, Mitch, Mitch! What was not new! He was new, Walter was new, the afternoon sunlight streaming in the kitchen was new, and so were the bushes, the hard ground and the gleamy stars.

"Any news?" Mitch persisted.

"You mean about *that*?"

"No, I mean the Vietnam War. Is there still a fucking cease-fire? Is the peace holding?"

Their own signals. This was the way they would speak from now on, in code, and they'd understand each other. "All quiet," Walter said.

"What do you mean?"

"Silent as the grave."

"You're kidding."

"Kidding? Would I kid about—"

"I've got an earache."

"So I thought," Walter said. Came from not wearing a hat. He loved Mitch's ears, loved the ridges along the top of his auricle and the fact that he had no lobes to speak of, that the pad of flesh attached so economically right to his head. "You know the old saw," he said, 'Always leave your campsite the way you found it'? I came home to check for bears, to air out the tent."

Mitch hung up. The phone was dead, no good-byes, no secret sign-off. It didn't matter. The message was delivered, the message received, it was understood, nothing further to discuss. Perfectly natural to keep it short, Walter said to himself. He'd go right to work to scrub away their tracks, get rid of the evidence. If Mitch was well he'd by all means be at Walter's side working until the dust had settled, until the attic felt as untouched and still as it had the day before.

First he shook the hall rug over the back-porch railing, so that Mrs. Gamble could see, if she wanted, his painty fingernails, Exhibit A. He beat the rug to a slow, even nyah, nyah. No need for Mitch to have said anything else, not so much as a So long. Hang up and get on with the operation. In the attic he examined the floor, the window and the roof for splatters and spills. With some turpentine and a rag he was able to remove the handprints on the sash and the sill. They were his prints and Mitch's prints, mixed up together on the wood, hand over hand.

The night before, he'd had a difficult time getting the paint off his fingers and sleeves in the downstairs powder room, and there'd been more trouble cleaning the sink. There was also the matter of the rag.

It seemed that the stain was going to transfer from object to object, damage after damage, Walter McCloud, the wily little perpetrator, like the Cat in the Hat. The paint under the blue rug in the attic was amazingly thick, as if it had not just spilled and dried but clotted. It was a significant amount of paint, but there wasn't any reason Walter could think of for his parents to take up the carpet, not until they moved, when Robert retired, when Walter was long gone, off into life. He opened the window and aired the place while he sawed the large cardboard box into scores of jagged strips with a kitchen knife.

It got dark early and he quickened his pace as the light faded. He would have to make two trips to Oak Ridge's brand-new recycling center, four blocks away, and he wanted to be done by the time the invalid and his entourage were home. The night was warmer than the last and the clouds hung low. It might snow, and he might leave tracks, coming and going and coming and going. Mrs. Gamble would have to investigate quickly as the snow got deeper and covered his traces; the double journey would make her wonder, would make her think through the logistics and the scope of their enterprise.

He sneaked out the side basement door, the only McCloud exit that commanded no view of the Gamble house. "You will heel," Walter said to the dog. "Do you hear me?" He put the leash around his wrist and in each hand carried a shopping bag. If Mrs. Gamble let the dogs out and if she stormed at him, tried to grab him or inspect the debris in the bags, he'd give Duke orders. "You'd go for her tough neck, wouldn't you, there's a good pup. You'd do it for me, wouldn't you, boy?" Walter asked kindly, as if Duke were his Old Yeller.

At the recycling center he pitched the half-empty paint cans and the strips of cardboard into a bin for glass. Misplacing the goods was probably an offense, too. But the work of a vandal had a wide range and very few limits. Walter pulled on Duke's chain, dragging him away from a ragged grease-stained sack caught in the fence. "Do you know that I could get used to talking to you, Duke the Puke? Do you? Do you know that?" It took considerable strength to haul the dog from one end of the center to the gate, and Walter spoke to him the whole way to cheer himself on. "You're actually my favorite one in the family now. That's a remarkable statement, you Gorgonzola turd. You don't even like me. You hate my guts, and I'm saying, You alone are my special friend. But the thing is, we're more alike than you might realize. You're neutered and in a way I'm neutered, too. We're both eunuchs, pal. You and me, we're the last stop. You're looking at a dead end, right here, buddy."

He stopped, hearing his own terrible words in the empty lot, and he felt as if he, the loather, had crept up on regular old Walter, as if he'd bitten his own leg. He almost wished the dog had snapped at him or stood his ground, snarling at the ugly intruder. He wished he could purge himself, be sick on the asphalt or weep with great shudders. "It's on to petty larceny," Walter whispered to Duke. "Let's go steal from Mommy's purse."

It wasn't until the third morning, Saturday, that she came. He was in the hall upstairs, in a hurry to get to ballet class, looking through the dirty clothes for a pair of tights that were even moderately fresh. Joyce didn't rinse out his clothes anymore, the way she used to in the old days. There were never clean things folded by category in his drawer. He used to deposit his underwear in the hamper, and a little while later he'd find a stack of briefs on his bed, the brown smears up the back gone without comment, the socks darned and mended. He belabored the point bitterly to himself as he burrowed through the hamper: his mother was going to join up with the angry, strident sisterhood, go on marches, canvass neighborhoods, take the bus to Washington to free womankind from household drudgery. The laundry was a thing of the past for Joyce McCloud. He could not find a clean shirt to save his life, the detergent barrel in the basement was empty, the lint in the dryer trap was thick as a quilt.

The Gambles' front door clanged shut. Walter went cold, looking into the maw of the wicker basket. It was the Maplewood Avenue Medusa, her pin curls turned to snakes. She rarely used the front entrance, and he knew instinctively that the noise meant she was coming. She was on her way, to stare him down, turn him to stone. He put his hand to his throat and peered out the diamond-shaped window. If she had looked up to the second story, she might have noticed one brown eye in the blue glass of the leaded circle. Walter noted that she was not making her way with her usual fierce stride, the one she used when she careened down the pavement cracking her bullwhip after the children in summer. She could have saved herself some time if she'd strolled across the carport and their lawn, but she was going the long route, cutting no corners in her turns. Could she be angry if she was taking such measured steps? There was a harsh wind, to judge from her bared teeth and the tilt of her body. She was not dressed to stand outside on the porch or inquire over the fence about Duke's health. She had nothing on but a long green cardigan, her apron, her stretch pants, a man's shirt that buttoned up to her neck and a knit cap that sat on the top of her head like a yarmulke.

She gave the classic sequence: three raps at the McClouds' front door. He was at the hall window even though she was out of sight, one floor below. He held the pair of smelly black tights. She knocked again, one, two, three. He stretched the thin cotton, in and out, in and out, as if he were conditioning a balloon before blowing it up. Perhaps no one would answer, and she'd go away. From her window she had seen them lumbering like hungry animals through the cage of the house and so she knew they were home. She knocked once more, and that time Joyce came running from the kitchen, wiping her hands on a dish towel.

"Florence!" she cried, opening the door. "Whatever—what is it?"

Mrs. Gamble's presence in the McClouds' entry was highly irregular. She did not set foot in the house, except for the Christmas party, when she and Mr. Gamble came in the back, ate a cracker, had one cocktail and then retreated to their own breakfast nook. A visit at the front door was an invasion, an assault upon the privacy and the sanctity of the McCloud home. Behind their front door, behind the white curtain that covered the glass, they were supposed to be safe from the neighborhood in which they lived.

Walter tiptoed to his room. He wished his mother had the bulk of Ma Kettle, including the .22 at her side, that Joyce could man the fort, protect the family from the stickup. In a pile on his floor he found a cleaner pair of dirty tights and a T-shirt, still damp from last night's sweat. He very carefully folded his ballet clothes and put them in his bag. He zipped it shut. Using hospital corners, he remade his bed, and after he'd smoothed his blanket so that it no longer had a single crease, as he would be expected to do at boot camp, he crossed the hall to the bathroom, to see if the mural on the carport had disappeared after three days. It could have worn off or been replaced by something even more modern, Art History bandits creating a Rothko effect, with horizontal bands and blurred edges. He flushed the toilet and turned the taps on at the sink, and while all that water was circling and streaming he climbed on the ledge of the bathtub for a look at the masterpiece.

Their work had remained the same. Nothing had happened to alter the splatters that were staring back at him this time like huge unblinking eyes. It looked fine. It looked good. Mrs. Gamble had had the carport built so that she could keep watch over her Chevy, so it would be close to her, right outside her kitchen, her living-room and her dining-room windows. Why wouldn't she want her roof to be so handsomely decorated? He hopped off the tub, put his bag over his shoulder, turned off the faucet and opened the door forcefully on purpose so it banged against the shower stall. He passed Daniel's room, where his brother was making revolting coughing noises, and went down the back stairs.

"I'm going to class, Ma," he shouted from the kitchen. He had never, in his life, called Joyce *Ma* but he might as well start sounding like an ordinary, cruel teenager. "Ma," he called louder, "I'm going downtown." At the point of departure in the past, before Daniel's illness, Joyce used to ask him if he had el fare, if he'd eaten a healthy breakfast. She'd wish him a safe trip. "I'm leaving," he yelled.

Joyce was in the living room, with *her,* doing something, talking, he supposed, although he couldn't hear them. Were they sitting, upright and stiff, or standing side by side or kneeling together at the coffee table? He couldn't think how they would speak to each other, what they'd do with their hands and their arms, without a fence to lean on, without a fence marking the boundary. He crossed the foyer to the coat hooks. "Always been independent and reliable," he heard his mother saying. She was either referring to his old self or to Daniel, the model citizen. He took his jacket off the peg and darted around, as if he had only then sensed a presence in the living room.

"Oh, hi, Mrs. Gamble," he said, facing them and at the same time adjusting the buckle on his duffel bag, fine-tuning it, getting it the right length, so that it couldn't possibly rub his shoulder bone, should the padding of his coat instantaneously wear thin.

I've always disliked you, Florence, he said to himself. What child on the block didn't mock her in the theoretical safety of his own room? She was a laughingstock, clearing her throat in long syllables, plucking at her shirt right above her breastbone as if the action released the phlegm. That motion and the noise of her sinus-drainage problem were her signature. You are the butt of the neighborhood jokes, he wanted to say. The butt. Thank you for giving us countless hours of amusement.

It was one thing to mutter about her under his breath, and another altogether to look up at her, to see her at the ready. Oh God, he thought. Help me, Father. Her exaggerated stance in front of the Mc-Cloud fireplace, her bent elbows, her splayed fingers had meaning to Walter: *Boy,* she was saying, *I'm not going home empty-handed.*

He stooped—steady now, steady now, he whispered—unzipped his bag to make sure, once more, that his ballet slippers were inside. He fished around as best he could, the trembling going all the way up his arms. Imagine her on the pot, he instructed himself. Better yet, imagine the dog shit, the volume of it, that she scoops up in the alley, day after day, year after year. It had to be a dog-do mountain equivalent to Mount McKinley, or higher, a Mount Everest coil of turds. The idea of her willingly taking on that kind of indignity emboldened him. He stood up, and bravely, without much fear at all, he walked into the living room. Mount Everest, he thought. She was squinting at him and he looked back, wide-eyed, trying to see beyond her, to the horizon, to the steaming pile of soft stink rising to the altitude of twenty-nine thousand feet.

"Good-bye, Mom," he said, going to Joyce. He kissed her cheek. He couldn't recall the last time he had touched her. She had a lilacky scent on her skin, from the bubble baths she habitually took in the evenings when she got home from the hospital. It was her one luxury, the way she spent her time instead of tending the house. It didn't seem like a canned fragrance. She was the only person he knew who could smell of lilacs in February. It was the delicate freshness of one lilac flower and not the overpowering sweetness of a row of trees blooming in a line. "Oh," he said, drawing away, unsure how long he'd been standing close to his mother, hovering at her ear. It might have been three seconds, or ten minutes, or half an hour. He glanced at Mrs. Gamble's beige Hush Puppies and the two inches of nylon stocking that showed above her shoes and below her pants. "So long, Mrs. Gamble," he said. He thought of doing something insolent, blowing her a kiss, mugging, asking her about the permafrost damage to her carport concrete—something to get a rise out of Mitch in a future telling. "I can't believe it's only six more months to the block party," he said, shaking his head. "It's amazing how fast the time goes." Chin up, back straight. He secured the button at the neck of his jacket. "I'll see you again," he said, in case either one of them had any doubt.

He went out the door with a spring in his step. It had been so easy to look her in the eye. He had stared at her without blinking, without faltering, and as he looked he had thought, I didn't do anything. Give him a few more hours and he'd have forgotten he'd done it; he'd be free of it. Mitch could probably put the incident out of his mind without much of a struggle, and there they'd be, the pair of them, innocent as lambs.

Mitch had missed Thursday and Friday at school, and was still sick on Saturday. Walter had tried to call him a few times but Mrs. Anderson always answered, and he felt obliged, under the circumstances, to hang up. He didn't want Mitch to be incriminated by association. Before ballet class that Saturday Mrs. Kenton came to Walter as he was warming up at the barre, trying to stretch. She called her pupils "dear" on the rare occasions she spoke to them about personal matters. "Is Mitch getting better, dear?" she asked.

For a minute her concern seemed so genuine that Walter forgot the sense of her question. He wished she were asking after him. Her hand was on her bosom and she was effortlessly standing in fifth position. "Fine," he murmured, "fine."

She smiled as if she understood his confusion. "And how's your brother? This must be a very difficult time for you."

"He's a fighter," Walter said, repeating his parents' standard reply.

She frowned and patted his leg that was on the barre. "That's good. Well! We're a small group today, aren't we?"

Mitch was out, Susan had been away for over a month, and one of the minor-league pets, Miranda, had had foot surgery. She meant,

Walter thought, that aside from her paycheck it was hardly worth her while to come to work. Walter guessed that by inquiring after Daniel she was actually trying to determine when Susan would return. *Is your brother dead yet,* she wanted to ask, *so we can have our star pupil back on the roster?*

Mrs. Kenton paid attention to him all through class, correcting his arms, kneeling on the floor and guiding his foot in the half-circle of a rond de jambe, lifting his arabesque a little higher, turning it out a degree or two more than his hip allowed. He couldn't really enjoy her notice because he knew it no more sincere than the compliments of a fair-weather friend. She'd disregard him once Mitch was on the mend. Maybe he didn't care. And anyhow he couldn't work up much interest in the usual exercises when there was a drama sure to be going on back home. As he was doing his grand battements Mrs. Gamble might still be in the living room, haggling over the punishment with Joyce. She'd insist on chopping off Walter's whole hand, and Joyce, always protecting her cubs, would skillfully negotiate for two fingers. His mother would work to save his thumb and the index finger for that prehensile advantage, using the pinkie as a bargaining chip. If only he'd pulled the stunt in the summer when all the windows were open, so the entire neighborhood could have been privy to the battle taking place between Joyce and Mrs. Gamble. A child with entrepreneurial talents could have charged admission, and it might have been spectacle enough that every year a group of punks would perform a reenactment under a big top.

Walter left the studio quickly after class and hurried down Michigan Avenue to get to the el stop. Once he reached Oak Ridge he took his time, prolonging the suspense. He went north on Maplewood for a good mile, west on Division, through downtown, east on Winthrop, back to his own block. Finally, at two o'clock, he went in the side door, listening, as he crept up the stairs, for his neighbor's voice. He expected to find Mrs. Gamble in the living room, talking to his mother, as if no time had passed in the Oak Ridge realm while he'd been away for several hours. He could hear Joyce running the water at the sink in the kitchen and his father making disparaging remarks about Henry Kissinger. He could smell Susan. The hall stank of every imaginable flower condensed into a few dark drops. It was nervy of her, to presume that she could barge right in and overpower not only his mother's fragile scent but the fragrance of the house itself. Daniel asked if he could have some more milk, and by the clanking of bracelets Walter could hear that Susan was pouring. So it was lunchtime, still, at two o'clock in the afternoon. Ever since Daniel had gotten sick the house had a perpetual frowsy holiday feel, late meals, dishes stacked in the sink, newspapers all over the place. Maybe if they straightened up, vacuumed, threw a load in the wash, got back to work, they'd be cured of what ailed them.

He was thinking that Mrs. Gamble was probably no longer in the living room hunting the quarry when Susan called, "Is someone there? Is that you, Walter?"

She had sensed him although he'd been standing on the landing without moving, without making a noise. She knew the box of the house better than his mother did, since she'd been sneaking around nights, looking to get laid. His mother had given up listening for danger, why bother when Susan was on the prowl?

"Hello, hello?" she sang out.

He came from the shadows into the white light of the kitchen. She was at the counter smiling at him, as if nothing as large as his brother had come between them. "Hi!" she chirped. "I thought I heard you."

"Oh," he said. "Hi." He wanted to say, I *smelled* you.

"You're just in time," his mother said.

Just in time. One more minute and there would have been nothing left for no-name McCloud. A crust of bread, the scum from the oatmeal pot.

"Pull up a chair," his father said.

At least he still had his place at the table, although of course they had neglected to put out a spoon and a bowl and a glass. Beyond Susan's perfume he could detect the smell of chicken soup. He supposed he should be thankful that they hadn't moved him in order to make room for the new child, that they hadn't set him up on the floor beside Duke's kibble dish. From his mother there were no questions, not so much as How are you? How was class?

"Walter," Robert said.

He couldn't remember the last time his father had spoken to him before he commanded him to pull up a chair. With the exception of

Christmas Day, he couldn't recall when his father had last been home. "Dad," he answered.

"Do you know anything about the roof of Mrs. Gamble's carport?"

So formal. Not Mrs. Gamble's roof, but the roof of Mrs. Gamble, as if he'd translated the sentence from a Romance language. Walter loved how the carport was always the province of Mrs. Gamble. He would have liked to discuss the subject at length. Mr. Gamble, for instance, had nothing to do with the building projects over at that house, or the customarily male domain of the garage. Did Robert Mc-Cloud have an opinion about the Gambles' reversal of roles? Did he think that Mrs. Gamble had burned her underwire brassiere, removing the hardware from it with her apron pliers before she torched the thing? And along those lines, he also so appreciated that his father, who was never around anymore, was supposedly the one to administer discipline and justice. He spoke as if Ward Cleaver were flashing the cue cards at the sink for his benefit. Neither Daniel nor Walter had ever misbehaved in an extreme way, and his parents had had to turn to television to learn what to say and how to act.

"What is it, Dad?" Walter said, his head back, squinting down at his father in the style of Mrs. Gamble. If only he had her glasses as a prop.

"You should take a peek," Susan said. "It's sort of incredible. It looks like the work of one of those artists."

He turned and stared at her straight on, in the manner he had recently begun to cultivate. It was phenomenal, that in a McCloud family inquisition, the first of its kind, she felt free to interject. "One of those artists?"

"Oh, you know. I can't ever think of the names."

"I'm supposed to shinny up the post, hoist myself over the downspouts, and *peek* at her roof?" He batted his eyes and held up his spotless palms for her to see.

She didn't know who he was anymore; he'd fooled her, changed his costume in the middle of the scene. It had made her go quiet. "You can see it out the bathroom window," she said into her soup. The rest of them, his relatives, were looking at him with a blankness that he was sure he would later find either pitiful or hilarious.

"I'll take a peek, then, one peek." He pushed his chair away from the table and trotted, happily, as a peeker would, up the back stairs. In the bathroom he crossed himself because Mitch would think it funny. He filled his lungs with air, and as he tanked up he pictured Mrs. Gamble coming at him with her frying pan and a hot slab of organic liver. When he could hold no more, he opened his mouth as wide as it went, shut his eyes and let the scream out in one long blast.

"Walter! Walter, what is it?" his mother cried from below.

"The carport!" he shrieked. "Oh, my God, the caaaaarport!"

He did not return to his lunch. He went up to the attic, climbed out the window in broad daylight, smoked a joint and surveyed his fiefdom. Once he'd had a good night's sleep he might consider decorating everyone's roof in the neighborhood. He'd learn the methods of a serial killer and operate in a similar fashion. He'd get Billy Wexler to help him. Old Billy boy would be in seventh heaven. They'd clamber along limbs in the trees at perilous heights, dropping balloons on the garages up and down the alley.

He went to bed midafternoon and slept until the next morning. When he woke up and saw that it was day again he felt sure that no one had bothered to check his breathing in the night, to see if he was alive. He was fairly certain that he'd folded his own clothes on the chair and put the glass of orange juice on his bedside table. There was nothing equal to the exhaustion that came at the end of a long sleep, the stiff joints, the cloudy head, the sensation of fur growing on one's teeth. At breakfast neither his mother nor his father mentioned the carport or his absence from the supper table. Mitch called while the Sunday coffee cake was being cut, and Walter stretched the cord to its limit and took the phone around the corner into the bathroom.

"News?" Mitch said.

"I think there's going to be a reaction. I think today something's going to happen."

"Come over, then," Mitch said, and he hung up.

"I'll do that, I'll come right now," Walter said into the silence of the receiver.

He didn't tell his mother he was leaving and he didn't take the time to find his hat. He ran the ten blocks to Mitch's, and when he got there he gently pushed open the front door and crept up to his friend's bedroom. Mitch was in his Nordic pose, sitting on his bed, leaning over his wastebasket, as if he were in the galley of a Viking ship, rowing. His infection had gone into his head and he was alternately spitting into the metal wastebasket and blowing his nose.

"Mitch," Walter blurted, "I'm so glad to see—"

"Are we in trouble?"

"No. No, not yet. But she figured it out, she's got to have her suspicions. She came into our house yesterday—do you understand? Into our house. Over the threshold. She came into enemy territory and she was not carrying a white flag. She was clearing her throat a hundred miles a minute, she was going for blood, I swear—"

"For Christ's sake, would you just tell me what happened? Did she report us to the police? Because if this goes on my record my mother will shoot me. I won't be able to get car insurance, and I might not get the money I need to go to New York this summer."

Poor Mitch! Walter thought. What they'd done wasn't so bad, in relation to the average juvenile crime, if you didn't count the fact that it was Mrs. Gamble's property. Mitch was scared to death by his mother, by the woman who had all of her bets on her big blond show boy.

"We might have gotten ourselves screwed, is what I'm saying. I don't know how I'm going to get the paint off my jacket, and I don't have another one I can wear." Mitch spit a hunk of mucus into the wastebasket.

Walter could hear Mrs. Anderson down the hall and he backed up and leaned against the door, as if the weight of his body could keep her away, keep her out. That his friend was frightened thrilled Walter. "I won't tell on you," he whispered. "I wouldn't rat on you, Mitch. If they get me I won't tell. You know I wouldn't." The wastebasket filled with tissues and the slurry of Mitch's spit was between them like a moat, but Walter reached across anyway. He hadn't seen Mitch in four days and he was grateful for the chance to let his hand rest in the sweaty palm for just a minute, before it was withdrawn.

⸺ ⸻

In the weeks that followed they waited for discovery. They wondered if Mrs. Gamble knew who was responsible. Did she know and decide not to press charges? They discussed it on the way to ballet class, talking into the wind out of the corners of their mouths, looking straight ahead, as if they were private eyes. They talked about themselves in the third person. Logically, Walter said, the vandals had to act from the McClouds' attic roof. Someone could have done it from the Gambles' roof, but surely the Missus had ruled out her own. It could have been a helicopter hovering soundlessly over the carport, Mitch said, a UFO, little green men. They were so obvious, Walter thought, wafting along the street in the fog and odor of the hash they smoked every day starting after breakfast, and through half the evening. There seemed to them no place to go anymore, and so they wandered down the alleys before school and at night, after class. They sat in the cold against a garage door or in the dirt of some dark alcove, and if Mitch was in the mood he'd clutch Walter and kiss him. It looked from a distance like a staged mugging, Mitch holding Walter by the collar, Walter floundering in the grasp, trying to maneuver his hands up out of the welter of their bodies to touch Mitch's face.

Walter supposed that what they were doing could be called Making Love. They had their routine. At Mitch's bidding, Walter fished down into Mitch's pants, and through Walter's attentions the former Mouse King managed to keep quiet, writhing against the metal garage door or the trunk of a tree. Mitch sometimes gave a grunt or two. It could be said, Walter thought, that there was satisfaction in Walter's giving and Mitch's taking, and in addition there was regularity. He wondered if it was greedy to ask for more than satisfaction and regularity, or if perhaps love itself had been falsely advertised. Maybe there was nothing better than routine, nothing better than coming down the alley after class, side by side, each, for his part, anticipating the moment. Mitch usually pushed Walter to the shelter of a fenced walkway next to a garage, drew him to the ground and jerked Walter's hands into place. Quickly, quickly, Walter did the job, and then Mitch would zip up and they'd sit, as if they were strangers in a bus terminal, waiting for their ride to Albert Lea, Sioux Falls and beyond, far into the plains, to Murdo and Kadoka.

A squad car came down the alley one night, when they were sitting cross-legged against a bank of empty garbage cans. They didn't know it was the police until the car turned on its beam, lighting the alley, framing them at the center of the circle. They were caught in the spot; they could feel their own eyes gone red.

The officer stuck his head out the window. "Come 'ere," he ordered.

Walter popped right up and went to the car.

"Open the bag."

He handed the cop the small brown sack full of the bananas his mother had asked him to buy at the Stop and Go. The policeman looked inside, removed the bananas and turned them over. "What are you up to, huh?" he asked, when he could find nothing illegal or delinquent in a bunch of green bananas.

"Right now, you mean?"

"Yeah, I mean right now."

Walter shrugged. They had been jacking each other off. That night Mitch had at last rubbed himself against Walter's pecker, flesh against flesh, and he'd also had the courtesy to finish the job by hand. It was the first time Mitch had touched him, and even though he went too fast and applied too much pressure where a little gentleness might have served, Walter wanted to scream with gratitude. He had banged up his mouth, kissing Mitch's head and face as the glory built. But what was left him when they closed up shop were bruised lips and sticky underwear. As soon as they were done it unaccountably felt like nothing. Somewhat in the same vein, it was disappointing to vandalize property and get absolutely no feedback. Maybe it just wasn't that interesting to be a desperado unless there was a chase involved and maybe it was the funniest thing that when a person finally was allowed in, allowed to love the dream boy, it sometimes, now and then, when you thought about it, ended up being far more lonely than sitting by yourself out in the gray night.

The officer handed Walter the bag of bananas. "Get yourselves home and away from trouble," he ordered.

"That's a good idea," Walter said, turning to Mitch to see if he concurred. "Definitely. Thanks, Officer. So, ah, well, good night, then. You take care of yourself too. I imagine it can get chilly, and well, forlorn on your beat—"

Mitch pushed Walter and made him trip. When the car had disappeared around the corner he said, "When will you ever learn to shut up, McCloud? I'll cram my dick down your throat one of these days, plug it permanently." The thought of such a thing made Walter woozy with desire. "Could we do that now?" he asked, choking on his own saliva. Mitch took off down the alley, and Walter soon fell behind, chasing from lamppost to lamppost, running after the flickering shadow.

On the morning of Valentine's Day in Otten, Walter had still been in bed at six o'clock. He was stuck, trying to imagine honoring the holiday in an appropriate way. His alarm had gone off twice while he imagined coming down the aisle after a bishop and a cantor, in the trail of the smoky incense. He was trying to think what he was commemorating. For an instant "I'm Going to Wash That Man Right Out of My Hair" obscured the cantor's Latin verse. "Maybe I should call in sick," he said out loud. Surely he was ill. Living in Otten had done it to him. He was damned to an eternity of high school, damned to the hellfire that was teaching youngsters against their will to listen to the word.

He sat up, and as if he were his own student, he said, "Look. The draft didn't claim you. That's number one. Number two, you didn't die at seventeen or at thirty-five." It was old-fashioned, a Victorian heroine thing to do, to count a person's blessings, but he supposed there was a certain stylishness in not being able to get beyond Number Two.

He got out of bed, put on his denim shirt, and his special *Great Expectations* tie, covered with the head of Charles Dickens right side up and upside down. His classes didn't like the book and it was proving impossible to woo them to it. The tie probably wasn't going to help any. Most of the students had no clue that there was pleasure to be found in observing character. They seemed to be afraid to look around themselves and find a world every bit as amusing, ridiculous and unjust as Dickens's London; they wanted to see no farther than the range of their own teenage selves.

Walter thought of Susan while he ate his toast, and he wondered if Lester had sent her a florid box of Valentine chocolates. Just the thing for a dancer who weighs 108 pounds. The star-crossed lovers were still corresponding, Susan reported, writing letters that she said just about broke her heart. For special occasions Susan's husband, Gary, usually gave her books that he got from publishers for free. His cheapness irritated her, even though she claimed to appreciate the luxury of a hardcover book. For just a minute, Walter let himself imagine life in Otten with Susan living next door, or across town. Walter didn't know what she'd do in retirement, but she'd said she had no interest in opening a neighborhood dancing school. She was not going to turn into Mrs. Kenton. She could get a library science degree, become the director at the Otten Memorial Library. She could beef up the popular collection with obscure literary novels. They'd have coffee together at Lee's before her morning aerobics class and they'd make private jokes that dated back to ballet school. She'd assist him when he had a show to direct, she'd choreograph the dance numbers and all the girls would be in awe of her, of Mr. McCloud's associate.

He saw the fantasy life so clearly that he was bereft when he returned to his breakfast cereal without her. He felt a little the way a cripple must, who has imagined walking only to find himself still strapped in the wheelchair. It would have been better not to have gone dreaming in the first place, better to drive off into the workaday world of Otten without the sense of farfetched possibility.

When he got to school Walter found a carton on the floor outside his locked door. He thought, A bottle bomb—someone is trying to kill me. He bent over it and saw the return address of a mail-order garden outfit. Nancy Sherwin was the only person who had ever given him flowers, and she had done it compulsively, before every performance of the Rockford *Nutcracker.* He opened his door and carried the box to his desk. He had never received a Valentine from anyone other than his mother, and Susan, and Lucy, when she was small, and recently little Linda. But he was a teacher, he remembered, and it wasn't out of the question that a brownnoser would think of him. Betsy Rutule might do such a thing out of real affection, or maybe the cast of *South Pacific* wanted to show their appreciation for the way Walter was whipping them into shape.

He very much liked the early morning before many people were in the building. It was like a conception of an artwork, complete in the mind's eye, before words or paint strokes violate the integrity of the idea. He was an excellent teacher in the silence of his classroom, before the bell rang, the floodgates opened and the students arrived. He had done what he could for Jim Norman, coaxing, giving him responsibility, ordering him to the principal. He more or less believed in the Dominican idea that you treat each person as if he were Christ. It was fine in the abstract. However, at some point if Jesus himself didn't respond, there was nothing to do but kick him out on his flat ass. Norman had skipped town before he'd been expelled for setting a fire in the hall, and no one on the staff was sorry to see him go. "Good riddance," Mrs. Denval had said.

Walter slit open the cardboard box and burrowed down through the biodegradable packing material. Although flowers in general had never moved him deeply, the dreamy pink Angelique tulips he brought up, in a green wooden crate, took his breath away. Not only were they pretty, but they seemed sent from another sort of existence—a clean life of calm and simplicity purchased so easily with a credit card. He couldn't help putting his face into them. They didn't have a sweet smell, but the damp earth in the box brought to mind the coming thaw and the twitter of robins.

"Who?" he said, tearing away the small white envelope taped to the side of the box. They were expensive flowers that had come the day before to the school office from an overpriced company in San Francisco. He yanked the stiff white card out of the envelope, saying, even as he read, "Who?"

"From your admirer."

Walter sat down. "From your admirer," he read again. No one in Otten could have conceived of the flowers—no one in Otten spent more than a few dollars for a flat of petunias for their window boxes. Betsy would bring him a handmade card or a chocolate, and Mrs. Denval might give him a sticky doughnut from the bakery but she would not charge up her account for a man who would never have lusted after her in her prime. "From your admirer." Julian, Walter thought. Julian Wright in New Orleans. Julian, sitting on a stool in his boxer shorts, legs crossed, flipping through the catalog, trying to think what Walter would like. Had Julian, in his bed at night, been pressing his hands to his lips, thinking of Walter? "Julian," he whispered. "Is it you?"

The flowers suddenly looked bright, fluorescent, their petals vibrating. "Good God," Walter said out loud. He could not possibly teach through the day with the flowers sitting on his desk or even hidden in his closet. How was he to concentrate, to think of anything but Julian's mouth, the circle of it lush as a plum? How was he to enjoy the flowers if they turned out not to have been sent by Julian? Julian in a suit, Julian in nothing at all, Julian wrapped in a towel. He had to get the tulips out of the classroom—it wouldn't do to have his pupils see him in a tizzy. He grabbed an index card and scrawled in red ink, "To Mrs. Denval. Happy Valentine's Day." Should he say Love, Walter? From your colleague, Walter? He didn't care—out! Out! He signed his name, plunged his face into the flowers one last time before he carried them over to Room 247 and set them by her door.

What a relief to have the box gone, away, where it could not exert its pressure! He could do nothing but totter around his room as if he were half in the bag. When he passed his desk the fifth time he picked up his notes for *Great Expectations.* He stopped at the highlighted phrases "Inverted Cinderella tale—two major social messages—Jaggers—his trade is the perversion of justice." He tried to reread his outline, but he was too agitated to make sense of the important points. Julian might still be sleeping, dreaming poetically of fields wearing scarlet gowns and carriages bringing death. Mitch, in California, two hours behind the Midwest, was certainly in bed, trying to dream developer dreams, boy dreams with bulldozers and dirt piles, sump crocks, all the while his innocent wife sleeping beside him.

Walter stared at the blackboard, letting himself drift back to his early-morning reverie; if genuflection and prayer were part of his tradition, he might go to Saint Catherine's in Otten after school and light a votive candle for therapeutic purposes. The February 14 candle wouldn't be for Daniel, not for Susan, Lester, Mitch, the wife, the two little girls. Not for Julian, with or without the Angelique tulips. Not for the present blessings and not for the gift of memory. His ritual was silly perhaps, and was not something he could explain to anyone, with the possible exception, in theory, of Susan. She would understand, but he would never tell her about his season with Mitch. It was the single omission, the secret he kept from her, and he'd guarded it faithfully because he did not want to taint her own remembrances of her high school flame.

At Saint Catherine's, if he were of that bent, he would light what looked like ordinary plumber's candles for the one perfect love moment. He had had it once, before he knew it was a moment, before he knew that nothing of its sort is protracted or protected from the revising powers of memory. It had taken quite a bit of work through the years to isolate the moment, to try to maintain it in its pristine form. He had hoped that in adulthood there might be endless time, time that was of a similar texture and weight, spun from the same thread as the love moment. He had not ever found it in its purity again. His had been that Valentine's night of 1973, lying on the cold ground, doing nothing more intricate than breathing, at last, the chill air, and finding under the bushes a tenderness that he long afterward associated with the word "grace."

The first bell rang, and even as it sounded the students' voices came up the stairwell and into the hall. "Thank you, Julian, or whoever you are," Walter said. He put his hands to his face, steadying himself, and then he went to the door and opened it to the here and now, to the noise and chaos and mess of this, his life.

Before Easter dinner at Lake Margaret it occurred to Walter that he could tell Lucy about the Valentine's Day when he was fifteen, about the Pollock roof, about how vigilantes had not come after him, even though he'd virtually begged for any little rebuke. He was still squatting by the fire in the living room when he realized that it was Lucy who could receive the story. She had so looked forward to his moving to the Midwest, and she was already sick of his one-liners. He should go find her and make amends for his bad joke about the virgins, and see if he couldn't talk to her. If he told her about that long-ago winter, about their parents, about Daniel, Susan, Mitch, would she look disapproving, he wondered, or would her clear brow furrow in sympathy? She was proving to be unpredictable, but it wasn't outside the realm of possibility that she'd be grateful for the light the story shed not only on him but on Joyce and Robert and, consequently, on herself. He suddenly very much wanted to be alone with her, to have some guarantee of peace so he could begin to know her and be known.

To know her and be known, not in a sugarcoated adopted-child-meets-birth-mother way, and not in the rush of an infatuation. He put on his jacket and went out, down the hill to the lake. She was probably indoors, but it felt right to first roam the property both in search of her and to gather some courage. He had wanted to talk to her in the same vein on other occasions, but he was frightened this time around. There was danger in an attempt to come close to her, and there was danger in letting her see a more truthful version of Walter McCloud. He wanted to go a distance. He wanted to try. If he failed he might not be able to reach her again, he might lose her, nothing left between them but polite inquiries and the expectation of birthday gifts for Linda. It was worth venturing, he knew it was, worth a dare.

The lake out of season was like a friend who has changed, who has dyed her hair or gotten a face-lift, become a widow and begun to live. Walter stood on the seawall, his hands shoved deep into his pockets, and he looked over the cold, rough waves. The summer water was never the color of the late-winter frothy blue. It was a wild lake for a time, no boats, no skiers, no swimmers or fishermen. It seemed to him to have an intelligence; it seemed to know that for a few months out of the year, without boats and without the sleep that ice brought, it was on its own, alive, free, and for itself. He would tell his sister the Valentine's Day story, and surely it would be a way of talking about everyone in the family. It was Daniel's illness, Daniel himself, who had provided refuge for Walter, protection from Mrs. Gamble. She had not come after him, although he was the only possible culprit. Dear old 646 Maplewood Avenue had been a safe house, and Walter as good as in a witness-protection program, without having to leave his birthplace, without having to acquire a limp or get a nose job. He had grown up that year into the lonesome world without realizing that his defenseless brother, the new McCloud family weakling, was his best champion. He would eventually get to some sort of conclusion, and he'd tell Lucy that Daniel died leaving them at first with a terrible grief, and then there came a hope, "the thing with feathers that perches in the soul." Hope for her. He'd fashion it as a happy story over all, one that ended with Lucy Rawson McCloud.

He found her with her cousins in the nursery looking through two garbage bags filled with girl clothes, five-year-old Christina's hand-me-downs from the lawyer mother, Kitty. The women were holding up the French and Swedish cottons one by one and determining what would suit which child, and also what would be fair in terms of distribution. Walter would not dream of diverting her from the spoils before the meal and so he went on into the parlor to prepare his unit on poetry for his American Literature class. His goal for the three weeks was to convert four people who had perfect contempt for verse. If he could bring four out of his sixty sophomores to Marianne Moore's idea of poetry as a place for the genuine, he would have amply done his duty.

When the dinner was ready the family again sat around the Ping-Pong table in the living room, with the two picnic tables as auxiliaries, as they had done at Thanksgiving. Aunt Jeannie had insisted on scattering jelly beans on the chairs, the dressers, the mantel and the sideboard for mood and decor, and just as the young mothers predicted, the children were full and irritable well before the meal. Sue Rawson glared at the two who spilled their milk at the cat table, and she yapped at spoiled Christina in her pink sweatshirt with the appliquéd Easter Bunny front and back. It was not an auspicious start to the feast.

The redeemer of Lake Margaret, Francie, ate quietly at the far end of the table while her husband of fifteen years lay upstairs with a stomach upset. The many Republicans and the few Democrats in the room did not discuss the new Congress, or the president and his wife, or the atrocities taking place at home and abroad. After a good deal of talk the group continued to agree that Michael Jordan had been right to return to basketball. Walter watched his relatives huddling in their jackets, eating the roast and pineapple salad. It was remarkable, he thought, that the collection of people around the table had very little in common but their phantom forefathers, years of shared summers in one place and their pleasure in Michael Jordan. They were not at a loss for words. After they'd exhausted basketball they talked among themselves about their software, their hardware, their vacations, their cars, their old houses, their new houses, their bikini waxes and their children's ear surgeries. Up and down the table they chattered. It seemed to Walter that Francie, chin to her chest, picking at her green beans, could not possibly be the agent of change. There was something ominous in her posture, in her slump. She was not a person who was preening for the role of the matriarch. She looked up, caught Walter's eye, quickly lowered her lids, bowed her head. That was peculiar, he thought. She was sitting between Marc and her cousin Celeste, but it was as if she were alone, in hiding under her bangs. She'd lost about forty pounds, and for the first time in her life, at thirty-nine, she was attractive. There was a delicacy to her features, now that her face had lost its plumpness, and she had that other certain something Walter recognized—it was a quality he'd noticed in women who were entering their middle years—a slow burn, a sizzle, the last-minute sultriness before the end. Francie had lost weight, he guessed, not because she had finally found the magic diet but because she was having a crisis of some sort. It came to him then: they were all going to lose Lake Margaret. He had seen it in her eyes. Francie and Roger Miller were not going to be able to pull together and buy the property out from under Sue Rawson. Francie, eating at the table, was not really present. She had ditched them, left them in the lurch.

Walter's salty pork all of a sudden tasted bland, the mash of the late-winter potatoes had no sweetness. He wanted to stand up and yell at them: Look, look at Mrs. Roger Miller! Does that hangdog pose, the stringy hair, the shifty eyes inspire confidence? Are you, or are you not going to come through, Francie? If the answer is no, understand that we will never sit around this table together again. You, every one of you here, need to ask yourselves what this is worth.

They would turn to each other, embarrassed again, again feeling cornered, while the question circled the room: What is it worth? What is it worth?

We die, Walter wanted to shout, and this place goes on. It is always here like a still small voice. If they could only think for a minute, think about standing in the living room one last afternoon, and finally the time would come. Someone would have to shut the door, leave it closed. One by one they'd go out the front gate, never to return, past the granite pillars that had "Rawson" spelled out in the stone.

Uncle Andrew's oldest, Nathan, was talking about his software company, telling his corner that he was doing work on the bleeding edge. "The bleeding edge?" Walter called across the table.

"That's right," Nathan said. "The cutting edge, forget it, that's history. I've got a technology so new, so virtual, it isn't perfected—hell, it isn't even invented. The bleeding edge, that's what we're on. People run down the hall at the office, no walking in our place, and I've got guys who sleep there."

"The bleeding edge," Walter repeated. It sounded distasteful, not something he wanted to think about during a meal. It sounded like the kind of edge he was probably on, living and working in Otten. He pushed back his chair, left his dinner and went upstairs to Sue Rawson's room. She hadn't stayed for the night at Lake Margaret in over a decade, but the room was hers. It would be her room when a stranger took it over. He stared out the window, wondering what he could do to galvanize his cousins. They seemed not to be the sort who believed they could make a difference, either singly or cooperatively. He began to pace the bedroom—stupid to pace, he thought, stupid to be so useless. They were going to lose the property and no one downstairs realized, and he was upstairs agitated, squandering his energy because he did not know what to do.

"Walt," Lucy said at the door. "There you are." She was smiling at him, ruefully, he thought, as if she wasn't mad at him anymore, as if she was sorry about her disapproval earlier in the day.

Easy, easy, he told himself. Don't blurt, don't blather. There were so many things he wanted to tell her. Maybe she knew why Lake Margaret was important, but it wouldn't hurt for her to hear it again. Lake Margaret was a piece of the story too, and she'd understand, he was sure she would, that if it went, another part of Daniel was gone. The old house was the steady center in all of their lives, the common heart. If he could keep her long enough he'd try to make a beginning; he'd sit her down in Sue Rawson's wing chair, get her a blanket and he'd start the story with the morning Daniel woke up with the lump.

"This is one of my favorite rooms," he said. "Sue Rawson used to invite me up here and we'd listen to music. Before you were born."

"Sometimes you talk as if you did all of your living before I was born," she said slowly, dreamily.

He stopped walking in circles and leaned against the old four-poster bed. He realized that she was often surprising him, that she was far smarter than he usually gave her credit for. "Have you done your living yet?" he asked.

"What do you mean, Walt?" And she laughed—"I'm in the middle of it."

He nodded and felt along the deep brown wood of the bedstead.

She was still at the door. She was nervous too, he could see, holding a yellow washcloth, pulling at a loose thread, unraveling it. "You know that sort of like fairy-tale thing you told me at Thanksgiving, about the beautiful sick sister and the living sister?"

"The life of Daniel," Walter murmured.

"I've been thinking about it, and I guess it has made me worry about you, because the sister in your story was—a little reckless, you know—her behavior with different men? If you haven't noticed I get cranky when I'm worried. And I've been wanting to say all these months—I know this might sound really queer—I mean dumb. But I've been wanting to say that if you were ever sick, if you get sick, you know? If you couldn't take care of yourself and didn't have anyone? If that happened, you could come live with Marc and I."

He caught his breath, inhaling as he spoke. "Marc and me."

"Okay, okay, Marc and me. Whatever. Maybe it's really weird to say that—but I've been wanting to for a long time. I wanted you to know that I'm not—ashamed or anything, of your lifestyle. I can't help thinking of you up there in Otten. You hardly have any furniture. When I'm old and sick I'll call out for Marc. What about you, Walt?" She came toward him and stopped just short of the bed. "Who will you call for?"

Nine

APRIL

1973

When it warmed up that spring, Greg Gamble tore off all the shingles on the carport and put on a new roof. Mrs. Gamble stood below, in her yard, smoking and watching him. If a shingle missed the trash heap she stepped outside the gate and threw it into the Dumpster herself. She'd open an upstairs window and lean out shouting, "G.G., you're going crooked!" It seemed to Walter that by ripping off the painty shingles Greg Gamble was erasing the bad deed. They might all forget it had ever happened. They might stop knowing who had done it. Mrs. Gamble's new goodness, born from overlooking their mischief, would be arrested in its relative infancy, and Walter could again dislike her for every one of the old reasons.

Daniel was in the hospital for three and a half weeks that month. Years later a boy in his condition would have been sent home to die, but it was not yet routine for cancer patients to spend their last days in their own bedrooms. Joyce and Robert took turns staying with Daniel through the night, sitting up in a chair next to the bed. Robert's factory was on the west side of Chicago, and he usually went to the hospital, to join his wife, as soon as he could get away. He and Joyce ate dinner from the vending machines. They were together when the doctor came for his rounds, and then one of them went home to Walter and to sleep.

In the evening, after ballet class, Walter and Mitch let themselves into the dark house. Finally they had a place to go that was out of the gutter, out of reach of the police. It didn't escape Walter's notice that Joyce never bothered to leave the light on for her stray son. She often told him that either she or Robert would be back when he returned from class but it was never true; they could not seem to pull themselves away from the hospital. "I'm home," he shouted to no one as he opened the door. "Come to Papa, puppy," he yelled into the kitchen. The dog came slinking out of the shadows, no wag to his tail, no warm tongue to the hand that fed him.

Walter couldn't stand thinking back to his younger days, when he prayed for drama in his life. His wish for tragedy had pretty much been granted, but it had not come out as he'd imagined. He was reduced, rather than ennobled, by his present situation. He couldn't keep himself from sweet talk with the dog that had always hated him, and when his parents were home he sat at the piano torturously banging away at a Beethoven sonata, so obvious, he knew, so childish in his appeal. He could do nothing but storm through the allegro, the allegretto, the adagio, ignoring the markings, playing each movement louder and faster than the last.

Mrs. Gamble often left a morsel at the door, an apple tart in a ramekin or a loaf of seven-grain bread, a bunch of asparagus all the way from California. Walter didn't like her food, on general principles. He brought the day's catch to the counter and uncovered it, exposing it to the air, to rot. Sometimes Joyce made his supper in the morning and left it wrapped in plastic in the refrigerator. Or she put a ten-dollar bill under the vase on the kitchen table, with instructions to order a pizza. She always signed off with an X and an O, as if that would do, in her absence. Walter usually gave Mitch the money so that they could pay their local dealer. He was afraid that with a fifty-dollar debt the little hoodlum would hire a hit man to knock off one of them. He was fairly confident that any self-respecting criminal, faced with a choice, would take the challenge of Mitch, no fun doing in such easy prey as Walter. Still, a person couldn't be certain, and he was always relieved to see the pizza money, to snatch it from under the vase and hand it over to the president of the corporation, the man of the house. They could survive on milk and cereal if it meant they'd live to see the break of day.

As if he wouldn't notice the dog, Joyce always left Walter a note, reminding him to take Duke for a walk. "Sure," he said to her handwriting, opening the front door, letting the bunwad out to run anywhere he pleased, to scrabble into garbage cans and gorge himself silly. If Joyce left a meal the boys opened the refrigerator and stood eating the baked potato, the pork chop, the green beans, the cookies, right from the plate on the rack. Mitch could eat a potato in one swallow, and Walter was quick to grab what he most wanted and tear it down the approximate middle. They drank the milk from the carton, passing it back and forth. When they'd finished, or when they'd grown cold, standing in the breeze of the refrigerator, they shut the door and went to the bread box. They ate what was left of the loaf. They ran their wet fingers along the bottom of the stainless-steel box to get the last crumbs. This, Walter thought, this easy domesticity, is what it will feel like when I'm an adult, when I have an apartment, when I have a real life.

They fixed themselves bowls of Kix. They added miniature marshmallows to the top, along with raisins, peanuts, bananas and chocolate sauce—anything they could find—and when all of that was gone they put their heads down into their bowls and sucked up the milk. Walter made popcorn, and once they poured melted unsweetened chocolate over the kernels. The bitterness surprised them, and so they added sugar and, for balance, a dash of salt. Duke ate the mess from the trash later that night and early the next morning he puked outside Walter's bedroom door. It was nothing less than a personal vendetta, Walter knew. The dog, although stupid in most ways, had a talent for vengeance.

The boys didn't clean up after themselves in the kitchen. The house was a wilderness, and putting away their plates would not have made a dent in the ruin. There were ants in the garbage, in the cupboards, in the drain, which was clogged with pieces of meat and cereal and carrot shavings. The can opener had a trimming of black scum on the blade; the floor was sticky with swill and muddy paw prints; the tap was busted, and there was a rusty stain where the water ran in the sink. Joyce brought groceries home and didn't put them away. The trash didn't get taken out. The mail wasn't opened and had piled up on the table. After they'd eaten, Mitch and Walter turned out the lights on the mess and went upstairs to Walter's room.

Every night, after Mitch left him, Walter imagined how with each next time they would begin a new sequence. He realized that becoming a lover might actually be something like learning a language, progressing from lesson to lesson, building on the previous skills until a person was speaking fluently and maybe even lyrically. Before he'd had any experience, he'd believed that sex, having sex, would be like riding a bike. You'd find your balance, wobble a little, figure out the steering and take off. After that first time you'd always know how. That's what he'd thought, but he'd been wrong. There was sport involved, it turned out, and probably artistry, and if you were a dullard you might go on for a long time without improving, without getting past the introductory lesson in simple conversation. Mitch seemed only to want to quickly finish the business in the dark. Their trysts inside had right away become habitual and perfunctory: eat in the light of the kitchen, go upstairs and fuck, more or less, in the grainy blackness of Walter's room. There had been a time or two, on a Sunday afternoon, in Mitch's unheated attic, when they had lain under a dusty coverlet on an old stained mattress, and Walter had ventured to follow the line of his friend's clavicle with his fingers, the outline he already knew so well without the benefit of touch. Mitch kept his eyes shut, as if he didn't want to see his admirer. He might let me kiss his throat, Walter said to himself. If I am careful, if I act with intention and speed, I might peel back the sheet and look. But Mitch rolled over before Walter made his move.

Night after night at his own house Walter wanted to back up and begin again. He wanted to take off Mitch's clothes, button by button; he wanted to light a candle so he could see the white skin, the blue eyes, the tangle of hair, and even his own proficient hands. It had been one thing in the alley, to make haste in the cold, but in the empty house they had the opportunity to take their leisure in a bed with cotton sheets, or they might have had a shower or a bath, or tried out the kitchen table like an adventurous married couple. It was not too diffi-

cult to look each other in the eye when they were passing the milk carton back and forth in the kitchen, easing their hunger and mocking
Mrs. Gamble, but somewhere during the trip up the back stairs
Mitch's footfall grew heavy, as if by the time he got to the upper hall
he was carrying a load, burdened by shame.

Years later Walter would tell Lucy about the night in the middle
of April, the night he and Mitch came home and between them ate a
pan of macaroni and cheese, a loaf of bread and also cleaned up a half
gallon of vanilla fudge twist. They left their dirty plates at the table,
along with the ice cream bowls, the soggy carton, the bum end of the
loaf and the plastic bag sitting in a pool of milk. Walter let the dog out
and turned off the lights. He was thinking what to say when they got
upstairs. He was going to whisper something to Mitch, a suitable
quote, a short affectionate line. Just a little pillow talk, nothing that
would threaten or bind. What it could be he didn't know. If he could
come up with a few words, a simple sentence. Something that was not
corny and would still do the trick. He was going to bust apart if he
couldn't tell Mitch a fraction of his feelings and if he didn't now and
then get a tiny, tiny response, a hello, a thank-you, the hint of a smile.
He wasn't asking for an ocean or a great lake and a major tributary. A
trickle, he would be satisfied with a drop or two.

They went up the back stairs. Outside it was raining and, inside,
the air grew damp and chill as they climbed to the second story. Someone had left the bathroom window open, and there they were, might
just as well have been hiking above the tree line into a fog. Walter
coughed and cleared his throat. If only he could get to the top step
and with a firm voice say the words that would bring peril to them and
throw them so fondly together. In the bedroom, as usual, they took off
their own clothes. They had seen each other naked for years under the
pink fluorescent lights of the dressing room at ballet school, but in the
darkness they always turned away from each other. Walter scrambled
under his sheets, pulled the cover up to his chin. He touched his own
nipples and he thought, as he often did, back to the first time Mitch
kissed him, in the bushes. He tried to remember what the gentleness,
the mercy, had felt like. The sensation was already as far away from
him as it would be years in the future, when he wished for it in his thir-

ties. Was there a word or two he could say, he wondered again, to get something of that feeling back? Or was it his own body, his repulsive, thin chest, his spindly legs, that made it impossible for a person so well proportioned to love him?

He opened his eyes and looked hard at the ceiling as if on the plaster there might be the right phrase. In a Jane Austen novel, he thought, the reader had to wait for hundreds of pages for a hand to press a hand. And then he remembered the line from *Persuasion*: "I have loved none but you." Mitch was going to grab at the sheets, as he usually did, grab where he supposed Walter's penis lay in wait. He was coming for it, his grasping fingers opening and closing as he came, his white teeth somehow shining. What Walter saw when his friend lunged for him were those teeth gleaming as if they'd been swabbed with glow-in-the-dark compound. Those glowing incisors were probably catching the light of some distant city or cities; the quad cities, he considered, all the way over in Iowa and western Illinois. Two can be abstracted at this game, he said to himself. Mitch lay flat out on top of the sheet, on Walter, rubbing against him. Neither one of them ever made much noise. How happy Walter would have been if Mitch could have afforded one ecstatic moan. He tried to name the quad cities: there were Moline and Davenport. What were the other two? Mitch, Mitch, he silently pleaded, Say something to me, something hopelessly antiquated and romantic. Say, *Walter, I have loved none but you, ever since I laid eyes on you. For you alone I think and plan.*

Mitch went on rubbing and breathing harder and digging his nails into Walter's bare shoulders. Walter wasn't going to hush this time, wasn't going to pretend they were in a convent. "What," he cried in a whisper, "are those two other cities in eastern Iowa and western Illinois? Oh, God, Mitch—what are they? Can you, can you say them?"

He was on the verge of getting Rock Island when the back door opened. They heard the knob turn in the lock. Mitch stopped rocking and let the full weight of his forehead rest on Walter's mouth. They heard the lights snap on, the door slam. They held their breaths and opened their eyes wide in the dark, as if eyes too, could hear.

"Or is it Bettendorf?" Walter said out loud, reaching down over the sheet to touch Mitch. In danger, he thought, breathing again. In danger perhaps something can be risked. "I have loved none but—"

There were footsteps on the back stairs and Joyce saying flatly, "I wish he'd clean up. I need to remind him." She spoke with no trace of anger or irritation. If a dead person could talk, Walter noted, it, the corpse, would speak in the same monotone his mother now favored.

In his moist hand Walter felt Mitch's member, as fine a dick as a stalk of asparagus out in nature, holding still in the winds on the prairie. He'd never seen a stalk of asparagus in the wind out on the prairie, but he was sure it would bring to mind Mitch's proud big daddy. His parents were climbing slowly to the top, wearily, heaving what sounded like two sets of orthopedic shoes up the fifteen steps. "For you alone," Walter murmured. "For you alone I—" Mitch pressed his hand hard over Walter's mouth.

"It's all right, Joycie," Robert was saying outside the door.

Mitch clamped down, a last squeeze for good measure before he let go, before he rolled over the side and slipped under the bed. Walter felt his mouth with both hands, trying to touch the hurt. Mitch might just as well have socked him, bloodied his teeth, or jammed a fist down his throat. He turned over, pulled the blankets up to his back, switched on his bedside light, reached for *The Great Gatsby* and began reading.

"Walter," his mother said from the hall, "are you in there?"

"Just about to go to sleep," he called through a fake yawn.

"Do you mind if we come in for just a minute?"

"I'm not exactly presentable," he started to say, but she was already in front of him in her navy peacoat, with her handbag over her wrist. She looked to have shrunk since he'd seen her last, or maybe it was his father, in his dark suit, behind, dwarfing her. Walter glanced at the floor, at Mitch's clothes in a pile by the bed, with his own, mixed up, cuffs sweetly around a neck, pant legs comfortably intertwined.

"What are you reading?" She sat down on the bed, her rump probably right over Mitch's private parts. Without the mattress separating his mother and his friend with the hard-on, the two of them could easily have been joined. Walter tipped the book so that she could see the cover. Robert moved forward, just into the room. This is not *like* being Lucy Ricardo, Walter thought. I *am* Lucy Ricardo. Joyce reached out and smoothed Walter's hair. The motion, ordinary only months before, seemed charged with meaning.

"Honey?"

She wasn't going to stop stroking his hair. She was patting him because his brother had died. Daniel, dead. Gone. What? Walter tried
to say. He couldn't speak over the noise of his beating heart. "What?"
he choked.

"We've been away so much," she said, tilting her head, looking at
him with a fondness he found unbearable. "Do you know that we care
about you? That we love you tremendously? Do you understand
that?"

This wasn't about Daniel, then, not yet. They knew about his
acts of sedition. They knew about the roof, the drugs, the homo sex
in the alley, the homo sex in their own house, and they were going to
forgive him, just like that. They were going to blot him out with their
singular compassion, overwhelm what was his wretched, bad self
with their pity and kindness. Soon enough his parents were going to
have their eggs in one basket. Walter was it, the one thing they'd
have for their own, the runt they would somehow have to learn to
treasure. All of them—Mrs. Gamble, Sue Rawson, his parents, and
Saint Susan—were finding in themselves love for Walter and all because of a sick brother.

"Sure," he whispered, "I know you do." He wished they would
blow out of the room. He closed his eyes, thinking at once to his
mother: Go. Stay. Keep touching my hair. Leave. And to Mitch: Love
me. Love me, and while you're at it, don't sneeze under there or
cough. Be still, and when you crawl out, come tenderly. His father
scooted to the side of the bed, and sat down next to Joyce, their collective weight making the mattress dip, the bulk of it pressing into
Mitch, pressing hard, Walter hoped, pressing hard into his chest.

"Daniel's very sick," Robert said.

Walter managed to squeak, "I guess I knew that, too."

"He's awfully sick and he's going to—"

"It's not going to be good, sweetie." Joyce put her head down to
her son's face as she spoke. Her tears fell down his cheeks, in whole
drops, as if he had made them. She made a retching noise, trying to
catch her breath, trying to hold herself together. She wiped at her nose
with the back of her hand, whimpering, "Dear, oh dear." But in that

slight movement she caught sight of his clothes on the floor. She was able to say, "I'll take your laundry."

"No, no, no, no, no, that's okay," Walter said, leaning over the bed, trying to reach for the pile. "I can wear those things tomorrow, they're fine, didn't get them too dirty, save the soap, they're as good as new."

She took his hand. "Is Duke set for the night?" She asked so kindly, smiling again at him, dabbing at her blurry eyes.

The mutt. Duke might have been mashed by the Klopers' station wagon or consumed by the Gambles' collies. "He had his walk," Walter muttered, and was still having it, he added, to himself: the dog, roaming the streets with a beret on his square black head, a cigarette hanging from his lips, no shirt on, tight pants, talking tough. Joyce squeezed his hand and stood up. His father slid over and kissed Walter on the cheek. That display was alarming too, something that hadn't happened in years. "We'll get through it, Wally," he said. His eyes were puffy behind his glasses. Walter had never noticed the small broken vessels all over his cheeks. "I wish this weren't happening to any of us," Robert said. He was talking under his breath, as if he were mumbling in his sleep. "I'd give up anything, everything, to stop all of this." Joyce came to the head of the bed and leaned over once more to kiss Walter. They couldn't wait to get out of there, he could tell, couldn't wait to get through with the conversation.

"It's a good idea to get an early night," Robert said, patting Walter's arm. "Don't read too long." As if he'd come in to dispense a bit of advice he said sternly, "Reading can strain the eyes. You take it easy. You'll end up like me, with trifocals."

"Okay," Walter said.

"Good night, son."

"Okay," he said again.

They closed the door and went back down the stairs to the kitchen. Walter turned over to the wall. His parents had probably been wanting to speak to him for some time. They would have wanted to find the right moment, and they might well have meant to talk in more detail, but his mother had begun to blubber and she'd spotted the laundry and changed the subject. His father butted in and took over on the topic of eyestrain. Walter didn't notice Mitch come out from under the bed or pull on his clothes. He didn't notice him slip away, and he didn't send out a prayer that Mitch have safe passage through the house. Over and over he read the inscription quoted at the beginning of *The Great Gatsby.*

> Then wear the gold hat, if that will move her;
> If you can bounce high, bounce for her too,
> Till she cry, "Lover, gold hatted, high-bouncing lover,
> I must have you."

"Then wear the gold hat," he read again. His brother was dying downtown in a hospital bed. For the first time in his memory Walter felt a kinship with Daniel. There was a stinging rush in the understanding, up his arms, down through his chest and his abdomen. They were united by blood and by history, by simple circumstances that couldn't be undone or changed. What was their essential brotherness could not in any way be taken from them. "If you can bounce high," he read, "bounce for her too." He hadn't been to the hospital to visit his brother in a long time, not since January, when Daniel was gone two weeks having surgery. The rooms had green tile halfway up the walls, and a lighter green paint job to the ceiling. Maybe the doctors didn't really know how to treat Daniel's sickness, and so they were trying any trick they could think of, hoping for results. He had already had several operations, and couldn't have much more inside him to remove. Walter imagined his brother's body, the firm swimmer's form hollowed out, nothing underneath the sheets but a shell of skin. The gravity of the illness was real to Walter finally because he'd been told by his parents. He was suddenly sorry for Daniel, very sorry he was going to miss all the rest of life. "Lover, gold hatted, high-bouncing lover." Walter tried to see himself, a hazy figure at forty, walking down the street. He would wake up every morning, for years and years to come, day after day, each day, each hour, every minute his brother receding, fading farther into the past. Daniel, lying in his hospital bed, might try to imagine the future, might try to live it quickly in his head, hoping to see what everyone would become without him. They would all go on without him. Walter had had a fleeting sense of the sadness of such a thing when he'd cracked his head at Christmas, but he had turned away from that truth. He'd let himself be distracted by Mitch, by what he supposed would be bliss. The news of death was something a person had to be told several times, he thought. It wasn't a fact you could absorb at one sitting. He felt as if he could not now, in the time that was left, lose sight of his dying brother. Nothing, he promised, could divert his attention from Daniel.

Not in years had he wept into his pillow. He stuffed the corner into his mouth to keep from howling. The tears ran cold along his neck, trickling across his chest. He wished his mother would come again and cry down his face. He wished one more time in a childish way, believing he might get what he was about to ask. He curled up, clenched his fists and hugged himself. He wished that Daniel would wake in the morning, climb out of bed, his old sick skin falling at his feet like a robe, and beneath he'd find clean new bones, new blood, new durable and long-lasting parts filling up his empty body.

The next day at school after the final bell Walter saw Susan in the hall. She did not dress up anymore, or wear eye makeup or spool her hair around her head. In her loose brown sweatshirt and a pair of faded jeans she looked as if she didn't care about anything. She was thinner than usual, and pale, and her braid was secured with a thick white band, the sort that holds broccoli in a bunch. When he caught up with her, she began talking as if she'd expected him; she launched in without looking at him, without a greeting, without the usual introductory guideposts for conversation. "My mother told me I shouldn't go to the hospital anymore, that it isn't a good idea to see Daniel. She thinks it's going to hurt me—hurt me—to see him waste away. I said to her, I said, 'No, Mother. It is not I who is hurting.' " She thrust out her dimpled chin and shook her head. "Not I."

Walter nodded. They walked on down the long hall. After several paces she said, "So why don't you ever come to the hospital? I know you're supposed to be sixteen, but I bet they'd let you since you're close enough. Why don't you visit?"

He felt as if he hadn't known anything until the night before, as if the months since the sickness began had been blank, unlived. He didn't visit because his parents were too absorbed with Daniel to think about him. He didn't visit because he hadn't understood, not really, that his brother was on the verge of death.

"So why don't you go see him?" she asked again.

He watched the speckled tile pass under his feet. "Because," he was whispering, "because, ah, they don't invite me."

It was clear right off that he'd said the wrong thing. She quit walking. "Because they don't invite you?" She was speaking out loud, with plenty of volume. There was no corner within range to scuttle around, nothing to hide behind. "Because they don't invite you." He winced when she said it a second time, as a statement, and he closed his eyes on the third, when she again made it a question. "Because they don't invite you?"

He was not going to suffer through her histrionics. There was truth in what he'd said—his parents no longer included him in anything. They were operating under the assumption that he was all right, that he was just fine. He didn't have to put up with Susan. The scene wasn't a job interview; he wasn't going to get graded; there would be no record of the dialogue that would follow him into corporate America. She snatched at his shirt with one hand when he started to walk away. She reeled him in like a practiced hoodlum. "Walter," she said, holding him tight. "Your brother is dying, do you realize that?"

"Really," he shouted, jerking his head, slapping at her arm to free himself. "Is that what's going on? I thought you were all going to the circus night after night. I thought you were having a—an orgy."

She dropped her three books, *V was for Victory, Sister Carrie* and *Variété du Conte Français.* She was shaking hard enough so that her silver earrings with three little bells tinkled. "Do you—know what, Walter?" She spoke slowly, and as if there were commas she had to observe between every two or three words. "You are—a disgusting— human being. I wouldn't shed—one lousy—tear—if you were dying. I'd thank—God—that another—evil person—was being wiped off— the face of this earth."

She gave a final shudder. She didn't stop to pick up her books. The other students parted down the middle to make way for her as she ran down the hall crying into her hands. Walter went quickly in the other direction to his locker for his ballet bag. Hysterical, he said to himself. Her sobs were echoing along the corridor. She was over the edge. He had been studying China in his World History class, and he tried to imagine her in the drab pants and tunics the men and women wore, each one indistinguishable from the next. She would never make it in a place like that. They'd capture her and torture her slowly, clanging pots and pans in her ears.

He went to the west door and sat along the brick ledge outside, where he always waited for Mitch. He had been thinking of Daniel, devoting his energy to his brother ten miles away in the hospital, and for the first time since the night before, it dawned on him that Mitch had heard his parents speaking to him. He'd been keenly aware that Mitch was under the bed at first, and then, once his mother began talking, the fact of Mitch's presence had faded. As Joyce ran her fingers through his hair Walter forgot to be afraid for Mitch. There was nothing fearsome after all about a live boy under a bed in a farce. If there'd been discovery there might have been a few angry questions, a lame excuse or two. No, Walter knew something about fear now, knew what it was meant for, knew that there were varieties of fear, bunny-hill types of fear that in no way prepared you, gave you any sense of the real ride on the big-boy mountain. They, Joyce, Robert and Walter, were about to slide down into a place they couldn't see, no way to judge the depth, the cold, the darkness.

Walter sat on the ledge for ten minutes while a good portion of the school's three thousand students poured past him. He wondered how Mitch had gotten out of the house the night before, if he'd gone unseen. Who cared? During third period Walter had been excused from Geometry in order to accompany the Girls' Choir on the piano for their state-fair audition, and he hadn't bumped into Mitch during lunch or after gym class. He felt as if he'd gone through the day with his eyes closed, seeing nothing, feeling his way along the corridor. It was their habit to wait for each other, and he supposed he was sitting on the ledge because there wasn't any reason to think their ritual had changed. They always rode the el to the city together. On Thursday they went downtown right after school even though their class was an hour later than the Monday and Wednesday routine. They liked to have coffee, to lounge in the dressing room and talk shop.

The school had emptied. The minutes ticked by. It was useless, Walter thought, time passing. They would move forward into a terrible end. There was only one possible conclusion, no hope for a last-minute deus ex machina, no hope for a wondrous presto-chango. He stirred a puddle with a stick and he thought he might stay put, stay on and on, sitting on that ledge. When the last loiterers had gone down the street, Walter stood up. He was cold and he had a class and he hated sitting and he hated his feet taking steps along the pavement. Mitch was probably sick again. The chamber of his middle ear, inflamed, bright as a strawberry, might well have filled with fluid. Walter walked slowly toward the el station. A person couldn't dance with ear troubles, couldn't keep his balance with a case of otitis media. He'd go to his class, that's what he'd do, and from there he'd find out how to get to the hospital. He could take a bus or ride a different train, or scratch together all his change from the bottom of his bag and hail a cab. It might be that Daniel wouldn't know him anymore. He'd go to class and think about what to say, and afterward he'd visit his brother. He'd try to apologize for not knowing what had happened to Daniel over the course of the year. During the barre work he'd dream up a short story, something to make Daniel laugh. Maybe he'd tell him about the Gamble roof and he'd say that he didn't really know why he'd done it anymore, that everything had become jumbled. He'd learned that you can start out doing something for no reason and then later you invent a slew of explanations, or maybe you discover a true source and motive, maybe you draw out something from a part of yourself you didn't know existed. He'd hold his brother's hand. It didn't matter anymore who was or wasn't the saint in the family. He'd say he was sorry, and Daniel would understand what was included in the apology.

The studio was often empty on Thursday afternoons. There might be one lone girl who had had a private lesson and was changing her clothes, or someone waiting around from the midday class, reading a book or knitting leg warmers. There was a sixty-year-old woman who rented out the studio on occasion to practice, an untalented woman who couldn't give up the dance but was too embarrassed to study with the young people. There were no Junior classes that day, and the Intermediate class didn't begin until five-thirty. Walter opened the door and stood in the waiting room. There was nothing to steal except a battered baby grand and the autographed pictures on the walls. The office, with the cash box, was locked. None of the partitions that made up the changing rooms and the office had their own ceilings, and any movement, a cough, the turning of a page, could be heard over the dividers.

Walter listened. There wasn't a rustle or the sound of a darning needle pulling through the boxy toe of a pointe shoe. He guessed that Mrs. Manka was out feeding herself, Mr. Kenton having an early one over at the Blackstone Hotel bar, and Mrs. Kenton down on fifth at the beauty salon. He thought himself alone, so that when he walked into the dressing room he had to clap his hand over his mouth to stifle his cry. Mitch was lying on the bench, his eyes closed, his hands folded on his chest with sepulchral neatness and solemnity. For a flash Walter's lips smarted again from last night's scene: he could feel Mitch's long fingers pressing down on his mouth to silence him. He had wanted to say, I love none but you. That was all. A basic declaration. He set his bag on the end of the bench and glanced up into the long tulle skirts that hung from the pole. Because there were so few boys, their changing room was used as a closet for the costumes Mrs. Kenton made for the Advanced classes' recitals. The skirts and satin bodices had been made for four of the oldest girls who were going to dance a divertissement called *Pas de Quatre* at a Chicago fund-raiser for the arts.

Walter went to the pole that stretched the length of the room and carefully removed one of the costumes from its hanger. He intended just to look at it. Mitch was dead or fast asleep and either way wasn't going to be good for conversation. Walter felt the creamy white satin and the puff of the short tulle sleeves. He untied the pointe shoes that were fastened to the hanger, shoes that were marked on the bottom, that belonged to Sonja Marendaz. The costume had attracted him, he would later explain to Susan, the way a coin glittering in the light of the alley draws a raccoon. He had read about *Pas de Quatre* and knew its lore, and he relished the idea of four prima ballerinas in 1845 overcoming their rivalries and jealousies to perform on the same stage in London. He thought, I'll put it on for half a minute, to see what it feels like. It couldn't do any harm. As he climbed out of his pants he imagined himself to be Marie Taglioni, the finest dancer in the world in 1845. The costume slid down so easily over his shoulders, and the satin was like cream against his chest. He walked around the room, straining to get the zipper back up, feeling in the costume as if he were swimming at night without wearing a suit. There was both freedom and luxury in the satin and gauze. He flounced down on the bench across from Mitch—he loved how the material of the skirt rose up around him, as if it were displaced water. He leaned over and put on the pointe shoes, tying the pink ribbons around his ankles. Susan had tied her own shoes, crisscrossing the ribbons hundreds of times in front of him, and he followed her motions from memory without much difficulty. The shoes were snug, but he knew they were supposed to be tight. He looped his undershirt around his head in the best approximation he could make of the soft, downy headdresses the girls wore in *Swan Lake*. How fabulous to be a cygnet, he thought. When he stood the skirt fluffed out nicely. There was no mirror and he could only feel, How divine I look! He rose on his pointes and with the tentativeness of a first flight he wobbled and fluttered his arms.

When Walter began singing a fragment of *Swan Lake* and hopping on one foot, the other stretched behind him in an arabesque, Mitch put his hands to his forehead, shielding his eyes, as if from a glare. Walter had seen *Swan Lake* four times at the Auditorium Theater, twice with Sue Rawson, once by himself, and once with Susan. He crossed his arms over his chest, as Odette, the Swan Queen, did at some moment in all of her variations. He bourréed on his tottery pointes to Mitch, humming the strains of Tchaikovsky's music as he came. It was so sad that the devilish look-alike swan stole the Prince from the beautiful good swan in the bad-magic-versus-true-love contest. It was not as hard to move on pointe as he had anticipated, although his toes were mashed and he couldn't exactly feel them.

"Help me, would ya?" he said to Mitch. "In the first place, I have no control over my destiny. That's why the stupid fucking ballet I ended up in is so romantic and miserable. The Prince has jilted me. He's going off to marry that bitch, my evil twin, Odile. He doesn't know three crucial facts about her: One, she's a divorcée; two, she sells Mary Kay products from her basement; and three, she has a drinking problem."

Mitch stretched and yawned. "You really are an honest-to-God fag, you know that?"

Walter sang in a higher register, exaggerating the pathos of the music. He flapped his fledgling wings and chugged across the room. "In *Swan Lake,*" he moaned, "love and sex can never be consummated, except in death." He moved in spasms back and forth across the dressing room wailing, "Only in death! Only in death! I think that's so beeeee—uuuu-tiful." He sputtered around in a pirouette and came to both feet, to fifth position. "I can do this," he cried. "Did you see that? I came back to a perfect fifth. I look good, you can't tell me I don't!"

"Shit," Mitch muttered.

"You'll never say I do, I know. You'll never admit it. I'm going to run to the mirrors and check."

"You're always going to be a homo!" Mitch called after him.

Walter paused outside the dressing room, considering that remark. Of course he was always going to be a homo. He had already figured out that his kind didn't reach the age of twenty-one and automatically and genuinely become marriageable material. He stuck one fluttering arm back through the door, as if to say in swan language, So will you too be a cream puff, and he hiked up his skirts and went slap-slapping into the studio.

The late-afternoon sun filtered through the clouds over the lake, and in the long bank of mirrors it was hard to see where the gauze of the skirt ended and the glittering dust began. He was no more flat-chested than half of the girls. He looked terrific, he did! He tinkered with the undershirt on his head, tucking the sleeves into the roll of the crown. If only they could wear costumes for class, instead of the drab black tights and the plain white T-shirt. He turned his head to this side, to that, admiring himself. He did a jump step called a pas de chat, one foot to the knee, step, the other foot to the knee, a sideways leap, the step of the cat. The pointe shoes made a pleasing noise as they came to the floor, wood against wood, and the skirt followed him, floating, a beat behind his movements. He sang, bringing his arms over his head, crossing them down to his knees, wavering on his pointes. His every movement, he thought, expressed the agony of rejection and the spell of sorrow. Poor Odette, he danced, who loves so purely and loses her chance of earthly happiness. He brought his trembling arms behind him, threw back his head, the way Odette does in both her passion and her grief. Mitch's words came to him— "You'll always be a homo"—and he thought too of the horrible things Susan had said to him at school. Daniel was lying in a steel hospital bed shoved up against a tiled wall, waiting to go from this world. How could that be real? Walter raised his voice and it cracked. Singing, dancing, he guessed, was the only way he could ever really communicate. It did cross his mind, as he so poignantly bobbled to his own strains, that he should be careful not to stay too long, one more look, and he'd pitter-patter back to the dressing room.

It was inevitable, he later thought, predictable, that Mr. Kenton flick on the lights and see him clearly. Under the white ball fixture Walter was no longer obscured by the deepening golden afternoon sunlight. He continued to move, shutting his eyes, laughing, as if he were already middle-aged and the scene was a past embarrassing moment. He had escaped the police in the alley, and Mitch, under his bed, had not been found out by Joyce and Robert. Still, it seemed so familiar, this getting-caught-in-the-light business. Mrs. Manka was standing behind Mr. Kenton, peering over his shoulder. Although it was April it was unseasonably cold. She looked like a Russian diplomat in her black-and-white-checked coat, with the big, black, plush fake-fur collar and a black fur hat.

"What in Sam Hill—" she began.

Mr. Kenton did not register surprise. "All right, then," he said simply. He came forward, pulled at the thighs of his trousers with his thumbs and index fingers and sat himself down on the white bench with the blue cushion, where he always sat when he watched their combinations. "We'll have Odile's fouetté music, please, Agatha."

Mrs. Manka seemed to be having trouble taking off her coat, or else, Walter thought, she was removing it reluctantly, stalling. She glanced at him once, shaking her head, pursing her lips, not a look of encouragement or amusement. He understood her to mean that the fouetté turns were difficult and that the man of the establishment did not have a forgiving temperament. There was no little pocket of mercy in Mr. Kenton and maybe he was going to give Walter a lashing he'd never forget, and who was to say that Walter didn't deserve it?

"Come to the center, Odile," Mr. Kenton said, clapping three times.

No, no! Walter was the good swan, Odette, not the bad swan. The wicked one had the hardest variations, the demanding turns. He was much better at expressing pain and misfortune; he couldn't possibly convince anyone, even through the dance, that he was conniving, out to spoil a prince's pleasure and happiness.

"Let's see your thirty-two fouetté turns," Mr. Kenton ordered. "You have two measures for preparation. About like this, Agatha." He hummed the music, setting the speed. It was far slower than the recording, but faster than a novice could manage. Mrs. Manka quickly lit her cigarette and took a sustaining puff.

Walter felt as if he were wearing flippers as he came to the center, as if he were all equipment, suited up for a horrific dive. Fouetté turns are sharp whipping turns, one after the next. He was to do thirty-two of them without stopping, just as Odile does in *Swan Lake,* when she's bewitching the Prince. He could sense the weight of the shoes but he didn't think he could find his own feet. It might be possible to turn around and around on half-pointe, without rising up on his toes. Walter's one strength in ballet was his ability to turn. It crossed his mind, just for an instant, that Mr. Kenton was appealing to his talent. But no, no, how could Walter forget? This was the hunter and his prey, the great big old cat with yellow teeth getting closer, closer, cornering the mouse, the resigned mouse, the I-am-already-dead mouse.

Mrs. Manka played her measures, and he did his preparation, arms to the front, arms and feet à la seconde, arms and feet to fourth position. He got three quarters of the way through the first turn when Mr. Kenton clapped to stop the music. "No, no, no, no. On pointe. You're a swan now, remember? You've got the costume and the shoes, now do the dance, GIRL."

Mrs. Manka again began the introduction. "And one and two and three and four," Mr. Kenton shouted.

It is trying enough for a seasoned ballerina to successfully execute thirty-two fouettés. There was a brittle anger in Mr. Kenton's voice as he counted. It's a long way down to the ground from the twelfth floor, Walter thought, and his sleeves would not have much wing action to slow the fall. He felt as if his feet were laced up in cement blocks; the numbness was rising from his ankles, spreading like dye along his calves. His hands were wet, his skin so cold, and the knocking of his chest was in his ears, overpowering the music. Those irregularities, he thought, meant that he was frightened.

"MOVE," Mr. Kenton ordered.

Walter turned. He went around in a burst, and again, and a third time. His feet were going to snap at the ankle with a few more rotations, he was sure of it, and he'd have to dance on the raw bleeding stub of a leg. He fell after the sixth turn. He lay still in the pool of his skirt. He hardly knew if he was crying, didn't want to feel his face to find out, couldn't in any case locate his cheeks or his eyes, all of him to the top of his head packed into the shoes.

"GET UP," Mr. Kenton shouted, with the force, the venom, of a sergeant. "Take it from the top, DEAR."

"I don't think I can—"

"FROM THE TOP." He was standing, banging the cane against the wall, shouting at Mrs. Manka, and at Walter, shouting, "Faster, faster, faster." Walter's turning foot bent and he skittered across the floor.

"Center, sweetheart," Mr. Kenton said with terrifying enunciation. "Again, lover."

Walter dragged himself, hauled his feet, to the front of the studio. He was preparing for the turns when he saw Mitch at the door, Mitch's right foot crossed over the left, Mitch resting against the jamb, Mitch's lip curling, Mitch sniggering.

"AGAIN," Mr. Kenton bellowed.

Walter looked at his teacher, at his flashing eyes, his red ascot bunched at his throat, that clot of color like a gaping wound. "It's not going to be good," his mother in her infinite wisdom had said the night before.

Why am I here? Walter thought. I need to go to the hospital. I need to see Daniel, my brother.

It's not going to be good, sweetie. He picked up his beaten, his quite dead, feet, and made for the door. He brushed against his friend, the one with the fiendishly long and hard winkie, the beauty of which he could only imagine because he had never been allowed to revel over it. He walked from the studio without hearing Mr. Kenton's invective, without listening to the demands to return, the threats, he supposed, and the insults. There were twelve flights of stairs, in the neighborhood of 240 individual steps and the walk around every landing. But he couldn't stand there waiting for the elevator with Mr. Kenton on his tail and he certainly didn't want to explain his girl getup to the elevator man. It was at the fifth floor that he felt his feet, suddenly, briefly, a stab of pain as if the nerves were finally being severed. His feet, he thought, were like two squashed hearts inside of Sonja Marendaz's pointe shoes, shoes that had been made by an old man cobbler across the ocean in England. He went down and down, the bloody pulp sloshing in his slippers. When he got to the last marble flight he sat and scooted on his behind down each stair to the lobby, where many of the girls in his class were waiting for the elevator.

He had a fair idea that he looked like a crippled pigeon. The girls were too startled to squeal or laugh out loud, and he was grateful for the silence. He got himself upright and walked out the door to the street. It occurred to him as he crossed Van Buren that he couldn't very well ride the el in the costume, and that he also could not go back to the studio to fetch his clothes. He stood on the pavement, the wind blowing his skirt up in the back. It was chilly and the tulle and satin weren't much for warmth. He realized that he couldn't ride the el anyway, because he didn't have his wallet. There were red stains spreading from the pink satin toe on each foot towards the instep. He had no money. It would be the first time in history a person bled to death from a wound to the big toe. He supposed that the newspaper would call it suicide first and murder later, after Mrs. Manka came forward and told the police the truth.

He turned back and hobbled up the block to the Pick Congress Hotel. In front of the porters in their green pants and green vests and green top hats, he walked along the curb and got into the first taxi in the lineup. He had no choice but to lift his skirts modestly and climb into the car. It was perhaps there, outside the row of grand hotels, that Walter found in himself a confidence that was later to hold him in good stead in Otten. There was nothing to do but be a fool in as dignified a manner as he could muster. The driver did not look at him, did not say a word, as if every day a boy dressed as a wili got in his cab. Walter took off the slippers and although he tried to massage his feet, one at a time, both of them remained in the shape of the shoe for the duration of the trip. The nails had come off seven of his toes and he let them bleed on the floor mat of the cab. He couldn't think what would have happened if he'd stayed on, if Mr. Kenton had planned to beat him or make him dance until he broke a leg. He put his head back and tried to find rest in the thought that it was over, he had gotten away.

When they pulled up to 646 Maplewood Avenue thirty minutes later Walter told the driver to wait.

"You bet I'll wait, kid, until I have every penny of the fare."

He limped up the sidewalk and into the house and through the rooms, opening drawers and looking in pots, searching for cash. Joyce had so thoughtfully left ten dollars for pizza under the vase. "Bless you," Walter whispered. He found three dollars in small change, and two dollars in Daniel's wallet that had been on the counter for a month. He went back out in his costume and his bare feet. It was when he opened the car door and handed the money to the driver that the man at last took notice. He looked Walter up and down and said, "What's the matter wich-you?"

"Is it extra for analysis, or do you do it for free?" Walter said, slamming the door.

In the following hour, in his living room, he considered killing himself by using a number of different methods. He didn't exactly want to die, but living was not something he wished to continue. He would have liked to go elsewhere, not as a traveler or a runaway—just elsewhere; to sit and wait, until his life was over.

He found he could not walk. He was sitting at the bottom of the stairs in the hall, and he could not move. It would be impossible, then, to climb the three flights to pitch himself off the attic roof. It would be out of the question to get to the medicine cabinet, to the full bottle of aspirin. His parents did not own a gun, as far as he knew. He didn't warm to the thought of stabbing himself with a butcher knife. It took more than enough effort just to take off his costume and ball it up and stuff it behind the piano. Getting his father's trench coat off the hanger almost did him in, and he collapsed on the sofa before he finished threading the buckle. He would pass out, that's what he would do. He had never fainted, and he didn't know if it was something that could be willed. It would be best, if he was going to lose consciousness, to go slowly, to music. He crawled to the stereo. If he could only manage to get the record on the turntable without standing, he'd have *Tosca*. It was worth doing for Tebaldi, never mind his bloody feet and all the rest of him that was hurt too.

When she came on in the second act singing "Vissi d'arte," Walter, in a pile on the floor, lifted his head and weakly sang along with her, feeling the meaning as he never had before. "Love and music, these have I lived for, nor ever have harmed a living being." He was with her all the way to the end. "Why, heavenly father, why hast thou forsaken me?"

Ten

MAY

1996

When he was in his early thirties Walter learned more from his father about Daniel's illness, about the botched surgery and the experimental drugs he'd been given. They stumbled into the conversation quite by accident one summer night when they were alone on the porch at Lake Margaret. Robert had been rambling on about the Cubs until the perfumed candle deep inside the frosted-glass bulb guttered down to the end of the wick and went out. The windy darkness was all around them, a wild August blow slapping the water up against the seawall and tearing branches from trees. There had been a memorable night like it years before, starting with a sweltering afternoon, a gust coming from the south and another, and pretty soon the waves were slopping out of the lake, the shutters flying off their hinges. Robert laughed out loud at the thought of it, and he said to Walter, "Were you there when Daniel tipped the sea boat over, turned it turtle? The boys worked for an hour righting the hulk, and when it was back up, Daniel wanted to go out again, into the eye of the storm. Brave fool!"

"Where was I?" Walter said. How had he missed the storm, and his fearless brother wrestling with the upside-down boat? Why hadn't he been there? "When was that, Dad? Was it the summer Daniel was sick? Had he become weak before anyone knew he was ill?"

That was the tumble, the two of them like blind men falling into a pit, groping to find a wall, a grip. Walter hadn't meant to ask a question that would require a long answer, a painful reply, but he'd gone and opened his mouth. The wind was unsettling, and he'd had a few drinks, and the night sky hung close, a dark hood over them, and he'd asked about his brother. It was done. Although Walter couldn't see the details of his father's face, he knew that Robert was alert, sitting straight in a chair meant for slouching, the tense line of his back in relief against the coarser blackness of the night. Carefully, slowly at first, Robert explained the progression of the illness. He told Walter that the exploratory surgeries they'd performed were not done in hopes of Daniel's recovery, but were last-ditch efforts, to keep up the fight as well as study the mysteries of the cancer. The medical community was working toward a treatment of Hodgkin's, a therapy that would in the future be improved and someday perfected. It became hit-and-miss as they went along, as Daniel steadily declined.

"Researching—using Dan," Walter said.

"The doctors were at a loss, trying what they could," Robert said, "but they just didn't know very much. That was the fact of the matter. We told ourselves that Daniel might have been slaughtered in Vietnam for no cause. He might have died in a car crash—there are any number of senseless ways to lose your life."

"Did you think of traveling to Mexico," Walter asked, "or feeding Daniel apricot pits, or trying a seedy place on the south side of Chicago for acupuncture or shiatsu? Was that sort of thing done in those days?" Had his parents, he wondered, been willing to suspend their suburban traditions and gamble with the exotic?

Robert leaned forward and scratched his leg. For some time he kneaded his calf. Walter understood as well as he ever had that his parents had been stunned by their son's disease, and that after all the years the disbelief and the guilt could so easily be renewed. They may have blamed themselves for a recessive quirk that had given Daniel the cancer, some glitch along one of their own wormy chromosomes.

"It must have been terrible," Walter said. "Awful." It was hopeless, the conversation, better to talk about baseball without even listening to each other.

"It was sly," Robert said suddenly. "The disease. A shyster. Nothing we could do about it, but still there were mistakes that have been hard to forgive. The operation they did early on, when they sutured the wound too tight, for one."

"Too tight?"

"Waiting for that mess to heal delayed the chemotherapy three or four weeks. It gave us something to blame for a while. The end was inevitable, we knew, but we focused on that bungle and I guess it didn't do any harm. Righteous indignation, not a worthless feeling. It got me through the most difficult part."

"What?" Walter said after a minute. "What part was that?"

"Telling my own son that he was going to die."

"Dad," Walter breathed.

"You probably won't be surprised that a day doesn't go by without my thinking of him, that several times a week I remember the talk we had. I told him I was sending him off on a trip, a journey I couldn't prepare him for." Robert shook his head and scoffed. "A journey. I said that he would leave his body behind, that he'd be the first of us to take the leap. There couldn't help but be something of an adventure in it. That's what I said, an adventure in it. I was drowning in sorrow and I was making out death to be an excursion to an amusement park. I have never even admitted the extent of my stupidity to your mother."

"Dad," Walter said again. He was shaken both by the confession and by his father's eloquence.

"How do you explain something you don't understand, don't want to understand, something you've had little experience with? I assured him. I talked about the great mystery. I said I trusted the plan. Death, I explained, as if I knew, was the ultimate act of generosity, the one magnanimous act we're made to do, like it or not, when our time comes. What was I to say, that I was afraid for him, scared out of my wits? I couldn't have put into words then that I was terrified for us, as much as I was for him. I didn't know if we'd get through it."

"You—you did best."

"No," Robert said, "I'm afraid not. I spoke as if I understood more than an ordinary man, as if I had conviction. I meant to be reassuring but I muffed it by being dishonest, by being prissy. I think about what I'd want at my end and prissiness is the last thing, the worst thing! Dan tried to see through it, but who knows if he did, or could. I think he gave up the ghost when I couldn't face him squarely and say, 'You're dying and part of us, a huge chunk, is going with you. I have no idea what in God's name comes next for you or any of us.' "

"No one wants to hear that—"

"I'm telling you that Daniel asked me for my truth, not some student teacher horse's-ass lecture. I sometimes think I spent all of my courage in that two-minute talk I had with him, that I spent my quota on the big lie. I don't know that it takes more guts to make up baloney than to talk straight. Get me another Bud would you please?"

Walter felt along the hall in the dark, and when he came back to the porch his forefingers to his father's hand as he gave the beer over was the best they could do to acknowledge the brief intimacy. They continued to drink and Robert maundered on about his own boyhood, his parents, his grandparents and the world wars. Walter half listened to the stories he had heard before. He couldn't shake the image of his father struggling to find a suitable truth, a palatable fiction, by Daniel's bed. If there was anything to regret, Walter thought, it was the shabby work of memory, that several good lines had become nothing more than doggerel in Robert's mind.

In Otten, Walter hated to admit that for his students at fourteen and fifteen there was already little hope for major rehabilitation. They might shed their fat, earn a lot of money, find religion, join support groups, but their basic natures were fixed. They would grow up into a complex future with uncertain skills and beleaguered backgrounds, and all he could do for them, it seemed, was focus on the small shortcomings that were manageable. Sometimes the only help he could give was correcting their grammar, fixing the length of a sentence. He thought he could predict with one hundred percent accuracy which members of his *South Pacific* cast would go on to become members of community theater, reliving their adolescent dreams of stardom on rickety, jerry-built stages. He had been asked to come forward on the last night of the show, and Kimmy Roth, the girl who played Nellie Forbush, had handed him one long-stemmed red rose. There had been a polite round of applause when he took his curtain call and a few whoops after he'd thanked the pit band, the stage crew and the actors.

All of the productions Walter had ever been involved with had come together at the last minute, and he had forced himself to believe that *South Pacific* too would gel in the final rehearsal. The students for the most part had worked hard and they seemed to be proud of their efforts. His seventh-hour bad girl, Sharon, had hideously overacted in her role of Bloody Mary, mugging and trying to steal everyone else's scenes. The Otten audience had loved it and given her an ovation at her curtain call. It pleased Walter to see her and the others wearing their makeup after the performances as a badge of honor, carrying their carnations and their dirty costumes with an exaggerated, vainglorious strain, hefting a great burden.

Walter had made an appearance at the cast party the first night; he'd done his best to be jolly, playing old show tunes on the piano while the ensemble sang, locking arms and swaying. They were each of them their own selves, certainly, and yet he could not help seeing his students as types. There was something of a Mitch in the crowd, the good-looking lazy kid who played Lieutenant Cable, and a well-rounded, kind Daniel or two. There was a Walter, a sophomore named Jacob Burkhart. He hadn't come to the party because he had a voice lesson early the next morning seventy miles away in Madison. He was the shortest person in his class and there was the problem of a tic in the lid of his left eye, but he had a respectable tenor voice. He had admitted to Walter during a costume check that he wanted to be in chorus lines in touring productions of Broadway shows. It was impressive, Walter thought, that Jacob had set his sights so reasonably on the provinces and on the back row.

At the cast party he played "Getting to Know You," and he looked over the top of the piano wondering who in the group was going to be the Otten sacrificial lamb. He had blocked the thought, gone to the buffet, eaten a brownie and excused himself, thanking Mrs. Roth on the way out. He had never stopped wondering why Daniel had been assigned his thankless high-profile role. From Walter's study of Otten he had concluded that in every four-year cycle a student died, usually in traffic, in an alcohol-related death. The 1973 Oak Ridge High yearbook had been dedicated to Daniel. He'd died right before the book went to press and they were able to squeeze in the full-page picture. Susan was the special girl who had had a poem printed, a memorial of some fifty lines to accompany the photo. As Walter recalled, the piece was titled "The Precious Nature of Life," but there had been some catchy phrases and sweet sentiments about the air in May, the smell of violets, the light in the morning, the light in the evening and the sound of mothers calling their children in for supper. It had demanded the reader to look around and take note of the bounty and the beauty. If a few of Oak Ridge's teenagers had heeded Susan's words, it could be said that Daniel and his sweetheart had made quite a contribution at the age of eighteen and sixteen. It was more than Walter could boast of doing in his profession, getting teenagers to snap to attention. He hoped that Daniel's classmates, at their reunions, still talked about the McCloud boy, the swimmer, and, for just a minute, felt the old sadness.

It was in the aftermath of his *Swan Lake* performance and disgrace that Walter realized he had been not the sacrificial lamb but the scapegoat. Mr. Kenton had in effect flogged him. Walter decided after the beating that he had been punished for the carport, for his shameful relations with Mitch, his hateful feelings toward Susan, his indifference to his brother. It was forty lashes for every one of his lapses, his hostilities, his perversity. Maybe, he thought, the beating extended beyond himself too, and Mr. Kenton had given him a lick for Mitch's cruelty and another for Susan's falseness. Add one more for his parents' silence, and why not a whop or two for their blanket forgiveness, when they should have mustered the strength to at least scold him. Walter had tried to see his thrashing as an impersonal attack on frailty and unkindness. It made him feel a little bit better, to think on a large scale, rather than the personal, to think that it wasn't really one sadistic man beating the shit out of an effeminate boy.

There were two pieces of bad news that May in Otten, both delivered by Joyce over the telephone. The first came on a Friday night, just as Walter was adjusting his covers, about to go to sleep.

"I hate to be the bearer of sad tidings," Joyce said. "It's Francie and Roger. I'm sorry to say that they are divorcing."

"D-divorcing?" Walter sputtered. "How come?"

"She has a young man, apparently. In Bloomington."

"In Indiana? A young man?"

"I don't know, honey. Younger than she is. She's gone, at any rate. Picked up and moved."

"You might think I'm faking," Walter said, "but I honestly had the sense that she was out of the picture at Easter. She'd gotten so skinny—"

"I feel for Roger."

"I feel for Francie's fellow, and for Aunt Jeannie, of course. Has she ever been humiliated before?" Right away Walter wished he could take it back. "Oh, Mom," he said. "This is a disaster. I don't want to know what it means about Lake Margaret."

"Your father and I are thinking hard about it. Trying to find some way to talk Sue Rawson down. I don't know. I can't tell if she'll bend or not. I really cannot call this one. We have to give thought and attention to some sort of plan."

"I will," he said. "I will." But it isn't thought and attention that's lacking, he wanted to say. If mental energy rather than cash could save the place, they'd have it handily. He hung up the phone, turned out the light and lay awake half the night. Before Francie and Roger had come forward with their offer, there had been two meetings with the cousins. None of them had money or time. They were all overcommitted with jobs and children, Scouts, school-board meetings, soccer games, conferences and sick in-laws. They wanted Lake Margaret, in theory, but they couldn't pay, and they didn't really feel like wasting their vacations painting the old house and ripping out the torn kitchen linoleum. It would be sold for lack of money and devotion.

Walter would stand at the gate and he'd look, and then he'd have to get in his car and drive away. Foreigners would move in and they'd knock down the walls and put in new bathrooms and hang cheap pictures and paint the upstairs pink and cover the floor with carpet and fill the porch with ugly wicker lawn sets. He would be left to make a miniature Lake Margaret. He had once had the idea of making a replica of his neighborhood in Oak Ridge, but if he was going to commit himself to construction in an inch scale he might be better off to create a tiny Lake Margaret. The project would allow him to exercise his memory and hold the house dear. This chronicle of his life would become an obsession for him, he knew. He'd become a consumer of little things, searching the country over for craftsmen who could build the parlor chairs to his exact specifications. He would get the details right if it meant going to Italy for the fabric and spending all his money in a given year on an ottoman the size of a Snickers bar. It would be humbling, to become exactly like the women he used to ridicule when he worked at the dollhouse shop in New York. Walter fell asleep thinking that Roger Miller was the only lucky one at the end of the story, the only character who was actually free.

In mid-May, Joyce called Walter and she didn't bother to say hello or prepare him for the shock. He was sitting at his butcher-block island in the kitchen, eating city granola with figs and cranberries, apricots and dates, a gut-cleansing mix an old friend in Brooklyn Heights sent him regularly. "Florence is dead of a heart attack," Joyce announced. "She got out of bed this morning, took a shower, put her clothes on, came downstairs, took a frying pan off the hook by her stove, and keeled over."

Not Florence! Funny, that he always felt closer to her when he thought of her as Mrs. Gamble. How could Mrs. Gamble be dead? Joyce had outlined a logical sequence, but he didn't want to picture her lifting up the covers, slowly swinging her veiny legs over the side of the bed, standing on the worn green paisley carpet, pulling her lacy nightgown over the quivery mass of her belly, that part which had always been concealed by the apron.

"Trishie called the ambulance, but she was already gone when they arrived."

"Already gone," he murmured. Mrs. Gamble had always been so reliable, lurking at the window, watching the McClouds, and he found it difficult to believe that she was truly out of this world. Now that it would never again be possible to catch a glimpse of her behind her sheer dining-room curtain, it struck Walter that he too had been a watcher, that he'd been as fascinated by Mrs. Gamble as she was by all of them. He had probably given her equal time, spying out the kitchen window into her breakfast nook.

He didn't want to listen to his mother describe the ambulance driver and the trip to the emergency room. In his New York days he had seen enough death to know that the process, the laboring toward the end, was at once awesome and hideous and ordinary as a boot. He had thought that at the moment of the unreal calm, when the heart finally stopped, just then what people knew left them; their body of knowledge, words, music and their suddenly unhoused spirit drifted up out of them like one last breath. It may not have been rational to believe such a thing, but there was a cosmic generosity about the idea that appealed to Walter. Perhaps that rich bit of air was left behind for the living to appropriate, to tap, all of the stuff of the dead in the public domain. If he inhaled at the right time, in the right place, he would instantly possess Mrs. Gamble's storehouse. He clapped his hand over his mouth and nose to prevent an accidental intake.

He told Joyce he was sorry, knowing as he said so that his sympathy was misplaced. Mrs. Gamble had been neither friend nor relation. The bond of neighbor was an uneasy one without exact rules and requirements beyond the village ordinance specifying grass length, the height of fences and the types of trees allowed in the parkway. "I have to admit," Joyce said, "that I'm sorry, too. I think I'm going to miss her. It's strange, unsettling, that a force of nature can so suddenly vanish."

"No," Walter said, "no, she's not gone. Not really. Not Mrs. Gamble. She'll pop up in a different form. You watch, that earthquake we've all been waiting for in San Francisco will happen tonight. The whole state of California will break off and be swept away in one stupendous tremor. If not that, at the very least her collies will go feral, after the requisite number of years pawing at her grave and making doggy crying noises."

"Oh, honey," Joyce said, laughing.

How could it be true, he wanted to say. How could she be dead? "I have a student who disappeared recently," he said, "a kid named Jim Norman. I don't think there's anything left of him except a bit of odorless, faintly yellow smoke. No one knows what's happened to him. The parents seem to have checked out too. I tried to reach him, in a teacherly capacity in class, but that proved to be beyond my powers. The school officials are trying to care, but I think everyone's relieved. I can't say I even knew him. So there's no sadness, the way there would be if a straight-A student got killed in a car accident, but on the other hand we're not allowed to be jubilant like the Munchkins. It's uncomfortable because his absence makes us reflect on our own carelessness and lack of interest. It's different from the discomfort Mrs. Gamble's passing prompts in us. Help me, Mother! I'm talking like an English teacher. I'd better say good-bye before I give you an assignment. Please convey my condolences to the family." They, he thought, were the true survivors.

After Joyce hung up he called Susan, to tell her.

"Oh, my God, Walter," she said. "I can't believe it. That old battle-ax! I was coming out of your house once and she was right on the sidewalk, waiting for me. Do you know what she said? She said, 'Young lady, I've seen you in the living room, doing what you do on the sofa, and it's a real bosom heaver.' She had that low, bloodless way of talking, you know? I was so startled by the term *bosom heaver* I couldn't get at what she was saying and I also sort of knew that she was the one at fault, snooping in other people's windows. I never did it with Mitch, you probably figured that out, by the way he didn't let up on me, always breathing down my neck. Everyone assumed we had, but you see, my mother had put the fear in me from way back. I come by my prudishness honestly. With Daniel it was different. For one thing, he didn't have a lot of extra strength, and so often we were just fondling each other without any expectations. I have to say that with him it was about the sweetest thing I've ever had in that department. About as poignant as it can get. I go all weak when I remember that I hoped I'd get pregnant! I thought it would be so romantic to carry his child and name it Daniel Junior, or Danielle—can you believe it, Walter?"

"I would have married you out of brotherly duty."

"Yes, and we'd have lived in those low-income apartments on the south side of Oak Ridge, and you'd have gone to work as a mechanic. It would have been so much fun! I can't help thinking that someone was watching over me, preventing me from going too far astray."

"Mrs. Gamble, angel. It was she who had her eye on you."

" 'A bosom heaver'! What nerve that woman had. How dare she spy on us. I'm not sorry she's dead, Walter, not a bit sorry. She spooked me. How are you, anyway?"

"I can't match you tidbit for tidbit, nothing to reveal about my high school sexual experiences. No long-buried secret." For the first time he was tempted to tell her about Mitch. Maybe he could tell her, in a way that wouldn't take away from her own fine memories. He could assure her that Mitch, after all, had only used him, that Walter had been convenient and so willing. Instead he said, "I told you about my cousin Francie's affair with a man who's studying rural sociology in Bloomington, Indiana. That's a lot of excitement for one family. I'm trying to figure out how to brace myself when Lake Margaret goes on the market."

Susan clicked her tongue and sighed.

"But let's see, I'm going to the prom tomorrow night. The theme this year at Otten, to go along with *South Pacific,* is 'Some Enchanted Evening.' "

"How awful for you! That sounds dreadful. You're a chaperone?"

"I'm responsible for pouring the punch and watching for signs of drugs and alcohol. 'Chaperone' is a gentle term for a bouncer. I'm supposed to be Them, instead of Us. Which means I'm not supposed to get plastered beforehand. You have no idea how these functions serve my memory. I guess I've already told you how my high school career is dredged up and re-dredged up daily. Sometimes I don't feel as if I'm in the present anymore. I'm in purgatory, suspended between then and now, alongside Mrs. Gamble. For me, Florence Gamble lives."

"I don't know how you stand it. Maybe the dollhouse shop was right for you—"

"When my students ask me what I did before I moved to Otten, I tell them, 'Construction.' Do you think they imagine me strapped to a girder ninety stories high in Manhattan, tanned, muscular, wearing a hard hat, whistling down below at the girls? What would happen, do you suppose, if word got out that I had worked at a dollhouse shop?"

"It might be ugly," she said. "You shouldn't think about it."

"Well, I don't. Much. How's Lester?"

"No word," she said mournfully. "Not for two months approximately, or sixty-five days specifically. It feels as if the wire has been cut. It was ill-fated and continues to be ill-fated, and yet, and yet, who knows? What about Julian? Have you done as I said and called him, or written him, or gotten on a plane and sat on his doorstep?"

"I did send him my Pollini program from 1977, signed by the master himself. It was my dearest keepsake."

"That was all the way back in February, Walter. It doesn't count."

"You mean there's a statute of limitations on offerings?"

"Yes. Frequency of communication is more important than the quality."

"I'm sure Julian is besieged by admiring students and Louisiana poets. He has no need to look back over the Mason-Dixon line, back to a one-night stand who spends his time trying to teach farm children to support the thesis sentence with three statements."

"You are sure of no such thing. Answer this next silly question kindly, will you?"

"Okay."

"What do you think happens to the—the love? I pitch it with all my might towards Lester. Breakfast, class, lunch, rehearsal, performance, dinner, sleep: I am radiating love for Lester. Other people may very well be hurling love my way and I don't have any use for it. Julian may be languishing down in New Orleans, dreaming of your arrival. What happens to the feeling once we've released it, do you think?"

"It's not a property that travels in any kind of measurable way, love isn't. The supercolliders can't track it, and on the other end the psychics rarely detect its glittery path. There's no mass to the stuff, no density. It's something that you have to take on faith, I'm afraid. If I were the Mother Abbess I probably wouldn't sing 'Climb Ev'ry

Mountain' at this point in the movie. I'd sing a snappy aerobics tune with the refrain 'Use the love, use the love, use the love.' You know, turn it homeward, where you can see its effects. But then she's a nun. What does she know?"

"No, no, of course you're right, damn you, Walter! Damn you. In your own sweet way you're telling me to be a grown-up. So okay, I'm trying, I'm trying almost as hard as I can. But as to love—if there is no such thing as love you would never have forgiven me."

"I only said love was difficult to trace. Forgiven you for what?"

"For every unthinking and ridiculous thing I did that year. That time we still don't mention very often."

"Oh, that year. I know the one. You did return the costume I stole from the Kentons before they sent me a subpoena. I owed you for that."

"You didn't exactly steal it. And that was selfish on my part, too. You should have kept it and sued them, you really should have. I hope they were worried sick about legal action. I did get the dress cleaned, it's true, at my own expense, but I got to carry it on a hanger, all clean and white and poofy when I went back for the first time in five months. Having the costume in front of me was a way to enter without having myself and my absence be the focus. I was aloof and superior when I handed it over. No, Walter, I've always been selfish. I'm even selfish saying I'm selfish because I expect to be forgiven for it, to be able to go right on being selfish."

"So you're a selfish pig."

"Thank you. I have to go rehearse for *Mystery of the Dancing Princesses,* and tonight it's the usual Dark Angel in *Serenade.*"

"When I told you the story of my disgrace, you didn't laugh. That's to your credit. I was so grateful to you for not laughing, for not even cracking a smile, not a quiver, not a twitch. You looked at my naked toes, bald without their nails, and you didn't flinch. You wept first, as I recall, before you laughed, when I demonstrated the fouettés. You had the purest response in word and in expression."

"Oh good. Maybe I did do one thing right then, a long time ago. I have to hang up. I'm late already, for class. Have a terrific time at the prom. And I'll even say a prayer for Mrs. Gamble before I go onstage, and one for you, too. But if love doesn't travel from live body to live body, my little prayer isn't going to reach the dead."

"We're talking about Mrs. Gamble," Walter said. "She'll get it."

Walter stood at the top of the bleachers during the grand march at the Otten High prom. The gym was unrecognizable, decorated in streamers, white lights strung around in potted trees, a red carpet underfoot and a chandelier hanging by ropes from the ceiling. There was nothing striking in the decor or the fashions to mark the year and it seemed to Walter that 1973 and 1996 were more or less interchangeable. A few of the boys had shaved heads and studs in their ears, but overall they were big and quiet and uncomfortable in their suits. As it had always been, and would always be, the girls could have passed for twenty-five with their hairdos and makeup and heels and slinky dresses, but the eagerness and shine belonged to their sixteen-year-old selves. There was so much talk about how students were different these days, but Walter wondered if anything fundamental had changed in twenty years. He wondered too, how long it would be before Otten sold single tickets or tolerated same-sex couples at their school dances, if such a thing would happen in his lifetime. Milwaukee, only a few hours away, was going to have its annual Pride Weekend at the end of the month, but Otten would certainly not feel any aftershock from the celebration.

He and Mrs. Denval watched the couples coming two by two up the gym floor and onto the stage. "Isn't it disgusting, what they're wearing?" Mrs. Denval shouted into Walter's ear. "Look at Cheryl Borgelt—why, you can see her G-string." The crowd went wild when Bill Pierce of the Otten Braves mounted the stairs with his date. He had opted for a classic black tux and crew cut. Walter resisted the urge to point out Bill's elegance to Mrs. Denval. She took his arm and said, "Did you go to your prom, Mr. McCloud?"

He was still clapping for Bill, and without thinking he said, "Yes."

"Oh, how nice. I don't think it's ever a good experience, but it's always lovely, especially if you're a girl, for the rest of your life to be able to say you went. Do you think all of our youngsters are going to go home, or wherever they go after this dance, and have sexual inter-course?"

Walter choked on his 7-Up. "I don't know. Probably some of them, Mrs. D., half of them? The ones you'd expect, and a few you wouldn't, but not all, no, not everyone."

"Did you, after your prom?"

"Of course not," he said. "I was a late bloomer. Actually, if you must know, I have yet to bloom. I spent my high school career playing *Name That Tune* with my aged aunt."

Walter had not gone to his prom or anyone else's prom, but he hadn't meant to lie to Mrs. Denval. When she asked him he had said yes, because in a way he felt as if he'd experienced the dance. He had gotten more out of the prom the year he was fifteen than a high school function was capable of offering. Maybe, he considered, that was the true nature of a miracle, that a person could take riches from a thing that inside and out was empty.

After he stopped going to ballet class that April, after the *Swan Lake* fiasco, Walter began to visit Daniel at the hospital downtown. It was beyond the time when he could have established a friendship with his brother. Daniel slept fitfully, and when he woke he lay waiting for his next shot of morphine. He was sometimes in pain, crying softly, or he was groggy, or he was asleep. When Walter sat beside him trying to make conversation, Daniel was unfailingly polite, but Walter knew that if he'd had the energy he'd have stolen past them, gone to another room, curled up into himself, away from talk and food and emotion.

That first week Walter quit dancing, Susan had a sinus infection and was home sick. The week after, her grandmother in Phoenix died and the family went west. Walter was thankful for her absence, and af-terward he wondered if she had somehow brought on her own sick-ness and her grandmother's death, if she knew to stay at a distance.

In the hospital, after school, he sat on one side of the bed, across from his mother. Joyce was knitting, what he couldn't tell. It was a shapeless pile, probably meant to be a man-size sweater. He assumed she was knitting to do something with her hands, instead of picking at her cuticles, that she didn't care what she made. She was long past fussing at Daniel to eat, but every few minutes she'd get up and swab his mouth with a cloth dipped in cold water, and she'd check his catheter, wipe his brow, hold his hand, speaking so quietly Walter could not hear what she said.

In the evening Robert joined them. He brought tacos rolled up in waxed paper or fried chicken in a bucket, or ham sandwiches from the cafeteria. They made a point to talk about anything, the elevator control panel, the doctor with the knee brace, the nurse who always grilled Walter about visiting privileges, the errant balloon floating down the hall. It was a relief to have words in the air. Walter had the idea that what was left in Daniel was the small hard core of his self, but the accumulated stuff of personality and learning and life was seeping away, bit by bit, hour after hour. How odd in the face of that, and also how good it was, to talk about the weather. Daniel's essential sweetness was intact, and sometimes when he opened his eyes he smiled weakly up at Joyce and as if he'd come a great number of miles and just arrived, he'd say in a thick, phlegmy voice, "Hi, Mom."

After supper Robert turned on the TV and watched the news, and Joyce moved her chair so that she could see the anchormen's familiar faces and hear their dispassionate voices. It seemed sacrilegious to Walter that his parents watched complete strangers talk about misfortunes in the city when Daniel was slipping away from them. He went to his brother when Bill Curtis came on, as if the six o'clock news were the McCloud boys' one occasion to unite against their parents, stand firm against authority. He found that he could remember playing with Dan, that in fact he could retrieve whole scenes, in the bath, in the wading pool, the sandbox, the attic on a rainy afternoon. It took concentration and will and a bit of invention to bring the episodes back. Walter had broken Daniel's train engine the Christmas he was five and there hadn't been hell to pay, not at 646 Maplewood Avenue, but Daniel had put his face in his new flannel pajamas and cried softly, in a way that presaged his adolescent stoicism. Walter would have liked to whisper to Daniel, to remind him of their joint past, but he felt shy in his parents' presence, and he wondered for whose benefit the unburdening really was, if it was actually for himself. He was so sorry about every little thing. It seemed possible that Daniel had some kind of knowledge and authority and that if Walter could confess to him there might in return be absolution. He couldn't tell. He didn't know anything.

Once, when Robert left to go to the cafeteria for coffee, Walter went to his mother, kneeled down awkwardly and put his head in her lap. Daniel's breathing was labored and Walter didn't think he could listen anymore. He blocked his ears. But she thought he was about to weep, and she leaned over him and patted him as if he were a baby, trilling, "It's all right, it's all right, it's all right." When he lifted his head she said in the same parrot voice, "You shouldn't be here, shouldn't be here." There had been a few arguments with various nurses but Joyce had stood her ground, and she had lied too, telling the administration that Walter was already sixteen. It was clear to him that she had lost her judgment, that it was the same to her if a person wept in her lap or blocked his ears in her lap or watched television or knit a suit of armor that no one would ever wear.

He got up and went to the window. There were no natural phenomena outside for inspiration or fortitude. The moon wasn't rising over the lake and there were no stars in the cloudy sky. The city was below them, all light and movement, and overhead he could hear the burr of a helicopter. The nurse came in and fiddled with the IV pole. He didn't want his mother to tell him to leave, not at this late date. There was no place to go, nothing he was interested in anymore. He and she were the same, set loose from their moorings. To divert her he said, "I'm going to quit ballet, Mom. I've had enough. I need to hang it up for good."

She nodded, as if she could have told him years ago that he wasn't suited for the dance, as if she'd known long before that they would someday have this conversation. "You're sure you want to?" she said.

"Yes."

"Maybe you should wait until—well, for a couple of months to decide. Or until you find something to replace it."

"No," he said. "It's time to stop. I'm ready."

Aunt Jeannie bawled Joyce out over the telephone for including Walter in Daniel's death vigil. She reminded her sister that she never interfered with her affairs, but that in this case she had to speak her mind. Her own daughter Francie was a year older than Walter, and she would never let Francie witness such a thing. She was worried, she said, about permanent damage to little Walter's psyche.

Mrs. Gamble also disapproved and spread the word up and down the alley. Walter had gone to the hospital that first afternoon following his run-in with Mr. Kenton, and he made it plain to his mother that he meant to stay for a few hours. His teacher had beaten him, but Walter could bounce back and tough it out with his parents, make his point, insist, storm, fight, have his way. Daniel was a ghastly sight, worse than he had expected, but he had seen and couldn't take the image back. "I'm going to be part of this family," Walter said to his mother, the re-solve, the strength of his feeling making his voice tremble. He was going to join the inner circle if it entailed watching every cancer victim in the hospital suffer; if it involved making conversation with Susan in the corridor; if it meant spoon-feeding his mother until she had enough starch to come home and sort the mail and sit herself down to a decent supper. He was going to face Daniel and find out what took place at the heartless end. He wasn't so afraid that he couldn't look, wasn't so terrified he couldn't try to help.

There had been no fond reunion that afternoon, no apologies or reminiscences, brother to brother. Walter followed Joyce's lead: he held Daniel's hand while he slept, and when he woke he adjusted the pillow and went to the hall sink for fresh water. Daniel opened his eyes halfway and said hello. That was all. Hello. And Walter said hello back and, without realizing, brought his own hand up and brushed the damp hair to the side, off Dan's forehead.

Walter always maintained that it had been right for their family to be together, and he never regretted those afternoons and evenings he spent with his mother and father, listening to the tortured breathing of his brother. He was not sorry, in spite of the nightmares, and the fact that for years when he thought of Daniel he often recalled the sick boy. It was not his experience that images of the healthy person soon supplanted the death scene. He knew that his relatives were looking askance at someone so young being subjected to the random cruelty of disease, and yet Walter could not have imagined taking up Aunt Jeannie's invitation to play backgammon and stay overnight with the cousins. He could not have explained to any of them that there was peace in the hospital room. It was a place where time seemed to have stopped, where the four of them might stay indefinitely. It was probably like being stranded in an elevator, or sharing a cabin at camp, or going to the moon in the same spaceship. Walter believed that when they came home they'd feel as if they knew the same songs, they'd have bruises in the same places, the shared memory of the northern lights and the sun rising red on the last day. Room 901 was a replication of heaven, he sometimes thought: the eternal life offered the consolation of sitting with your family in a small well-lit cubicle with kind women in white uniforms whisking in and out, and every now and then the head physician passing through to make his pronouncement. Jeannie could not have known that for Walter it was a privilege to be let into the privacy of Daniel's final month, and that the bewilderment, the wounds came later, in all of the following years that his parents never spoke of that time in the hospital.

Either Joyce or Robert spent the night with Daniel in May, and sometimes they were both there, sleeping in recliner chairs at either side of the bed. Joyce was determined to be with him when he went. She did not want his going it alone. Walter knew without words having passed that she planned to hold Daniel's hand as he took the last breath. He knew by the way she clutched her purse when she left, and looked at Daniel all the way out the door. When she returned there was panic in her eyes as far back as the elevator. She rushed into the room, her arms going as if she were swimming, trying to find her way to the bed, to see if he was still there.

On the Saturday of Oak Ridge's prom Walter went to the hospital at four in the afternoon to spell his mother. She'd been in Room 901 for three days and had agreed to run back to Maplewood Avenue for a shower and a quick nap. There had been assurance from the doctor that the end was not imminent. Robert had a head cold and was on the sofa in the den at home with the thermos of chicken soup Walter had made for him. It took Joyce fifteen minutes to gather her things and find the car keys, and when she was gone Walter pulled up a chair and sat by Daniel. He looked at the short thin eyelashes, the crust between the lids, the stubble on his chin, the chapped open mouth, the bloody scab at his nose, where the oxygen tubes had irritated his skin. He wondered if Daniel dreamed anymore, or if he had exhausted all of the material from his eighteen years. His lids looked like dried apple slices. Walter wondered if the dream was always the same, if Daniel was forever walking down a long dusty road under the hot sun to the shady place in the distance. He wanted to ask him what he thought about his life and the unexpected turn of events, if there was anything a person should do to prepare for the finish, if he had advice for his kid brother. And what, if anything, was there that Walter could do for Daniel, any small thing to make the passage smoother? He wanted to say that sometimes he was so scared he sat up in the dark shaking and crying, and other times he felt an inexplicable calm and it was as if nothing was as sad as he'd thought. He wished he could ask his brother why that was. Maybe Daniel would have explained that every terrible thing he could think of was about wanting and not having. Walter could almost hear his voice. Dan would elaborate; he'd say, "Wanting. Wanting to live, or to walk, or to see, or wanting peace, or children back from the dead, or wanting food or fame or love, a voice, a home— Humans have been made to want, Wally. But the problem with you people down below is that even if your wish is granted, even if you get the happy ending, you right away turn around and want something else, or an accessory or an improvement, a bigger diamond, a fancier car." Daniel, Walter willed himself to believe, was already speaking to him as he would from beyond the grave.

At six o'clock the nice nurse, Betty, brought Walter a bowl of soup and some oyster crackers in a Baggie. It was so strange to sit with food in front of his sleeping brother. He held the bowl in his hands for the warmth of it. There were strands of what looked like algae floating on the top of the soup, cream of asparagus, he guessed. When there was no more heat in the porcelain, he went and stood at the window and looked down at the traffic. He thought about being older and driving past the hospital and glancing at the window, the very window on the cancer floor, knowing that another family on nine was having a similar tragedy. Maybe someone on the street with a difficult past was driving by, looking up at him, thinking the very thought. What he was living through at the moment would become something that happened long ago. How futile everything was—how empty life was! He moved so quickly to Daniel's bed he almost toppled over on his brother's chest—he seized the limp hands, crying, "Don't go, Dan! Don't go!"

Walter didn't hear the elevator bell, didn't notice a sound until the swishing was right outside the door. It was the panting noise the Gamble collies made when they stood at the fence with their mouths hanging open. He was imploring his sleeping brother to live, and in his panic it seemed logical that Mrs. Gamble would bring the dogs, both to entertain Daniel and to say good-bye to him. It was not usual but he had to admit it was a great idea. The nurses couldn't say no, couldn't object when Mrs. Gamble was so adept at cleaning up after the animals. He cocked his head, straining to see the dogs, to get the first view of them trotting through the door, obedient at their master's side. He had to look twice to see Susan. It wasn't the blond dogs with the ears that had been trained to turn down in velvety triangles. It was Susan. Susan in a brassy turquoise dress. A shiny strapless hooker getup with puckers in the material on top, the place for a normal girl's breasts. She hadn't knocked or called or as much as peered around the corner tentatively. The dress was tight to the ankles with satin bows at the sides and festoons, he believed such decorations were called, festoons of fabric flowers dripping from the waist down the front. Her hair was piled in a cone that looked unstable, likely to tip if she did anything more vigorous than sit. She stared at Walter, as if he was the last person she'd expected to see. She was wearing blue rhinestone earrings that came to her shoulders, a blue velvet choker with a pink-and-white cameo pinned at her throat, and she'd installed one gigantic red hibiscus blossom at her left ear. Walter hadn't talked to her since the day she'd hoped God would take him from the face of the earth. She had never called to apologize, and for his part he hadn't said he was sorry about her grandmother's death.

"You look—nice," he lied.

"Thank you." She came forward a few steps, her purple high heels sounding on the tile like coins spilling out of a pocket. With great care she shook her head haughtily. "How is he?"

Walter put his hand to Daniel's brow and said, "Alive."

She didn't chastise him. She understood that his response was one of two possible answers. She came to the other side of the bed. They stood looking at him. Walter swallowed, fighting the emptiness that seemed again to be rising in him. How curious it was, he thought, that a thing like emptiness could take up space, could overwhelm a person. He turned to Daniel to keep himself firmly in place. Funny that he looked to his brother for fortitude. Odd that he expected Dan to give him guidance.

Dan in his steel bed, nothing to be done. What to fasten on, to move away from the sorrow? Walter looked up at Susan. The dress. It was unspeakably ugly. She looked frightful in it and not least because it wasn't a good color for her. A girl didn't wear a slut dress unless she was going to a costume party or planning to get good and drunk and let come what may. It was Saturday, he figured, she was going out—and he realized then, he understood that the prom was about to begin. "A Night to Remember" was the slogan for the 1973 Junior Prom. That was hilarious, a scream. A night to remember. "You're going to the dance," he blurted. "You're all dressed for the prom."

"No," she whispered. "No, Walter. I don't exactly have a date."

"Of course not. I didn't think so," he said.

"Will the nurse kick me out?"

"Betty was in here a while ago. She probably won't come unless we buzz."

"Could we get him to open his eyes, so he could see me?"

We shouldn't, Walter thought at first. They might wake Daniel up to pain. But he considered how Dan was going to die any second and there Susan was shimmering like a gladiator. It occurred to him that she had meant to go overboard, that she had chosen to be an exaggerated prom girl so that Daniel, through the blur of the morphine and his sickness, could see her. "You try," he said to Susan. "If anyone can wake him, you can."

She took Daniel's hand and folded it to her satiny, flat bosom. She was already starting to cry. "Daniel, I'm here. It's our prom, you know, what we planned for. I've come to have this dance."

The idea was inspired, no doubt about it, Walter thought. The drama could only have been improved if she'd brought a band along, but she was blowing it, going off course. It wasn't going to be worth it for Dan to wake up if she was going to dissolve and be maudlin. He went to the other side of the bed and shook Daniel's shoulder. "Wake up, Dan. Your girl is here, your buffalo gal, the delight of your dreams." He remembered the poem from Gatsby and he recited, " 'Then wear the gold hat, if that will move her; If you can bounce high, bounce for her too.' " Susan gave a long honk of a sniffle and Walter said to her, "Don't cry. Do not cry if you can possibly help it, do you hear me?"

"Okay, okay, I won't," she said, taking her bottom lip and holding it between her thumb and index finger.

"Wake up, Daniel," Walter called. "You do not want to miss this. Come back for just a minute." He shook his brother. "Look, look at Susan." When Daniel opened his eyes, Walter grabbed both his shoulders. "Open up, stay awake, look what we have here, don't close the shop, that's it, wake, wake, wake."

"Dan, Dan, dear Dan," Susan said, coming to Walter's side. "Remember how we were going to go dancing? Remember how we practiced in the kitchen? You had such rhythm. You were—you're a natural!"

He tried to lift his head and when he couldn't do that he raised his hand, reaching for the flower in her ear. He was off the mark and got her mouth, instead. She pressed his fingers to her lips and through them she said, "I'm going to hold you. And Walter's going to put your arms around me, all right?"

She lay against him and Walter, one at a time, put his brother's arms in place at her back and kept them there. She lay draped over him. Walter was afraid she might crush him. She might put a fraction of her weight down on his heart and he'd go up in powder. Help, God, he thought—would that be considered murder? A boy mashed by his date, or pulverized by a vulgar dress. "Careful," he whispered to Susan. "Careful."

She lay there on him until the elevator sounded. "That might be my mother," Walter said from the door. "You better get off him."

Slowly she pulled herself away. Walter watched her, thinking how it is to get a leech off a person's leg, how it bends to the flesh and won't easily let go. By the time she'd gotten herself upright and set Daniel's thin white arms back at the sides of the bed he was already asleep again. She felt her hair, to see if it was still on top of her head, and yanked at her dress, both top and bottom. When Joyce and Robert walked into the room, she was holding Daniel's hand, gazing at him.

"Mom," Walter began.

"Hello, Mr. and Mrs. McCloud," Susan said. "I haven't been to see Daniel—"

"We've got to go now." Walter took Susan by the elbow. "Betty knows she's here, Mom—she didn't have to sneak or anything. Dan woke up and saw her. He couldn't believe the, um, ensemble and the real flower. It smells, by the way." He nudged Susan forward.

"I'm—glad," Joyce said.

Susan was not moving fast enough, so Walter gripped her wrist and took her past his parents. "She's got her car and she'll drive me home. I had soup before and I'm fine. He was awake for just a minute, but he saw her."

They were out of the room at last, going down the hall to the elevator. She could hardly walk in her sheath, the straight tube with no vents. "Why are you in such a hurry?" she whined, taking her little Japanese steps. "Stop jerking me."

He had felt it necessary to get her away from his parents because the gown was such an embarrassment. It was gaudy and glaring and obscene in just the right way for some other girl, but on Susan the luridness seemed accidental. It was as if she had a breast hanging out without knowing, or a stain spreading on her backside. "I'm hurrying," he said to her, "because they want to be alone with him."

"Well, we're out of the room now, so can we slow down? Please. I can't walk in this thing."

He drew her to him. It had been such a long time since he'd embraced her. He felt the satin down her back and he said, "Your dress reminds me of an item I got recently."

"What kind of item do you have that could possibly remind you of this piece of shit, Walter? It was the best I could do at Goodwill, last minute."

"I'll show it to you at my house, if you can spare the time."

She leaned against him. "Oh, I've got time all right." He had noticed that her face had no color and he wondered if she would look the same when she was fifty, after the ballerina life of cigarettes and

Coke and barre work had done her in. Anyone who glanced at her might think she was old and haggard, already a widow.

"It's sort of a story," he said, "about a dress that I managed to appropriate. It's a horror story, in a way, but the kind of vignette certain people would think is humorous in a slapstick, yuk-it-up kind of way." He was tired of the hand of God, of death, of cancer, of the smell of bedpans and canned soup, and it would be a blast of fresh air to talk about Mr. Kenton and ordinary human malice.

"I'm not in a laughing mood," she said.

"No, no, I'm not either. That's why I'd like to tell it to you now, when you're more liable to cry. I'd prefer it if you could muster a tear or two."

They went down in the elevator to the parking lot. When she got into the car she slumped on the wheel and she said, "This feels like the worst day of my life."

He could see that she was going to spill over, that she was cranking up for a long, racking cry. It was hard for him to think about anything being the worst anymore because all the days were unreal. Each one was more blandly worse than the next. He was moving through his life without thinking or understanding, and he hoped she wouldn't start sobbing because there was no telling if he could hold on or not. And if he had a choice he would prefer not to begin the Vesuvian display on the freeway, in her hatchback car.

"This might not be helpful?" he said, as if it were a question. He was speaking too loudly, but he couldn't help it, couldn't turn it down. "Probably nothing a person says can make a difference, but it, all of this, could get a lot worse. Maybe today is nothing. It's possible that tomorrow could be even more terrible."

She was quiet, pursing her lips, before she said, "That's just brilliant, Walter. So smart." She was spitting at him with every other *t*. "What makes you think your genius statement is true? How do you know?"

"I don't really." He shrugged. "It's just a hunch."

"I'm supposed to be grateful, aren't I, because I'm not in Vietnam and my legs aren't amputated at the knees, and my mother isn't an alcoholic and my father isn't running off with his secretary. Is that it? Because if that's what you mean you can go to hell in a handbasket. If you think I'm going to sit here in this dress and count my blessings, then you better get out and walk."

He could see that there wasn't actually much steam in her anger. She was too tired to work herself into a frenzy. "Forget it," she said, under her breath. She started the car and turned on the radio and all the way home they listened to a Dvořák symphony. He was relieved not to have to make conversation with her while she drove in the tight dress and her three-inch heels. It probably took all of her concentration just to feel the gas pedal through the shoes. He wouldn't want to distract her, and he also had nothing to say in his defense. With her present handicap they could easily get in an accident and have to have their legs amputated at the knees, and then her mother would become a drunk, and her father might escape with the neighbor, and he and Susan would have to be brave and cheerful and study hard and deflect everyone's pity. He felt he was correct, that everything around him— the car, the buildings, the whole food chain—could collapse. It was a little bit of a comfort—but he didn't say so—to think that the entire world might fall to pieces, that it wasn't only Daniel who was failing.

She drove up on the curb at 646 Maplewood Avenue. Walter wasn't sure if it was the elm tree at her fender that stopped her or if she shut off the motor of her own volition. "Could you hand me the screwdriver from the glove compartment?" she said. He dug through Lou Ann's grocery coupons, empty gum packets, the crumpled foil wrappers. With one motion she slit the dress from the thigh to the ankle with the Boy Scout knife he had found. "There," she said. "Now I'll be able to make it up your front stairs."

He came around to the driver's side and opened the door for her, and they walked arm in arm up the walk and into the house. Although she could move freely they went one step at a time. She rested against him like an elderly woman. When they were inside he guided her to the bench in the hall and sat her down. He went straight to the piano, reached behind it, removed the balled-up costume and came toward her, holding it to his front. He turned around, glided into the living room, turning again, as if the blue line of the rug were the runway. It would be best, he thought, if she came to the knowledge herself.

"Isn't it?" she finally said in a whisper. "Isn't it what Tracy, Sonja, Maureen and Alberta were going to wear for—for *Pas de Quatre?* Oh, my God, Walter, did Mrs. Kenton make that? Does she know you have it?"

He told her the basic story, including the carport crime and omitting the fact that he had had sexual contact with Mitch. He also did not tell her that his flogging happened on the day she had yelled at him at school, when she told him she'd be happy if he died, that he was a worthless human being. He took off his shoes to show her his toes that were still partially without the nails, and she bent over his feet and she petted them, as if they were kittens.

"It's just going to be the two of us pretty soon, Walter," she said. "Sure, I'll go back to dancing school. Sure, we'll finish our sophomore year and summer will come. I'm never speaking to Mitch again, the way he laughed at you, the way he supported Mr. Kenton. Oh, Walter, pretty soon it will really only be the two of us who know anything."

They put on Daniel's Moody Blues album, *Nights in White Satin.* Walter opened the curtains so that Mrs. Gamble could watch them if there was nothing good on television. They stood holding each other, rocking slowly from side to side. "I've never gotten what this song means," she said. " 'Nights in White Satin.' Does it mean the kind of knights riding on horses in good clothes, or is the song about clouds wrapped in material?"

"I don't know," he said. "It's probably about fucking. And magic. Most songs are about the two of those things, trying to put them together." He pulled her closer. "It's a remarkable dress," he murmured in her ear.

"I don't think I ever want to get married to any—you know— dumb guy." He understood her to mean a straight man, a clod who would expect satisfaction and regularity. "But I'd live with you, Walter. I'd marry you, just so we could talk after work and cook dinners and dance around the living room in our stocking feet. If you wanted to, I'd do it in ten or, say, twenty years."

"In twenty years Mr. Kenton will be dead, darling," Walter whispered. "Mitch will wear a Mountie's outfit and be in forestry up in Alaska, macho as Smokey the Bear. You'll be a principal dancer in the New York City Ballet. I'll be someplace close, like Dorothy is in Oz, closer to Kansas than she thinks, but far away, of course, too. No one will know me there. I won't let anyone know me."

Eleven

JUNE
1973

Daniel's memorial service took place on June 7 at Lake Margaret, outside, down by the water. Joyce and Robert had not been regular churchgoers and for years they had had no affiliation with a congregation or a minister. Jeannie urged the family to hold the service at First Presbyterian for the sake of simplicity, to spare them the headaches of travel, but she also wanted to say, and finally did, that she thought it was a little tiny bit unfair to use the property on such an occasion. "No one, after all, wants our home to be associated with tragedy," she said, making clear that she had conferred with the others, that she did not stand alone in her opinion. Sue Rawson advised an Oak Ridge ceremony for her own reasons. The Lake Margaret property had already exerted a strong hold, a mawkish grip over the McClouds, to her way of thinking. They were soppy enough about the house as it was, no point in adding extra freight.

Joyce thanked her older sisters for their advice. She asked them to remember Daniel, and how much he loved his summers at the lake. If they could picture him swimming out to the raft, his beautiful slender arms coming over his head in the butterfly stroke, if they could see him sailing the Sunfish on a windy afternoon, they would surely understand that there was no question about Lake Margaret. To Robert she said that it was the only place she could stand to be, that the porch and the long green hill and the sound of the water were as good as any church, and furthermore the eleven acres were spacious enough and old enough to absorb every one of the family's rituals. "Let Jeannie and Sue stay home," she said evenly. She kicked the roasting pan that was hanging out of the cupboard and slammed the door after it.

The service was meant primarily for the relatives, but word of the date and time and location got around in Oak Ridge. On that June afternoon a number of Daniel's classmates and the parents, and his teachers made the drive to Lake Margaret. There were over seventy cars parked up and down the road, and Aunt Jeannie herself chased to the grocery store in search of three more plain sheet cakes and the makings for punch. Joyce went into the upstairs bathroom and wept into a towel. There had been plenty of hospitality already—"Goddamn it," she cried. "Goddamn these people." She and Robert had put up with a steady stream of visitors through the living room since Daniel's death on May 22, friends and acquaintances, hospital and school staff paying their respects, the able-bodied women on Maplewood Avenue bringing food. "I can't bear it," she said, bending over the sink to wash her face.

Walter stood on the lawn before the service, watching the swim team come along the path, walking shoulder to shoulder, as if they were one organism, as if all that was missing was the costume of the dragon or a horse that would fit over the bulk of them, twelve pairs of big feet shuffling underneath. He couldn't think why they had appeared, when they'd already dropped by the house in Oak Ridge, standing nervously in the hall while Joyce spoke to each of them in turn. Even as they came in formation Walter could see that they couldn't figure out what to do with their hands, that they didn't know how to move. They seemed to think that swinging their arms backward and forward naturally was too wild a motion for the occasion. Their discomfort was so naked Walter had to turn away from them, stand with his back against the old walnut tree.

Susan came from the porch and went to him, adjusted the collar of his brown shirt. It was nice of her to attend to him like a girlfriend just when the boys showed up. "You have spaghetti sauce on your mouth," she whispered, and as furtively as a mother she spit on her finger and dabbed at his upper lip. "Don't look now, but Mrs. Anderson is getting out of the car, leaving it by the kitchen door like she expects valet parking. Mitch is in the backseat—asleep. Did you know he was coming?"

Walter closed his eyes. Did animals who were smart enough to play dead under trying circumstances half believe they were a dream, a flicker of light, a spume? Maybe I could expire right here, he thought, if I pretend hard enough, if I clap clap clap because I believe in fairies and other unseen wonders.

"I realize it's not an invitational sort of thing," she gabbled on, "and his mom probably made him come, but you'd think he would have asked if he could—"

"It's okay. It doesn't matter."

She slapped her hand over her mouth. "I'm sorry, Walter. You're right. What difference does it make?"

She moved the waistband of her lavender-and-pale-green print skirt to the left and the right, trying to get the front seam down the exact middle. In the two weeks since Daniel's death she had begun to regain her bloom. She had not seen him again after the prom night; she told Walter that for her it was as if he had died then, in her arms. She no longer looked battered at school, and she was back to washing her hair every day and coordinating her outfits. Walter was grateful to her for not dressing up in black for the service. Instead of a dingy bombazine tight to the neck, skirt to the floor, she was wearing a white knit shell, her rayon skirt with the shamrocks and a purple belt, a thin gold chain around her neck with no locket, no cross, no diamond. She had fixed her silvery hair in one braid down her back.

Joyce and Robert were moving through the guests like a pair of generals greeting the good soldiers. Walter could only think, How? How could they rise to the occasion so admirably? It was horrific that they had to, and in a way it was horrific that they were capable of such heroics. "Would you mind coming to get me when this thing starts," he said to Susan. "I'm going up to my aunt's room, to ah—"

He was going to say, hide, but she nudged him toward the front door. "Shoo," she said. "I'll knock twice. Quick, before Mitch opens his eyes."

Thank goodness, thank God he was getting away, if only for a few minutes. Run, run like the wind, through the cool living room, shut up against the heat, and two steps, four steps, eight, sixteen, to Sue Rawson's chamber in the back of the house. No one would look for him there. The shadows from the trees outside, the young summer leaves and the dark branches, moved in waves, back and forth across the white coverlet on her bed. Keep still, he said to himself, clutching a pillow, curling up into the swirl of the shadows. "Keep me safe," he said to the room.

Maybe he didn't have very high expectations anymore for his friends, his family, the walls of a house, but he couldn't help feeling grateful half the day lately for shelter, for a few people here and there, and only because they sometimes had the ability, for a minute or two, to dull the nagging ache in the hollow of his chest. You never knew when someone was going to appear out of the blue and not make things worse. That was the astonishing thing he'd learned so far in his short life, the fact that had come through to him the night with Susan in the hospital, that sometimes a moment, or even a few hours, weren't as bad as they could have been. It was possible, too, that even death was like some great call to the dying, a lovely beckoning that the rest of them left behind couldn't hear or know. Maybe the saddest detail in the last year was the fact that Daniel had once been a skilled chess player and as his disease progressed he couldn't think through the moves anymore. He had cried when Joyce made the awful suggestion that he try checkers instead.

Walter went to the window and looked down through the heart-shaped leaves of the catalpa tree to the guests below, shaking hands, talking quietly. For one ridiculous instant he missed Mrs. Gamble, but of course she was back in Oak Ridge, watching over the McClouds' house. How out of whack he must be, to want to see her pin curls, her deadly green-eyed glare, her little gray teeth. How funny, wasn't it funny, like so many other funny things, that Mrs. Gamble was as familiar and dear as an old pair of slippers, a book that has been read a hundred times. Maybe he should be thankful for the fatigue that had reduced all his feelings to sentiment. He guessed he could take baby steps from melancholy to gratitude, or he could lie back down on Sue Rawson's soft mattress with the trough in the middle, and finally let loose for the enormity of his brother's death. He could take his pick, the way the urchin pack in the alley used to, both feet in the circle to be counted, to decide who was It for kick the can. *My mother and your mother were hanging out the clothes. My mother punched your mother right in the nose. What color was the blood?* How fragile any sort of peace was, he thought then, in a family, in a neighborhood. He should go downstairs, probably, embrace, shake hands, fight back tears as was expected, receive the benediction and carry on as Daniel surely would want him to.

In Oak Ridge Robert had told Walter, in passing from the bathroom to the bedroom, that they might easily go under in grief, but if they had willpower and resolve they might lick it, they might find something to hold on to, a power within themselves to keep standing. His brief speech was like the hopeless appeal a coach might give his losing team, the last pep talk, but Walter had understood his father and had done his best to see what good remained. Susan had helped him more than she realized. They were together once more, companions through the march. Walter was thankful that she hadn't walked through the halls crying in the final days, and after. She had kept her sorrows nearly private, acknowledging her distress only to Walter, and then with nothing more than a look or the brush of her fingers over his arm. They had managed not to see Mitch at school, or perhaps Mitch had gotten in the habit of taking any long way around them in the hall.

Daniel had died in the early morning, and already that same evening Walter could see that Susan was prepared for the old life to seal over. It seemed to him that she, out of all of them, was following the proper and sensible course. He did not hold her fortitude against her. She had said, "I think I can both hold him here"—she tapped her heart—"and"—she flung her hands up to the heavens—"let him go, at the same time. It's hard, takes effort, concentration, like psychically patting your head and your stomach simultaneously and forever, but it's possible. I think it's possible."

That night they were sitting on the McClouds' porch swing, and she cried a little into Walter's shoulder. They were too tired to wail. It had rained all afternoon and into the evening, the heavens grieving too, they thought. They sat, wiping at their eyes, and Susan blew her nose for so long they couldn't help laughing. How dumb it was, she

said, that they couldn't have an emotional moment without her sinuses draining. The night air, steamy and thick, was closing around
them, and although they didn't mention it, both of them believed the
moisture and the heat were part of Daniel's loving presence. They
walked over to Susan's house, bumping gently against each other,
stumbling through the puddles without noticing, without speaking.
At the gate they clasped hands, held on. Walter had hated her only
weeks before. Don't let go, he wanted to say. If there was anything to
look forward to, it was seeing her again, in the morning. Suppose he
went home and took off his clothes and got into bed and closed his
eyes and, while he slept, suppose the earth spun and the sun rose and
he opened his eyes and found clean underwear, washed his face, went
down to the kitchen. It might be worth going through those motions
if he could spend an hour with her, if she'd come over and sit with
him, or sing in his ear, or show him a pretty little nothing, or take him
for a walk. He might stay on the sidewalk all through the night, waiting for her, hanging close with his head over the fence like a girl's loyal
horse. "Good-bye, Walter," she said, kissing him on the lips. "Good-
bye, dear friend."

She disappeared into her foyer. He followed her movement
through the house as it went dark downstairs and light upstairs; room
by room, into the bathroom she went, her parents' room and her own
room. He waited at the gate while she read a chapter of a Hermann
Hesse novel, while she drew up her covers and plumped her pillows,
set her alarm clock, leaned over and snapped off her Tensor bedside
light. She would sleep, he was sure of it. After breakfast she'd wake up
and call him, and it might not be so bad, the day, the endless hours
stretching before them. They'd talk about Daniel for a while, Daniel,
who had paved the way. It was Daniel, Walter knew, who had given
Susan back to him.

"And what do you have, Dan?" He had asked out loud into the
haze of the night. "What priceless gift is left for you?"

Better not to ask, better not to think of the limited prospects. He
had died alone, in his sleep, while Joyce went to the bathroom and
Robert stepped into the hall to take a break from the rasping noise of
their son's breathing. It was intolerable to sit through, hour after hour,
and no one had been able to say how long it might go on. When they

came home from the hospital to tell Walter that the long wait was over, he felt let down, disappointed in the final scene for his mother's sake. Joyce poached eight eggs out of habit for the old family of four, toasted a package of English muffins, made coffee and orange juice, sectioned the grapefruits. The three of them sat at the table. Everything was in place: napkins, teaspoons, cream and sugar in the wedding china. Robert sat moving his muffin around his plate with his knife as if it were a hockey puck. The food was like a prop, a useful something to handle to give a feel of reality and depth to their own characters and their conversation. They all knew they weren't really going to eat. Joyce stirred her coffee and Robert began making a list on his napkin of people they should call, looking up occasionally and saying, "Who else, Joycie? Who else?"

Walter wondered if it was a perk for a nurse to be able to whisper into dying people's ears, to have your words float on into the next world. His parents didn't hear, or maybe he hadn't spoken. It was the beginning of the weeks to come, the time when he felt nothing. He didn't know anymore how to think a thought from start to finish. He couldn't feel his bum heart ticking. And there didn't seem to be any point to eating or swallowing or blinking or sleeping. Big deal, living and breathing. Maybe it wasn't so bad, to have gone out in the middle of a dream.

On one of those gray mornings in the kitchen, after the end, Joyce stood at the table and asked him right out what he thought happened in the hereafter, and if he had religious inclinations. "Is there anything for you to fall back on?" she said. "I don't know if we've given you boys a foundation."

"A foundation." Walter didn't want to offend her, or make a blunder if she'd suddenly come upon Jesus, if it was he who was going to get her through the next few decades, but he knew she'd catch him if he recited some fakey inspirational line. "I don't know, Mom," he said. "God isn't the architect and he's not exactly the main character either, but I think he's something, um, literary. He's the setting, maybe. That's it. God is all of Mrs. Gamble's backyard, and as for Jesus, I've always thought he was in the wrong line of work. I mean, he might have been happier and developed a sense of humor if he'd kept at his carpentry and gone into inspirational speaking, just on weekends, part-time, charged money and made cassettes for people to listen to in their cars. The whole Christianity thing got out of hand when maybe it was only meant to be a fad from a warm climate. Still, if you want to enough, I guess you could probably become a believer and it might make a person feel better for a while. I don't know much of anything, as you can tell. I feel kind of—" He couldn't say, didn't have the knack to describe what it was like to feel nothing.

There was concern, he guessed it was, in her wrinkled brow, and the strange crooked smile, the tremble in her lower lip. Her cockeyed mouth was making him jittery. "I did figure out one small piece," he blazed on, looking down at her faded pink tennis shoes. "I think that Daniel was working, laboring, to get there, wherever there is, and that we watched him make his passage. That's what the pastor at the hospital kept calling it. 'His passage.' " Joyce's shoes had rips in the rubber around the toe as if someone had carelessly tried to make scallops, and the laces were frayed, so that if they came unstrung it would be difficult, if not impossible, to rethread them. The shoes were pitiful, and for the first time in a week Walter felt as if he might sometime in the future be able to cry. "And anyway," he went on, "it doesn't matter that you weren't right with him because he had already crossed over. That's what I think. For all intents and purposes he went the night Susan showed up in that sensational dress. She chose it, incidentally, only because she knew he'd see it, if he opened his eyes. He wasn't going to understand some elegant understated million-dollar little black number and so she pulled together that wild hairdo and the tacky choker and the dress. The dress! She found it at Goodwill. They wanted to pay *her* to take it off their hands—"

The sound of his mother's "heh," the syllable of laughter, startled him and he stopped talking. She moved to the sink and he went back to his cereal. That conversation, as it turned out, was not the first of many but was instead the only one they would have for years about Daniel. Before the final illness Walter had not had much interest in his brother, but in the last months he wanted to know everything that had gone on in Daniel's head, what he thought about when he woke up, what it had been like when Susan loved him ardently, what he would have hoped to become, what he looked at underwater, in the pool, when he swam for two hours without stopping. He wanted to know what understanding Daniel had had, what he thought of his death, if he had had faith, and what Joyce and Robert had said to him in their efforts to give him assurance. At breakfast that morning his mother turned away and began removing the stems of the strawberries a neighbor had brought. Walter was afraid to say more, afraid to begin the long search, asking, asking. He said to himself that soon, tomorrow or the next day, he would start to name all the things he didn't know about his brother, to see if in identifying the questions Daniel would somehow come closer.

In Walter's memory the service at Lake Margaret was always set against a backdrop that was nearly blank. There were the shapes of the guests, their flat gray faces. There were stray sentences floating by in the airless, white hours. The local minister from the Methodist church came out of the house and stood surveying his congregation, the strangers of many denominations from Illinois. Walter would not forget how the beefy man in his vestments raised his arms, and without words the whole group walked after him down the hill to the lakefront, to the grassy plot, the bit of land that year after year irked Sue Rawson. It was those two hundred feet that made the difference on the Lake Margaret tax bill, two hundred feet of prime lake frontage. Walter couldn't help thinking of her annual outrage. She had investigated conservation easements and zoning changes, but there seemed no way around the fact that the Lake Margaret Corporation owned the longest stretch of undeveloped frontage on the lake. It had irritated her for decades that she, and her siblings, paid the hefty bill for the homeowners across the water, for their pleasure, their view.

Sue Rawson went down the slope and stood at the end of the property, as if she were marking it for the mourners, so they would understand the dimensions of the holding. At dawn Uncle Ted had walked around blasting Raid into the thickets, but it was the sun and the breeze that were keeping the mosquitoes at bay. Susan and Walter had to cut through the guests to get to their places next to Robert and Joyce. Walter smelled the traces of the repellent and the freshly mown grass, the honeysuckle and the lilies of the valley. I should learn the trees and the shrubs and the vines and the plants, he said to himself. He loved the Lake Margaret flowers and he didn't know what any of them were called. There were plenty of books inside the house that he could use to identify the Wisconsin flora. Pretty soon, he figured, he might wake up, back into ordinary life, and then how he'd look alive, bright-eyed and bushy-tailed, boning up on the kingdoms and the phyla and the genera and the species. In a while he'd know exactly what was missing if there was the smallest loss: a violet swiped by a child, a trampled gentian, an iris with the blossom lopped off.

The relatives stood on the flat of the land in front of Reverend Bentley, and the others fanned out up the hill. Francie had been enlisted to play a dirge from the hymnal on her violin. Concentrate on Francie, Walter said to himself. Don't think about the purpose of the event. Notice her orchestra skirt, black and straight to the middle of her kneecaps, as well as the white shirt, buttoned at the neck and the cuffs, and the nylons and black pumps. What was different about her? The uniform was complete with the exception of the Oak Ridge symphony maroon blazer. It took Walter a few bars to realize that she was playing her instrument in tune. The music! "Take My Life and Let It Be," the song that Joyce had allowed would be all right, as a concession to Jeannie. Walter had never heard his cousin play three consecutive notes in tune, and she was sawing away as if she'd acquired an ear for pitch. Here was another check for the plus side, better not to question it, to wonder how or why.

Mitch was behind them, lost somewhere in the throng among the young sycamores and the quaking aspens. You are nothing to me now, Walter thought. The Reverend was saying his opening prayer, praising the Lord both for his unfathomable ways and for the power of his love. You once saved my life, Walter went on, but so what? The drone of the motorboats and the shouts of the children jumping off the piers came across the water, blending with Bentley's mournful tones. *You are nothing to me now.* It was easy enough to say those words. No difficulty stringing together a subject, verb, object, the complete sentence. Once the service was over and everyone had gone home, Walter knew he was going to have to set out, and it would be an unfamiliar landscape to travel through, a terrain that had no guideposts or trails, a country with mountains of glassy black stone and, beyond, the uncharted waste. A place where a person so blithely said, You are nothing to me now. There was no returning to the village, to dear old Mother.

He watched the ducks sitting on the waves, rising and falling. Bentley was saying something about Daniel going on a ship over the rim of the world. That terrible emptiness rose up in Walter's throat. Over the rim of the world. Daniel is gone, Walter thought, headed west, and the rest of us are left behind. Aren't we? Are we all here? Roll call, he wanted to shout. Roll call! I think I'm accounted for, he said to himself. Joyce, present. Robert, yep. Susan, right beside him. If anyone wondered, snaky Mitch was way in the back. One person, only one, had left them and that departure had changed them all. He understood suddenly that the real sadness about death was the fact that there was no way to follow to the limit. Daniel's body had been burned and was already ash. Over the rim of the world. Walter was going to choke, couldn't breathe. He reached for Susan, found her hand and she pressed it, let it go, put her arm around him, nudged him close. Yes, that was it, something in her that held him in place, that allowed him to take a breath. What he'd do is try to remember, aim to keep the details clear for the rest of his life. Waking up Daniel was the single thing he had been able to do for his brother. On prom night, the Night to Remember, he'd slapped him about the ears and called into his face and jostled his frail arms. It wasn't much, rousing Daniel so he could see Susan. It hadn't required thought or much effort or a charitable heart. But it was something, a small deed that had perhaps made a difference.

He tried to imagine the year 2000, a number that sounded so white and clean and empty. Where would he live at the turn of the century when he was forty-three, and what sort of profession would engage him? Where would he be in ten years, five years? Twelve months? Another June. The same flowering shrubs bursting into bloom and smelling, again. What, he wondered, would keep his interest; what, if anything, could ever thrill him? There was no light in the beyond, not so much as a glimmer. No sign for a while yet that on June 5, 1974, his mother, well into her forties, would give birth to a six-pound baby girl named Lucy Rawson McCloud. In her honor Walter would pass out pink bubble-gum cigars in his European History class.

Mitch, in the front row, would thank him and Walter would say, "You're welcome," the sum of the words they'd exchange through the rest of high school. He'd spend the next summer walking the baby in the night after her feeding, checking her in her bassinet to make sure her back was rising and falling. By day he played the piano to her, he tried to teach her to roll over, and he pushed her down the street in her buggy with the air of a proud father.

Standing side by side at the service Walter felt as if he and Susan were married, in their misty future, as if they'd been together for twenty-five years, as if Daniel were something like their child, a boy they'd given up for adoption long ago and come to know briefly before his premature death. The idea came to him then that he'd trip along behind her, that he'd go to college in New York City, to study whatever he could fix his mind on, so he could be close to her, so he could watch her dance. Reverend Bentley had never met Daniel, and his eulogy sounded like an astrological description of a teenage boy born in the month of November. As far as Walter could tell, Aunt Jeannie was the only one who could not restrain herself, who was crying. A different sort of ceremony might have served them all better, he thought, something that would shake them up, make them fall to the ground and howl. If he'd gotten whisked away into a straw hut for a bloody ritual he might emerge with wisdom and spirituality, and afterward there'd be song and dance, the suckling pigs and stories from the elders. Surely it was preferable to have high drama, the funeral pyre floating off, burning on the sea, rather than the calm of the present gathering, the pretending that over the horizon Dan was being received, that there was a fond welcoming.

Sue Rawson was picking the burrs off her sleeve. She'd have favored an Isadora Duncan type of dance, Walter supposed, girls in white tunics running around barefoot, paying homage to Diana. Joyce was looking across the lake at the one hundred steps that led to the top of the bluff. Walter hoped that all through Bentley's gibberish she was thinking of the teapot she'd found on the fiftieth stair when she was a girl, a blue-and-white-speckled treasure she threw a fit over, had to have, and eventually carried back with her in the duckboat while her mother rowed. It was the one tantrum in Joyce's oral history. He guessed that his father, head bowed, eyes closed, was trying to obey, that he was doing his best to focus on the goodness, the strength and the mercy of the Lord Jesus Christ.

After the benediction the crowd moved slowly up the hill, to the porch. Joyce had brought a sheet cake with mocha frosting and small red roses along the edge. There were lemon bars and chocolate chip cookies, macaroons and brownies, and the extra carrot cakes that Jeannie had drummed up well beyond the last minute. The pastel mints were in the silver dishes, and the green punch, made with ginger ale and lime sherbet, was in Grandmother's crystal bowl.

Susan and Walter stood in the corner, watching the guests. "The last time we were here together," she whispered, "was that amazing party for your aunt's anniversary."

"Aunt Jeannie's busy bossing the kitchen help around," Walter said. "The coffee is always so much better when you have two or three women standing over the urn. Dad was worried that she'd turn on her hostess charm, that she'd forget this wasn't a golf outing. It's a good thing she has a job so she's out of the way."

"Remember when she stood at the door in her wedding dress, waiting for everyone to look at her? I'll never forget that. Will Mitch come to us, do you think? Oh my gosh, my mom's talking to his mother. Should we—or I—approach him? Should I behave as if I'm an adult, as if nothing has happened between us, as if his being here is a peace offering? Or should I wait for him to take the lead? I wish he'd get back in his car and go home."

She was chattering in the way Jeannie might have if she hadn't been relegated to the scullery, but Walter didn't think the talk was hurting anybody. There was a pleasant lilt to Susan's voice. Let her warble on for the rest of the afternoon. He considered her questions for a minute. It had been nice of Susan to be outraged at Mitch in his behalf, but he knew he couldn't expect her to keep up the stance indefinitely. On the plus side, being furious at Mitch for Walter's sake had given her the upper hand in her future relations with the ex-boyfriend. She had loved a dying young man and she had evidence of Mitch's disloyal, scumbag soul, both points that surely would serve to reinstate her virtue in his mind. She could have him any way she liked and there was probably no reason, except for the fun of coyness, to keep her distance.

"I think," Walter said, in one of her pauses, "that if you're up to it, you should go say hello, and I should take a walk and do the sort of thing people do when they stroll in the woods. Maybe I can come up with some meaningful new saying, something like 'Beware of all enterprises that require new clothes.' "

"You should never let bygones be bygones, you know? Not after he laughed at you."

"I'll never forgive him, then, if I have your permission."

"It's just that you can tell he feels like a dope, standing out there with his mom."

"Uh-huh," Walter said.

"And it wouldn't take that much for me to say something." She gave Walter a peck on the cheek, a token of her affection for the fifteen minutes they would be apart. "Good-bye," she said.

He walked down to the lake without looking to see if the old twosome were reunited. Mitch had once, and for some unknown reason, given him a moment of—what? Walter supposed he could call it a moment of unutterable loveliness. Where that tenderness had come from out of the cold night he didn't know. He felt a flutter in his chest, a sign that his wounded heart was still inside of him and up to the usual tricks. Maybe that February night in the bushes was another thing, besides living and dying, that he'd never understand. One foot in front of the other, he said to himself. Left, right, left, right, down the hill. Daniel had had plenty of affection and devoted attention. Walter could say—and who could tell, perhaps it was true—that Daniel had had a full portion, to the finish.

He could see Sue Rawson in the stretch of woods by the boathouse, wearing a straw hat, poking her nose into the last tattered blossoms of the wild apple tree. She nodded at him, and together they climbed the stairs to the upper boathouse. They leaned over the railings and they could see all the way up to the north end, where the canal went through to Hank's Pond, and to the south end, the marshy place with the leeches, and across the water to the pastures in the next county.

"What are you going to do with yourself," Sue Rawson said, "now that you're not dancing? Will you take up the piano again?"

"Not formally," he said. "No."

There seemed to be such a long time ahead of him, days and months and years that would have to be spent in some way. What he wanted right then, he realized, was to be ten, in Sue Rawson's bedroom, listening to opera, to Puccini. Madame Butterfly's life had been a mystery to him when he was a boy, but it had become real to him in the last few weeks. She had to kill herself because she hadn't been able to stand the thought of the years before her, all that time, without the one thing she wanted. If I could fasten on anything, he thought, something. One thing to want. A milk shake. A pair of new shoes. The days would fill up of their own accord if there was something to want.

"I'd like to stay here," he burst out, like a child. He right away felt foolish for saying so, but it was what he could see to want for the next hour.

"This place won't always be here," she muttered.

"It will," he said firmly. "It's ours."

Twelve

JULY
1996

As a student Walter had vowed never to be the type of distracted, halfhearted teacher who counted the days until the end of the school year. If he'd learned anything after nine months of experience in the classroom, he understood that his pledge was ill-considered, that even a tired nag picks up its hooves and plods after a carrot. Without the eye on that one sweet thing the old mare would buckle at the knees, fold up, quit. Walter had a calendar in his kitchen by the telephone and another on his desk in the classroom as well as his lesson-plan spiral and a leather-bound engagement book. He did not cross off the squares with indelible black X's, but at any given moment he could have announced down to the respectable rough measurement of an hour how much more time he and the young people were required by law to attend Otten High. The golden sunshiny joy of his imminent release was tempered only by the fact that the month of June inevitably followed the end of May, no seven-league boots anywhere in sight to step over the thirty troublesome days that he would so much like to avoid.

No viable proposal had been put forward to save Lake Margaret, and Sue Rawson appeared firm in her resolve to sell the property. At Thanksgiving she had told the relatives that she expected to host a

June 1 meeting to settle the question of ownership. Walter hoped—in vain, he knew—that there was nothing really to worry about, that the family was only going through a melodramatic spasm for the sake of entertainment. Word had it that cousin Maxi had had the impudence to go to her aunt's front stoop to plead her case through the screen door. The Grande Dame reportedly flicked the lock, as if Maxi might try to bully her way in, and said through the mesh that she had no sympathy for beggars and weepers. Francie had left her rich husband for a penniless graduate student, and if no one else had any money the family must face the consequences.

It was common knowledge that Francie had told Roger about her affair with the idea, according to cousin Celeste, that he'd let her continue her spree until she was used up and ready for a square meal. Roger had filed divorce papers immediately. The few relatives who had called him agreed that the soft-spoken man whose passion was hand-pollinating lady's slippers no longer felt even-tempered or generous. Maxi whispered around that he fully intended to screw Francie royally.

On the other side of town, Jeannie had reputedly beseeched Sue Rawson to wait another few years before throwing the summer home to the wolves. The conversation had by most accounts taken place over the telephone, but it was said that Jeannie actually beat one of her breasts and moaned. Sue Rawson, everyone supposed, spoke to her sister right over the histrionics. "It is unfortunate for you," she apparently said, "that your daughter had the poor taste to tell her husband about her transgression." It was not ever clear how the exchange had been overheard, or by whom, but for Walter the important part of the story was the fact that Jeannie had been rendered speechless for an extended period, for the better part of an afternoon. "How sad," Sue Rawson concluded, "that Roger is taking his revenge, but just as well that he showed his true colors, don't you think, before the younger generation was under his sway?"

For some of the cousins the Lake Margaret issue was obscured by what seemed the bigger question: how was Jeannie going to retaliate, or was she done for, her fire extinguished by her witchy older sister? It was an interesting question, to be sure, but Walter tried to keep the focus on the place itself. His mother, he knew, had had a number of conversations with Sue, but Joyce was not forthcoming about the sessions and Walter guessed that there was little or no progress. He assumed that on June 1, at dawn, Sue Rawson would call the family together, and in a neutral site in Oak Ridge, most likely the meeting room of the public library, she'd outline her plan for the dissolution of the family corporation. He tried not to think about the speech she'd give to the group, but her voice was often in his ear, her image before him as he stared at his ceiling in the night, trying to fall asleep. She'd walk around the room, rapping on the chair with a ruler, lecturing the cowering relatives. "You've all been living out of the pockets of your ancestors," she'd say, "living a life that no longer has a place at the end of this century." She would not be delicate in pointing out that even if they could afford to buy her shares they would be hard pressed to pay the taxes without her support.

In the last week of May, in the final days of school, Walter tried to keep his sense of impending doom at bay. He was grateful for work, for the diversion of his students. He knew that if he gave an inch they would overtake him with their jangly energy and their pop-culture lingo. He tightened his belt, sharpened his red pencil and banged his ruler on their desks as he walked around the room, in a way that would have done Sue Rawson proud. He ran the pupils in his American Literature classes like dogs in the parking lot, with a concept he called Emily Dickinson relays. It would have been helpful in some cases to have Mrs. Gamble's whip to snap at them. With the promise of all the pizza they could eat, his sophomores went scrambling across the asphalt to their teammates, shouting as they tagged the waiting hand, "I'm Nobody! Who are you?" Off the second tier runners went, presumably with the next line on their tongues, "Are you nobody, too?"

Inside, Walter had them dancing to waltz music in a Gatsby and Daisy contest, and they played charades using any first sentence in a work they'd studied in the year. He let them laugh, he assumed they were having fun, but he did not allow them to forget that he was their lord and master. He had the grade book open on his desk, and furthermore he had the strength of what he fancied was his imposing head-of-the-Gulag self. Never mind that Betsy Rutule had the gall to come right up to him, tickle him under his arm, that he collapsed into his chair giggling like a girl at a pajama party. "Off with your head," he shouted when he had regained his composure. He got through the teacher-appreciation dinner at the Red Oak Supper Club without a drink or a mishap. There were final exams and report cards and graduation, and when it was all over he cleaned out his desk, turned off the lights, locked his room and said good-bye to the janitor. He went home and lay down in the grass in his backyard. There was a colony of biting red ants in the peonies two feet away, and still he fell into a deep sleep. He felt as if his arms and legs had a gorgeous sinking weight, that they were holding him in place, and when he woke he knew he'd been productive, that with an hour's rest he'd accomplished a full day's work.

The summer opened before him with a few specific dates and a lot of spare time. He had to plan his courses for the coming year, and he was thinking about going to a workshop in Chicago on techniques for teaching Shakespeare. His chairman, Bob Kressler, had given him a junior honors section for September and the promise of a drama class in the second semester. They'd read some of the old standards: *Hamlet, Uncle Vanya, Waiting for Godot, The Glass Menagerie,* but Walter might slip in a few scenes from *Angels in America,* or go for broke, buy twenty-five copies with his own money and assign the whole thing. There was a fair chance that Mr. Kressler would not know enough about the prize-winning play to be alarmed. It would be good to have a comedy or two to balance the gloom and doom, an Oscar Wilde, a Woody Allen, an Elaine May routine. He might try to drum up some money to take the class to Louisville, Kentucky, for the annual Actors and Playwrights Showcase. Traveling out of state, and for the theater, was a bold idea for Otten, a revolutionary concept, but it was worth a try.

He might also think about someday beginning to create a groundswell, a few students at first, gathering after school for an alternative sexual orientation club. For starters, the organization could figure out a snappy acronym, as well as lobby for same-sex couples at the dances, and in general work to catch up with more forward schools in cities and suburbs around the country. They could have a support group, nothing wrong with that, and go to films and concerts in Madison, and they could take trips to Washington to protest legislation. It was hard to say how his life would have been different if Oak Ridge High had had a similar group. He had necessarily built his character around the need to conceal his true nature, and it was impossible to imagine himself without that dimension. There was no point in speculating at this late date, and Walter meant to concentrate on the coming generation of Otten High queers. As in all undertakings, timing was key. He would have to wait and watch for the issue to show itself. He would have to be alert. It was improbable that he'd get support from anyone besides Mrs. Denval, but he would do his best to behave like the Walter who moved so confidently through his favorite bedtime fantasy: Mr. McCloud, impeccably dressed, a few inches taller, the original hairline restored; but more important, certainly, Mr. McCloud, courageous, dignified, a man with the obstinate conviction that no matter the ridicule, no matter the danger and limited resources, all things are possible. Once he brought the idea of the club forward, and if he was not fired on the spot, at the very least it would be fascinating to listen to the Otten High board grapple with a topic that was not related to bus scheduling and delinquent football stars.

Aside from the course work, Walter was planning to take Mrs. Denval to Milwaukee on the fifteenth anniversary of her husband's death in July, to see the Florentine Opera perform *L'Elisir d'Amore*. He had an invitation mid-June to watch Betsy Rutule receive her black belt in karate at the Dodgeville Academy of Karate, and he'd by all means go down to Schaumburg for Lucy's birthday on the fifth. There were a few appointments set in stone. In August he might travel with Sue Rawson to Washington to see Susan dance in *Jewels* with a temporary company their beloved ballerina, Suzanne Farrell, was throwing together. So many amazing Susans in one auditorium. He probably should go to New York to visit the old crowd and to feel the city play on his nerves and to remember that in America there are people of color and various creeds. He was also thinking of buying a giant schnauzer. A litter had been born down the road, and if he was going to get one he needed to claim it. He liked the idea of walking a big animal out in the county park, through the backwoods, the dog woof-woofing when anyone came close. It would be nice to hear the noise of someone else eating in the kitchen, to hear the crunch of Purina Dog Chow. The dog might end up to be evil in the way Duke had been, but

he might have satisfying canine mannerisms too, wiggling his stub of a
tail every night, and jumping up when Walter came in the door.

It was all very well to make plans, but Walter found he could not
think about the summer or the coming year until he knew about Lake
Margaret. It was clear, now that he'd come up to June, that everything,
the rest of life, hinged on whether or not the house would become a
stranger's property. He had only gone so far as to imagine the shadow
of a man standing with boxes and suitcases, waiting at the door to
move in. But undoubtedly there would be a wife too, and children and
cousins, parties, holidays, a ski boat, a sailboat, tackle boxes, storms
coming up across the lake, sultry afternoons and down the hill—to
run down the hill—the relief of the cool spangly green water three
miles across. Oh, he hated that the ousters might not have any interest
in the previous owners, and even more he hated that they might be in-
trigued, scraping around in closets, prying up floorboards for some
clue about the past. Whoever they were and whatever they were going
to do was wrongheaded, unpardonable.

June 1 came and Sue Rawson did not call a meeting as she had
threatened back at Thanksgiving. Walter waited at home in Otten, inside, while the sun shone and warm air blew in the open windows.
From across the way came the waft of black dirt that had recently had
an application of manure. The field was ready to be seeded with corn.
That's what I should do while I wait, he thought, take up gardening,
plant blue-ribbon beefsteak tomatoes and best-of-the-fair collard
greens. He was sure that the phone would ring, certain that there'd be
an announcement. Of course if he really wanted to know he could call
his mother. Or he could wait, wait for the message to come to him.

June 2 also passed without a word. In Walter's experience no
news usually meant nothing more than delayed bad news. He wished
Sue Rawson would stop menacing him and get on with it, plunge the
knife in up to the hilt, draw it out, wipe the blade clean and be done.
On June 3 he woke to the sound of rain, then hail for a minute, and
heavy rain again, beating on the windows. Although lately he professed not to believe in signs and portents, he gave himself the warning: nothing good happens in foul weather. As soon as he was awake
enough to navigate, he drove to the lake, as if being there he could
somehow hold on to it, press his claim like a homesteader.

He wandered from room to room looking carefully at the furnishings, the drapes, the paintings, the driftwood, the lanterns, the candlesticks, the faucets, the marble of the sinks. My house, he whispered. They would have to take the place apart when the time came, strip it to the bone. It was remarkable that in the nomadic American culture of the late twentieth century one house had so defined a family and each of the individuals within that family. There was an antique, tribal aspect to the Rawson heritage. The furniture, the letters, the violet-soap smell of the stiff cotton sheets in the linen closet, the musty old books, the sketches in the composition tablets—all of it had made men and women who were long dead real, and they in turn, with their benevolent presence, had given the plaster and lath spirit. Great-aunt Lydia had featherstitched all the blankets, and there were scratches on the wooden benches in the cookhouse from generations of children, including a gouge his own mother had made with her pocketknife. The clamshells were on the mantel, along with the snail shells that had always been there, and the smooth stones and ungainly stones and flat stones, and the bristly bird's nests falling to pieces. He picked up each thing and examined it. He studied the watermarks on the ceiling, the speckles on the linoleum, the train painted on the wall over the bed he'd slept in as a boy. He wanted to remember every detail; indeed he could not do with anything less than exact recall if he was going to spend the next thirty years constructing the property in miniature.

The yellow slickers hanging on the hooks in the hall were at the ready, as if firemen were upstairs sleeping on the edge of their narrow beds. Walter remembered his uncle Andy, years before, urging the cousins out into a dreary day, telling them that with the proper gear and sharp tools they could accomplish anything. They didn't know if what he was saying was true, and they grumbled and went outside and climbed up a tree. They forgot all about Uncle Andy. Walter put on a black plastic hat and he chose a green-and-white-striped fashion raincoat because it came to his ankles. It was slippery down the wet steps to the pier, and he went carefully to his place in the Adirondack chair. He sat wrapped in the mangy quilt from the boathouse wishing he could somehow distill the sound of the water's lapping and its live, fresh smell. He closed his eyes and felt the drizzle on his face, running down his neck, past the dark green corduroy collar. Losing Lake Margaret, he knew, was an extension of losing Daniel. It seemed for a moment as if time had both compressed and extended, that childhood and the link from the past to the future were gone, that the death of his brother and this next loss were nearly one and the same. Walter remembered feeling at Daniel's memorial service that what lay beyond, in all of his future, was unmapped territory, streets that had no names, rivers with no bridges, twisting paths that disappeared behind a person, gone, no way back. He had that sense again, and he wept, wondering what there was that could possibly take the place of his faith that was soon to be so permanently ruptured.

He cried out of anger then, at himself, at his sloth, his inability to have drummed up some sort of coalition to save Lake Margaret. He had given in to Sue Rawson and he had let teaching suck him dry. He should have sold pizzas door-to-door or slept with someone rich; he should have seen to the preservation of the property. The quilt was soaking and the batting was coming out of it in soggy clumps. Jeannie's bargain raincoat was useless, which was why she kept it at Lake Margaret, for someone else to wear. He was wet down to his briefs, nothing left to do but go back up to the house and try to start a fire with the damp wood; nothing left to do but beat himself for his own shortcomings. What had he learned so far? He was a failure in every department. He'd always suffered like a nitwit from unrequited love. With hindsight, after he'd been dumped, the boyfriends were such amazingly obvious jerks. He'd never mastered anything, had no technique for the arts he'd pursued, hadn't practiced the piano religiously as a child, didn't have techniques for just plain living, hadn't done well by the farm boys in Otten, had no source beyond the family home for his strength. "Sit yourself down," he said, "because you could go on and on for an entire day in this vein."

But he was sick to death of his tirade by the time he got to the kitchen. He'd call Joyce if only to hear a voice that was not coming from his own spleeny brain, and to find out once and for all if there was any word. "I give up," he said under his breath. "I'm calling." If there was no news he would try to think of something to fill the afternoon that did not involve self-laceration, and if there was a plan he would try to begin to imagine the next day, and the day after that, the end of Lake Margaret creeping up on them, hour after hour.

What was both an admirable quality and a failing in his mother, he would later tell Susan, was her ability to pull off scenes that had great theatrical potential, and all without any sense of drama. His mother had probably cultivated her talent as a result of growing up with a sister like Jeannie. Joyce had never stormed out of the house or broken a dish in a temper. When he was small she had always reproached him quietly, and when Daniel died there was no apparent outrage against God or the doctors. It was what he might fault her for if he had to make a grievance about his upbringing.

In the matter of Lake Margaret she remained true to form. Walter, shivering from his chill, clutched his mug of steaming Swiss Miss with one hand, and with the other tried to dial Oak Ridge's number on the large black rotary phone. It was an ancient skill, he thought, finding the correct number on the face of the relic, moving the circle around just so, to the exact spot, not getting the index finger stuck, letting go at the right time. Rotary dialing, the vanishing art.

"Hello, Mom," he said, when she answered. I'm desolate, he wanted to say. I have three months of freedom and I'm already lost. What you are about to tell me will make it even worse.

"I'm glad you called," she said. "Dad and I were going to get ahold of you tonight. We've been putting the final pieces of the—"

"What?" Walter said. "What?"

"I hardly know how to speak anymore, honey. These dealings are ticklish, and for weeks I've been going after Sue so gingerly."

"Gingerly," Walter repeated.

"But then when it came time to make the move—well, I don't know. It was such a peculiar thing."

He didn't know what she was talking about. Could it be that his dainty mother, deep down, had the constitution and cunning of a Mafia don, going after the thing she wanted, zooming in for the kill?

"I think it was because of you that Sue Rawson agreed," she was saying. "She is glad—yes, I'd say that she's glad—that you will be the principal shareholder, that you'll have more than anyone else. Perhaps it was what she'd hoped for all along. That is, if you'll agree, if you'll take our offer, and really hers too, if we can put the shares in your name. Sometimes I think that it's really what she meant from the beginning. It must have thrown her for a loop when Roger and Francie tried to take the ball. We had to play the game, you understand, beg her to come down in the price, walk on our knees. There are tax implications, of course. She and Dad are still working on the IRS part of the puzzle, and there's the issue of maintenance, but your father seems to think it will come out more or less in our favor."

She had spoken in English, in her usual quiet way, but she had begun the story in the middle. He was not sure that he'd understood her. "Are you there, honey?" she said.

"I'm here, at Lake Margaret," he managed.

"Is this something that you'd like to take on, because if—"

"Mom." His mother, a Gambino family baby who had been set out in the bulrushes, presumed dead while she drifted west on the river to Illinois.

"Please," he said. "Hold on. I think you need to tell me this news in person. I've been feeling pitiful, so sorry for myself just two minutes ago and I haven't quite switched gears. I've got to shift up through desperation, depression, standard unhappiness—here we go—to absence of malaise, to satisfaction, pleasure, felicity—I've got a way to go to euphoria, to ecstasy. Bear with me. If it's okay I'll drive down to Oak Ridge now. I'll get in the car and I'll be there in a few hours and then what I'd like to do—if you're not in the middle of something—I'd like to sit down on the porch, or in the kitchen, and you could explain the deal, if that's what it is, from the start to the finish. And I say this only because I'm getting older and I have a feeling that this could be one of the biggest moments of my life. I want to prolong it. I don't want to have it happen over the telephone. If you could have some kind of music playing when I pull up, that would add to the sensation, certainly. Brahms, I think, would be fitting. The Fourth Symphony. I'll bring a bottle of wine and an enormous half-dead Wisconsin fish flapping in the bottom of a bucket. It's really too bad that Mrs. Gamble isn't here to join us—but I'm getting ahead of myself. I'd like to come and hear the plan, if you don't mind."

He ran outside without a wrap, he slammed the door, he went down the hill. "Oh golly," he was saying as he slid on the wet grass.

"Oh, golly, oh dear God." Was he asleep, was he awake, was he dead? Was it a hoax, an April fool sort of prank? He should pause to kneel by the all-generous lake and give thanks. "Thank you. Thank you, Jesus." How good the rain felt on his face, streaming into his shirt, down his hot chest. How cold and refreshing. "Thanks so much, Sue Rawson. Is it true, you tall stern imp? You ogre aunt? You angel! Please make it come true!"

If he had gotten any of his mother's drift he might dare to hope for noisy Lake Margaret Thanksgivings and Easters. He'd dare, but he'd take the dare tentatively. Could it be that there was the chance for future boys, summer after summer, sleeping down in the boathouse, playing with matches and reading inappropriate magazines? And the hope, too, for girls long after the year 2000 giving each other back rubs at night in the large yellow bedroom, and doing their hair and getting mad at each other and making up, getting mad, making up. His parents had arranged to buy out Sue Rawson, and if he understood, they were going to give him the shares. He reached out to hold the drooping limb of the willow, their expensive-shoreline lachrymose willow. There was the possibility that in his dotage he'd sit at the head of the table and Lucy's children would take his dinner plate away and bring him pie. He'd be the matriarch, demanding Cool Whip. It would be up to him to make the Easter lamb cake every year because he had watched Aunt Jeannie mix it up with the secret ingredient. There was no underestimating the effect of a half pound of lard. He'd be Aunt Jeannie and Sue Rawson, all in one, the two biddies in a single harmonious body, something on the order of the Platonic ideal. Uncle Walter, the man who put on elaborate puppet productions, the tough who patrolled the grounds, making sure there was decorum, no boys in the girls' room, the cake-maker who further won the children's hearts by inciting them to throw mashed-potato balls around the room at dinner. He'd invite little Linda up to his room to listen to Puccini, and he'd let her touch his Liberace jacket, and on summer nights, in the fluttering light of the candle on the porch, he and Lucy would take an hour to follow the thread of each other's lives. This is how a woman must feel, he thought, when she learns she's going to have a baby. Solemn and afraid and giddy. In the long future ahead there would be lawn care and putty work and foundation troubles, leaky faucets and rotting floorboards, and there would be conversation and food and sound sleep, and in the family there would be marriages and deaths and the squall of infants. It was green pastures, still waters, goodness, mercy and the cup flowing over.

It took several weeks for Walter to absorb his parents' plan. He had known as a teenager that Daniel had had complications with a surgery and that Joyce and Robert had sued the doctor. He had inferred from his father's comments through his college years that part of the settlement had been used to pay for his education, and some of it, he'd learned later from his mother, had gone for the general upkeep at the lake, for a new roof, plastering the living room, resurfacing the old bathtub. In November, after Sue Rawson's bombshell, Joyce had told her husband that even if they'd had the money she wouldn't rush into the fray, that she was going to let Jeannie's group take hold if they had the means. It was no use, she said, borrowing money and then getting into a bidding war with her own sister after they'd been friends for sixty-some years. When Francie went off to Indiana and Roger bowed out, Joyce called on Sue Rawson and began the negotiations, making an offer that was two hundred thousand dollars lower than the asking price. She and Robert had no qualms about giving Sue Rawson what was left of the settlement money, which had always seemed to them to be tainted cash. It was clear to Joyce, considering the relative ease with which Sue Rawson capitulated—indeed, the relief with which she yielded—that her older sister had never had any intention of selling her portion to Jeannie or any of Jeannie's children.

Walter and Joyce reviewed the chain of events, starting as far back as the anniversary party in 1972, and for several days they went around and around, favoring first one theory about Sue Rawson's motives and then another. Perhaps at the start, Joyce told Walter, Sue had not realized how much the place meant to all of them. Or maybe she'd wanted to test them, to see if they did care, to see if in fact they were worthy. Or she might have believed that she should get cash from the estate, that the money was rightfully hers; and maybe, too, she had been genuinely concerned about the upkeep and the responsibility of ownership. Or perhaps, in the end, Joyce ventured, Sue Rawson lost her nerve.

"Lost her nerve to be the wicked queen," Walter said.

It was the idea they came back to again and again, the failure of nerve. How thankful she must have been, Joyce said, to have such a graceful way out.

Lucy was to get part of Joyce's shares upon her death, but Sue Rawson stipulated that Walter hold the keys to the kingdom, that he have the majority of the stock. She was a no-nonsense fairy god-mother; she wrote him a terse note ordering him to call her lawyer to discuss the trust that she had established to assist him with the annual maintenance.

Both Joyce and Walter were concerned about Jeannie's response to the McCloud ascendancy, a rise in their fortunes that was going to sorely test her sportsmanship. There was petulance in Aunt Jeannie's new expression, a chronic pout in her lower lip, but it was the silence, so unnatural, that worried Walter. He came up with the idea of having a thirty-year-overdue housecleaning extravaganza, a weeklong party that might serve to make everyone feel included and helpful, and on the final Saturday they could rent a metal cooker and roast a pig. It was Joyce who organized what turned out to be a small party and, with time and patience, lured Jeannie to the lake for the occasion. Through June, Joyce called her big sister every morning, and once or twice a week they went to the tennis club for dinner. Joyce listened while Jeannie complained about everything but Lake Margaret, and she said soothing words when Jeannie put her head in her hands and whimpered over Francie. When Joyce invited her to help scour the lake house, to sort through the junk that had accumulated over the generations, Jeannie said she couldn't possibly get up to Wisconsin before August. But the thought of the others rifling around in the rooms that she had always claimed disturbed her, and she later phoned Joyce and said in her lackluster voice that she guessed she'd come along if they thought she could be of any use.

In early July it was the three of them, Walter and Joyce and Jeannie, who spent a week going room by room, each of them armed with the Gamble-style aprons that Walter had purchased and equipped with cleaning supplies. They took down all the photographs from the famous wall and dusted each frame. They went through the dishes, the sculptures, the books, the bedding, the jars of loose coins in the grandfather's collection, the fusty issues of *Boy's Life* dating back to 1925, the odd assortment of zoris and tennis shoes that had been piling up since the fifties, and the swimsuits and jackets and hats from the turn of the century. There were family letters that no one had looked at in decades, and scrapbooks, broken toys and board games with faded paths to the treasure. They knew they were not exactly making progress—there was very little they actually discarded, but the project, taking stock and cataloging and dusting, gave the three of them a sense of satisfaction.

Walter took it upon himself to pull down the wine jugs on the porch ledge, those that had been put there through the years after a notable feast or celebration. There were places on the glass and the labels where the dust was matted, thick as scum. The bottles were arranged in a loose chronological order, and he let himself work at his task slowly, polishing, sniffing the corks, imagining the drinkers, their arguments, the puns, the songs. He remembered a few scenes from his childhood, the discussions Uncle Andy and Uncle Wally used to have about civil rights and the Vietnam War. He tried to imagine farther back, the decorous, well-bred great-aunts and great-uncles raising their voices over the United Nations and suffrage, prohibition and that old boozer F. Scott Fitzgerald. He was in the 1920s section when he came upon a California champagne out of place, bottled, he noticed, in 1994. He turned it over—he almost dropped it when he saw, above the Surgeon General's warning, the names, Francie and Skip, and the date, September 10, 1995. He passed the thing back and forth, from hand to hand, as if it were hot. Obedient Francie had flown in the face of her mother and her ancestors and used Lake Margaret as a love nest! Which room? Or had they done it in every room, his room, Sue Rawson's room, like Goldilocks trying out each piece of furniture for the best fit? He wondered if Francie would be happy once her defiance was spent, blissful in Bloomington with her impoverished sociologist. What to do with the bottle? If he put it out with the recycling it would be ground up and it would become part of someone else's container, the mystery specks of cerise in the otherwise clear glass. If Jeannie saw it she might have a breakdown, take to the heath in a blowing rage. No, it was better to put it back up on the shelf, leave it. Fifty years hence, the next time the bottles were cleaned, someone not yet born could come upon it and try to piece together all the relations. The bottle would guarantee Francie a place in history even if she never returned from the good life in Indiana.

For two days Joyce and Walter made their province the downstairs living room and they talked as they sorted the books. "You could take the old davenport for your house," Joyce said. "It really looks as if it has had it, and I don't think anyone else wants it—not with the gash in it. There's got to be someone, somewhere, for a price, who would love to work on an heirloom that has so much class and history. We could bring Grandma's settee from home, the one that was here originally. Then we could say that we were actually at the work of restoration."

The sofa in front of them was made of red leather and had been at Lake Margaret since 1922. "I might get a dog," Walter said, looking up from a book about Eleanor of Aquitaine. "The dog hair probably wouldn't cling to the leather." Without planning, without having thought through his announcement, he said, "I'll either get a dog or a boyfriend." No! What was he saying? What had he said? It wasn't even what he meant: he had no prospects, no one, nothing. He went on in a rush—"There are disadvantages to both, of course, as I'm sure Mrs. Gamble would be quick to point out."

"Did I tell you that the two Gamble dogs died?" Joyce said. "Both of them went within three weeks of Florence."

"What?" Walter's heart was racing from his admission. He had come out to his mother, officially, and she hadn't even noticed. Or else the short jokey sentence had slipped so quietly from his mouth that she hadn't heard.

"I guess we had so much to talk about the last time you were home that I forgot to mention it. The two collies, bing, bing, dead. One of them got bitten by a squirrel, the other had to be put down because of bowel trouble."

"Bowel trouble. That makes sense."

"It's so still over there. It's unnerving."

"They followed her," Walter said. "I had the feeling those dogs would do something strange in her absence. Let's hope she traveled with a good supply of Baggies and her precious trowel."

Joyce laughed. "It is odd, isn't it? Well, I don't see why you have to choose. You could have a dog *and* a boyfriend. I don't suppose Otten would be the easiest place for it," she said, perfectly understandable in her vagueness, "and being your mother, I'm biased—but I love everything about you and I would think they'd be lining up."

Walter blinked back the tears that had so quickly and unreasonably filled his eyes. It wouldn't do to have an outburst, to cry on the Eleanor of Aquitaine book. Lately everything, absolutely everything, seemed sweetly precarious and poignant, and in his happiness he often wanted to bawl. As a young teenager he had been inexperienced and cynical in an affected fifteen-year-old way, and with Daniel's death he'd become prematurely wise and nostalgic. The finished product, the grown-up, he was sorry to say, had the fiber of a sentimental old lady who must at all times have a hankie up her sleeve to dab at her runny eyes. This is what life has done to me, he said to himself.

Jeannie came into the room carrying a basket of sweaters, for the moment saving him from his own emotion. She had missed her hair appointment and strands of white showed at the temple. Her lapse made Walter feel more than usually tender toward her. "What do you think?" she said, dropping her load. "Should these be saved?"

She and her flesh and blood owned less than one third of the Lake Margaret stock, and in her impoverished state she was asking the Mc-Clouds to make decisions that were obvious, that she could easily make herself. She was rubbing it in, Walter knew, making the point whenever she could that he was the primary owner, that every detail was now his concern.

"Pitch them," Joyce said.

"Wait." Walter went to the basket, taking what was a gray sleeve, drawing it out from the middle of the heap. "Oh," he said. He held the shapeless wool sweater to his chest. Joyce had knit for months the year Daniel died, and here was the result, her handiwork, the garment that would fit a giant. It was nothing more than twelve skeins of yarn and thousands of loops, but it had the power to bring back in a flash the green-tiled walls of the hospital, the sound of an ambulance trying to cut through city traffic in the distance, the beating of a helicopter's blade in the clouds, the breathing of the dying boy, his father staring at the ceiling, the full greasy bucket of fried chicken on the bed table.

"I'll take this one," Walter said, balling up the sweater as best he could, stuffing it into a shopping bag that was half full of the books he was taking home, that he was borrowing.

"Oh, honey," Joyce said. "You don't want that old scrap."

"You made it. I remember your making it." Keep it light, he said to himself, that's a boy. "There's a use for it. Don't you think so, Aunt Jeannie? No offense, Mom, but I could invade the Huns with it or strap the sleeves to my car tires in a blizzard, for traction, or protect our nation with it out in space, a shield against nuclear attack."

Jeannie tittered in her usual way in spite of herself. "You always did have that sense of humor," she said as she went upstairs. When she was out of range, Joyce went to Walter's bag and retrieved the sweater. She laid it on the card table, the long arms hanging down, and she fingered the stitches. "Will you look at the mass of it," she exclaimed. "I don't even recall making it."

" 'Memory—that strange deceiver,' " Walter quoted. He bent over a stack of books on the floor. "I'm starting to revise my own history, and wishing, naturally, that Daniel was around to refute and corroborate. Do you remember, for example, how Mrs. Gamble used to tear out of the house with her whip when we asked the milkman for ice? She used to crack the rawhide on the cement—she scared the daylights out of us. I used to think she was protecting the milkman from us, from our annoying presence. But I don't know anymore. I've started to think that she had it in mind to protect the children, snapping that whip, keeping us away from a driver who could have run over us accidentally, or done us bodily harm in the back of his truck."

"It's possible," Joyce said. "It's very possible that she cared that much."

"Revising my idea of Mrs. Gamble is unsettling, I have to admit. I feel as if I've been making paintings all my life and then I go and look at them and they don't, after all, say what I intended. I suppose I'm free to invent her now, to make her fit my story as I'd like, to take the paint tube and go wild."

"She was never sure, speaking of going wild with the paint, if it was Greg Gamble's disreputable friends who ruined the carport roof. She couldn't put her finger on it. G.G. did have some good-for-nothing sidekicks and she knew for a fact that one of them hid in her attic once for a few days. She couldn't get a word out of the boys."

"Whoever it was can take satisfaction in having outsmarted her, I guess," Walter said, kneeling, inspecting the yellowed paper of a book on Western philosophy. "It was probably the only mystery in her life, the one thing she didn't know for sure."

"Dad and I got to laughing about it a while back. We couldn't stop. It was vandalism, I know, nothing funny about that, but there was never a more fitting crime for the victim. The way she lavished attention on her carport, and the way she harassed the builders! But as we were saying, a boyfriend is easier than a dog, I think. When you go on vacation you wouldn't have to pay for the kennel cost, and vet bills can be out of sight."

"True," Walter said, "but a dog loves you, and only because you feed it."

"They live for such a short time, though."

"That could be positive."

"Duke lasted for ages."

"I guess I could have a boyfriend and a dog. Maybe it's not being greedy to ask for the summer house, a dog and a boyfriend."

"It is sometimes hard to know when to stop asking," she said, "but I think your requests are within conservative limits."

Before supper Walter went into the room his parents shared downstairs, the large bedroom with casement windows that opened onto the woody ravine. He sat on the great-grandmother's chaise and flipped through the mildewed copy of *Stalky and Company,* the novel his father read every summer, taking up wherever he happened to open the book. Walter was too tired to read. He closed his eyes, wondering about an old pair of canvas lake shoes that in his memory, at least, had been the most comfortable pair of shoes he'd worn as a college student. The two rum and tonics he'd made for himself had been potent and he felt pleasantly loose and a little hazy. He had made the drinks strong in an effort to cheer Aunt Jeannie, or failing that, to assist Joyce through her sister's black mood. Maybe his favorite shoes were in his parents' walk-in closet, the narrow windowless place that he used to think had supernatural potential, a gateway to another dimension. As a boy he had probably spent hours all told hiding in the back, waiting to be found.

He made his way past the rack with the windbreakers and pants, a few of his mother's old housedresses. On the floor his father's bluchers and heavy-duty boat macs were in line on one side, and on the other, the neat row of Joyce's sandals and loafers and Keds. When Walter saw the cylinder on top of the hatboxes on the upper shelf he knew immediately what was inside the standard crematorium urn. He had known that Daniel had been cremated. Although there had never been a ceremony for the purpose, he'd always assumed that the ashes had been let go somewhere or buried in the cemetery, in the family plot, beneath the stone marker that read, *Daniel Robert McCloud, 1955–1973*. At an earlier point in his life he might have been shaken by the remains in the box but he felt, staring in the twilight murk of the closet, that he was in the presence of his parents, rather than his brother, that he had caught Joyce and Robert in their small act of deception, their weak attempt to hold on.

His mother was safe in the kitchen with Jeannie, whipping the mashed potatoes and dressing the salad. He lifted the urn down from the shelf, took it out to the desk, removed the lid. Inside he found the Baggie with the bits of bone in the gray dust. The sweater that Joyce had made in the hospital had been a painful reminder of both Daniel and his death, far more than the sprinkle Walter took on his finger and blew into the air. "This, what is not you," he whispered, "bless our house." The dust caught the late-afternoon sunlight and shimmered as it floated off. Daniel had again come through, in his mysterious and unpredictable way. Without the settlement from the surgery, Joyce and Robert would not have had the means to rescue the family. Must his brother have had to die to make this part of Walter's life possible? There was no way to know, no good in dwelling on the question. It was better to give up a prayer of thanks to the long-ago boy who was providing for them, still affording safe passage. Walter smelled inside the urn—no scent, nothing left after all the years—put the lid back on, and returned it to the closet for his parents to someday care for, in their own time.

That night he sat on the pier wrapped in his lumpy quilt listening to the water. He had half a mind to stay out until dawn, to watch the steady, bright stars fade into the blue of the morning sky. He could take off his clothes and swim, and lie on the pier watching for meteors, or he could go upstairs and sleep in the deep quiet of the house. In a while he'd decide. There was no rush. He thought about how nothing at the lake would change for some time, not until the older generation died. Sue Rawson would still come to the family functions because he'd insist upon it. His cousins would try to sustain their dislike for Sue, but Walter would do what he could to be her champion. She chewed with her mouth open and didn't care if she was disagreeable. What love she had in her she had showered upon Walter, but they would probably never speak of it. He counted on her living another twenty years and keeping her guard up well past the bitter end.

He thought that even though it was probably much too late he might take a trip to New Orleans. There had been one note from Julian in the course of Walter's letter campaign. A postcard had come with a few lines of an Elizabeth Bishop poem, but he had found nothing revealing or pertinent in the verse. It wasn't out of the question that he might run down to Louisiana for a short visit. There was very little, after all, to lose. Maybe his mother was right, and a person could have a house and a dog and a boyfriend. Buying a motorcycle would tip the scale, but having the three wasn't exactly an embarrassment of riches. With or without true love there was bound to be a future even in a place as seemingly inert as the home of the Braves. Living and teaching in Otten was something like being assigned to write a villanelle, he thought. The nineteen-line poem, as he recalled, was supposed to have five tercets and a final quatrain on two rhymes, with the first and third lines of the first tercet repeating alternately as a refrain at the end of the succeeding stanzas, and joined as the final couplet of the quatrain. Those, more or less, were the rules. His New York City life had been free verse, but there was something to be said for some stringent guidelines, for boundaries, for finding a different sort of liberty within the constraints.

They would never know him in Otten, and maybe if he got down to it he wouldn't understand too many of them. The people in his town moved slowly and were afraid, not only of bigger highways, new roads to the cities, but of change on general principle. What had been good enough for them was adequate for their children, no reason to put more tax dollars into a school that had worked since 1937. Change would be thrust upon them by state mandates, but they would not welcome it. It was sometimes difficult to identify the fearsome thing in a person or a community, and Walter guessed that if a few of his students could spot what was genuinely frightful he could say he'd done his job teaching literature. He would try to think of his solitary self, his loneliness, as that one best thing, shining with the stubbornness of the eternal flame, inside himself. If he never found a Julian he would probably find some roundabout way to be grateful for the longing, for the keenness of desire.

The future would come and come, constant and continuous as air. He'd walk down the streets in Otten, as time went on gradually wearing more and more clothes from the Farm and Fleet, along with his townspeople. He'd drink their coffee and occasionally hear their bright overstressed vowels in his own sentences. It might take a few years but eventually with the staging of the right musical comedy, with the success of a student or two, the people of Otten would begin to see him. In the meantime, they might feel the vibration, the sound of his own quiet voice echoing out into the town, the words he'd been saying since the beginning: I am among you.

JANE HAMILTON lives, works, and writes in an orchard farmhouse in Wisconsin. Her short stories have appeared in *Harper's* magazine. She won the PEN/Ernest Hemingway Foundation Award for best first novel for *The Book of Ruth* in 1989. She is also the author of the best-selling *A Map of the World.*

ABOUT THE TYPE

This book was set in Simoncini Garamond, a typeface designed by Francesco Simoncini based on the style of Garamond that was created by the French printer Jean Jannon after the original models of Claude Garamond.